By NICKI BENNETT

Always a Bridesmaid
The Cattle Baron's Bogus Boyfriend
Evan's Heaven
Flight
Home for Christmas
New Traditions

With Ariel Tachna
Under the Skin

ALL FOR LOVE
Checkmate
All for One

HOT CARGO STORIES
Hot Cargo
Something About Harry

THE EXPLORING LIMITS SERIES
Exploring Limits
Stretching Limits
Refining Limits
Breaking Limits
Transcending Limits
No Limits

Published by DREAMSPINNER PRESS
www.dreamspinnerpress.com

By Ariel Tachna

At Your Service
Best Ideas
Château d'Eternité
With Nessa L. Warin: Dance Off
Fallout
Her Two Dads
Highland Lover
Home for Chirappu
In Search of Fireworks
The Inventor's Companion
The Matelot
Music of the Heart
Once in a Lifetime
Out of the Fire
Overdrive
The Path
Rediscovery
Revelations in the Dark
Rose Among the Ruins
Seducing C.C.
Stolen Moments
A Summer Place
With Madeleine Urban: Sutcliffe Cove
Testament to Love
Why Nileas Loved the Sea

GAMES LOVERS PLAY
Amorous Liaison
Best Behavior
Ride 'em Cowboy

HOT CARGO
Healing in His Wings
With Nicki Bennett: Hot Cargo

With Nicki Bennett: Something About Harry

LANG DOWNS
Inherit the Sky
Chase the Stars
Outlast the Night
Conquer the Flames
Cherish the Land

PARTNERSHIP IN BLOOD
Alliance in Blood
Covenant in Blood
Conflict in Blood
Reparation in Blood
Perilous Partnership
Reluctant Partnerships
Lycan Partnership
Partnership Reborn
Partnership Reforged

With Nicki Bennett
Under the Skin

ALL FOR LOVE
Checkmate • All for One

THE EXPLORING LIMITS SERIES
Exploring Limits • Stretching Limits • Refining Limits Breaking Limits • Transcending Limits • No Limits

Published by
DREAMSPINNER PRESS
www.dreamspinnerpress.com

CHECKMATE

Nicki Bennett
and
Ariel Tachna

Published by
DREAMSPINNER PRESS

5032 Capital Circle SW, Suite 2, PMB# 279, Tallahassee, FL 32305-7886 USA
www.dreamspinnerpress.com

This is a work of fiction. Names, characters, places, and incidents either are the product of author imagination or are used fictitiously, and any resemblance to actual persons, living or dead, business establishments, events, or locales is entirely coincidental.

ISBN: 978-1-63477-462-8
Digital ISBN: 978-1-63477-463-5
Library of Congress Control Number: 2016907027
Published July 2016
v. 2.0
First Edition published by Dreamspinner Press, 2009.

Printed in the United States of America

This paper meets the requirements of
ANSI/NISO Z39.48-1992 (Permanence of Paper).

To Carol, whose birthday started it all
and who still provides the best inspiration.
Special thanks to Rita for our first lessons in sword fighting,
and to Saura for her expertise in all things Spanish.

ONE

Spain, 1624

SIR LOWELL St. Denys stood in the shadows of the dank alley outside the seedy tavern in Madrid, waiting impatiently for his contact. He searched the face of each person who passed, but none gave the gray-haired man a second look. That suited St. Denys fine. The last thing he wanted was to be recognized here, in this setting, except by the man he was supposed to meet. Teodoro Ciéza de Vivar had been recommended to him as a sword for hire, a mercenary with enough honor to complete the job, but not so much as would prove troublesome. With that thought in mind, St. Denys had worked out the perfect story to get the swordsman to go along with his plan.

Movement at the corner of his eye caught his attention. A man stood at the entrance to the alley, clothed in dark leather over a paler linen shirt despite the heat. The brim of his hat was wide and slightly tattered, and he wore a sword at one hip and a dagger tucked in his belt on the other. As the man approached, St. Denys took note of the thick moustache that obscured his upper lip and the expressionless brown eyes that pierced even the deepest of shadows for any threat. St. Denys's eyes lingered appreciatively on the breadth of the shoulders revealed by the leather jerkin, the trim waist, the narrow hips and long, long legs, a frown marring his face only when he reached the battered, mended boots. With a regretful shrug, the Englishman stepped out of the shadows. "Ciéza de Vivar?"

Teodoro Ciéza de Vivar had been watching the older man for some time before he was ready to approach him. His finances were always uneven, and the coin for this job, if he decided to take it, would be most welcome, but he had enough in hand at the moment that he could afford to decline the offer should it come to that. He did not always have the luxury to be so discriminating, though there were some undertakings to which nothing could compel him to agree, but this did not feel like one of them. Teodoro had learned that observing his would-be employers could often reveal to him whether he would agree to their task, even before hearing the details or the terms. His instincts told him that this richly dressed, silver-haired gentleman would at least be worth hearing out. "I am Ciéza de Vivar," he replied. "And you?"

"St. Denys," the noble said with a courtly bow, seeing no reason to admit his title to the swordsman. It would likely only raise his price. "Lowell St. Denys. I'm hoping you can help me, señor. My friend is most distressed at his son's behavior."

"Shall we take some refreshment while you tell me of it?" Teodoro inclined his head toward the tavern—surely not the type of place his prospective employer would normally frequent, but even if he chose to decline the job, he could at least get a decent bottle of wine from the meeting.

St. Denys frowned a little, not accustomed to such common taverns, but he understood the game. He would buy the mercenary food and drink in exchange for being heard. The rest was up to his powers of persuasion. "I would be pleased to dine with you," he said magnanimously. "Lead the way."

Teodoro had met enough men of a certain type at this tavern that the serving girl knew to seat them at a quiet table against the back wall. Declining his prospective employer's offer of a meal—he would have St. Denys's measure first—Teodoro asked her to bring a bottle of their best vintage, then settled in his chair, stretching his long legs and turning his attention back to the Englishman. "Why is your friend not here to see me himself, if he is so concerned about his son?"

"He is still in England," St. Denys explained. "His son was supposed to return from the Continent last month. Instead, he has run off with his... friend... and refuses to return home." In another place, St. Denys would not have minced words, but he had seen the burnings in the town square the week before; the Inquisition had no mercy on sodomites. Still, he was well experienced in concealing his own inclinations and would not hesitate to play upon the mercenary's undoubted prejudice in that regard, if it would gain St. Denys what he sought. "His father asked me to approach him as an old friend of the family, but the boy will not be swayed. So his father requested that I employ whatever means necessary to separate him from the current bad influence in his life and return him to England at once. Thus my message to you."

"So the boy is not being held against his will?" Teodoro asked, frowning. "Is he of age?" The original message had implied that the lad in question had been kidnapped, but St. Denys was describing a spoiled runaway. If the boy was unwilling to return, Teodoro's task would be that much harder—and his fee that much higher, he decided as he waited for a response.

"He is twenty-three," St. Denys replied, "but his father retains control of his purse and his future until he is twenty-five, so it remains his father's decision what he should be doing. If after that, he chooses to consort with... men like Hawkins, that will be his choice. For now, his father insists that he come home."

There was a moment's pause as the serving maid brought their wine, poured them each a glassful, and set the bottle in the middle of the table. After raising his goblet to his companion in a silent toast, Teodoro took an appreciative swallow, letting the flavor of the rich red wine mellow his mood. "So I will be fighting both the... friend, and the youth himself?" he mused. "That will make the task more difficult, especially since I expect the father wishes them both unharmed."

"Hawkins is unimportant," St. Denys declared with a wave of his hand. "He is the reason the boy has neglected his duties in the first place. But I will increase your pay by half for dealing with him. All that matters is bringing Blackwood to me unharmed so that I can get him home where he belongs."

Teodoro's well-developed sense of self-preservation made him immediately suspicious of anyone to whom price was no object. Still, St. Denys met his eyes steadily, and what harm could there be in returning a young man to his own father? "Where can I find this Hawkins and... Blackwood, was it?"

"Christian Blackwood, and they are in Valencia," St. Denys replied. "He seems to think that by not returning to England, he can avoid his father's disapproval. I am quite sure you can reach him faster than I would be able to get there to hire someone local."

"It will take me some days to ride that far," Teodoro calculated. "And no guarantee the young man and his... friend... will not be gone by the time I arrive."

"You can be there in nine days if you ride hard," St. Denys countered. "If they have left by the time you get there, follow them. The boy's father will pay you well to make sure he recovers his son."

Teodoro fingered the end of his moustache, his thoughts troubled. The easy way St. Denys countered his every objection only strengthened his distrust. Still, the man was paying well—too well, his judgment told him, but he would be a fool to refuse to profit from the foreigner's ignorance. "I will take your commission," he declared. "How will I recognize Blackwood when I get to Valencia?"

"He should be quite easy to pick out of a crowd," St. Denys assured him. "He's reasonably tall—about your height, I think—with blue eyes and blond curls long enough to brush his shoulders. Hawkins is tall— very tall—dark-haired, but also obviously English. None of the swarthy skin so common in Spain."

"And what should I do with the young man once I find him?" Teodoro inquired.

"Bring him back to Madrid," St. Denys instructed, his face carefully calm, only adding to Teodoro's unease. "I will make sure he returns to his father from here." He reached in his pocket and withdrew a purse. "Here is the first installment of your fee. I will have the rest for you when you bring me the boy."

Teodoro opened the purse and let the coins spill into his hand. As he expected, they were gold—enough to satisfy his obligations and some to spare. Pushing aside the misgivings he could not afford to indulge, he nodded shortly. "If all goes well, we should return within three weeks," he said. "I will send word to you when we arrive." After draining his goblet, he stood, his blade settling at his hip. "Until then, Your Mercy."

St. Denys watched the mercenary disappear out the door and leaned back against the wall of the inn, his eyes closing. Close. He was so close. Surely this time his plan would succeed.

TEODORO CLIMBED the stairs to his rooms in the upper level of the parochial residence of *la iglesia de San Pedro*—rooms he occupied at the insistence of his son's uncle, though as often as he had needed to leave the boy in the priest's care during his early years, there had been little choice but to accept. He found Esteban where he had left him, practicing his letters at the small table that served them as desk and dinner table as well, when he could afford to put food on it. "Fetch my saddlebags," he said. "I have a commission, one that will take me out of town for several weeks. Don Inocencio will see to you while I am gone."

Esteban was full of questions, but he knew better than to ask for answers his guardian was unlikely to give him. "*Sí*, Teo," he replied, rising from his seat and then putting the items Teodoro was likely to need in the pouches. He returned with the bags and offered them to Teodoro. "Be careful," he added unnecessarily.

"Stay out of trouble while I am gone," Teodoro countered. Esteban was at the age, no longer a child but not quite yet a man, when he was most ripe to get into any kind of scrape, but there was no way Teodoro could take him along on a journey where speed was of the essence—even if he could afford to hire a second horse. Reminded of his change in finances, Teodoro took the Englishman's purse from his belt and tossed one of the gold coins to Esteban. "That should keep you fed while I am gone. I don't want to find you've used it on anything but food when I return!"

"What else would I spend it on?" Esteban asked innocently, pocketing the coin with a bland stare.

Teodoro lifted an eyebrow, his dark eyes kindling until Esteban blushed and dropped his own. "You might buy a new shirt," he observed. "You've nearly outgrown that one."

"Food, and a new shirt," Esteban agreed, cursing himself for the blush that gave him away. "Anything else will wait until you return, Teo, I promise."

Teodoro nodded, ruffling Esteban's dark hair before dropping his hand to the hilt of his blade. He ran a checklist in his head—his sword, the *daga izquierda* tucked into his belt, the smaller dagger hidden in the top of one of his boots. Sighing to himself, he crossed to the small armoire in his bedroom and took out the box containing his pistol. It was a weapon he disliked, preferring the grace and elegance of the rapier, but his gut told him this affair was one in which he would need every advantage he could get. After pouring powder and shot into a small pouch, he moved the dagger to the back of his belt, tucked the pistol in its place, and gathered up his saddlebags.

"Three weeks, Esteban," he said as he headed toward the door. "Expect my return sometime after that." He did not mention what would happen should he not return—he no longer needed to.

"Be careful," Esteban said again, softly this time, as he watched his guardian, the only father he had ever known, disappear out the door.

TWO

Teodoro sat at a table in a shadowy corner of *la taberna Galesa*, nursing a tankard of ale and watching the tavern slowly fill with patrons as the evening wore on. He had arrived in Valencia around midday, and after a quick ride about the town to orient himself, he had spotted several señoritas of less than sterling virtue taking their ease under the shade of a portico on one of the less fashionable streets. A few minutes of conversation and light flirtation had gained him the location of the inn he sought, the girls assuring him they had seen only one golden head in town in recent days. St. Denys's *reales* had made it easy to procure an adequate room, and now he sat, eyes narrowed as he scrutinized each newcomer who entered the common room for one that matched his quarry's description.

The patience learned on many a weary campaign during the wars was rewarded when, shortly before ten, two men who could only be those he sought entered the tavern. The larger of the two was tall, heavily muscled, with the unconsciously arrogant air of one who had every confidence in his own strength. But it was the younger of the two who caught Teodoro's attention. St. Denys had described his target as a boy, but it was no stripling who accompanied the bravo into the common room. Though slender, the young man moved with a dancer's easy grace, and the face, surrounded by a halo of dark blond curls, could have served Velázquez as the model of an angel. Teodoro sank deeper in the shadows as the pair found empty seats at a table a short distance away.

Christian Blackwood flagged down a passing barmaid and ordered ale for himself and his bodyguard, Gerrard Hawkins. The tavern itself was no less oppressive than their room upstairs, but at least it was less confined, and the ale would provide some refreshment. He suspected Gerrard would not do more than sip at his, but Christian could finish it if Gerrard did not. "Relax," he urged his friend. "There is nothing here to worry about, just the same familiar crowd. No one followed us, and no one but my father knows we are here."

"That is not a reason to be less careful," Gerrard growled. "Your father is paying me well to keep you safe, and I intend to reward his faith by doing just that."

Though the noise of the tavern made it impossible for Teodoro to overhear the pair's conversation, enough carried to his ears to recognize that the two were not speaking Spanish. If he had needed any further confirmation that these were the men he sought, that affirmed it. Taking a sip from his tankard, he settled back to watch and wait. It would be much easier to separate the youth from his hulking companion after they both had a few ales under their belts.

As Christian had predicted, Gerrard drank little, but that did not bother him. He was relaxed and comfortable and drank enough for both of them. There was nothing else to do to pass the time; at least nothing that Gerrard would let him do. The bodyguard had proven remarkably resistant to Christian's charms. "How much longer will we stay in Valencia?" he asked again, though the answer had been the same since they arrived.

"Until the end of the month, as you well know," Gerrard replied. "Then we will find somewhere else to stay for another month. And we will keep doing this until the negotiations with Spain are finished and the threat to you is lifted."

Christian sighed. He knew Gerrard was right, knew this was for his own protection, but he was ready to return home, to return to his familiar haunts where he could be himself, rather than this overwhelmingly conservative country that looked askance at everything and everyone. He didn't know how much more heat and humidity he could stand when he could not even loosen the collar on his shirt to provide some relief.

It did not escape Teodoro's notice that the larger man—Hawkins, St. Denys had called him—barely touched his drink, while Blackwood was imbibing freely. Though their heads were bent close to each other over the small table as they conversed, he saw nothing that hinted at the relationship his employer had indicated between the two. Perhaps they were simply being circumspect in public, though that pointed to more control than the younger of the two was currently demonstrating. As the night wore on along with the number of tankards he consumed, Blackwood's expression became more animated, his gestures more sweeping, as if he was trying to convince his partner of something Hawkins was reluctant to undertake.

Giving up on persuading Gerrard to do anything more exciting than stare at the walls of the tavern, Christian rose from his seat. "I need some fresh air. I promise I won't go any farther than the alley outside the door, but the smoke in here is getting to me."

Privately Gerrard suspected the ale, not the smoke, was the culprit, but he dutifully rose as well. "I will walk outside with you," he offered, not wanting to neglect his charge.

A tight smile curled the corners of Teodoro's lips as the two finally rose from their table, Blackwood energetically, Hawkins with seeming reluctance. He waited until they had exited the common room before rising to follow them, tossing a coin on the table as he left. If all went well, he would not need to return.

Gerrard stood in the shadows of the alley, grasping the hilt of his sword. He had not seen anything to make him suspicious, but his instincts were shouting at him that his charge was in danger. Christian had come to mean much to him. He thought of Christian as a younger brother and had every intention of seeing him safely back to his father.

The alley in back of the tavern stank of stale beer, rotting trash, and urine—pretty much like any other alley in back of every other tavern Teodoro had ever seen. He paused in the shadow of the door frame, quick to notice Hawkins's hand resting on his sword hilt. Teodoro revised his estimation of the guard dog—for so he had come to think of the larger of the two—upward. He would not be able to depend upon surprise. No matter; he had another trick or two that would work as well.

"Christian, we should go back inside," Gerrard insisted, nerves jangling for no reason he could name. Maybe it was the heat combined with the putrid smells. Maybe it was the boredom mixed with constant vigilance. Either way or something else entirely, Gerrard wanted his charge safe behind locked doors again.

"Just a few more minutes," Christian wheedled; despite the alley's lack of fresh air, he dreaded being confined to their rooms yet again. He understood why it was necessary, but that did not mean he had to like it.

Tossing the light cloak he had donned to conceal his weapons behind him, Teodoro exited loudly and clumsily from the back door of the tavern, staggering over the filthy cobblestones and managing a convincing belch as he neared his quarry. "Hola, amigos!" he slurred, managing another few calculated, weaving steps before stumbling. He flashed a hand out to grab Hawkins's sword arm, as if for balance, while he drew the dagger he had tucked in the back of his belt with his other hand.

Gerrard's annoyance flared when the drunkard grabbed his sword arm. That turned into anger when he saw the knife in the man's other hand. Shaking off the confining touch, he drew his own sword with a hiss of steel. "Turn and walk the other way," he warned in a soft but authoritative voice, the Spanish words heavily accented but perfectly comprehensible. "I do not want to hurt you."

Behind him, he could hear Christian sinking into the shadows as Gerrard had instructed should a situation like this ever arise. Content that his charge was following orders, he focused entirely on the Spaniard facing him.

Teodoro knew he ought to have struck as soon as he drew his knife. That would have been the prudent move, but it was not an honorable one, and he found himself strangely unwilling to descend to that level before these two. The feint had not been wasted, in any case—he had a good idea now of the big man's reaction time, as well as his strength. Drawing his own sword with a quiet flourish, he inclined his head toward his adversary. "And I do not want to hurt you, but it seems unlikely both of us will get our wish."

When the other man drew his sword, Gerrard tensed even more. Clearly this was not merely some drunkard, but rather a man with a purpose. "What do you want?" he asked, hoping it was something simple like gold rather than a far more complicated answer involving the young man behind him.

"I want many things," Teodoro responded, "but I imagine the only one you are concerned about is your companion hiding in the shadows over there." He gestured with his sword, watching for the opportune moment. "I don't suppose you will be reasonable about this and let him go, will you?"

"Not in this lifetime," Gerrard replied hotly, following the other man's movements with the tip of his sword. "I don't know who sent you, but you can tell him to go to hell."

Pleased at his opponent's impassioned response—for a hotheaded swordsman was often a careless one—Teodoro decided to fan the flames. "Is it not enough that you have seduced this young man away from his family, but you must insult those who are justly concerned for his welfare?" he taunted.

So that's the lie the old man is selling, Gerrard realized. It was a dangerous game, one that could have Christian dead if he whispered it in the wrong ear. "You insult me by suggesting such a thing," he replied, consciously tamping down his temper. "En garde!"

Teodoro spared a quick glance at the young man who stood motionless in the shadows before making a quick lunge at his opponent. Hawkins would have the advantage of strength over him—he would have to counter with speed and cleverness. His blade slid along his adversary's steel, opening a slice across the back of his hand from knuckles to wrist.

Cursing as pain danced up his arm, Gerrard drew back and parried the Spaniard's thrust, using brute strength to push the other man away, giving himself a chance to regroup before attacking again. Their blades crossed, and Gerrard met implacable dark eyes through the gap. "I will not let you take him."

"Selfish, are you?" Teodoro sneered, freeing his blade and then countering with a dancing thrust of his own. "Looking at him, I cannot say I blame you."

There it was again, the implication that made Gerrard see red. He knew Christian's preferences and did not hold them against the younger man, but they were preferences he did not share. "'Tis self-interest, not selfishness," he retorted, his blade catching the Spaniard on the arm, enough to nick the cloth and, Gerrard hoped, the skin beneath.

"Self-interest?" Teodoro hissed, though the other man's blade had barely scratched his skin. He riposted fiercely, following through with a series of quick strokes that drove Hawkins backward over the slimy cobbles. "I have no doubt it is only yourself and your own... needs... that interest you."

Gerrard met the Spaniard's steel each time, but he could feel his breath quickening. His assailant was no simple blade. If he could not turn the tide quickly, he would lose this battle. "Christian," he called over his shoulder, using his strength to press his attack, hoping to give Blackwood a clear path to the tavern door. "Get inside."

The words, even more than the sudden attack, drove Teodoro to return thrust for thrust with equal ferocity. He could not afford to let Blackwood out of his sight and risk losing him.

Christian watched, tensed and ready to run if the opportunity presented itself, but Gerrard did not succeed in pushing their attacker toward the head of the alley. The Spaniard fought like a demon, and if Christian had not been so afraid of what would happen if Gerrard lost, he would have admired the lean lines of the older man's form.

It was apparent his adversary was tiring, but Teodoro could feel his own muscles beginning to weary as well, and he knew he had to make an end of this. Feinting to the left, he darted back quickly, avoiding the other's blade and sinking the tip of his sword into Hawkins's shoulder. At the same time, he stabbed with his other hand, his dagger sliding between two lower ribs.

The dual bolts of pain drove Gerrard to his knees, clutching at his shoulder and his side. Looking back over his shoulder and meeting Christian's eyes, he gave one last desperate order. "Run!"

Christian hesitated, not wanting to abandon his friend and defender, but the look on Gerrard's face was implacable. He turned on his heel and ran as though his life depended on it.

It grated at Teodoro's honor to leave so worthy an opponent simply lying in a growing pool of blood, but he could not spare a moment if he was to catch the fleeing youth. Hoping the next drinker who needed to relieve himself would find the wounded man, he hastily sheathed his sword, tucked his dagger into his belt, and raced after his prize down the dark alley.

Christian heard the pounding footsteps behind him, cursing under his breath as he swerved unsteadily. Fear had driven away a healthy portion of the alcohol he had consumed that evening, but not all of it, leaving him less fleet than usual. Added to that, he kept seeing Gerrard go down. Gerrard had drilled him over and over on what to do if they were attacked, and Christian had done it, though he had always promised himself he would not leave Gerrard if a fight went ill. The constant lectures had apparently done their job, because curse himself for a coward, Christian had run when ordered to do so. He veered around a corner, lost his footing, and stumbled, his ankle giving out beneath him as his head hit the cobblestones with a resounding thud.

Teodoro was so focused on closing the gap between them that when Blackwood fell suddenly, he nearly ran into the crumpled body. Dropping to his knees, he lifted Blackwood's head from the stones and ran his free hand over the motionless form to check for injuries. Finding no obvious breaks, he drew a deep breath into his heaving lungs and rose, holding the limp body in his arms.

As he slipped through the back streets to his room, Teodoro pondered the evening's turn of events. He had learned over the years to trust his instincts, and the young man in his arms set every one of them on alert.

THREE

TEODORO HAD made a point, when he left his few things in his room earlier that afternoon, of prowling the lodging's narrow corridors until he found a second staircase—probably a servants' passageway from the days when the inn was new enough (and clean enough) to cater to patrons who could afford servants. He owed his continued survival on more than one occasion to always knowing the location of an alternate exit. Tonight he took advantage of the little-used access way to carry the unconscious young man to his room without having to return through the crowded tavern.

Blackwood had not stirred, even when Teodoro let his legs slide to the floor so he could dig the key out of the pouch at his belt. Once inside the dingy accommodations, he set the bolt and deposited his quarry on the bed's thin mattress. After moistening a kerchief from the pitcher of water on the dresser, he cleaned away the traces of dirt from the slackened face. *Madre de Dios*, but he was beautiful! The honeyed tone of his skin, the long, dark lashes, the silken profligacy of his curls surpassed any Englishman's he had ever seen or imagined. Teodoro rinsed the cloth, then daubed at the rivulets that had run down the long, graceful throat. Beneath the sweat and the lingering scents of the rank alley and of too much beer, he could still smell something sweet and tangy, lime oil and sandalwood, perhaps. He tucked a strand of hair behind Blackwood's ear, staring at the golden ringlet curled around his finger.

The cool moisture on his face roused Christian from his stupor. His eyelids fluttered open to reveal the face of the man who had attacked Gerrard earlier. His blood chilled even as he struggled to regain his wits enough to speak. He wanted to rant and rail at the Spaniard for depriving him of his bodyguard and friend, but he doubted it would do any good. It was a shame, for the swordsman was everything Christian sought in a man: strong, fearless, cunning, ruggedly handsome. The thick moustache, so typical of this country, promised sensations aplenty as the mouth it topped brushed over his skin or closed around his cock. Christian frowned at his wayward thoughts. He had obviously knocked his head harder than he realized because he knew better than to fantasize about strangers, especially here, where the mere whisper of scandal could send a man to the stake.

Teodoro watched Blackwood's eyelids open to expose eyes the color of warm summer skies. A thin trace of gold edged the black pupils, dilated now as he fought his way back to consciousness. Satisfied that he saw no sign of concussion in the orbs that were beginning to flash with anger as awareness returned, Teodoro sat back, dropped the cloth onto the nightstand, and tugged at the end of his moustache in consideration.

"What do you want with me?" Christian asked defensively, sitting up and pulling his knees to his chest as if to protect himself. He had seen the man fight. It would be little help if he decided to attack.

"I mean you no harm," Teodoro answered, his captive's defensive posture reminding him—a reminder he would do well to heed, he told himself—that Blackwood was an innocent, or nearly so. "I do not intend to hurt you, only to return you to your family in Madrid."

"I have no family in Madrid," Christian exclaimed. "My only family is in London, and my father sent me here for my protection. Who told you I had family in Spain?"

Teodoro frowned. "Running away with your—" He bit off the word "lover," knowing in these days it was not safe to talk of such things openly. "Running away as you did is a poor means of protection," he replied dryly.

"Gerrard!" Christian gasped, realizing he had not given his friend a second thought. "Where is Gerrard?" he demanded.

Somehow, Teodoro found himself unable to tell Blackwood that he had left his lover bleeding to death in a filthy alley. "You need not worry about him," he answered gruffly. "You will not be seeing him again."

"He's dead, then," Christian said softly, lowering his forehead to his knees as he realized he would never see his friend and steadfast defender again. He took a deep breath to steady himself. "I'm no match for you with a sword, but I will see him avenged," he spat.

"He lived when I left him," Teodoro admitted, surprised at the need he felt to comfort the youth who would, he knew, just as soon see him lying in a pool of blood in place of his lover. "He is a strong man. It is likely he may survive."

Christian brightened immediately. "Let me send for a surgeon," he pleaded. "I have the means to pay for one. I can't just let Gerrard die, not after he protected me for so long."

His eyes narrowed, Teodoro considered Blackwood's plea and noted, for the second time, his claim that Hawkins was there as his protector. "I will see that a surgeon is called, on one condition," he answered. Though in truth he had meant to return downstairs to ensure his opponent had been found as soon as he knew Blackwood was unharmed, he would not dismiss the chance to turn his captive's concern to his advantage.

"What condition?" Christian asked warily. He wanted desperately to agree, but he knew better than to rush in blindly.

"It is nine days' ride back to Madrid," Teodoro countered. "I have no mind to keep you restrained all the way there. Give me your word you will return with me without resistance, and I will make sure your companion is well cared for."

Nine days. That was nine days Christian could use to find out what this man really wanted from him and to convince the mercenary to let him go. Nine days of cooperation in return for Gerrard's life. "Agreed," he said softly, knowing he had no real choice.

Teodoro was not a man who trusted easily, but looking into those deep blue eyes, he had no doubt Blackwood would keep his word. "Gather what you need from your room," he instructed. "I will see to your... friend, and perhaps order some dinner as well. We will leave at sunrise tomorrow."

"Gracias," Christian replied, knowing he could well be signing his own warrant into hell in return for Gerrard's life. He knew what Gerrard would say about it as well, but to Christian's mind, it was worth the risk. He started toward the door, cataloguing what he would need to take with him and what he could leave for Gerrard.

Using the main staircase this time, Teodoro returned to the tavern in search of the innkeeper, only to find the short, stout man wringing his hands over the vicious attack that had taken place outside his very doorstep. "This is a good, safe neighborhood," the man bemoaned. "What will happen to my business if guests are afraid of being attacked by robbers if they but step outside to relieve themselves?"

"Who has been attacked?" Teodoro asked, feigning concern. "My young friend's companion has been gone for some time, and we were becoming worried about him. Is it possible he was set upon?"

"If you mean the big man who has been staying with the blond-haired lad, then he's the one," the proprietor affirmed mournfully. "Bleeding all over my storeroom floor, he is."

"He is fortunate you found him," Teodoro responded, taking his coin pouch from his belt. "Will you send for a surgeon to tend to him? The lad and I have urgent business to attend to, but I will pay for their room, and a little extra for your trouble as well, if you will ensure our friend is taken care of while we are gone."

The innkeeper's eyes lit at the sight of the gold coin in Teodoro's hand. "Of course, Your Worthy. My wife will care for him as if he was our own son," he promised.

Teodoro nodded as he dropped the coin in the innkeeper's eager palm. "See that you do," he insisted. "I should be most displeased if I returned and found he had died while we were gone." Teodoro had no intention of returning to the inn, or indeed to the city, ever again, but the innkeeper had no need to know that. Adding a request for two bowls of *guisado* and a bottle of wine to be brought to his room, Teodoro headed back up the stairs, wondering if he was a fool to expect the youth to still be there.

Christian entered the room that had been both his prison and his escape for the past three weeks. As he gathered up his clothes for the trip to Madrid, he pondered what he knew so far. Obviously someone had sent this Spaniard after him under false pretenses. The swordsman had said he was taking Christian back to his family, but Christian's father had sent him to Spain with Gerrard. Even if he wanted Christian to return home, he would not have sent a stranger to attack them and would not have requested they come to Madrid. That meant this was another kidnapping attempt, only this time it would be successful if Christian did not keep his wits about him. His captor seemed an honorable man. If Christian could convince him of the truth, perhaps he would be willing to let him go. After picking up his things, Christian left the room he and Gerrard had shared for the one he would share with his captor for his last night in Valencia.

Teodoro had just reached the door of his room when he saw Blackwood approaching down the corridor, his belongings in his arms. "You are a man of your word," he acknowledged, gesturing for his charge to precede him into the chamber. "Your companion lives," he continued, settling into the single chair and stretching his legs out before him. "I have arranged for a surgeon to be sent for, and the innkeeper promises to care for him as his own until he has recovered."

"Gracias," Christian said again as he set down his bag. "I realized while you were away that I don't even know your name."

"Teodoro Ciéza de Vivar." He sat forward enough to execute a mock bow. "A su servicio."

"Christian Blackwood, Viscount Aldwych," Christian replied, returning the bow and completing the introduction. He took a seat on the bed since there was not another chair. "Who sent you, Ciéza? My father is in England and sent me here with Gerrard for my own protection. I don't know what you were told, but it was a lie."

Teodoro bit back a curse. In his experience, getting involved with nobility, even foreign nobility, was nothing but trouble. He would be lucky to come out of this with his skin intact. Unconsciously, his hand rose to stroke the tip of his moustache between thumb and forefinger, a habitual pose when deep in thought. "The man who commissioned me to find you said his name was St. Denys," he answered slowly. "He claimed to have been sent by your father to convince you to return to England—that you refused to comply in favor of spending your time with your—friend."

"That old bastard!" Christian spat. "I should have known."

"I take it he is not an old family friend?" Teodoro murmured, amused at the vehemence of Blackwood's reaction.

"Not hardly," Christian replied. "Perhaps an old family enemy."

"What does he hope to gain by my bringing you to him?" Teodoro asked. "He did not seem the type to hold you for ransom." In fact, St. Denys had paid handsomely for his services, but Teodoro was not anxious for Blackwood to realize that fact.

"For money, no," Christian agreed, "but my father is the Duke of Ranleigh, England's chief negotiator with Spain, and St. Denys has tried more than once to persuade my father to his point of view concerning a series of treaties. My father doesn't think St. Denys's plans would benefit anyone but the old goat. The last time my father refused him, St. Denys made some very pointed threats, and since then there have been four attempts to kidnap me, including yours. My father hoped I would be safer on the Continent, so he hired Gerrard to protect me."

"Canalla!" Teodoro snarled, thinking back to the older man's putative concern for the safety of his dear friend's son. Between the two, there was no question which one Teodoro believed—Blackwood's sincerity all but radiated from him. Teodoro cared little for the negotiations between their countries—it was preferable to open warfare, though he doubted much would be gained by either in the end—but using a man's son against him was despicable. A wave of disdain at his own actions swept over him. As a hired sword, he had done many things he was not especially proud of, but his role in coercing this young man and all but murdering his bodyguard sickened him. Wishing he had his hands around the old liar's throat, Teodoro was about to speak when a knock sounded at the door.

Ingrained habit took over, and Christian rose from the bed, backing into the farthest corner of the room. Gerrard had always made him do this to give the bodyguard space to move in case of a fight.

Noting Blackwood's cautious withdrawal, Teodoro felt even more guilt at having deprived him of his protector. "That will be the dinner I asked for," he reassured him, though his hand was on the hilt of his dagger as he cracked open the door. The serving wench who offered their tray was hardly a threat, unless the coquettish smile she threw at his young companion could be considered a threat to his virtue. *Just as well the lad will be sleeping with me tonight.* That thought brought an unwelcome flare of heat, which Teodoro was quick to smother. It had been a long time since he had felt such an impulse, and in any case his new companion had several times implied that despite St. Denys's hints, his bodyguard had not also been his lover. After setting the tray on the dresser, Teodoro poured a deep draught of the rich red wine into one of the mugs. "Eat," he prompted, picking up a bowl of stew and settling back into the chair. "It will be a long ride back to Madrid."

"I thought... I thought you believed me!" Christian said plaintively as he approached the tray and picked up a bowl, then backed into the corner again to eat. He had hoped, when he saw Ciéza's reaction, that the Spaniard would leave him here with Gerrard rather than drag him to Madrid.

"I do." Teodoro scowled, knowing that the prudent thing to do would be to take the old man's money and ride away from Blackwood and everything he represented. He also knew there was no way in hell he could do it.

"Then why are you taking me to Madrid?" Christian demanded, stirring his spoon through the cooling stew. "I'm safe here, or at least I will be when Gerrard recovers. St. Denys is in Madrid. That's the last place it's safe for me to be right now."

"You said there have already been three attempts to kidnap you," Teodoro pointed out. "Whatever game St. Denys is playing, he obviously means to have you at any cost." He thought again with shame of the gold coins in his belt pouch and the equal amount he had been promised upon his return. "If I don't bring you back, he'll just find someone else to send in my place." He took a bite of stew and gestured with the empty spoon. "We need to find some way to stop him for good."

"All I have to do is stay out of his grasp until the negotiations are complete," Christian countered, still trying to dissuade his captor. "He won't have any use for me after that. It shouldn't be but another month or two."

Teodoro snorted. "Spain and England have been 'negotiating' since before you were born," he retorted, "and like as not they'll be at it still when both of us are gone. Do you *like* living in hiding? Never knowing if any man who approaches you is friend or foe?"

"No," Christian admitted. "I hate it, but going to Madrid seems incredibly risky. What if we can't find a way to stop him?"

"Then you're no worse off than you are now," Teodoro insisted. In truth, he wasn't sure himself why he was pressing the matter so urgently, except that he wanted to pay the old man back for playing him for a fool—and to redeem the debt of honor he felt binding him to this young man's fate.

Recognizing he was clearly not going to win this argument, Christian turned his attention to his dinner with a sigh. When he had finished, he looked back up. "Can I at least say good-bye to Gerrard before we leave?"

"In the morning, before we depart," Teodoro agreed, thinking it would be best to give Hawkins as much time as possible to recover before letting Blackwood see him. "We should get some rest while we can."

Christian eyed the bed nervously. It had been one thing to sleep beside Gerrard at night, but to share a bed, however innocently, with a stranger made him more than a little uncomfortable. Pulling the quilt off the bed, he laid it on the floor, intending to make himself a pallet in the corner where he could sleep.

"What the hell are you doing?" Teodoro demanded as Blackwood made to lie down on the floor. The knowledge that his companion couldn't bear to share a bed with him shouldn't have surprised him, but he found it galling nonetheless. "Take the bed—I'll sleep here."

"That's not necessary," Christian insisted. "I'll be perfectly fine here. I couldn't deprive you of your bed."

"Believe me, I have slept in far worse accommodations over the years," Teodoro scoffed. "Take the bed, Your Excellency."

"Really, I couldn't," Christian protested. "And don't call me 'Your Excellency.' Call me Christian, or Blackwood, at least. Nobody calls me by my title, not even my father's servants."

"Take the fucking bed!" Teodoro thundered, losing what little patience he had left.

Reluctantly, Christian spread the quilt back over the mattress and removed his shoes and jacket so he could rest more comfortably. With Gerrard, he had stripped down to his long undershirt and smallclothes, but he did not know Ciéza that well yet. He slid between the sheets, then closed his eyes to pretend to sleep, sure he would not get a moment's rest. But within a minute, sleep had overtaken him.

What the fuck have I gotten myself into? Teodoro asked himself. If Esteban had challenged him so persistently, he'd have boxed the boy's ears by now. But Esteban had never tied his guts in knots the way one evening with this blue-eyed youth had done. Stretching out his long legs and leaning back in the hard wooden chair, Teodoro settled in for a watchful night.

FOUR

ESTEBAN STARED out at the street from the window of *la taberna Castellán*, as he had for most of the past three days. Teodoro did not like him to visit the tavern where they sometimes took meals when they were in funds, but the small window in their rooms at the parish residence did not give much view of the street, and after three weeks had come and gone and Teodoro had still not returned, Esteban could no longer sit upstairs and pretend to study the lessons his *tío*, Inocencio, had left for him. If he had known exactly where his guardian had gone, Esteban would have set off in search of him, but since Teo had neglected to provide him with that information, he could do nothing but wait, watch for him, and worry about what would happen should he not return.

It was growing dark, and Beatriz, the tavern owner's wife, had started throwing him looks (which he was doing his best to ignore) to indicate it was time to return home before the night's heavy drinking began, when Esteban caught sight of a figure in a familiar wide-brimmed hat and worn brown jerkin. When he was younger, he might have run out the door, crying out to anyone with ears to hear that Teo had returned, but with age Esteban had learned some discretion and also some self-preservation. Slipping quietly outside, he tried to appear as if he were simply strolling the street to take some air and just happened to notice that Teodoro was approaching. He was so relieved to see Teo that he did not at first realize he was not alone.

As soon as they turned onto *el calle del Badajos*, Teodoro spotted Esteban doing his best to look as if he had been loitering innocently on the street rather than just coming out of the tavern. He knew Esteban would have begun to worry, since the trip from Valencia had taken longer than he had expected. They had not gotten off at first light as he had intended—Blackwood had insisted on seeing the bodyguard, Hawkins, to confirm for himself that the man's injuries were not life-threatening, and then had subjected the innkeeper to an exhaustive list of instructions for the wounded man's care. Nor had Hawkins taken with equanimity the news that his charge was planning to travel to Madrid with the very man who had almost killed him. A loud and colorful argument had ensued, ending with Blackwood declaring that he had given his word, and that since Gerrard was in no position to stop him, he might as well shut up and accept it. Teodoro had been forced to admire his charge's determination, though he was well aware that had he been able to, Hawkins would have gladly torn out Teodoro's guts and used them as restraints to keep the *vizconde* from leaving. He had made his position clear when, after Blackwood had embraced him warmly and left the room, Hawkins had caught Teodoro's arm and growled to him, "I swear that if any harm comes to him, I will hunt you down wherever you are and kill you." Teodoro had simply nodded, his dark eyes expressionless as he bowed to the wounded man and took his leave.

Since then he had endured nearly two weeks of riding (if it could be called that, since the horse he had hired was none too pleased at having to carry a double burden and refused any gait beyond a walk) with Blackwood clinging pillion behind him. In retaliation, Teodoro was certain, the nag had thrown a shoe midway between Alarcón and Honrubia. It was half a day's walk to reach the nearest village, and they'd had to wait for the blacksmith to sober up before the shoe could be replaced, which had cost them another day. But as bad as the endless hours in the saddle with Blackwood pressed against him had been, the nights were worse. Whether they stopped at an inn or slept wrapped in their cloaks under the stars, Teodoro had been achingly aware of Blackwood's presence. That he knew the ache would remain unsatisfied had done little to improve his temper.

Christian had sighed with relief when Ciéza pulled the horse to a stop. He was sure this was Madrid, though he had never been there before, which perhaps meant they had reached the end of their journey. Even if they had not, they were stopping for the moment, giving him a much needed break from Ciéza's proximity. The last near fortnight had been... difficult, the Spaniard's nearness a constant prod to Christian's libido, until his erection seemed to nag at him day and night. Ciéza had not seemed to notice, but Christian needed a respite. Fortunately, they had left the horse at a livery stable and were now on foot. He glanced around to see an inn of slightly lesser quality than the one he had inhabited in Valencia, but that seemed to be their destination. A youth some years younger than Christian's own age lounged against the wall, pushing off when he saw them and approaching eagerly. Christian frowned, wondering who this was.

"You're late, Teo," Esteban said accusingly, stopping in his tracks when he noticed the gentleman accompanying Teodoro. The man was elegantly dressed, if somewhat dusty and rumpled, and he was undeniably handsome, but something about way he dogged Teo's steps like a shadow set Esteban's teeth on edge. "Who is this?" he demanded, nodding at the stranger.

"My commission," Teodoro answered shortly, amused that Esteban sought to distract him by taking the offensive. "Your Excellency, this whelp is my son, Esteban. Esteban, this is Don Cristian Blackwood." He didn't bother with the Englishman's full title; it wouldn't mean anything to Esteban, and if all went well he wouldn't be around long enough for it to matter in any case. The younger men bowed to each other with the air of two dogs sniffing each other warily.

Christian had already discovered a weakness for Ciéza's voice, but hearing his name spoken, not with boring English rhythm, but with the Spanish flair that made everything more alluring—Cristian, not Christian—only increased his susceptibility.

"Now, since you've obviously made yourself familiar with the tavern in my absence, make yourself useful and have Beatriz send us some food—and a bottle of wine." He gestured to Blackwood to precede him into the taproom, his gaze following the graceful sway of the younger man's backside as they entered. "Better make it two bottles," he called to Esteban, forcing his gaze away.

"Thank you," Christian murmured, hearing Ciéza mention wine. He turned back with a grateful smile. "I could do with a drink," he admitted ruefully as Ciéza gestured toward a table in the corner that offered an unimpeded view of the rest of the room.

Teodoro dropped his saddlebag on the scarred tabletop, stretching his aching muscles as he hung his hat on a hook near the table. Perhaps after a decent meal he would be able to decide what to do with his reluctant guest. Though the tavern rented rooms, it was far too public for safety, as Teodoro himself had proved in Valencia. He had not brought Blackwood over sixty leagues only to lose him his first night in Madrid. He could likely convince Aldonza de la Cerda, proprietress of the brothel where he had served as a hired protector until Esteban had become old enough to notice where he spent his time, to hide the *vizconde* in one of her rooms. It would cost Teodoro a night in her bed—certainly no hardship, though the idea did not appeal as much as it once had—but he could only imagine Blackwood's scorn at hearing he was expected to sleep in a *prostíbulo*. If Blackwood did not decide to sample the wares for himself.... No, there was nothing for it but to take him back to their lodgings, where he could be kept out of danger until Teodoro could decide how to deal with St. Denys.

After removing his plumed hat, Christian took a seat beside Ciéza, not sure how far his "host's" hospitality extended. He reeked of sweat and dust, wanting only to sink into a tub of warm water and refresh himself. The city was clearly Ciéza's home. Surely he would know where to procure a bath. "Would it be possible to bathe after dinner?" he asked hopefully. "I stink of our travels." As he spoke, the image of sharing that luxury with Ciéza drifted through his thoughts, sending a fresh spike of lust to his reawakening erection.

Teodoro glanced sharply at Blackwood, a sudden vision of his companion reclining naked in a tub of steaming water flashing across his mind. He smoothed his moustache and forced his thoughts away from the tantalizing image. He would deliver the *vizconde* to safety and that would be the end of it. Blackwood had no place in his life. "It should be possible to arrange one after we eat," he conceded, determined to find some errand that needed to be done elsewhere while his charge performed his ablutions.

"Thank you again," Christian answered evenly. He could tell Ciéza was not terribly happy with him at the moment, but then the man never seemed particularly happy, regardless of what Christian did or did not do. He had hoped to win Ciéza over with his charm, but it seemed he was immune to that as well.

The innkeeper's wife came over with a platter of roasted chicken, a loaf of bread, and several plates and tankards, Esteban trailing behind her with two bottles of wine.

"So who's this fine gentleman?" Beatriz asked, lingering after setting the food on the table. "He's a cut above the ones you usually drag in here."

"And what kind of gentlemen does he usually drag in here?" Christian interrupted, not wanting his identity revealed and not sure his new protector would have thought of a believable excuse for his presence.

"None as pretty as you, that's for sure." Beatriz simpered with a bat of her eyelashes and a swirl of her skirt that revealed a hint of ankle above her functional shoes. "But you didn't answer my question, Ciéza."

"Fencing lessons," Teodoro answered shortly, knowing that whatever he told her would be all over the neighborhood by nightfall. "If we can negotiate acceptable terms over dinner." He stared at the tavern keeper's wife until she flushed and turned back toward the kitchen, no doubt to share the news with her husband, the cook, and anyone else in earshot.

Teodoro relieved Esteban of the wine, opened a bottle with the ease of long practice, and filled the two tankards, then offered one to Blackwood before taking a deep draught of his own. Esteban was not allowed wine, except sometimes when Teodoro soaked stale bread in it for their breakfast when funds were low. Seeing the way Teodoro watched their guest swallow his portion made Esteban vaguely uneasy, though it didn't stop him from tearing into the provender with the impatient hunger of youth.

Blackwood sat quietly, sipping his wine. Careful not to stare at the way the younger man's throat worked as he swallowed, Teodoro emptied the bottle into his mug and split the remaining chicken between them, considering again whether he had made a monumental mistake in bringing Blackwood back to Madrid.

Christian nodded his thanks at Ciéza, wondering about the youth who had joined them. Ciéza had identified Esteban as his son, but the youth had called the swordsman "Teo," not "Father." He had seen nothing to suggest Ciéza was married, but that did not mean he had never been. Was the youth perhaps his son from some past relationship, legitimate or not? Or was it something more sinister that bound them? Esteban was young, fourteen or fifteen, perhaps, but old enough to be considered an adult. And he had called Ciéza by his given name. Was the title of son a way of hiding an illicit relationship of a different kind? If either of those were true, they meant a disappointing end to the attraction Christian could feel growing despite his reminders to himself that such feelings were dangerous in this place. "Will we be staying the night here?" he asked, uncomfortable, as always, with the lengthy silence.

"Perhaps your funds are limitless, but mine are not," Teodoro answered, wiping his moustache clean with the back of his hand. "Nor is a public inn the safest venue, as you have seen," he added wryly. "We will return to my lodgings until a more permanent solution can be found to your current difficulties."

"I wasn't sure where you made your home," Christian replied softly, feeling like the worst kind of cad for having unintentionally pointed out the difference in their stations. He didn't spend a lot of time dwelling on his money because it had never been an issue one way or another. Nor did he view those in less stable financial straits as inferior, unlike many of his peers. Ciéza had already proven himself a more honorable man than the much wealthier, "nobler" St. Denys. Unfortunately, he doubted Ciéza would believe him if he made that assertion at the moment.

"If you are finished, Your Excellency, we will make our way there now." Teodoro rose, dropped a coin from St. Denys's rapidly diminishing purse to the table, and tucked the second bottle of wine under his arm. Blackwood's presence had not appeared to have drawn unwarranted attention yet; he would like to be gone before it did.

"I thought I told you not to call me that," Christian muttered as he followed Ciéza out of the tavern and back into the street, Esteban trailing along behind like a lost puppy, except that he was the one who belonged here, far more than Christian did anywhere.

Gaze darting watchfully down each *calle* and *avenida* they passed, Teodoro led them through the darkening streets, turning down a narrow alleyway when they reached the front of a centuries-old church. Blackwood paused, looking up at the carved saints adorning the stone façade.

"I didn't know you could rent rooms in a church!" Christian exclaimed. "Are churches that different here than in England?"

Knowing the Church considered the apostate English as little better than heathens, Teodoro's lips twitched beneath his moustache. "As to that, I could not say," he replied. "But we do not sleep in the church. The boy's uncle is *el cura*—pastor—here at *la iglesia de San Pedro*. He allows us rooms in the upper story of his residence." He glanced back at Blackwood, his expression hardening. "It is perhaps not up to the standards to which Your Excellency is accustomed, but I can assure you it will be safe."

"Will you stop calling me 'Your Excellency'?" Christian demanded, noting that Ciéza had referred to the priest as Esteban's uncle but not his brother-in-law. The mystery of his kidnapper-turned-protector deepened with each passing moment. "And safety is my first priority, so if it is indeed as safe as you say, then I will be perfectly content."

Deciding not to spring their new houseguest on Don Inocencio unannounced, after leading them down the alley to the priest's residence, Teodoro entered not through the front door but around back, through a separate entrance that led to the kitchen and up a narrow set of stairs to their rooms. Originally a small servant's quarters and storerooms, the two men had converted the space into a bedroom for Teodoro and a slightly larger room that held a table and chairs, several bureaus and cabinets, and a cot for Esteban.

After locking the door behind them, Teodoro hung his hat on the hook beside the door, then unbuckled his sword belt and leaned the rapier against the wall beneath it. He removed the pistol from his waistband, then returned it and his saddlebags to the armoire in the bedroom before turning his attention to lighting the oil lamp in the center of the table.

Christian removed his hat and sword, holding them awkwardly as he waited for some indication of where he should put them. Looking around curiously, he was pleased to see that. while simple, the room was clean and welcoming, obviously a home and not simply rented rooms.

Teodoro couldn't interpret Blackwood's expression as he glanced around the unadorned room, but he doubted the noble was impressed. Even the rooms at the inn in Valencia were larger. Gritting his teeth, he dropped his eyes to the items the nobleman held out to him, for all the world as if Teodoro was his valet. *He likely considers you even lower than that*, Teodoro reminded himself, nodding toward the second empty hook. "Make yourself at home," he said, knowing as he spoke the words how laughable they would sound to Blackwood, whose home was certainly nothing like this.

Christian took Ciéza at his word, hung his belongings on the indicated hook, and unbuttoned the top button of his doublet. "I have yet to get used to the heat in Spain," he admitted. "I always feel like I have too many clothes on."

Against his will, Teodoro's gaze was drawn to the curve of throat and the vee of smooth skin revealed by the gap in the fine fabric. He could imagine all too clearly freeing the remaining buttons from their closures, slipping his hands inside to explore the warm skin beneath. The room suddenly felt too small to hold them both. "I am going back to the tavern," he said, buckling his sword back on, "to learn what has been happening in my absence." And to get his inappropriate lust for Blackwood under control. The sooner the *vizconde* was out of his rooms and his thoughts, the better it would be for all concerned.

Stomach jumping with nerves at the unexpected announcement, Christian's eyes flew to Ciéza. Had he been wrong in trusting his instincts, which, even now, insisted Ciéza meant him no harm? He knew Ciéza's type, despite the oddities that set him somewhat apart. With a youth of Esteban's age to feed and clothe, money was surely a motivator for him, even more so than for many of his fellow blades, and St. Denys had it aplenty. Christian also knew enough of the way St. Denys operated to guess that only half of the commission had been paid in advance, meaning that Ciéza still had much to gain from turning him over to the old bastard. The trip could be as innocent as Ciéza claimed. Or it could be a chance to alert St. Denys to his successful return. And that was a chance Christian could not take. "Whatever St. Denys offered you to kidnap me, I will match it," he offered slowly. "Just do not turn me over to him."

Teodoro slammed his fist on the table, his dark eyes flashing. "I brought you here to find a way to free you from St. Denys's threat," he growled dangerously. "I do not require your gold to remind me of my obligations." He strode to the door, then paused to glance back at Esteban. "Lock this behind me," he instructed, and then, despite his intentions, his gaze returned to Blackwood. "I will set water to heat for your bath," he said tightly, turning away and closing the door behind him.

Esteban glared at the stranger who stood across the table from him, still staring at the doorway. "How dare you insult Teo's honor?" he demanded. "I don't know who you are or why he brought you here, but as long as you are under his protection, he would give his life to keep you safe." His gaze raked over the foppish figure disdainfully. "I only hope you're worthy of his regard."

He probably was not worthy, Christian mused sadly, but still, Ciéza's departure gave him a chance to question Esteban. "Why don't you call him 'Father'?" he asked.

"Because he isn't really my father," Esteban admitted. "He married my mother after my father died. We came here with my uncle, Don Inocencio, when I was only a few years old. Teo is a good man, an honorable man," Esteban insisted, stung that this interloper could even doubt it.

"He has been kind to me," Christian assured him, not wanting to tarnish the image the lad had of his guardian. "My life depends on his trustworthiness, though, so you must understand that I will do anything to ensure my safety."

"If Teo has promised to protect you, then you need have no fear," Esteban countered, still angered that this stranger would partake of Teodoro's hospitality with one breath and impugn his honor with the next. "He is a man of his word."

The sound of the door banging open drew their attention. "I told you to lock that behind me," Teodoro growled from around the wooden tub he carried. After depositing his burden in the bedroom, he fixed them both with a reproving glare. "The water will be hot enough in a few minutes. Do not let me find this door unlocked again when I return." His dark eyes pinned the *vizconde* with his stare. "And do not be so foolish as to think of leaving in my absence."

"I'm not a fool, Ciéza," Christian retorted. "I'm not going to expose myself to danger when I have nowhere else to go."

"See that you remember that." Teodoro pulled his hat from the hook and turned to go. "And lock the door!" The heavy wood slammed at his heels.

Esteban flushed darkly at being scolded like a child. At fifteen, he felt the weight of his impending adulthood, and any slight to that status angered him. He dared not take his frustration out on his revered guardian, which left the unlucky Englishman instead. "I'll fetch the water for Your Excellency's bath," he said mockingly. "It wouldn't do for you to be caught gossiping with those so far beneath you."

He was out the door before Christian could protest. With a sigh, Christian frowned. At least he knew what the relationship was between them now, but that provided little comfort in the face of Esteban's open hostility. It would not take much for that to carry over to Ciéza, Christian was sure. He sighed. When had his life gotten so complicated?

TEODORO EXAMINED his worn boots as he took another long draught from his mug, trying to distract his thoughts from the residence a few blocks away, and the *vizconde* who would even now be lowering himself into his bath. He'd made the rounds of the tavern, picking up whatever news he could of events during his absence. The weeks had been quiet, it seemed; he'd heard nothing more noteworthy from his acquaintances than a jealous dispute over a shared lover between two of the leading ladies of the *teatro*, and the usual depredations of the Inquisition. Determined to avoid returning to his rooms until he was sure Blackwood had completed his ablutions, Teodoro sat in a quiet corner of the tavern, unable to prevent his mind from imagining the young man stripping off his clothes to enter the tub, the water closing over his honeyed skin, gilding it in the candlelight…. He bit back a curse and forced himself to consider instead what his next steps should be to rid himself of his all-too-tempting responsibility.

The sensible action would be to deliver Blackwood to St. Denys and collect his *reales*, Teodoro thought, but he knew he was not mercenary enough to do so. His pride chafed at being used as the old man's pawn, though he had no doubt that was how both St. Denys and Blackwood saw him—common and readily expendable. Still, he mused, even a pawn could bring down a king. For better or worse, he'd taken on responsibility for the *vizconde* when he'd incapacitated his protector. His thoughts turned relentlessly to Blackwood, picturing him reclining in the bath, the water rippling around him as he settled deeper into the tub, his elegant hands sliding over his chest and shoulders to wet them.

One of the serving girls passed by the table to ask Teodoro if he wanted more wine. He must have done something to fall out of Beatriz's good graces, since she was not serving him herself. Bautista Garza might own *del Castellán* in name, but everyone knew his wife was the one who really ran *la taverna*. Teodoro wondered if she would have been better pleased had he brought the intriguing stranger back with him. Well, Beatriz would just have to suffer his absence—he would not bring the *vizconde* back to the attentions of the tavern keepers or its patrons again. Nodding his thanks to the serving wench, his gaze was caught by one of Aldonza de la Cerda's courtesans, who offered him a simpering smile that was clearly an invitation. He had taken his pleasure at the *burdel* in the past in exchange for dealing with customers who got too drunk or too rough, but even if he was not sharing his accommodations tonight, he knew that thoughts of Blackwood would have kept him from visiting Aldonza or one of her stable. An image of supple hands lathering over smooth flesh invaded his mind, and he scowled. Inclining his head with a tight smile that was both acknowledgment and dismissal, he stretched wearily. This was going to be a damned long night.

Try as he would, Teodoro couldn't keep his thoughts from returning to the enticing image of the naked young man in his chambers, imagining his own hands gliding over that alluringly lithe body. Heady with arousal, he drained the mug and dropped a coin on the table, then rose to return to his lodging. Blackwood had better be finished bathing, Teodoro thought grimly, because he needed to find some way to deal with the growing hardness concealed beneath his leather jerkin.

HAVING UNDRESSED with a relieved sigh, Christian trailed his fingers over the steaming water Esteban had carried up in sullen silence. It would be so good to be clean again. Gerrard had laughed at him for his insistence on bathing every night, but the heat and the dust were overwhelming compared to home, and Christian had found he could not sleep well without being clean. There had been neither the time nor the privacy to bathe during the trip from Valencia to Madrid, and Christian intended to relish every moment tonight. He stepped into the small tub and sank into the water, knees bent nearly to his chest, another sigh escaping his lips as he relaxed against the side of the tub. Idly, he stirred the water, splashing it gently over his upper chest, not submerged like the rest of him.

Christian reached for a rag, then worked the bar of soap into a lather and began to wash away the dust of the road. His thoughts strayed, as they always seemed to these days, to his rescuer. Ciéza had probably reached the tavern by now and was catching up with old friends, surely the center of everyone's attention, for how could he not be? They would gather around him, laugh with him, slap him on the shoulder and back, demanding to know of his latest adventure. The ladies would fawn over him, hanging on his every word, and if he knew their type, the caresses they bestowed would linger, making offers that most men would accept without hesitation. Christian had always been immune to their blandishments, preferring a different kind of caress, but he had seen no sign that Ciéza might share that interest. No, he was almost certainly trying to decide which one to pick tonight. A frown marred Christian's features as he realized the depth of his jealousy. *Stop being an idiot*, he scolded himself. *You have no claim on him and no hope of ever having one.*

Thoughts of Ciéza had a predictable effect on Christian's body. Glancing around to assure himself he was truly alone, he lowered his soapy hand to the heavy flesh between his legs. Stroking gently at first, then with ever increasing vigor, he imagined it was Ciéza's hand, not his own, that caressed him thus. He muffled his moans out of habit, not sure where Esteban was, as his cock swelled and his passion mounted.

The trembling started low in Christian's body, almost against his back, the telltale sign that his climax was nearing. Closing his eyes, he gave his imagination free rein, sliding one hand lower to cup the heavy sac and then beyond to dance around the tight pucker of flesh. He was close... so damned close. Arching his hips, he groaned as he pushed the tip of one finger inside. Another moan escaped him as he imagined it was Ciéza's finger inside him, preparing him. That thought was enough to trigger his release, and he came hard, Teodoro's name escaping in a sigh as he collapsed into the water. A sound in the next room caught his attention, and he muttered a curse, rising quickly and wrapping the towel around his waist. He had no desire to be caught pleasuring himself with Ciéza's name on his lips. That Ciéza's given name had slipped out would only add to the impropriety. They did not have enough of an acquaintance to excuse that liberty, even under these circumstances.

Esteban had delayed in the kitchens as long as he could, chattering with Isabel, the elderly woman who cooked for Don Inocencio, but eventually she finished all her chores and left to return to her own home. He said his good-byes, along with a promise to go to the market for her in the morning, and made his way reluctantly back upstairs. He'd hoped the intruder would have finished his bathing by now—it certainly never took him that long to clean himself!—but the door to the bedchamber was still shut. Esteban hesitated when an unmistakable sound filtered through the closed doorway. He knew the sounds of passion from the rare nights Teo had brought a woman to warm his bed, and that was definitely the moan of someone finding pleasure. A knowing grin spread over his face—so the snobbish Englishman was no better than Esteban in that regard after all!—when the moan turned into a name. His guardian's name. The stranger moaned "Teodoro" as he pleasured himself!

Teodoro strode into the common room of his chambers after relocking the door behind him, to see Esteban standing in uncharacteristic awkwardness in front of the bedroom door. "Isn't he done yet?" he growled, his voice clipped with frustration.

"He... no, Teo, he...." Esteban flushed, too shocked to tell Teodoro what he had heard.

Looking around the bedroom, Christian realized he had not brought his valise into the room with him. Sighing against the inevitable, he wrapped the cloth more tightly around his waist and opened the door. He hesitated when he saw Teodoro and Esteban standing there, but there was no help for it. He needed his clothes. Without speaking, he crossed to his bag and rummaged through it for a clean shirt, breeches, and hose.

Teodoro's already hard cock throbbed against his breeches when Blackwood entered the room clad only in a towel, his bare chest and limbs even more alluring than he had imagined them. Nodding to Esteban, he unbuckled his sword and leaned it against the sideboard. "Be sure he doesn't wander off," he instructed, then entered the bedroom and closed the door firmly behind him. Leaning his head against the dark wood, he fought against the urge to send Esteban on some errand so he could strip the scrap of fabric from Blackwood's hips and bare him completely to his hungry gaze. *Fool*, he told himself as he quickly stripped off his own garments and sank into the cooling water. Knowing that Blackwood had reclined there only moments earlier did nothing to tame his passion.

Christian flushed a little when Ciéza left so quickly. He did not know what else he could have done, but he still felt incredibly awkward as he dressed in front of Esteban, deliberately keeping his back turned and putting the shirt on first so the long tails would cover him if the towel slipped. Eventually, dressed and feeling more in control of himself, he turned around and took a seat at the table, tapping his fingers idly as he tried to keep his mind on anything other than the knowledge that Ciéza was probably settling into the same tub where he had found his release only minutes ago.

After washing himself quickly, Teodoro wrapped his hand around his insistent erection, clenching his teeth to prevent himself from crying out as he pumped into his callused fist. Imagining himself thrusting into the *vizconde*'s willing embrace, he felt his balls tightening as his climax overtook him quickly, easing the physical ache but doing nothing to relieve the pull of desire that still drew him to Blackwood.

The sounds of Teodoro bathing traveled through the thin walls, adding fuel to the fire of Christian's thoughts. He shifted uncomfortably on the hard chair, trying not to draw attention to his state. He had absolutely no desire to explain himself to Esteban. If Teodoro were the one asking…. He reminded himself that was a foolish, impossible notion. A part of his brain marveled that he could react so strongly when he had climaxed mere minutes ago. He had plenty of experience with passion, but never had his desire refused to be quenched, at least temporarily, by an orgasm as strong as the one that had taken him in the bath. He looked toward the door, speculation clear on his face. If just the thought of Teodoro could make him react this way, what could the man's touch do?

Esteban watched the Englishman shift awkwardly at the table, as if he found the chairs too hard for his taste—or, Esteban realized suddenly, as if he found it uncomfortable to sit at all. The look on the stranger's face as he stared at the closed door raised an uneasy suspicion in Esteban's mind. He knew that some men felt passion for other men—the Inquisition dealt publicly and cruelly with those it discovered. Suddenly he felt an urgent need to ensure that the man sitting across from him harbored no such impression about Teodoro.

"I am surprised Teo did not find other accommodations tonight," he offered casually, watching Blackwood's expression. "Especially after being gone several weeks... the señoritas cluster around him like flies around a honey pot. A man like Teo can always have his choice of women. They say he is as skilled with the ladies as his renowned kinsman, Don Rodrigo Díaz de Vivar," Esteban continued proudly.

Christian's heart clenched even as he reminded himself that this should not have come as a shock. Of course the señoritas flocked to Ciéza. They would have to be blind not to appreciate his powerful physique and wry smile. "You said yourself he takes his responsibilities seriously," Christian replied dully. "I am sure that is why he has not made other arrangements for the night."

Esteban frowned as the implications of the discussion dawned upon him. Their small quarters contained two beds—the one in Teodoro's bedroom, and the cot Esteban slept on in the common room. Where was the stranger going to sleep?

After he pulled on his only other clean pair of breeches and a loose shirt, Teodoro left his boots in the bedchamber and padded out silently into the common room. His two companions sat at the table, tension clear in both their attitudes. "Perhaps you should wash as well, Esteban," he suggested, "before we remove the tub."

"I bathed in the river yesterday—some of the other boys and I went swimming," Esteban said hastily, hoping Teodoro would find nothing unusual in his disinclination to bathe. Changing the subject quickly, he asked, "Teo, where is this—" He hesitated at the sharp look in Teodoro's eyes, biting off the insult he had been ready to utter. "Where is the English gentleman going to sleep?"

FIVE

CHRISTIAN HAD been in the bedroom. He knew the bed was large enough to sleep two. From the sound of Esteban's previous comment, it had likely slept two more than once. As much as he longed to be the one to sleep at Teodoro's side, he recognized it was a hopeless wish, one it would be easier, in the long run, not to indulge. He knew his benefactor, though. Ciéza had insisted he take the bed at every inn between Valencia and Madrid, much to Christian's chagrin. There had not been an alternative then. Here, though, there was one.

"I shall take the cot," he suggested. "That way, I do not deprive you of your bed, señor."

Esteban shot the infuriating Englishman a resentful glare. Of course the pampered noble thought nothing of depriving Esteban of *his* bed! Before he could protest, Teodoro shook his head with a tightening of his lips Esteban had learned it was best not to challenge.

"That is most considerate of you, but it would leave me to bed with Esteban, who has a distressing habit of sprawling over every available space when he sleeps," Teodoro countered dryly. "I do not choose to spend my first night home fighting for a few inches of my own mattress. You will share my bed, *vizconde*." Teodoro had spent enough awkward nights drowsing in chairs or on the ground during their journey from Valencia— he'd be damned if he was going to be put out of his own bed in his own home. The thought of lying only inches away from Blackwood's nearly unclothed body set a curl of lust tightening in his groin. He knew he was condemning himself to a night of frustration, but the chance to have Blackwood in his bed was one he could not force himself to pass up.

Christian glanced away uncomfortably, his actual title barely preferable to Ciéza's slurred use of "Your Excellency." He should have known Ciéza was too much of a gentleman to make the lad sleep on the floor, and he already knew he would not be allowed that option, but he wished wildly that he dared suggest it again. Anything to avoid the hellish torture of being only inches from the man who had fueled his fantasies, waking and dreaming, since he first laid eyes on him. He had no idea how he would be able to lie there and not touch, not roll against him. "If you are sure you don't mind sharing," he answered finally, realizing that Ciéza was awaiting a reply.

"I think we will be able to endure a night together," Teodoro replied, hoping in his own case that it would be true. His recent release notwithstanding, he remained aroused by his mental image of Blackwood's nude body as he bathed. Willing his expression to remain impassive, he nodded toward the door. "Fetch the ewer and bowl, Esteban. We will empty the tub and then retire. Perhaps a night's rest will help us decide our next steps."

Esteban nodded, careful not to let his resentment show on his face. Teodoro was not asking anything more than he usually did, the full tub too unwieldy for either of them to manage alone, but the fact that Esteban's efforts would benefit the snotty Englishman as much as Teo bothered him more than he would admit.

"Help me drag this into the other room," Teodoro asked Blackwood, certain the nobleman had never had to deal with the aftereffects of his own bath before. "Then you can retire without being disturbed again."

Not likely, Christian thought. *Not with you in bed next to me.* "Are you sure I can't help with anything else?" he asked instead, following Ciéza into the bedroom, embarrassed at having to be asked to help with the tub. Perhaps because the apartment had once been an attic and servant's quarters, the bedroom was quite small, with room only for the bed, a small night table, and an armoire along one wall. The addition of the tub had left the space crowded so that to remove it, they had to stand quite close together, closer than they had been except when riding had forced them into the same saddle. The proximity sent a fresh surge of lust through Christian, leaving his cheeks hot and his cock hardening. He forced his gaze to the tub, refusing to look at Ciéza. He knew his discomfiture and his arousal would show on his face if he did.

Teodoro had not considered the impact the constricted space in the bedchamber would have on his already heightened senses. The clean fragrance of Blackwood's skin teased at his nostrils as they bent over the basin; the tousle of damp hair curling against the pale arch of his neck tempted him to push it away and feast his lips on the delicate flesh. Keeping the bulk of the tub between them to hide the effects of his reluctant guest's closeness, Teodoro hauled the bath over the threshold, careless of the water that sloshed over the sides to splash their bare feet.

Returning with the pitcher and bowl from the sideboard, Esteban handed the basin to Teodoro and dipped the ewer into the tub, filling it with soapy water. "Open the window," Teodoro directed, submerging the bowl and then tossing the contents out the open casement. "Once we've emptied it about half, the three of us should be able to lift it enough to dump out the rest."

Christian watched in uncomfortable idleness as the two emptied the bathwater out the window. He wanted to help, not wanting them to feel he took them for servants, but with only the two containers, he could do nothing but twiddle his thumbs until they were ready for his help. His father wouldn't have even watched, going about his business as if the doings of two servants were beneath him, but that had never been Christian's way, even when he lived under his father's roof. And he certainly didn't want to insult or antagonize Ciéza any more than he already had, since he seemed so determined to highlight the difference in their stations.

"That should be enough," Teodoro said, setting the bowl aside. "Now, Your Excellency, if you will be so good as to lend your muscles to dispose of the rest?" Squatting to wedge his shoulder against the wooden tub, he waited until Blackwood and Esteban took their places on either side, the three lifting in unison to tip the remaining water to the muddy ground outside.

"Gracias, mi señor vizconde," Teodoro said, latching the casement and then dragging the empty tub to the landing outside their door. He'd carry it back downstairs in the morning, when it was light. After setting the lock behind him, Teodoro extinguished the oil lamp that burned in the center of the small table and pulled his shirt over his head as he turned back to the bedroom.

Christian swallowed convulsively when Ciéza removed his shirt. He clearly felt safe here if he was comfortable enough to undress, even partially. As they traveled, Ciéza had remained constantly on guard, even sleeping with his sword around his waist, ready to protect Christian at every moment. To see him so obviously unconcerned now reassured Christian on the issue of security while adding to his concerns about what the night would bring. Would he walk into the bedroom and find Ciéza down to his smallclothes? And if he did, would he be able to stop himself from begging for Ciéza's attention? He did not have the answer to either question, but he knew he could not avoid the inevitable, especially not after telling Ciéza that he was looking forward to the rest. "Buenas noches," he said to Esteban, and then he followed Ciéza into the bedroom.

Teodoro dropped his shirt over the small stool that sat beside his armoire, then hesitated a moment before removing his breeches and climbing into the bed clad only in his smallclothes. After so many fitful nights of broken sleep, he knew he needed rest if he was to have his wits about him to come up with a plan to deal with St. Denys. He could only hope Blackwood would fall asleep quickly, leaving him free to fight off his own insistent desire enough to allow himself to find some repose.

Christian stepped into the bedroom, shutting the door behind him and looking anywhere he could except at Ciéza. Even staring at the farthest corner of the room, he could see the other man in bed, his chest bare, the sheets covering his lower body so that Christian could not tell what he still wore. Then his eyes landed on the pile of clothing on the small stool: shirt and breeches. *Damn!* he cursed silently, struggling to get his own body under control so that he would not embarrass himself as he undressed. That brought him to another problem: undressing with Ciéza's gaze on him. The man was not his lover, however much he might wish otherwise, and to strip down in his presence, beneath his watchful gaze, seemed too fraught. His gaze averted from Ciéza, Christian approached the bed, still fully clothed.

Lying on his back, Teodoro let his gaze rake over Blackwood's body, wondering how much of his clothing he would remove before climbing into the bed. He could feel his cock thickening, and he shifted slightly under the bedsheet, watching from beneath hooded lids as Blackwood hesitated at the foot of the bed. "Are you going to stand there all night?" he growled, his voice rasping. Turning to his side, he blew out the bedside candle. The moonlight filtering through the latticed window provided enough illumination to reveal Blackwood's unsettled expression. A pang of anger twisted in Teodoro's chest at the thought that the *vizconde* could not even bear to share a bed with him. "Get into the bed and go to sleep," he husked.

The lack of light and the absence of Ciéza's gaze gave Christian the courage he needed to slip off his shirt and climb into bed. He lay there awkwardly, afraid to move lest he roll against Ciéza. He could smell the soap the other man had used, and the deeper musk of the man, the scent enough to have him shifting restlessly as his erection returned. He shivered with suppressed desire, certain he would stare at the ceiling all night.

Teodoro swallowed deeply as the mattress dipped beneath Blackwood's weight. Even though he stayed well on the far side of the bed, Teodoro could feel the warmth radiating from his body, heating his own blood. He shifted to his side, his erection pressing into the bedding as he turned his back on Blackwood. He didn't need to face him to imagine the lissome body, to picture himself straddling Blackwood's hips, tasting the honey-colored skin. His cock twitched as he imagined Blackwood moaning his name as he pleasured him. He knew it was madness to allow himself to indulge in such hopeless fantasies, when Blackwood could obviously barely stand to sleep in the same room with him, but his body refused to listen. Stifling a groan, Teodoro exhaled roughly and fought to prevent himself from rubbing against the sheets to relieve his need.

Each time Ciéza moved, Christian imagined what might come from it, saw with vivid clarity the older man moving over him, working his way down Christian's body, the moustache tickling his skin in sensitive places, driving him out of his head with lust. The sudden burst of breath he heard from his bedmate sounded far too much like the sounds of passion for Christian's composure. He buried his face in the pillow, biting the cloth to keep his own moan from escaping. He wondered how Ciéza would react if he suggested procuring another cot, because he could already tell he would never get enough sleep in this bed.

Blackwood's restless movements made Teodoro imagine him writhing in ecstasy. He cursed himself silently, knowing if he did not bring his lust under control he would not be able to stop himself from turning over and reaching for the alluring body beside him. He circled his erection with his hand, squeezing tightly as he fought for control, willing himself to breathe deeply and clearing his mind of all thoughts, his weariness finally allowing him to drop into an uneasy sleep.

With the cessation of movement and the ensuing silence, Christian finally settled to sleep, his fantasies following him into dreams where the handsome mercenary ravished him to their mutual delight.

THE TEASING dance of sunlight through the fluttering curtains awoke Teodoro the next morning. Stretching and groaning, he rolled onto his back, only to find the other side of the bed empty. A momentary panic seized him, and he feared Blackwood had stolen away while he slept. Swearing beneath his breath, he hastily pulled on his breeches and flung open the door to the common room, his racing pulse calming when he saw Blackwood seated at the small table with a sheet of paper before him.

Christian looked up when the door to the bedroom slammed open, revealing Ciéza clad only in breeches, barely fastened, so that Christian caught a glimpse of his smallclothes beneath. He smiled at his protector with open delight before he registered the frown on the handsome face. His smile faded as he took in the annoyed expression. Glancing back down at the paper, he signed his name and waved the letter back and forth to dry the ink. "Could I send this letter to my father?"

For a moment, Teodoro thought he had discerned an expression of pleasure crossing Blackwood's face when he entered the sitting room. Berating himself for allowing his nighttime fantasies to carry over into waking hours, he scowled and reminded himself that his only concern should be keeping Blackwood safe until the threat from St. Denys's machinations could be eliminated. Approaching the table, he rubbed the back of his neck, glancing over to where Esteban still slept on his narrow cot. "We can walk to post it as soon as we have broken our fast," he agreed, wondering how much the *vizconde* had revealed to his father of the danger he faced. He was shocked to discover how much it pained him to think of Blackwood returning to England.

Seeing the scowl but not sure what had caused it, Christian hastened to say, "I only told him I was no longer in Valencia, and that I was safe. I write to him once a week, and if I don't, he'll worry and might send people to search for me. I didn't want that to alert St. Denys." He handed the letter to Ciéza to see if he wanted to approve it before sending it.

Wondering at the *vizconde*'s offer to read his letter, Teodoro shook his head, pushing the document back to Blackwood. He retrieved his shirt from the bedroom and shrugged it over his head, about to speak when a knock sounded at the door, causing him to tense. Motioning Blackwood to silence, he picked up his dagger before turning the lock and opening the door just enough to peer outside.

Christian waited silently as Ciéza answered the knock. He wondered what it meant that Ciéza had returned the letter without even glancing at it. He feared he'd insulted the man with his assumption that Ciéza could read English. Could he read at all?

"There is a visitor below for you, Teo." Teodoro stepped back, setting the dagger on the sideboard as he opened the door enough for

Don Inocencio to enter. The priest was carrying a platter of freshly baked pastries. "I believe it is one of the women from Aldonza de la Cerda's establishment. I wish you would curb your association with her—she is not a fit person for Esteban to know." Setting the platter on the table, Don Inocencio smiled. "Isabel made an extra batch of churros this morning. I thought perhaps you might care to share them with your guest."

Teodoro was sure it was curiosity about his "guest" as much as concern about his unwelcome visitor that brought Don Inocencio upstairs, but since he was using the cleric's residence to shield Blackwood, it was unrealistic to expect them not to meet. "Your Excellency, allow me to present *el cura,* Don Inocencio Guzman. Inocencio, this is Don Cristian Blackwood, *el vizconde* of Aldwych in England."

"It's a pleasure to meet you, Don Guzman," Christian said, stepping forward as Ciéza introduced him. He pointedly ignored the shiver that went through him at the sound of his name on Ciéza's tongue. He wondered what sort of establishment this Aldonza de la Cerda ran for the priest to be so disapproving, but he didn't ask. "Thank you for the hospitality of your roof for the few days I'm in Madrid."

Their voices and the aroma of the pastries roused Esteban from his sleep. He yawned widely and stretched before rising to snatch a churro from the platter. "I will see to Aldonza's message," Teodoro said as he pulled on his boots, though he suspected he knew why the brothel keeper had sent for him. He'd just have to make clear to her that his services were no longer available, at least at present. "Thank you for sharing your breakfast, Inocencio." He fastened his leather jerkin and turned toward the door, clearly expecting Don Inocencio to accompany him downstairs.

"I think I will visit with your guest until *terce,*" Don Inocencio said, taking a seat at the table. "See to your business, Teo. I will keep him company until you return."

"I would enjoy some friendly conversation," Christian admitted, thinking how hostile Esteban, in particular, had been toward him. And perhaps, if he could think of some errand for the boy, he could find out more about his new protector since both Esteban and Ciéza himself had proven rather closemouthed on the subject.

Since he had no real reason to protest, Teodoro fastened his sword belt and took his hat from its hook, determined to deal with Aldonza and return with as much speed as possible. When he had started down the stairs, Don Inocencio turned to Esteban. "Isabel tells me you offered to go to the market for her this morning. That is kind of you, *hijo mio*."

"She is always sending things up, even though Teo tells her not to," Esteban said. "I try to repay her kindness by running errands for her. I'll dress and go down right now."

"Teo did not mention what brings you to Madrid," Don Inocencio said once Esteban had left for the kitchen.

Christian debated how to respond to the question that was not really a question. He could tell the priest the same tale he gave everyone else, but his presence put his host in danger, however obliquely. Don Inocencio deserved to know the truth. "Trying to stay out of the hands of a man who would use me as a pawn against my father in the treaty negotiations between our countries," he answered honestly. "He hired Señor Ciéza to bring me to him, but I think I've convinced him that St. Denys is the real threat. He's offered to help me deal with St. Denys once and for all rather than turning me over to him for whatever treachery he had planned."

"That is Teo, rushing in to save the innocent," Don Inocencio murmured in a voice so quiet he might have been speaking to himself.

"He has done something like this before?" Christian asked, seizing onto the comment. He couldn't decide what he hoped the answer would be. A part of him wanted to be unique, to mean something to Ciéza that no one else had. The majority of him, though, needed the reassurance that his trust was not misplaced.

"Teo would deny it, as if it were something to be ashamed of, but he would not turn a blind eye to injustice if it lies within his power to remedy. He is a good man at heart," Don Inocencio insisted as though he suspected his visitor would doubt it.

"I want to believe that," Christian said, "but it's unsettling knowing he took money to kidnap me. He... dueled with my former bodyguard—this is not the first time St. Denys has attempted to take me against my will—and nearly killed a man considered to be one of the finest swords for hire in all of England. I would be no match for him if he turned on me."

"I cannot justify all Teo's actions, but I can assure you of this—if he promised to help you, he will never go back on his word. He would not bring you here, would not introduce you to Esteban, if he meant to do you harm."

"I had already told myself the same thing, and yet I cannot seem to lay my fears to rest," Christian sighed. "You have clearly known him for some time."

"I have known Teo since we were both children. We grew up in the same small village in Castilla, though his family is far older and higher placed than mine. During the wars, I was chaplain to the *compañia* Teo served in." Don Inocencio's expression saddened at his memories.

"How fortunate that you were together during such terrible times," Christian mused. "If nothing else, you both had the comfort of a familiar face."

"They were terrible times," Don Inocencio agreed, shaking his head. "Teo was badly wounded in one of the battles, and he is convinced my care for him afterward helped save his life, though I think his gypsy friend had far more to do with his recovery than I. Still, he insists to this day he owes me a debt, despite everything he has done for me, and for my nephew, since."

"Surely such debts do not exist among family," Christian replied with surprise. "You both want what is best for Esteban, as I'm sure you both wanted what was best for your sister when she was still alive."

"Teo is a proud man, as no doubt you have already noticed." Don Inocencio's solemn face broke into a shy smile that underscored the resemblance to his nephew. "It was kind of him to agree to reside here, so that I could have a part in raising Esteban. The boy is all I have left of Margarita."

"Has she been gone long?" Christian asked curiously. Don Inocencio spoke of her with something approaching reverence but very little grief. He knew it was petty of him to wonder how long Ciéza had been without his wife, but it seemed safer to get such information from his brother-in-law than from Ciéza himself.

"She died shortly after Esteban was born." The smile had left Don Inocencio's face. "He never knew her."

"How sad," Christian said softly, thinking of his own mother, who had died when he was about Esteban's age. He tried to imagine his childhood without her, but the thought was too painful to contemplate. "At least he has your memories of her, and Señor Ciéza's, to give him some knowledge of her. I'm sure it was hard on Señor Ciéza as well, raising a newborn baby without his wife at his side."

"It is hard for any man to raise a baby alone, though Teo—"

Before Don Inocencio could finish his comment, the door opened and Teodoro entered, the scowl on his face fading at the priest's presence.

"Still here, Inocencio? I did not expect you and *el vizconde* to have found so much to talk about."

"Your brother-in-law has kept me in fine company. Perhaps you should thank him instead of berating him," Christian suggested sharply.

Don Inocencio rose, not at all put off by Teodoro's remark. "I enjoyed our conversation, *vizconde*. Perhaps we may speak again before you leave Madrid." Turning to Teodoro, he added with a smile, "Esteban has gone to the market for Isabel. If you have no other duties, perhaps you and your guest would care to attend morning prayers with me?"

Teodoro's moustache twitched. "Do I ever attend prayers with you, Inocencio?"

The priest's mournful expression was belied by the warmth in his eyes. "No, but I never give up hope."

"I am sure your prayers more than suffice for us both. In any case, His Excellency has advised me he wishes to post a letter this morning."

"To assure my father I am in good hands despite my unplanned change of location," Christian explained. "Thank you again for your hospitality, Don Guzman. It has restored my somewhat tarnished view of mankind."

"I will pray for your difficulties to be resolved quickly," Don Inocencio offered as he took his leave.

When the door had closed behind him, Christian reached for his hat and sword. "What are the rules for our outing?" he asked as he fixed his attire for going out.

"Rules?" Teodoro asked, raising an eyebrow before taking a churro from the platter to break his fast.

"There are always rules," Christian said with a roll of his eyes. "'Stay within arm's reach. Don't meet anyone's eyes. Don't stand to my right because that's my sword arm.' So what are your rules? I don't want to spend all day trapped inside."

Swallowing the last bite of the sweet churro, Teodoro nodded. "Then if you know there are rules, I expect you to obey them without argument. No one at the tavern has seen or heard anything from St. Denys while we were gone, but without a doubt he will be expecting me to contact him soon. Keep your eyes and ears open, and if you see or hear anything unusual, tell me at once. If anything happens and I tell you to run, you will do it, immediately and without questions, and return here. Understood?"

Christian nodded slowly. Ciéza's orders were not so different than what Gerrard had insisted upon. In one respect, Ciéza seemed to expect even more than Gerrard had. He expected Christian to help keep watch. Deciding that was compliment enough to excuse the curt tone, he added, "I will do as you say."

"Bien," Teodoro replied, surprised but pleased that Blackwood had not protested his strictures. He watched with a critical eye as Blackwood buckled on his sword, finding that he seemed adept at handling the weapon. That did not mean he would be as adept at wielding it, Teodoro reminded himself. It was his job to ensure that he never needed to find out. After tucking his dagger into his belt, he gestured for Blackwood to precede him down the stairs.

The two men walked in silence through the early morning streets to the central plaza, where Christian could deliver his letter to the posting office. Questions darted through Christian's mind incessantly as they strode—about the city he was visiting for the first time, about the man walking at his side, about Ciéza's plans for foiling St. Denys once and for all—but he saw Ciéza's gaze darting back and forth as they walked, saw the way his hand rested on the hilt of his sword, the other hovering near his side, ready to pull the long knife Christian had seen him slip into the small of his back at need. So he held his tongue, his own hand ready, his own eyes watchful even as he drank in the sights of the city.

"Did you settle your business with Señora de la Cerda?" Christian asked as they passed an open-air market. "I understand you may have commitments already, but if I can expect you to be gone for long periods of time, I should consider finding an additional protector."

Teodoro considered telling Blackwood exactly what business Aldonza was in, but the reasons for keeping him well away from the brothel still held. "Judging by how ineffective your last 'protector' proved to be, I am not sure I would trust you to make that choice," he said instead. "In any case, Señora de la Cerda has no further claim on my time."

"My father hired Gerrard, and he proved perfectly effective against three previous attempts to separate us," Christian said in his own defense. His curiosity would not let the matter rest. Don Inocencio had been far too disapproving. "What claim did the señora have on you? Were you one of her employees?"

Smoothing his moustache, Teodoro fought a smile at the question. "The señora has on occasion secured the use of my sword."

Remembering the priest's comment, Christian looked at Ciéza sideways. "Which sword?" he muttered under his breath, not expecting Ciéza to hear him.

One hand still on the woven hilt of his rapier, Teodoro gestured to his *daga izquierda*. "Both were at her disposal, but the señora prefers a longer sword." His brow rose at the flush that stained Blackwood's fair cheeks at the suggestive comment.

"Her loss is my gain," Christian replied gamely, refusing to back down despite the suddenly bawdy turn of their conversation. Silently he cursed the blush he could feel heating his face, but he could do nothing about that. Not even the color he had gained from his time in Spain could completely hide the effects of strong emotion on his face.

Certain Blackwood could not know how much he might wish that were true, Teodoro let the remark pass without further comment.

They reached the posting office without incident and began their return. Christian was tempted to ask if they could go somewhere other than the tiny rooms in the parish residence, but he doubted Ciéza would feel as confident protecting him elsewhere. If he did, they would surely have gone there already.

Even as he watched their surroundings for any hint of danger, Teodoro could not help but be aware of the presence at his side. Blackwood was obviously holding back his usual conversation about the streets and buildings they passed, his blond locks bobbing as he turned his head back and forth as much to keep watch as to take in the sights. The unconscious grace of his carriage tempted Teodoro's eye, but his acquiescence and confident manner made Teodoro question whether there was more to the *vizconde* than the spoiled child of privilege he had initially dismissed him as being.

They were only a few minutes' walk from the church, and Teodoro's gaze was lingering appreciatively on the curve of his companion's backside when something moved in the periphery of his vision. Grasping Blackwood's shoulder and thrusting him behind him, Teodoro's hand tightened on the hilt of his rapier as two men stepped out of the shadows of the alleyway ahead of them. Recognizing their faces as two of the many men who since the end of the war had made their livings by putting their swords up for hire, much as he had, Teodoro had no doubt as to their intentions. Not waiting for them to approach, he drew his sword and gave Blackwood a backward shove. "Run," he commanded, pulling the *daga izquierda* from his belt as the mercenaries drew their own swords in turn. "Run, now!"

Christian hesitated only a second before doing as Ciéza commanded. He knew the dangers of sword fighting, knew that the odds were against Ciéza even without the additional distraction his own presence would add. Hand on the hilt of his sword in case he needed to draw it, he ran in the direction of the tavern where they had dined the night before, hoping he could reach it in time to roust the aid Teodoro would need. He had just found the older man; he was not about to lose him to two ruffians now.

As Blackwood reluctantly obeyed his order, Teodoro gripped both his rapier and the dagger and faced the two men. Both were shabbily dressed but armed with serviceable swords. Studying them warily as they neared, he identified them as Batiz and Cascos. He'd seen them before, drinking in the local taverns, boasting of their prowess. Though he'd never seen either of them fight, in his experience men who had to boast about their skill rarely lived up to their bravado. Still, there were two of them, and if they had worked together enough to coordinate their attack, they could be dangerous. He glanced quickly between the two, determining that the closest man, Batiz, was hesitant, and the grip he used on his sword's hilt was awkward and far too tight. He would be the easiest to dispatch with speed. The longer Teodoro had to fight two opponents, the worse the odds that he could be wounded… or killed.

"You know you can't beat both of us, Ciéza," Cascos sneered. "Just walk away and nobody has to get hurt."

Not deigning the taunt worthy of a reply, Teodoro circled until his back was to the nearest building, blocking either of the two from coming at him from behind. He might have let a lone assailant make the first move to judge the degree of skill his opponent possessed, but two attackers would necessitate a different strategy. Batiz having moved out of reach, he advanced slightly to the right and lunged for Cascos's sword arm. The larger man parried nimbly, and Teodoro countered with another thrust, again for the sword arm. Cascos smirked at the simple moves, clearly thinking Ciéza's reputation had been exaggerated. The look changed to surprise when Teodoro turned the lunge into a feint and let his sword arm drop to avoid the answering parry. Withdrawing slightly, he immediately countered with a lunge to the opposite arm, drawing the rapier back quickly and leaving two bloody slices across Cascos's left shoulder.

The tight space of the alleyway interfered with the plan the two men had developed. Cascos was supposed to keep Ciéza's sword occupied while Batiz attacked him from behind. Ciéza had anticipated them, however, keeping the building at his back. Seeing his partner injured roused Batiz's anger, and he threw himself at their opponent's side, determined to keep Ciéza from killing his friend.

Leaving Cascos dazed and grunting with pain, Teodoro spun quickly to catch the second man's sword as he lunged for Teodoro's side. A circular parry wielded with strength and speed was enough to dislodge Batiz's unsteady grip, and his sword spun away, clattering to the side of the alleyway. The fool stood still in shock as he realized he had been disarmed. Ciéza had neither time nor patience for fools and amateurs.

Sparing a quick glance at Cascos, who seemed to have changed his opinion of the ease with which he would earn his pieces of gold, Teodoro moved quickly across the cobbles toward the weaponless Batiz. While it would even the odds if the smaller man simply fled, Teodoro couldn't take the chance that the ruffian might overtake Blackwood. True, Blackwood had a sword and Batiz did not any longer, but Teodoro still had no idea how proficient the *vizconde* was with his weapon. It was a chance he was not willing to take. The question proved moot when Batiz confirmed Teodoro's appraisal of his foolishness by scrambling for his lost blade.

Batiz cursed when his sword went flying. If he had been fighting with anyone else, he would have abandoned the field, knowing himself outmatched, but he could not abandon his friend. Scrambling for his sword, he did his best to defend the other man until Cascos could recover enough to fight again.

Using the moment while Batiz regained his sword to catch his breath, Teodoro's gaze flickered between the two assassins. Seeing Cascos wounded seemed to have impaired his partner's judgment—his attack was driven by emotion, not forethought, always a dangerous mistake. With as little effort as another might flick away an insect, Teodoro deflected the sword.

Teodoro had killed men before, both in war and for pay. He was not proud of it—a man did what he had to do in battle, or to earn enough to live—and unlike some who wielded a sword for hire, he did not enjoy watching his antagonist suffer. So instead of slicing the *daga izquierda* up into his opponent's kidneys or stomach, he thrust the point of his rapier into Batiz's heart. It wasn't a deep thrust. It didn't need to be. It took only three fingers'-width of steel to kill.

With one of his opponents dead, Teodoro turned his attention back to the other before the body of the first had crumpled heavily to the street. He knew it was likely that the sounds of the fight had alerted someone. A constable could have already been sent for, and Teodoro could not chance being delayed by questions while Blackwood was alone and unprotected. It was time to end this.

Cascos was wiser than his partner, or at least better able to control his emotions. Though his eyes flashed with anger, his attack was measured. Teodoro might wonder at the unusual concern between two mercenaries, but he could not allow himself to become distracted. He needed to get back to the *vizconde*. This time when he engaged the wounded man, he did so with harder blows and greater speed.

The tempered steel of good Spanish blades clanged and clanked as both Teodoro and his adversary moved quickly over the cobblestones. Their boots scraped against the rough street and their exhalations puffed in the humid air between them. Parrying another cut that sliced dangerously close to his shirtsleeve, Teodoro wished absently that it hadn't been too warm to wear his cloak. He might have wrapped it around his arm as a makeshift buckler, or tossed the cloak in the other man's face while he dove in for the kill. Not a strictly honorable way to dispatch an opponent, but no one had recently accused him of being overly honorable. Judging by Cascos's experience, though, Teodoro doubted he'd be taken in by that ploy.

Cascos fought with all his skill and determination, but he was no match for Ciéza. In an attempt to rid his opponent of one of his weapons, he slashed hard at Ciéza's left hand. The attack failed and left him with yet another slice, across his own wrist. Angry now, he attacked with renewed strength and speed, determined to finish the fight once and for all.

Christian had run at Ciéza's command, not questioning the order since it had been part of the terms of this outing, but the farther he went from where he had left his protector, the more doubt crept in. He had seen Ciéza fight, knew the man was a whirlwind with his sword, but against two mercenaries, even the best blade was at a disadvantage. His feet slowed as his concern grew. He had not Ciéza's skill, but surely he could help somehow, even if only to distract one of the attackers long enough for Ciéza to finish off the first. Skidding to a halt, he turned back, determined not to leave Ciéza to his fate as he had done with Gerrard.

Sword in hand, he made his way back to where he had left Ciéza, stumbling over a body lying at the entrance of the alleyway. "Teodoro!" he gasped, falling to his knees in horror, thinking his protector had been felled by the attackers. He started to roll the body over, fearing to see Teodoro's face set in a death mask. The sound of steel biting steel reached his ears as his hand touched the cold shoulder, and he realized Teodoro was still fighting, that the body under his hand must be one of the attackers. Rising, he tightened his grip on his sword, determined to help his protector in any way he could.

Parrying to escape a blow that would have impaled him, Teodoro heard his name called out in anguish. More than twenty years of fighting in pitched battles and street engagements such as this one had taught him the folly of being distracted, but no distraction had ever called his name with such pain and fear. He turned his head toward the sound for no more than an instant, but it was enough time for his opponent to strike.

Even as Teodoro realized that Blackwood had disobeyed his order and was returning with his own sword drawn, Cascos took full advantage of his quarry's divided attention. The assassin lunged for Teodoro's heart, and Teodoro barely diverted the blade with a parry from the dagger in his left hand, catching the incoming steel from the side and bearing it upward. The turning sword pierced Teodoro's right shoulder instead, the tip of the rapier grating against bone. The sharp pain and the power of the blow took him to one knee, and he dropped the *daga izquierda* to brace hard against the force of the fall.

Cascos advanced to deliver the stroke that would end the fight, only to be met with a handful of dirt and filth that Teodoro swept up from the cobblestones and flung full in the man's face. Cascos staggered back in surprise and disgust, shaking his head to clear his vision. By the time he had wiped the offal from his eyes, Teodoro was back on his feet.

Cascos spit and sputtered as he tried to clean his face. Finally able to see again, he looked beyond his adversary to the object of his commission, returned to the fray. Ciéza was wounded badly, surely out of the fight. All that remained was to engage the younger man. The old Englishman had insisted the young one was no threat with a sword, so Cascos was quite sure he could disarm the youth and force him to accompany him as he made his escape.

Acting as rashly as the swordsman he had just dispatched, Teodoro stepped full into Cascos's path, an action born not of strategy or cunning but of pure fear at seeing the assassin turn on Blackwood. Switching his sword to his left hand, Teodoro thrust his rapier into Cascos's right shoulder with as much force as he could muster due to his own wound. But it was enough.

Unlike Teodoro, Cascos couldn't retain his hold on the rapier, the sword falling to the cobbles as he clasped his wounded shoulder. He fled down the narrow street, cursing the other mercenary and Englishmen in general. As he rounded the corner, he called on the full pantheon of saints to see that they met a suitably unpleasant end.

Seeing the ruffian flee, Christian sheathed his sword. "Teodoro!" he shouted in dismay when he saw the blood already staining the leather jerkin. He rushed to Teodoro's side and put an arm around his waist. "How badly are you hurt?"

"I told you to return to the church," Teodoro countered through gritted teeth. The wound in his shoulder seeped steadily, but he judged he would be able to make it back to his apartments before the loss of blood became critical. Despite the throbbing pain, his nerves hummed at the clasp of Blackwood's arm around his waist. Fighting off the temptation to allow the embrace to support him, Teodoro pushed away, cleaning his bloodied sword on his bandanna before sheathing it. He stooped to retrieve his dagger, staggering as a wave of dizziness swept over him when he rose.

"Do not be foolish," Christian scolded when Teodoro wavered on his feet. He returned his arm to its place on Teodoro's waist, inserting his shoulder under Teodoro's unwounded arm to support him. "Let me help you back to the rectory. Then you can scold me all you wish." He felt the shiver that trembled through Teodoro, but he discounted it as an effect of his injury. He did wonder, though, how Teodoro would interpret the answering shiver that went through his body at the closeness of his oft-desired fantasy.

Teodoro knew he should push away, but his pulse was hammering and his body felt disconnected from reason and good sense. Every instinct told him he needed to remain on his guard, though he doubted St. Denys had sent more than the two mercenaries he had just dispatched to retrieve

Blackwood. He settled for leaning as slightly as need demanded on Blackwood's shoulder, keeping the dagger at the ready as best he could in his right hand as they walked. He set a steady pace, the imperative to keep Blackwood safe overriding the temptation to draw out the feel of the younger man's body pressed flush against his, their hips brushing each other with every step.

Teodoro was not a man who asked for help lightly, but he recognized in that moment that, weakened as he was, he would not be able to keep Blackwood safe without aid. He needed someone he could trust to protect Blackwood, both from his enemies and from Teodoro himself.

When they entered the alley that led from the church, Christian spied Esteban loitering outside the parochial residence. Had the situation been less dire, he would have had a few choice things to say about the boy wasting his time in idleness when he could be improving his mind or learning a trade, but for the moment, he was simply glad to see another familiar face. "Get hot water and some linen from the kitchen," he ordered. "Your father is hurt!"

His initial concern eased at seeing Teodoro on his feet, Esteban's first thought was to help Teo up to their rooms, but it seemed the Englishman had that matter well in hand. Scowling at being usurped by the foreigner, he ran, nevertheless, to the kitchen to tell Isabel that Teodoro was injured. That should foil any plans the aristocrat had for Teo. As soon as the señora heard Teodoro was hurt, she would be up the stairs to hover as was her wont. He delivered his news with the appropriate urgency and watched as his prediction came true. The elderly woman started preparing water and linens and bustled off, muttering prayers under her breath as she climbed the stairs to rap firmly on the door.

Christian had just gotten Teodoro seated and was about to remove his boots when he heard the knock at the door. Surprised that Esteban had not simply come in as he always did, he frowned. "Wait here," he told Teodoro. "I will be right back." He opened the door to see a grandmotherly looking woman he did not know. "Did you bring the water?" he asked.

"Esteban will bring it as soon as it is hot," she replied. "How fares Señor Ciéza? I should see if he needs stitching."

"He is injured, but I am taking care of him. If you want to help him, go back and hurry Esteban along. The longer he is allowed to bleed, the harder it will be for him to get better." Christian all but pushed her back out the door, closing it firmly behind her.

Esteban climbed the stairs with a bucket of hot water, scowling when the door to his own home was slammed in his face. Who did this Englishman think he was, upturning their lives, causing Teodoro to be wounded, and now taking over as though he had more of a right to care for Teo than Esteban himself? As soon as Isabel started back down the stairs, muttering about finding needle and thread, Esteban thrust the door open, ready to confront the interloper, but the sight of Teo's face drawn with pain stopped him before he could speak. Animosity forgotten, he dropped to his knees at Teodoro's side, his eyes wide with fear. He had seen Teodoro injured before, but he had never seen a wound that bled as badly as this. "Will he be all right?" he asked, grasping the hand that hung limply at Teo's side. "What can I do to help?"

"Go get Raúl," Teodoro grated, clenching his teeth as Christian began to ease off the blood-soaked leather jerkin. "Tell him I have need of his assistance."

Esteban ran for the door. He knew the gypsy healer and swordsman Teodoro had served with during the wars, and he had always been told to go to Raúl if Teo did not return from a commission, but Teo had never sent for Raúl's assistance before. Fear gripped him at the thought that Teo was badly injured enough that he was sending for Raúl, speeding his steps down the stairs and through the city streets.

When the jerkin was removed, Christian started pulling free the laces on Teodoro's shirt, his hands trembling with the restrained need to hurry, knowing that undue haste could worsen the injury yet wanting to help as quickly as possible. The shirt was bloodied already, so once he got it off, he pressed that to the wound. "Can you hold it there while I bring the water over here?"

Teodoro nodded, the movement of his head enough to make his vision swim alarmingly. "Bedroom," he managed to rasp, pressing the blood-sodden shirt to his shoulder as firmly as he could. "Rags... use to... bandage." He leaned back into the straight wooden chair, trying to steady his uneven breathing. He meant to add an instruction to lock the door, but Christian had found the bundles of cloth and was back kneeling before him, his hands soft on Teodoro's chest, stealing Teodoro's breath.

Christian was just sorting through the rags from the armoire when another knock sounded at the door. Quite sure it was not Esteban returning with the mysterious Raúl, he almost called for the person to enter. Self-preservation, well ingrained by Gerrard's constant lectures, stopped him from that mistake. He went to the door, checking to make sure it was someone familiar returning. Taking a second bucket of hot water from Isabel and thanking her but refusing her offer of aid, he returned to Teodoro's side. He dipped one of the rags in the water and wiped it carefully over the injury, washing away the blood and sweat. When it was as clean as he felt he could get it, he grabbed another handful of rags and made a pad to cover the wound. Using another strip to bind them in place, he knelt beneath Teodoro's uninjured side. "You will be more comfortable in bed."

"Not until Raúl arrives," Teodoro protested, the bloodied dagger still clutched in his right hand. Though he was not sure how long he would be able to stand if another hired sword arrived to threaten Blackwood, he would fight to his last breath to protect him. Teodoro was about to direct Blackwood to lock the door when it swung open suddenly. He struggled to his feet, switching the long knife to his good hand when Esteban burst into the room followed by a slender black-haired figure. Blackwood rushed to his side, wrapping his arms around Teodoro's bare chest to hold him steady as he tried to block Blackwood with his body.

"Now there's a sight I haven't seen in a long time," Raúl drawled suggestively, following Esteban into Teodoro's rooms.

SIX

CHRISTIAN STIFFENED. Given that Esteban was standing right there, having brought the other man into the room, he assumed the newcomer was this Raúl whom Teodoro trusted so completely that he called for him in time of need. That did not bother him so much. It made sense that Teodoro would have trusted friends. What bothered him, set his nerves on edge so much that he could feel his hackles rising, was the familiar, lustful way Raúl was watching *his* Teodoro.

Teodoro eased back into the chair, grinning at his old comrade-in-arms. "You saw it often enough during the war," he agreed, "though I would have preferred to spare you the sight today." He shifted his shoulder tentatively, testing the range of motion the bandage permitted, and then grimaced. "As it is, I have a… situation… in which I could use your help."

"A situation?" Raúl asked with amusement. He knew Teodoro would not have sent for him if the "situation," as his friend called it, was not serious, but he could not help but notice the way the young man behind Teodoro reacted. It had been a dozen or more years since Teodoro had a steady lover. Raúl had always known that their relationship was as much about convenience as anything else and had let it end willingly along with the end of the war. Since then, he had watched Teodoro satisfy himself in the arms of the willing señoritas, but nothing had satisfied his friend's heart. Raúl suspected nothing would as long as he lived the solitary life of a hired sword. Something in the stranger's mien, however, suggested a more than platonic interest. "Would it have something to do with your young man?"

Teodoro frowned at the tone in the gypsy's voice. He and Raúl had never pretended their time together was any more than it was, and they had remained friends after the end of the war that had drawn them together. There was no one else he would trust to keep Blackwood safe, even if it meant enduring Raúl's innuendos in return. He had no idea how Raúl had sensed his interest in Blackwood from a single glance, but the gypsy had always had ways of knowing things that nothing could explain. "He's not *my* young man," Teodoro answered dryly. "He's my responsibility to keep safe. As you can see, it is not an easy task."

Christian frowned at the gypsy's words. *Your young man....* The words echoed in Christian's heart, wishing as he did that they were true. Teodoro's response, though, dashed what little hope remained. He dropped his eyes, backing away from Teodoro's chair.

Raúl raised an eyebrow at Teodoro's comment. He would watch and wait, but he decided immediately that he would find a way to encourage the undercurrents he felt in the room. "Apparently not," he agreed. "So what do you want me to do?"

Briefly, Teodoro described to Raúl the pretext under which St. Denys had hired him, and the truth Blackwood had revealed after Teodoro had incapacitated his bodyguard. "We need to find some way to stop St. Denys from simply hiring someone else to capture Cri—*el vizconde*," he concluded.

"You never have simple problems, do you, *amigo*?" Raúl asked with a smirk. He'd heard Teodoro's slip and was surprised by it. It was rare to hear a given name from Teodoro's lips in this society of formality in which they lived unless it was someone Teodoro had known for many, many years, to the point of considering them part of his family. "No, you could not have needed me to just patch up your shoulder or your heart. You have to bring me something complicated."

"I do my best to alleviate the tedium of your existence, and this is the thanks I get?" Teodoro retorted, knowing Raúl would remember similar comments from the time they shared together in Flanders. He beckoned for Raúl to join him at the small table. "Let us put our heads together and see if we can find some weakness on St. Denys's part we can exploit."

"You shouldn't be sitting up!" Christian protested, jealousy surging at the familiar way the two men addressed each other. "You told me you'd go to bed when Raúl arrived."

"Esteban didn't tell me *that* was what you needed me for," Raúl replied with an arched brow, amusement growing at the young man's reactions.

Used to the pair's interaction, Esteban merely shook his head as Teodoro grinned at Raúl. "You think because I'm injured you can finally keep up with me?" Teodoro jested. He would not be so bold with anyone else, or if they were in a public place, but with Raúl he could let his guard slip a bit and display the humor he so rarely allowed himself to express.

Christian's frustration exploded along with his jealousy. It seemed Teodoro did enjoy the company of men—or one man, anyway—so it must be Christian he did not want. Christian could deal, had dealt, with much in his life, but he did not think he could stand to watch another man flirt with the man he wanted. "This is not the time for casual jests and flirtations! Two men attacked us today, and St. Denys is not likely to stop simply because those two failed. They are not the first he has hired to kidnap me, and they will certainly not be the last." He focused on Teodoro, making himself concentrate on his face, not the alluringly bared chest. "You said we would stop him. How is this... this gypsy supposed to help when all you do is trade insults and innuendos?"

"Raúl has all manner of unexpected talents," Teodoro answered, biting back his anger at Blackwood's outburst. He told himself he should not be surprised at Blackwood's impatience with his spending a moment laughing with his friend—the *vizconde* obviously had no use for anything other than Teodoro's prowess with a sword. Reminding himself that freeing his charge from St. Denys's threat was his only responsibility, he thrust his useless fantasies out of his mind and returned to business. "Can you find where St. Denys is living in Madrid?" he asked Raúl. "Perhaps by searching his rooms we can discover something we can use to stop him."

Embarrassed at being scolded like a child and mollified by the suggestion, Christian subsided, sulking.

Across the room, Esteban hid his grin at seeing the aristocrat called down like the spoiled brat he was. He had been afraid Teo would not see it, but he should have had more faith in his guardian. Teodoro Ciéza de Vivar was nobody's fool.

Raúl shook his head at the foolishness of youth, except it appeared Teodoro had caught that malady as well. "I will find where he is living," he assured his friend. "After that, we will see about searching his rooms. Even one of my unsurpassed talents cannot gain entrance to all quarters. Before I go, though, I will take a look at that wound. You always were worthless at the healing arts. Let us get you into bed."

Knowing it was useless to argue, Teodoro let Raúl help him up and lead him toward the bedroom. As they reached the threshold to the other room, Raúl turned back to Esteban. "Fetch some more bandages, *mijo*," he ordered. "These are too dirty to reuse."

Esteban started downstairs to ask Isabel for some clean cloths, knowing better than to protest being sent away again. He might occasionally question Teo, but he was far too in awe of Raúl to say anything.

Seeing that Esteban was following orders, Raúl turned back to Teodoro and helped him into the bedroom. He kicked the door hard enough that it swung shut but did not quite latch. Looking around the room, he saw it had changed little. "So where did your young man sleep last night?" he teased. "I see Esteban's cot and your bed, but nothing else. Do not tell me you made him sleep on the floor."

Lowering himself onto the rumpled sheets with a grunt of pain, Teodoro scowled. "He slept here," he admitted, settling against the pillows. "Don't," he added in warning as Raúl's expression changed to a knowing grin. "He slept. That is all."

"And why is that?" Raúl challenged, seeing the resignation on Teodoro's face. "Why would you not take what he is offering you?"

Outside the room, Christian flinched at Raúl's words. If his interest was so obvious even a stranger could see it, then he could not pretend to himself that Teodoro was unaware of his desires. He would do better to banish this infatuation before it turned into more.

"Offering me?" Teodoro scoffed. "He sees me as a mercenary who tried to kill his friend. He puts up with me because he has no one else. As soon as he is free of St. Denys's threat, he will be gone."

"I see you are as blind as ever, *amigo*. The question is not if he wants you, but if you want him," Raúl said, shaking his head as he untied the bandage Blackwood had fashioned around Teodoro's shoulder. He examined the wound critically before reaching into his pouch for some crushed herbs. "Do you have fresh water here? These will be more effective wet."

Christian flinched again. He already knew Teodoro did not want him. Ciéza thought him little more than a child, incapable of defending himself or of knowing his own mind. He slumped in the chair Teodoro had just vacated. Perhaps it would be better to return to Valencia and take his chances with Gerrard.

"In the pitcher—in the other room," Teodoro hissed as Raúl dabbed away the blood still oozing slowly from the wound. "When have we ever had the luxury to indulge our own wants?" he added dourly as Raúl turned toward the door.

"Would you, though?" Raúl challenged, pausing at the threshold. "If things were different, would you want him?"

For just a moment, Teodoro let himself imagine Christian entwined with him in his bed, imagined there was some possible way the two of them could be together. Sure that Raúl could read the naked longing in his eyes, he dropped his gaze to the spot where Christian had lain the night before. "Why do you ask questions to which you already know the answer?" he complained. It did not matter what he wanted. He would fulfill his duty, and that would be all.

"I wanted to make sure you knew the answer," Raúl replied, stepping into the other room.

Christian looked up at Raúl, wondering how to interpret the expression on his face. Teodoro's words had given him pause. He had been so sure Teodoro had no use for him, yet his last words seemed to suggest otherwise. Rising to his feet, he declared, "You should show me what Teodoro needs done to help him heal. If you go after St. Denys, tending to him will fall to me."

"Come with me, then, *guapo*," Raúl replied, gathering the pitcher of water. Before they went back into the bedroom, he caught Blackwood's arm. "Teodoro deserves only the best," he growled. "Hurt him in any way, and you'll answer to me, *comprendes*?"

Christian blinked, his surprise growing. Was Raúl giving him… permission? And if so, did that mean he thought Teodoro was interested in Christian? "I would never hurt him intentionally," he settled on for an answer.

Raúl nodded, silently appraising Blackwood. He saw a depth of character there he would not have expected in one so young, but he recognized an old soul when he saw one. His instincts told him this one would be good for Teodoro, if only the stubborn Spaniard would let him. Caring for Teodoro would give Blackwood plenty of opportunities to get close. He only hoped Christian had enough experience to take advantage of the situation. "Vamos," he said, leading him back into Teodoro's room.

Teodoro tensed when Raúl motioned for Christian to take his place beside the bed. Instinctively he twitched his hips away from contact with Christian's thighs as he settled onto the edge of the thin mattress. Teodoro shot a glare at Raúl, who raised an eyebrow and returned an innocent smile. "If I am to find St. Denys's lair, *el inglés* will need to care for you while I am gone," Raúl explained reasonably.

"I will be fine. Just bandage me up again," Teodoro demanded. As much as he wanted to insist on accompanying Raúl to find St. Denys, he knew Raúl would not allow it in his current condition. He had conceded to himself that he needed to rest and regain his strength so he could take action once they determined how to approach St. Denys, but he had not counted on having to fight his growing desire for the *vizconde* at the same time.

"And if it gets infected?" Christian demanded. "If Raúl is searching for St. Denys, he will not be free to come tend to you. Better that he shows me what to do now." He looked up at Raúl and waited for directions.

Raúl grinned pointedly at Teodoro as he handed the herbs to Blackwood. "Dip them in the water, spread them across the wound, then bandage him as before. You will need to change the dressings twice a day until the skin closes." He almost wished he could stay to watch his friend struggle against his attraction to his self-appointed charge, but Teodoro was right. They needed to find the source of the threat. He would give them one more push in the right direction. The rest would be up to them. "You should also bathe him during the day to keep his temperature down. Even with the herbs, he will probably develop a fever, and if it gets too high, it could kill him. Make sure to keep him cool at all times."

Fixing a pointed glare at his supposed friend, Teodoro braced himself for the touch of Christian's hands against his chest. He would consider a way to repay Raúl for his treachery later; right now all his consciousness was focused on the ripples of heat that fanned over his skin wherever Christian's slender fingers spread the paste of herbs over his wound. He concentrated on the pain, and the realization that the fingertips were uncallused, confirming his suspicions that the *vizconde* had little experience wielding his sword—anything to distract himself from the growing ache that had nothing to do with the pain of his wound.

Raúl watched for a moment, observing Christian's care. Seeing nothing to fault in it, he addressed Teodoro once more. "Since you are in such capable hands, I will begin my search. How long it will take me depends on how determined this snake is not to be found. I will return when I have news." He looked at Christian one more time, his gaze hardening. "Remember what I told you."

Christian nodded as Raúl disappeared. Then he turned his attention back to Teodoro, tied off the bandage, and laid a hand across his forehead. "Raúl is right. I can feel the fever starting already." Picking up a rag, he dipped it in the water, then brushed it across Teodoro's neck, slipping the tips of his fingers off the edge of the cloth to lightly caress the stubbled skin.

A shiver shook through Teodoro's frame, the gentle scrape of Christian's fingertips more overwhelming than the cool trickle of water down the side of his throat. He caught the hand holding the cloth in his own, his gaze flickering up to lock with Christian's blue eyes. The heat in his blood grew as he recognized an answering flare. So Raúl was right, as he always was—the *vizconde* did want him. It changed nothing. Letting his eyelids fall to hood his gaze, he plucked the cloth from Christian's slackened grasp and rubbed it wearily across the nape of his neck, knowing the cool water would be powerless to dampen the fever that consumed him.

"Let me take care of you," Christian asked softly. "Let me...." He could not say what he wanted, not without some greater assurance that his interest was returned. He met Teodoro's eyes, holding his gaze, willing the other man to acknowledge him, his interest.

Teodoro shook his head, unable to prevent another shudder from racking him. He wiped a hand over his burning forehead, recognizing the beginning stage of fever. Damn Raúl for always being correct! He let himself settle deeper into the pillows, closing his eyes, hoping the *vizconde* would think he had fallen asleep.

Christian saw the high color and the closed eyes and recognized them for the fever they were. Cursing under his breath, he looked around for another rag, soaked it in the water, and wiped Teodoro's brow and down over his chest, all attempt at seduction gone now. Yes, he wanted Teodoro, but he would not risk his health in a game of desire.

The door to the apartments slammed as Esteban rushed in, his arms full of clean rags and a pitcher of fresh water. "I brought everything Isabel had that could be used for bandages," he announced, his gaze flickering around the bedchamber before coming to rest on Teodoro reclining on the bed. "Where is Raúl?" he demanded, his voice rough with concern. "Why did he leave Teo with you?"

Christian waved his hand at Esteban to get him to lower his voice, continuing his gentle stroking as he felt Teodoro react to the noise. "He went in search of the man who hired your father," he told Esteban softly. "He showed me what to do before he left." His gaze fell to Teodoro. "He's asleep now, but when he wakes, we'll have to change the bandage again."

Esteban's first instinct was to order the Englishman away from his father, to demand to care for Teo himself. But watching the gentle way in which he used the moistened cloth to cool Teo's fever, and the way his gaze never left Teo's face, gave Esteban pause. He realized with surprise that Blackwood was as worried about Teo as Esteban was himself.

"Raúl would not leave if he thought Teo was in danger," Esteban said to reassure himself as well as Blackwood. He recognized also that Raúl would not have left if he did not trust the Englishman—another point in Blackwood's favor. Esteban paused, remembering how Teodoro had reacted on other occasions he had been wounded. "He will not be able to eat much until the fever drops," he considered. "I will ask Isabel to make some broth for him to drink when he awakes."

Floating in a hazy state between sleep and wakefulness, Teodoro lay with his eyes closed, listening to the quiet voices surrounding him. He supposed he ought to let the others know he was not unconscious, but the soothing strokes of the cool cloth over his heated flesh and the musical tones of Christian's soft voice were lulling him into a state of peacefulness he felt all too seldom.

"That is a good idea," Christian agreed. "Do you suppose she could spare some stew or something for us as well? I do not know how long we will have to watch him, but I would rather not leave his side or the rooms, not without him to protect me. I was foolish in Valencia, an experience I would not care to repeat." He brushed a cool hand across Teodoro's forehead. "My next kidnapper would probably not be as honorable as Teodoro."

Pleased to see that Blackwood was beginning to recognize Teo's worth, Esteban nodded. Hungry himself, and more comfortable now that he had another useful task to perform, he decided it would be safe to leave Teo for a short time in Blackwood's hands. "I will see what I can find for us to eat," he agreed, offering a small smile before he hurried back downstairs to the kitchen.

When he was alone with his patient again, Christian brushed the shaggy hair away from Teodoro's brow and lowered his head, brushing his lips across the creased forehead. Even in repose, it seemed, Teodoro could not abandon all care. "Rest," he urged. "I will keep watch until Raúl returns."

Rising, he went into the other room to retrieve his sword. Though unwieldy in close quarters, he felt better in command of it than of Teodoro's long knife. Setting the sword across his knees, he retrieved the cloth and used it to idly bathe Teodoro's neck and chest, hoping to keep him comfortable.

Teodoro struggled to open his eyes, but an unwelcome and ill-timed weakness weighed them down. He had been wounded enough times before to know he would do better to give in to the lethargy and let his body mend itself, but it warred with his duty to keep Christian safe, and his desire not to lose any portion of the time he had in his company, knowing as he did it would be all too brief. When he felt the gentle brush of what felt like a kiss on his forehead, he could not tell whether it was real or merely a product of his longing and his delirium. His eyelids fluttered as he fought once more for wakefulness, but it was a battle he was destined to lose. Cool hands caressed his chest, and he gave himself over to the dream in which he had the right to touch in return.

SEVEN

GHOSTING THROUGH the afternoon's lengthening shadows, Raúl made his way back to *la iglesia de San Pedro*. He had done all he could for the day in his search. His contacts had not failed him, but it would be another day or two before he had the information he needed. In the meantime, he wanted to check on Teodoro. He would certainly want to participate when it came time to search St. Denys's apartments. That meant getting him on the mend. While he knew the *inglés* would not do anything to harm Teodoro, Raúl had more tricks up his sleeve than he would share with a foreigner, even one who was caring for his friend.

As he headed up the stairs, he wondered what he would find. He had meddled as much as he dared between the two men. He was curious to see what his efforts had wrought over the day. Knocking at the door, he waited patiently for someone to admit him.

Esteban had been waiting anxiously for Raúl's return and ran quickly to the door when he heard his knock. It was not that he did not trust the Englishman to care for Teodoro—each time he had entered the bedroom, Blackwood was wiping Teo down or helping him to drink some soup or water the few times he was alert enough to swallow. But the fever had not abated as the day wore on; if anything it seemed to be getting higher. It frightened Esteban to see Teo lying so still and quiet, or worse yet, muttering and tossing restlessly in the grip of some vision only he could see. Esteban hoped Raúl would have some potion or spell that would help restore Teo to health—for he fully believed that Raúl had unexplained powers that the elders of the Church would no doubt consider unholy.

"Do not open the door," Christian shouted from the bedroom. "You do not know who it is." He set down the cloth and picked up his sword, then headed toward the other room. He would not be much match against a determined intruder, but at least he would put up a fight if need be.

"It's Raúl—that's his knock," Esteban called as he threw open the door. "Teo is still sick—you must come and help him at once," he insisted, all but dragging Raúl into the inner chamber.

Christian scowled reflexively, but in truth, he was glad to see the mysterious man again. He had done as Raúl directed, but it did not seem to have helped. Teodoro had been delirious or nearly so almost since Raúl's departure. Though Christian had almost emptied the pitcher of water washing him down, the fever was still high.

Entering the bedroom, Raúl took in the scene. The *inglés* hovered at Teodoro's bedside with all the care and concern he could have desired, but it seemed Esteban was right. "Wait outside, *mijo*—the room is too crowded with four of us," he ordered. When Esteban obeyed, he turned to Christian. "Help me here. We need to finish undressing him. The more skin we can expose to the air, the more quickly we can cool him down."

Christian averted his eyes, trying to hide his reaction to the simple thought of Teodoro naked. "If you think that's best," he agreed softly, moving to the opposite side of the bed from Raúl.

Raúl hid a grin. The situation was potentially too grave for that. He unbuttoned Teodoro's breeches. "Lift him up and I will work them down his legs."

Christian could not hide his flush this time as he slid his arms around Teodoro's hips, raising them so Raúl could remove his clothes.

Lost in an erotic fever-dream, Teodoro moaned as his lover caressed him, stripping away his clothing to draw him closer to his own naked flesh. "Cristian," he whispered, his voice hoarse with desire.

Christian jerked away reflexively, sure he had committed some grave error, even as his body reacted to the way Teodoro said his name.

"Careful!" Raúl scolded. "'Tis the fever talking. Hold him steady until I get him undressed."

The fever talking. Christian sighed. He should have known better than to think Teodoro would say his name that way while in possession of his senses.

Raúl heard the sigh and looked up sharply. "Fevers are interesting things," he said conversationally as he pulled Teodoro's breeches off, gesturing for Christian to release him. "Teodoro has little control over what he is saying and will probably not remember having said it, but he cannot lie while he is like this. Anything that falls from his lips will be the truth as he understands it to be. It was your name he called just now, not mine."

Christian looked up sharply. "What do you mean?"

"I mean that you have nothing to fear from me," Raúl replied, easing the bandage from Teodoro's shoulder.

Teodoro bucked against the sudden sharp pain, his face twisted in a fierce snarl. "*Cabrón*, Bernardo," he hissed, closing his hand into a fist around an invisible blade. "En guardia! "

"Easy," Raúl soothed, running calming hands down Teodoro's arms. "Bathe his legs while I check his shoulder."

"Who is Bernardo?" Christian asked, dipping the cloth in the cool water again.

Glancing at Christian while he gently explored the wound, Raúl frowned at the heat of the torn flesh. "Has Teo told you anything of Esteban's history?" he asked in a voice too low for Esteban to overhear in the next room.

"Esteban told me Teodoro was his father in name only," Christian replied honestly. "That's all I know. I take it it's not quite that simple?"

Raúl shook his head. "Nothing is ever simple when it comes to Spaniards and their honor. Teo insisted, as soon as he felt Esteban was old enough to understand, that he be told the truth, but even so, the boy does not know the full story."

"And you do know it, I suppose," Christian commented, not quite comfortable asking but burning with curiosity to know the full truth of Teodoro's relationship with the woman who once bore his name.

"Teo and I have few secrets from one another." Raúl wet a clean cloth to swab the dried blood crusted around the wound. He doubted Teodoro would admit his part in the tale to Christian, but Raúl had no such scruples. "Bernardo de Celadilla y Zarzaguda was an *hidalgo*, a minor noble in the province where both Teo and Inocencio—Esteban's uncle—lived. While most of the men in the province were conscripted into the war in Flanders, Celadilla became enamored of Inocencio's sister. When she refused him—for his reputation was not one to recommend him to a chastely raised maiden—he kidnapped her and took his pleasure of her."

"No wonder Teodoro called him *cabrón*!" Christian exclaimed. "He challenged the man, obviously, and won."

"Celadilla refused to redeem the señorita's honor through marriage. Teodoro saw that he paid for his actions and then offered the protection of his name to the young woman and, though he did not know it at the time, her unborn child."

"He must have loved her very much," Christian said slowly, turning to the task of washing Teodoro's legs. "Don Guzman said she died soon after Esteban was born. I can't imagine how hard that must have been on him."

"Celadilla y Zarzaguda's family did not take his death well," Raúl answered, though he was aware that was not what Christian had meant. While he was willing to help matters along, Teodoro would have to answer for his own emotions. "When Esteban's uncle was offered a pastoral office in Madrid, Teo found it expedient to remove with him."

Christian shook his head. "No wonder he has so little patience for the nobility. His secret is safe with me. I would never do anything to harm Esteban, even if Teodoro occasionally makes me want to scream." After dampening the rag again, he returned to bathing Teodoro's legs, working his way higher in an attempt to keep him cool.

Teodoro stirred restlessly as the sensual touch raised prickles of sensation over his heated skin. Amorous images flitted behind his closed lids, the heat of desire replacing the heat of battle in his blood. When a tantalizing hand slid up his thigh, he reached out to grasp it, holding the wrist in a grip strengthened by a lifetime of swordplay.

Christian gasped when the hard hand closed around his wrist. He looked up at Raúl frantically, wondering what to do now.

Frowning, Raúl bent down and whispered softly in Teodoro's ear, words meant only for the two of them.

Raúl's voice drifted through the erotic haze that filled Teodoro's thoughts, soothing the ferocious pounding of his pulse. His grip loosened and his disturbed movement calmed; his eyelids fluttered, trying to respond to Raúl's words, but he still lacked the strength to force them open.

"What did you say to him?" Christian snapped jealously when Raúl lifted his head and Teodoro's grip eased.

"I told him he was safe, and that you and I were here looking after him," Raúl assured him. It was partially the truth. Some secrets were not meant to be shared with anyone. "Keep bathing him. I need to send Esteban out for fresh herbs. It seems that what I used earlier has lost its potency."

Christian nodded as Raúl went into the other room, calling Esteban's name.

Anxiety and intimidation marked Esteban's face as he answered Raúl's call. "Will Teo be all right?" he asked fearfully. "What can I do to help him?"

Raúl pulled the pouch of herbs from his pocket and handed it to Esteban. "Take this to the herb seller off the main square. Tell her I need fresh ones. The freshest she has. Do not waste time, but do not fear, either. I have no intention of losing your father now."

There were few people in his life Esteban trusted without question: his *tío* Inocencio, his guardian—and Raúl. If Raúl told him not to fear, he could leave knowing Teo was in the best possible hands. Nodding gravely, he took the packet of herbs and headed at a run for the marketplace.

"Did you tell him the truth when you told him not to fear?" Christian challenged when Raúl came back into the bedroom. "Or were they simply words meant to reassure a frightened child?"

You are just as frightened as that child, Raúl thought, *and not nearly as talented at hiding it.* "I would never lie to Esteban. Teodoro's wound is serious but not beyond my ability to heal." He examined Christian critically. "When did you last eat?"

"Esteban brought some broth up from Isabel earlier," Christian replied. "I didn't want to leave his side."

"I am here now. Go downstairs and see if Isabel can find something to eat for both of us."

Christian nodded and left Raúl alone with Teodoro.

Hearing the door shut behind the *inglés*, Raúl turned back to Teodoro's prone form. "Now, *amigo mio*," he muttered, "let us see what we can do for this wound." Closing his eyes, he laid his hands on either side of the injury, concentrating on it as he murmured softly in the secret language of his people.

Trying to focus on the low hum of Raúl's voice, Teodoro clung to that thread, following it out of the fog of swirling and seductive images that ensnared him. He stirred fitfully, finally forcing his leaden eyelids to crack apart. Wincing at the harsh stab of light, he let them fall closed again, muttering thickly, "Am I dead?"

"Not on my watch," Raúl retorted mildly, "but it may be a while before you regain your normal strength."

Before Teodoro could reply, Christian burst back into the room. "You're awake," he cried, rushing to Teodoro's side and resting a hand familiarly on his stomach. He thought nothing of it. After all, he had been caring for Teodoro all day, touching him in any way necessary to help ease his fever.

Teodoro flinched at Christian's touch, the gentle pressure merging with the sensual dream world he was still struggling to escape. His hand shot out to catch Christian's wrist in unconscious repetition of his earlier action, with one significant difference. The first time, he had welcomed, even encouraged the touch. Now, with returning awareness, he realized the danger and knew he could not allow it to continue. "No," he ground out, his voice harsh and raw. "Do not."

"What?" Christian asked, confused. "Why not? I have spent the entire day taking care of you on Raúl's orders. He is not going to mind that I touch you now."

Another shiver shook through Teodoro as he realized not everything in his dreams had been his imagination. He felt himself beginning to harden beneath the clammy bedsheet, and wondered how much he had revealed in his febrile state. Whatever he had imagined in his delirium, he knew he could not allow the fantasies to cloud his waking mind. He could not allow himself to believe that Christian's touch meant more than it did, merely because Christian was no longer holding the damp cloth to his skin when he touched him. Even if Raúl was correct and Christian did share Teodoro's desire, he could not afford to give in to it. Releasing his grip on Christian's wrist, he sank back onto the pillow. "It is not safe," he rasped, the few words leaving him panting for breath.

"Safe?" Christian repeated. "What do you mean it is not safe? It was a simple touch, no different than any of the others as I cared for you today." He did not mention the times he had bent and brushed his lips over Teodoro's forehead or the times he had simply rested his hand against the hot skin, not to test for fever but because he feared he would only ever have this chance.

Perhaps his perception was still colored by his fever-dream, Teodoro thought wearily. Christian was insistent that his touch was no more than caregiving; curse Raúl for feeding his hopes and then proving wrong for the first time Teodoro could remember. He shook his head as another tremor shook him. "Raúl, damn you," he muttered hoarsely.

Raúl shook his head in frustration. "Why do you each insist on lying to the other?" he asked. "I know all the reasons for keeping such things behind safely closed doors, but the doors are shut now. There is no one here who would see either of you come to harm. Explain this to me. What is it you fear?"

Christian's gaze flew from Raúl's face to Teodoro's and back to Raúl's. "That he will send me away," Christian replied softly, addressing his words to Raúl rather than Teodoro. It seemed easier somehow to confess if he did not have to look at the object of his desires. "That he will refuse even a helpful touch because he fears to encourage a more intimate one." He drew a deep, shaky breath. "That he will not want me the way I want him." The last slipped out a mere whisper. Christian had trouble believing he was saying these things to a complete stranger, but Raúl's gaze was compelling, drawing the truth from him with a force he could not begin to understand or explain.

"It is not safe," Teodoro whispered again, closing his eyes against the hunger to reach for Christian, this time to pull him down against him and take what he knew now Christian was willing to give. It would satisfy them both for the moment, but he was under no illusion that Christian wanted more than to temporarily slake his lust. He would not risk exposing them both to the condemnation of the Inquisition for a few hours or days of pleasure.

"Why not?" Christian demanded, turning to Teodoro, eyes hot with anger as he heard himself refused, his declaration denied. "Raúl would never do anything to hurt you, and I certainly would not. I would be as badly hurt if I did. What harm is there in the pleasure we could give each other? Or am I that repulsive to you, that you would use safety as a pretext to keep me away?"

Teodoro's eyes flew open at the bitter comment. How could Christian possibly think he was repulsed by him? Sure his expression revealed the depth of his emotions, Teodoro tried to push himself up on an elbow to meet Christian's eyes on the same level. "St. Denys... has spies," he rasped. "If they were to see... to condemn you... to the Inquisition...." He drew an unsteady breath at the thought of Christian in the hands of the merciless Inquisitors. "I swore to protect you," he insisted.

"Here?" Christian challenged, pride still stinging from Teodoro's continued rejection. "In this room? I understand the need for discretion within the public sphere. I am not an imbecile, but you see betrayal where there is none. Unless you think perhaps Esteban would betray you?"

"Never." Teodoro rejected the suggestion out of hand. Esteban might not understand, perhaps, but he would never condemn Teodoro's choices. "But outside these rooms... a look... a touch... could be enough. A hint is all St. Denys would need... I will not risk you—your safety," he corrected himself, hoping Christian would ascribe the slip to his labored breathing.

Every word Teodoro said was true, Raúl knew, but he also knew when Teodoro was concealing something. Moving to stand so he could look directly at him, he said, "Tell us the rest of it."

Teodoro's stormy gaze locked with his former lover's, refusing to allow it to stray back to Christian. "This is… different," he husked, knowing Raúl would understand. "More… than comfort and distraction." His lids closed, shutting out Raúl's too-perceptive gaze. "I will see him safe, and then he will leave."

Raúl's eyes dropped in defeat. His skills allowed him many things, but he could not make the *inglés* fall in love without compromising more of himself than he was willing to do, even for Teodoro. And if he did and his friend found out, Teodoro would never forgive him.

Christian had no answer to Teodoro's words either. While he believed he could be discreet enough to avoid the Inquisition, he had no rebuttal for the contention that he would leave when the threat was gone. He had never intended to stay in Spain as long as he had, but St. Denys had given him no choice. If Raúl and Teodoro could do as they promised and end St. Denys's threat, there would be no impediment keeping him from home any longer.

And no reason to stay.

Even though he knew his words were true, some part of Teodoro had hoped Christian would dispute them. When Christian remained silent, confirming his belief, Teodoro's determination to smother his unwanted longings redoubled. Sagging into the mattress, he forced his mind back to the practicalities that would allow them to disarm St. Denys's threat—and speed the *vizconde's* departure. "What did you learn?" he asked Raúl tiredly.

"Not as much as I had hoped," Raúl replied honestly, "but I will know more come morning. By tomorrow evening, we should have the information we need. Then it is simply a matter of waiting until you are well enough to go with me to St. Denys's lodging, since I doubt you will let me go alone."

Tomorrow evening. Twenty-four hours. Was that all the time he was to have left with Teodoro? Christian wondered hopelessly. Looking back at the vividly red gash on Teodoro's shoulder, he thought perhaps he might gain a little more time than that. Surely Teodoro would not be up to a fight again so soon.

"You know me well," Teodoro admitted, unable to hold back a grim smile. "As soon as you discover St. Denys's location, I will be ready." He closed his eyes again, refusing to allow himself to look in Christian's direction. The sooner they disposed of St. Denys, the sooner he could begin to forget he had ever met the alluring, unattainable *vizconde*.

EIGHT

IF ANYONE had told Esteban two days ago that he would come to not merely accept, but actually like, the interfering Englishman, he would have told them they were crazy. The intervening days had done much to soften his attitude toward Blackwood. The *vizconde* had not merely cared for Teodoro, following Raúl's instructions to the letter and protesting any attempt by the irascible invalid to rise from his bed. During the hours when Teo slept, overcome by his own weakness and the potion Raúl had insisted he drink in place of the wine Teo would have preferred, Blackwood had used the time he left the sickroom to talk with Esteban, asking about his past and telling him some of his own history.

Esteban found that rather than being the selfish aristocrat he had at first deemed him to be, Blackwood had a dry sense of humor and an uncomplaining acceptance of the plain food and limited space that were all they could afford. Rather than demanding Esteban give up his cot to him, Blackwood spent each night in a chair at Teodoro's bedside, dozing fitfully, ready to respond to anything his patient might need.

IT WAS time.

Raúl hoped his potion had done its work and that Teodoro was recovered enough to go with him, because he did not relish the argument that would ensue if Teodoro was not. He had deliberately stayed away since the night he had delivered the news of St. Denys's location. That news had been accompanied by information that the old man would spend this evening dining in the royal palace with the king. Raúl had no idea how the conniving bastard had arranged that invitation, but he had no qualms about taking advantage of it to search the man's quarters.

He was curious to see as well what had developed between the inhabitants of the little apartment above the priest's residence in his absence. He knew with a prescience that struck him far too rarely and vaguely that the *inglés* could make Teodoro happy, but he had no sense of how that would happen. He had learned the hard way that such visions were best kept to himself, lest the revealing of them change the outcome in less desirable ways.

Lifting his hand, he knocked and waited for Esteban to admit him.

Esteban welcomed Raúl's arrival, ushering him into the common room with a sigh of relief. "They're arguing again," he told Raúl, though the sound of raised voices was evident through the closed door of the bedchamber. "Teo insisted on dressing, and *el vizconde* does not believe he is recovered enough to accompany you." He grinned, knowing Blackwood had no hope of dissuading Teo from anything he had made his mind up to do.

Raúl gave Esteban a conspiratorial grin. He knew how stubborn Teodoro could be, and if Christian was daring enough to argue, then he was probably equally stubborn. While their argument would likely be quite entertaining to watch, he and Teodoro had other business to attend to this night. Thoughts of his vision still fresh in his mind, though, he did not want to dismiss the *inglés* out of hand. He wanted Teodoro to take Christian's concerns seriously, to see him as an equal rather than merely someone in need of protection. "Do you suppose they will accept me as the arbiter of their dispute?" he asked softly. "Surely I know more than either of them how well Teo's wound has healed."

"You are welcome to try," Esteban answered dubiously, knowing how ineffective his efforts had always been at swaying Teo. If Raúl were able to manage it, Esteban would believe he indeed had mystical powers.

Raúl winked at the lad and walked into the bedroom. "Take your shirt off, Teodoro," he ordered when he saw his friend lacing it up. "I want to look at your shoulder."

Both men looked up in surprise at the barked order. "Raúl!" Christian exclaimed. "Am I glad to see you! Make him listen to reason. He refuses to accept that he is not healed enough to go with you tonight. He can barely lift his sword. What is he supposed to do if it comes to a fight?" He turned and glared at his recalcitrant patient.

"You needn't worry on that account," Raúl assured Christian. "Teodoro is deadly with either hand."

Teodoro winked at Raúl and directed a smug grin at the overprotective *vizconde* before unlacing his shirt and pulling it over his shoulder. The wound still ached, but far less than it had, and nothing was going to keep him confined to that bed for another hour.

"Do not be so sure of yourself," Raúl warned. Certainly his preference would be to have Teodoro by his side that evening, but he would rather go alone than have him become a liability. "Let me look at your injury first."

Hearing Raúl's words, Christian smirked back at Teodoro, sure the gypsy would take his side once he had a chance to examine Teodoro's shoulder.

Ignoring them both—they could glare daggers at each other for all he cared as long as they continued to interact—Raúl focused on Teodoro's shoulder, pulling aside the bandage. The wound was still more inflamed than he would have liked, but he could see it beginning to heal on either end, even knitting together in the center despite the redness that remained. He looked over at Christian. "When was the last time there was blood on the bandages?"

"Last night," Christian replied. "He spent a good part of the day sitting up, trying to teach me more than the basics of playing chess."

"Do you still have that small set you carved while we were in Flanders?" Raúl asked in surprise as he probed the wound, watching Teodoro's face closely for a reaction.

Steeling himself against Raúl's probing, Teodoro kept his face impassive as Raúl examined the wound. "It still serves well enough to pass the time," he countered, dismissing the attempt to distract him. "Do not think you can stop me from accompanying you. You may be able to slip in and out like a ghost, but if it turns out to be a trap, you will need assistance. And two of us can search faster than one."

Satisfied with Teodoro's lack of reaction, Raúl laughed. "I am not stupid. I would have arranged for other assistance if you were not in any shape to accompany me. As it is, I see no reason why you can't. Get dressed and we'll go."

Christian frowned and reached for his own sword belt. "I'm coming too," he declared firmly.

"Like hell you are," Teodoro growled. "You're staying here with Esteban."

Christian's temper flared and he stepped forward until he stood nose to nose with Teodoro. "I have more invested in this than anybody," he ground out. "I also have a better chance of knowing if something is truly important since it's *my* father who is involved in these negotiations.

Can either of you even read English, if St. Denys's correspondence is not in Spanish? I can, in case you've forgotten where I'm from."

"And you're also exactly what St. Denys has been trying to get his hands on for months," Teodoro retorted, clenching his fists to keep from grabbing his infuriating charge and shaking him until his teeth rattled. "He knows you are here in Madrid with me. His latest hired sword has undoubtedly reported back to him by now to confirm this." He did not add that Christian's return to the scene of the ambush had been the distraction that caused him to let the second attacker escape. "Do you think we're stupid enough to deliver you to him? This could be a trap, and I *will not* put you at risk," he insisted. "Though you obviously think we're illiterate fools, both Raúl and I can read enough English to recognize your name. And as Your Excellency and St. Denys are at present in Spain, those corresponding with him are more like to do so in Spanish than English."

Robbed of his most convincing argument, Christian's shoulders slumped in defeat. He had not meant to insult either man, but he had never spoken anything but Spanish with either of them. He hadn't considered that the letters would probably be in Spanish. The idea that they could be walking into a trap rattled him. Watching Teodoro with Esteban the past two days, he had seen a different side of the man, a softer side, and it had touched him in unexpected ways. The thought now that he might never see Teodoro again scared him. They had spent so little time together. He was not ready for it to be over! He had things he still wanted to learn, to say, to do. Raúl was ready to leave, though, and Teodoro lacked only his sword. Gathering his courage, he grabbed Teodoro's hand, reaching up to press a hurried kiss to his lips. He wanted more, to linger and taste and explore, but he knew better than to insist. At least, if something happened, he would have this to remember. "Come back to me safely," he whispered, turning away to hide his flush and the tears of frustration and fear that shimmered on his lashes.

Surprised at Christian's actions, Raúl stepped quietly out of the room, leaving the two men alone to say the rest of their farewells in private.

Stunned by the kiss, Teodoro reached instinctively for Christian, only to draw his hand back when Christian broke away and turned his back to him. The past two days had only deepened his feelings, as well as his determination to free Christian from the danger St. Denys threatened. Giving in to his impulses now would only make it harder to endure when the threat was vanquished and there was nothing left to tie Christian to him.

Christian's words gave him pause and kept alive the spark of hope that his best efforts had not been able to smother completely. "We will return," he answered gruffly, "and we will bring back something we can use against St. Denys." His voice softened, and against his will his hand settled on Christian's shoulder, drawing strength and purpose from the innocent touch. "I give you my word on it."

Christian turned, eyes still downcast. "Come back safely," he repeated. "I do not care about the rest."

"I will," Teodoro vowed, moving his hand to Christian's chin to gently lift his head. A thrill ran through him as he met and held Christian's glittering gaze. He caressed the smooth, honey-colored skin of Christian's cheek with his thumb, and then he turned and strode out of the bedroom.

Raúl looked up when Teodoro came into the sitting room. "Are we ready?" he asked, wondering what had passed between the two men but unwilling to ask with Esteban sitting right there.

"We're ready," Teodoro said shortly, buckling on his sword and tucking his *daga izquierda* into the belt. "Vamos."

Christian stepped to the door, standing silently as the two men made ready to leave. He still believed he should be going with them, but he would not argue anymore. He murmured a prayer for their safety—for Teodoro's safety—under his breath as Teodoro settled his cloak around his shoulders. He hoped silently for one last look, one last glance to show that Teodoro was thinking of him, but he did not expect it. They had said what they dared already in the bedroom.

Settling his hat over his head, Teodoro nodded to Esteban. "Lock the door behind us, and should there be any trouble before we return, go to Señor Narvaez," he instructed. The high constable was not above taking coin for questionable actions, but the same could be said of Teodoro himself, and if their errand at St. Denys's turned out to be a trap, Narvaez had the authority of his position to protect both of Teodoro's charges. Esteban nodded his understanding, and Teodoro could not prevent himself from turning to meet Christian's gaze one last time. His dark eyes locked with Christian's worried blue ones, and with a curt nod, he turned to Raúl and started out the door.

Christian took a step forward, pulled toward Teodoro, but Teodoro was already leaving. Schooling himself not to run after him like a lovesick woman, Christian turned instead to Raúl. "Keep him safe," he said softly, his heart in his eyes.

"Always, *mijo*," Raúl assured him. "I'll bring him back to you, but you have to decide what to do then."

Before Christian could react to that, Raúl had followed Teodoro out the door, leaving Christian alone with Esteban. He turned to face the youth with an uneasy smile. "So what do we do now?"

"We wait," said Esteban glumly, slumping into one of the hard chairs around the small table. "It will probably be hours before they return."

Christian frowned, joining Esteban at the table. Hours. Hours to sit and worry. To imagine everything that could happen. To see in his mind's eye Teodoro lying in the street bleeding to death, or captured by the city guards, under arrest for breaking and entering. He shook his head to chase away the morbid thoughts. "Perhaps we might uncork the bottle of wine Teodoro brought from the tavern to help us pass the time," he suggested.

Esteban grinned; he was liking the *vizconde* more and more. Teodoro did not normally let him drink wine, but he could see that Blackwood was as worried about Teo as Esteban was himself, and it would be a gesture of friendship to share the bottle with him, would it not? "I think that is a fine idea," he said as he rose to retrieve the wine.

RAÚL LED the way through the narrow back streets of Madrid, purposefully avoiding the wider avenues where they might be seen by those who would interfere with their plans. His strength was stealth, not steel, and he had every intention of delivering Teodoro safely back into the arms of the *inglés*. Judging from the look on Christian's face before they left, he had begun to realize how much Teodoro meant to him. That was good. Now if Teodoro could just be persuaded to listen…. Reminding himself that they had other concerns right now, he stopped at the end of a dark alley and pointed to the building across the street. "St. Denys has rented the second floor," he told Teodoro in a whisper. "He has bodyguards who travel with him, a coachman, and two maidservants. I've seen no sign of a butler. The maids generally go home in the evenings, but they may have lingered because he has gone out and will need their services when he returns."

"What do you suggest, then?" Teodoro asked. He might be the more skilled swordsman, but this was Raúl's province, and he would follow the gypsy's lead to find a way into St. Denys's rooms.

"A simple knock at the door will reveal if the maids are there," Raúl replied, pulling out a small packet of herbs. "We can use delivering these as a pretext to get past the concierge in the front. If the maids answer, then we will have to convince them to let us in. If they do not, then we pick the lock and search unhindered."

"Let us hope they are not there," Teodoro said wryly. He wanted to get into the English dog's apartments, find something they could use against him, and get out, not waste time playing the gallant to some giggling housemaids.

"Indeed," Raúl chuckled. "Arrange your cloak so your sword is as inconspicuous as possible. After all, we are delivery boys, not swordsmen."

As he wrapped his cloak around himself and pulled his hat lower on his head, Teodoro thought privately that no one would mistake either of them for delivery boys, but he followed Raúl's lead as they crossed the quiet street.

Raúl tapped at the door and waited patiently for the concierge to answer. When the man did, he showed the package and explained their ruse, making a point of meeting the concierge's eyes, deploying all his powers of persuasion. The man gave no more than a cursory glance at the packet and let them pass. When they were out of his hearing, Raúl grinned at Teodoro. "See? I told you it would work."

"Let us see if you are as successful in cozening the ladies as you are one gullible old man," Teodoro murmured. In truth, he suspected Raúl would be able to get them past any obstruction if it became needful to do so.

Raúl smirked. "You're just jealous because the ladies prefer me to you." He tapped at the door and waited to see if anyone answered.

"That's hardly surprising, as pretty as you are," Teodoro retorted with a twinkle in his eye. "'Tis what attracted me to you in the first place."

"You do know how to pick the pretty ones," Raúl agreed. "Just look at the one waiting for you to return tonight. A prettier young man I haven't seen in years."

The reminder of the nobleman awaiting their return in his quarters made Teodoro grimace. "There is no one inside," Teodoro growled, ignoring Raúl's observation. Yes, the *vizconde* was beautiful. He was also beyond the reach of a mere hired sword. "Open the door and let's find what we came here for."

Shaking his head at his friend's stubbornness, Raúl withdrew a long, thin file from his pocket and knelt to work the lock free. If Teodoro had replied any other way, Raúl would probably have made a joke about it and left well enough alone. This refusal to even consider the topic, though, worried him. Teodoro's happiness was on the line, yet he did nothing to realize his dream. With a sigh, Raúl finished with the lock and pushed the door open, gesturing for Teodoro to precede him into the apartment.

St. Denys's rooms were luxurious, the opulent furnishings a vivid contrast to the shabbiness of Teodoro's modest lodging. Reminding himself that these were the type of surroundings to which Christian was accustomed, Teodoro glanced about with a critical eye, wondering where to begin their search. A chess set, the pieces skillfully carved in ebon and pale wood, stood arranged on a low table between two chairs. "It seems our host has an interest in games of strategy," he observed, wondering who St. Denys played against. He traced the features of one of the knights with his finger before moving on to examine the rest of the room.

An ornately carved writing desk caught his eye. "There," he said quietly to Raúl. "Let us see if St. Denys is fool enough to leave his correspondence in plain sight."

Keeping his ears open for the sound of the maids returning or St. Denys arriving home, Raúl nodded and padded on silent feet to the desk, then began to riffle through the loose papers. Nothing caught his eye right away in the letters, but he handed them to Teodoro nonetheless, in case his friend saw something he did not. He turned his attention instead to the desk itself, opening the drawers carefully. "Look at this," he said, calling Teodoro's attention to the writing table's proportions. "The drawers are not as deep as the desk."

After pulling the drawer free from its channel, Teodoro knelt to probe at the interior wall of the desk, sliding his roughened fingertips over the smooth wood. "I feel something," he exclaimed, following a tiny groove until he encountered a small catch. Flipping it upward with his thumbnail, he released the concealing veneer to reveal a thin compartment filled with papers. "It seems our friend has something worth hiding after all," he drawled, extracting the documents and spreading them over the desk.

"Let us hope it's something we can use against him," Raúl agreed, skimming the first of the letters and setting it aside when he saw nothing of interest to them. A name in the second one caught his eye. "Aldwych," he murmured. "That is your young man's title, no?"

"*El vizconde* Aldwych," Teodoro confirmed, leaning over Raúl's shoulder to scan the document. "What have you found?"

"Plans or orders, I cannot say for sure," Raúl replied, "but 'tis proof that the old man was behind the attempts at kidnapping your young man. Half the Spanish court is guilty of such plots, though."

"It confirms *el vizconde* was telling the truth, but that in itself means nothing," Teodoro replied, no longer needing the proof of Christian's word. "No one will care what two *ingléses* do to each other. Give me some of the papers—I would not wish for St. Denys to return and find us reading his correspondence."

Raúl handed him a stack of letters and continued to peruse the rest. There had to be something else, some crime they could pin on St. Denys that would rid them of his meddling. They just had to find it.

Teodoro scanned the first few documents in growing frustration, recognizing that these were the type of carefully worded letters that hinted much but proved nothing—certainly nothing substantial enough to use as a weapon against St. Denys.

Raúl skimmed the unfinished letter in his hand, dismissing it as the sort of billet-doux any wealthy gentleman might write to his lady love. He was about to toss it in the growing pile of worthless papers when the direction caught his eye. *El conde* de la Rocha was a name well-known in the Spanish court. He blinked a couple of times and looked at the letter again. "This will land him in front of the Inquisition for sure," he observed, showing the letter to Teodoro. "If we choose to use it, that is."

Teodoro frowned. "We will take it, but that is not how I would choose to disarm him," he countered, knowing Raúl would agree. There were many epithets that could be leveled against him, but *hypocrite* had never been one of them.

Raúl nodded, slipping the letter in his pocket. It would be a last resort. "Blackmail is always an option," he commented as he continued to read. "The threat of the Inquisition could well be enough to keep him away."

"Perhaps," Teodoro agreed. "He would be a fool not to fear it, but I—" He broke off, whistling soundlessly as he read the letter in his hand a second time to be sure he was not mistaken in what he saw. "Take a look at this—it is more than enough to put his neck in a noose."

Raúl took the letter and skimmed it. "Why would he keep this?" he asked. "Why would he not burn it the minute he read it? This is treason!"

"Perhaps he thought to use it against the author?" Teodoro shrugged, though the letter was unsigned. "He will find it a blade that cuts both ways." Even a hint of threat against the king would be enough to lead to St. Denys's arrest, and this was no less than the outline of a plot to murder Philip should the negotiations go awry. "I would say this is more than sufficient to put an end to his menace."

"Whatever the reason he kept it, you are right about the rest." A noise on the street outside caught his attention. "'Tis time for us to go," he declared, heading toward the window rather than the door through which they had entered. "We dare not let anyone see us until this is turned over to the proper authorities lest it be turned against us rather than him."

Teodoro gathered up the handful of incriminating letters and shoved them inside his shirt. After returning the rest to the hidden compartment, he quickly replaced the drawer. Raúl had already opened the window and disappeared. Teodoro paused a moment, then crossed the room to the chessboard and moved the knight to place the dark king into check. Smiling grimly, he returned to the window and threw his legs over the sill, twisting to pull the casement closed behind him before dropping silently to the ground.

Resisting the urge to hurry, Raúl looked back at Teodoro, handing him the last letter. "Home first, to reassure Cristian you are safe? Or would you rather take these to the authorities now so you do not have to leave him again?"

Teodoro raised an eyebrow at Raúl's baiting. "I doubt the high constable would appreciate being roused from his bed at this hour, no matter how serious the provocation," he answered dryly. "The letters will keep until tomorrow, I think."

Raúl smiled. "He will be glad to see you safe," he declared as they began threading their way back through the maze of alleys and lanes, knowing Teodoro would not think he was speaking of the high constable. "He was worried about you."

"He is worried about his safety," Teodoro rejoined dourly, his shoulder beginning to ache from the strain of clinging to the window ledge. "Now that we have found a way to assure it, you will see how quickly his concern will fade."

Raúl frowned. "You do him a disservice," he said mildly. "His actions before we left were not those of a man worried only for his own well-being." He did not mention the kiss directly, knowing it was not safe to discuss such things in public. Teodoro would know, though, and remember. And hopefully that would be enough.

"You saw St. Denys's rooms," Teodoro countered. "That is the life *el vizconde* is used to. If there was—interest—" He lowered his voice, cautious even though there were none but the two of them to hear. "—it would burn itself out soon enough. Better never to let it begin," he concluded grimly.

"You don't know that," Raúl insisted as they neared the church. "You have never even asked him. Has he complained of your life these last few days? Has he said anything to suggest he is in a hurry to leave?"

"He is alone in a strange land—because I nearly killed his protector," Teodoro protested. "He thinks he is the cause of my being wounded. If he feels anything, it is gratitude, infatuation—would you have me take advantage of that? When it would only put him in more danger should his... tastes... become known?" He shook his head. "Once the threat St. Denys represents is gone, there will be nothing to prevent his return to England. It is better for both of us to leave it at that."

Raúl shook his head in turn. He had seen Christian's face before they left the apartment. He was quite sure Teodoro was misreading the situation, but his comments did not seem to be helping. It appeared the *inglés* would have to fight his own battles. "I think you will find differently," he said finally, "but I will speak no more of it unless you ask. Go see how much trouble your charges got into while we were gone. I will join you in the morning so we can deliver our find into the hands of the appropriate authorities."

Teodoro clasped Raúl on the shoulder. "Gracias, amigo," he said simply, knowing that Raúl would understand his thanks were not only for the assistance against St. Denys. He watched as the gypsy disappeared into the night before climbing the stairs to his chambers.

The sound of a key turning in the lock drew Christian's attention from the cup of wine he was contemplating. "Teodoro!" he exclaimed, rising to his feet even before the door opened. "He's back!" he said to Esteban. He started toward the door, intending to open it and make sure his protector was safe, but it swung open to admit Teodoro before he could get there. As soon as Christian reached his side, he ran his hands over Teodoro's body, checking for injuries. "Are you all right?"

The heavy fumes of wine reached Teodoro's nostrils even before Christian explored his body. "I see you found the means to keep yourself entertained during my absence," he muttered, glancing about to glare at Esteban, nodding sleepily on the far side of the table.

Finding no sign of any injury, Christian breathed a sigh of relief. "Did you find anything at St. Denys's?" he asked, ignoring Teodoro's comment. As long as that hung unresolved between them, Teodoro would never believe any declaration he might make. He had come to that conclusion—and several others—as he and Esteban finished off the bottle of wine. Reminding himself of that, he waited patiently for an answer.

"Enough to hang him twice over," Teodoro answered, capturing Christian's hands and holding them still.

"Thank you," Christian replied softly. "I owe you a debt I will never be able to repay. I will finally have a choice in my life again instead of having to make every decision out of fear of his machinations."

Teodoro glanced back to Esteban, who blinked at him apprehensively. "Get to bed before you pass out," he growled, frowning. He had no intention of conducting this conversation with Esteban as audience. He stripped off his hat, cloak, and sword, hung them beside the door, and strode into the bedroom, certain Christian would follow.

Surprised, Christian trailed behind Teodoro into the bedroom and shut the door behind him. "May I see what you found?" Christian asked hesitantly, not sure yet of Teodoro's mood.

Teodoro reached into his tunic, pulled out the sheaf of letters, and dropped them onto the bed before setting his dagger in the armoire. "Raúl and I will deliver these to the authorities in the morning," he muttered. "I expect Álvaro Narvaez will have St. Denys in irons by midday."

Christian picked up the letters, taking the gesture as permission. He scanned the first one, seeing the plans for his own kidnapping. The second one was far more damning. "A plot to kill the king?" he asked in a shocked whisper. "This will send him to the gallows for sure!" He picked up the third letter and read it, the paper dropping from his hand in dismay when he realized its import. "No… you can't!"

Glancing over Christian's shoulder at the third letter, Teodoro caught it as it fluttered toward the floor. "We found that before we discovered his designs against the king," he admitted. He glanced away, uncomfortable with the thought that Christian believed he would use such knowledge to expose St. Denys. Holding the damning letter to his bedside candle, he watched it flare and crumble into ash. "I would not turn any man over to the Inquisitors for such a cause," he averred, rubbing his soiled hand clean against the leg of his breeches.

"Lo siento," Christian said softly. "I should have known that." He went to Teodoro's side, encircling his waist with his arms. "You are a good man, Teodoro Ciéza de Vivar."

For an instant, Teodoro stood unmoving, letting himself absorb the warmth of Christian's arms around him before grasping his hands and stepping free of the embrace. "And you are an inebriated one," he said lightly, trying to ease the suddenly heated atmosphere in the close room. "Was the wine your idea or my not-so-innocent son's?"

Christian shook his head, ignoring the comment about Esteban. "No," he insisted, approaching Teodoro again. "I did not have enough to intoxicate me, only to help me endure the waiting for your return. I am free now, you know. I could go wherever I wanted, do whatever I pleased. Do you know what would please me, Teodoro? Do you know what I want?"

Cursing himself for twelve kinds of a fool, Teodoro could not resist the low, seductive tone of voice, nor release Christian's hands from his clasp. "Tell me what you want," he answered, his own voice sounding harsh in his ears.

"You," Christian replied simply, leaning in close enough that his breath brushed over Teodoro's lips. "Your mouth, your hands, your body. On mine, against mine, in mine. You want it too. I know you do. Take what I'm offering, Teodoro. There's no harm in it."

A surge of pure lust flooded Teodoro at Christian's words. His body responded to the invitation as he imagined himself claiming Christian's lips, touching him, tasting him, taking him. Their mouths were so close that he could feel Christian's warm breath as he exhaled, could almost taste the wine he had been drinking. All he would need to do was lean forward a fraction, swipe his tongue over those alluring, intoxicating lips....

And in the morning, his passion satisfied and his freedom secured, there will be nothing to stop him from returning to England, Teodoro reminded himself. Releasing his grip on Christian's hands, he drew a deep breath and stepped back, away from the temptation to clasp Christian's body to his.

"Why do you back away?" Christian demanded, following Teodoro, crowding him. "You cannot pretend I am repulsive to you. I can smell your desire. Why will you not take what I am offering? All I ask is for one night." He tilted his head and nuzzled Teodoro's neck enticingly. "One night, Teodoro. Then I will leave you in peace if that is what you wish."

"I do not want one night," Teodoro growled, grasping Christian's shoulders and thrusting him away. "You are drunk, Excellency, and I am not of the mind to serve for your amusement. Put yourself to bed and sleep it off—you will doubtless wish to make an early start in the morning."

"First of all, I am not drunk," Christian declared, catching his balance and advancing on Teodoro again. "Yes, I had a few glasses of wine, but hardly enough to impair my judgment, if that is what you're suggesting. Secondly, I am not looking for amusement. I want to make love with you. And what makes you think I am leaving in the morning? Are you planning to kick me out? You can try, but you will not get rid of me that easily."

"Do not expect me to believe that you plan to remain in Spain once St. Denys's threat is ended," Teodoro retorted. "I expect you will collect your former… bodyguard"—he was less certain than ever that the man he had wounded had not been the *vizconde*'s lover—"and return to your home as soon as you can arrange passage."

"Gerrard will have already left for England if he is well enough," Christian replied. "His contract with my father ended the moment he was too injured to protect me. I was supposed to hire someone else, but that seemed unnecessary since you stepped in. And I cannot force you to believe anything, but I have unfinished business here, and I do not plan on leaving until it is settled." He hoped his business with Teodoro would never be settled. The past few days had opened his eyes to the kind of man his protector truly was. Watching Teodoro leave that evening, not knowing if he would return, had cemented those feelings. Christian had fallen irrevocably in love. Now he just had to convince Teodoro to return his feelings. And if he could not have that, he would have one night to remember, one night to warm his thoughts for the rest of his empty life.

Despite his resolution to withstand temptation, Teodoro could not deny his relief at Christian's insistence that unfinished business would keep him in Spain. He had learned long ago, in the trenches of Flanders, how fleeting life could be. Determined not to make the inevitable parting any more difficult, he would nonetheless savor each remaining day with Christian, storing the memories to recall when he was once again alone.

Deciding he was taking the wrong tack, Christian took a step backward from Teodoro. "If you truly do not want me, then I will retire for the night," he said softly, determined not to make this easier. Keeping his gaze locked with Teodoro's, he shed the loose shirt he wore, then removed his breeches as well so that he stood in only his flimsy linen undergarment. He stepped back again until he could lie down on the bed. Folding the covers back, he made himself comfortable and patted the empty space beside him. "Come to bed, Teodoro," he urged. "You are still recovering. You need your rest."

Not want him? Teodoro managed not to snort at the idea, keeping his expression impassive as Christian disrobed before him. He briefly considered trying to sleep in the bedside chair again, but though he would not allow Christian to discern it, the night's activities had left his wound throbbing. After snuffing the candle between his thumb and finger, he quickly removed his own outer garments and reclined on the mattress, keeping a distance between himself and his bedmate and trying to relax his aching shoulder.

Immediately, Christian shifted on the bed so that his arm brushed Teodoro's side, his leg bumping against the other man's thigh. He wanted to scoot even closer, to rest his head on Teodoro's shoulder, but he held back. He did not want to press so hard that Teodoro pushed him away. He just wanted to make sure Teodoro understood that even now the offer of intimacy was still open. Inspiration struck, and he draped his arm across Teodoro's chest, gently working the muscles below his injured shoulder, trying to help them relax.

Teodoro's conscience insisted that he ought to pull away from the intimate touch, but he was too weary to fight both Christian and himself any longer. Letting his eyes drift closed, he allowed the tender massage to continue, imagining what it might lead to if he were free to indulge his own desire.

This was hardly the first time Christian had touched Teodoro in recent days. This felt different, though. First, he was in bed next to Teodoro instead of sitting on a chair nearby. This time he knew Teodoro was awake and fully aware of his touch instead of unconscious or caught in a fever-induced dream. Most important of all, though, this time Christian had offered himself to Teodoro, an offer that still stood and would continue to stand until Teodoro accepted it. The thought made him tense with desire. He ignored it as best he could, focusing on Teodoro, on getting as close as he would allow. Christian shifted, as if to get a better angle for the massage, and pressed up against the side of Teodoro's body. With a sigh, he relaxed, never faltering in his attentions.

Christian's touch and the warmth of his body seeping into Teodoro's side incited him even as it soothed him. Turning slightly on his hip to hide the stir of his arousal, he bit his lip to hold back the groan of pleasure the contact elicited.

Sleep came slowly, Christian's unsated desire making him restless, but he pushed it aside in favor of stoking Teodoro's desire instead. Eventually he fell into slumber, still curled against Teodoro.

NINE

TEODORO RESISTED awakening, the dull but still present ache of his wounded shoulder discouraging his return to full wakefulness. He let his mind drift, nestling closer to the warm body entangled with his, the steady rise and fall of the head pillowed on his chest, the leg thrown over his thigh and cradled between his own. Soft curls tickled his chin; he turned his head to feel them slide along his cheek, breathing in the sweet, clean scent.

Stirring in his sleep, Christian shifted, trying to get more comfortable. He drew his hand closer to his face, the palm coming to rest over the reassuring beat of Teodoro's heart. He was not awake enough to realize what he had done, but the steady pulse soothed him, and he fell deeper into slumber again.

Still adrift in the hazy imagery of dreams, Teodoro felt the soft hand settle over his heart. Without thought, his larger palm moved to cover the smaller one, holding it still, even as his lips brushed the silky hair that teased him with its caress.

Drifting in the fantasy of being held, of being loved, Christian shifted again, his hips seeking friction as his dream lover caressed him intimately. He had felt Teodoro's roughened hands, even if they had been pushing him away, and that sensation echoed now in his dreams, not pushing him away, but pulling him close. His fingers tightened reflexively as he rubbed against the hard body next to his in the bed.

The feel of his lover moving against him kindled Teodoro's arousal. Turning to pull the enticing body more firmly to his own, he nudged the head resting on his chest upward, lowering his own to claim a welcoming kiss.

The feeling of lips moving on his own drew Christian out of his dreams to a different, better reality. The sensation of Teodoro's mouth on his was better than any fevered dream, any nighttime imagining. He returned the kiss eagerly, not about to miss any opportunity to kiss Teodoro.

When the lips beneath his parted eagerly, Teodoro deepened the kiss, plundering the willing mouth hungrily, mapping its contours with his tongue as he drank in his partner's heady taste. His hips arched to press his arousal into the friction of the body rubbing against him, seeking more contact, more warmth. A firm chest brushed against his, and he shuddered, his passion spiraling.

Christian twined his tongue around the one invading his mouth, moaning in his throat at the touch. Teodoro was pulling him closer, and he went eagerly, shifting his weight so he lay halfway on top of him, his hips pulsing eagerly against Teodoro's solid form. He lifted his head, looking down at the closed eyes, his passion taking control. "Teodoro," he moaned softly, lowering his head for another kiss.

The sudden weight of a body settling atop his, its arousal pressing hotly against his own, and the earthy moan of a voice calling his name broke Teodoro from the lingering wisps of sleep. His eyes snapped open as Christian's lips closed over his, his tongue instinctively parrying the one that slid into his mouth, stopping his words of protest. He grasped Christian's hips, halting their undulation, their cocks separated only by the thin linen of their smallclothes.

Christian thrilled at the feeling of Teodoro's hands on his hips… until he realized they intended to stop him from moving. He moaned in protest this time, determined not to let this moment end in another rejection. He could feel how hard Teodoro was, how much he wanted this. Surely he just needed a little encouragement. Christian had every intention of giving it to him.

Holding Christian's hips still with one strong hand, Teodoro plunged the other into the deep blond curls that had tantalized him in his dreams. Cradling Christian's head in his palm, he broke the kiss, holding Christian back when he tried to recapture his mouth. "Enough," he commanded, his voice roughened with sleep and desire.

"Not enough," Christian rasped, trying futilely to lower his head again, to recapture the bliss of Teodoro's lips moving willingly beneath his. "Never enough."

"Basta!" Teodoro ground out, moving his hands to Christian's shoulders and rolling them to one side so he could slide from beneath Christian's weight. He pushed onto one elbow, his chest heaving as he fought to steady his racing pulse and will down his ferocious arousal.

"Why?" Christian demanded, sitting up in bed. "You kissed me, Teodoro. I didn't start this. Why are you pulling away now? I'm not drunk. I'm not asleep. I know exactly what I'm doing, and I want this. I want you."

Teodoro swung his legs to the ground and sat on the opposite edge of the mattress, facing away from temptation. His shoulder ached as he raised his hands to run them through his hair, reminding him of the danger of allowing himself to become distracted. He had managed to keep Christian safe the last time he was attacked—barely. He could not take the risk of losing his focus, of concentrating on a pair of sky-blue eyes rather than the danger that surrounded them—especially when his attentions could put the *vizconde* at even more risk, should they become known to those who would not hesitate to use any tool against them.

"This is a war, Cristian," Teodoro muttered, rubbing the back of his neck and cursing himself for giving in to his weakness. "We do not have the luxury of indulging our wants."

Christian shivered in delight at the sound of his name on Teodoro's lips, the first time he had called him "Cristian" that wasn't an introduction or a fever dream. "So you do want me, then." It was some balm to his wounded pride. "I thought you said St. Denys would be arrested. We hold all the cards. I do not see how you can call this a war."

"St. Denys is not acting alone," Teodoro reminded him. "He has at least one partner, perhaps more. The letter disclosing the plot against the king was unsigned." He turned to face Christian, his dark eyes intense with the need to make him understand. "You are not out of danger, even once St. Denys is arrested. His counterpart has as much to gain by taking you hostage." He did not mention his fear that the unknown conspirator might seek to disrupt the negotiations completely by disposing of the son of the chief English negotiator.

Christian frowned. He had not considered that aspect of the situation. "Yet last night you wanted to send me back to England unprotected," he pointed out. "Are you tired of me already?" He was quite sure he knew the answer to his question, but he wanted Teodoro to admit it, to say that he wanted Christian to stay, that he was willing to continue in the role of protector.

"I deprived you of your bodyguard," Teodoro countered. "I promised to protect you in his place, and I hold to that promise." He rose to his feet, reaching for his shirt, hoping to defuse the sexual tension that still shimmered between them. "Until St. Denys's partner is in irons as well, I will continue to see to your safety. Nothing is more important than that." He pulled his shirt over his head, his face set against the pain. "Nothing."

Christian shook his head and rose from the bed. "Stop," he ordered, going to Teodoro's side, heedless of his near nudity and of the still-hard cock that tented his smallclothes in a most obvious fashion. "Don't hurt your shoulder again. You can hardly protect me if you make your injury worse." He reached up and straightened the linen, pulled the laces together, and tied them closed. He picked up the breeches and held them out as well, hoping for that much opportunity at least to get his hands on his lover's body. He refused to think of Teodoro any other way now. It might take time, but he would find a way to seduce the stubborn Spaniard. Fortunately, Teodoro's inherent nobility had assured him more time to try.

Conscious that the thin cloth of his undergarment did nothing to hide his blatant desire, Teodoro held out his hand for his breeches. He had steeled himself to endure the brush of Christian's hands against his chest as he laced his shirt, but leaning against Christian, allowing him to pull the worn leather pantaloons over his legs, over his erection, was a test of endurance he was not sure he could withstand.

Christian frowned but eventually released his hold on Teodoro's breeches, stepping back to let him dress. He pulled fresh clothes from his valise. The pouch of coins his father had given him tumbled onto the floor. "Since you have stepped into Gerrard's shoes as my protector, you should have the coin I would have paid him for his services," Christian declared, tossing the pouch on the bed. "'Tis the least I can do since I am living under your roof, eating your food, and sleeping in your bed. If you will take nothing else from me, at least take this."

Teodoro tensed at Christian's offer. It was apparent that despite his words, Christian still saw him only as a mercenary, someone whose services could be purchased for a handful of coins. He was not proud that his introduction to Christian had been due to exactly such a monetary transaction, but to Teodoro it had come to mean far more. Obviously, to Christian it had not, making the shallowness of his desire all the more evident. "Keep your money," he growled, bending to pull on his boots. "You need not pay for my protection. I owe you a debt of honor." Shrugging awkwardly into his jerkin, Teodoro picked up the letters that would seal St. Denys's fate. "Wait here until Raúl and I return. Keep the door locked and do not open it to anyone but the two of us."

Christian cursed Teodoro's stubborn pride under his breath. He had not meant to insult the man, but did Teodoro not see that his own pride resented living off Teodoro's charity? He would have to set him straight when he returned, but he could hardly run after Teodoro in nothing but his smallclothes, especially not with Esteban in the other room. Christian had a feeling Teodoro would not appreciate the boy finding out about them that way. He sighed. Of course, if he did not stop making blunders where Teodoro was concerned, there would be nothing to find out about. "Be safe," he said instead, hoping Teodoro heard him before he left.

Leaving Esteban snoring quietly on his cot, Teodoro resisted turning back at Christian's response. It would be so easy to allow himself to hear real concern in the musically accented words. Reminding himself that the *vizconde* had just proven exactly how much he considered his attentions to be worth, Teodoro used his key to lock the door. He was not surprised to find Raúl leaning against the side of the church when he exited into the early morning sunlight.

"You took your time this morning," Raúl observed casually, pushing away from the wall. "Shall we find Narvaez? I would have those letters out of our possession as quickly as possible."

Teodoro nodded, keeping his head down lest Raúl's all-too-knowing eyes detect the lingering remnants of desire on his face. He was having enough difficulty fighting his own wants—he did not need his well-meaning friend urging him toward what he knew was beyond his reach. "I disposed of one of the letters," he admitted instead, sure that Raúl would understand of which he spoke. "We have enough evidence against St. Denys without it."

"That was well done," Raúl agreed, "although I wonder if the lover could also be the author of the unsigned letter." He did not mention the plot against the king. Saying such words aloud where any could overhear was far too dangerous. "I suppose it does not matter. After all, 'tis St. Denys we're after."

"So I thought at first, but now I am not so sure," Teodoro countered. "This unknown compatriot of his worries me. We know he has as much interest as St. Denys in swaying the negotiations, and we know he is aware of the plot to use *el vizconde* as a hostage to control his sire's actions." He paused, knowing Raúl would make the connection. "Cristian is not yet out of danger."

Raúl frowned, not having considered the situation from that angle, though he filed away the easy use of Christian's given name for later thought. "So what do you propose?"

Shaking his head, Teodoro grimaced in frustration. "I do not know. Perhaps St. Denys will reveal something when he is questioned, though I doubt it. His lover will bear watching, to see if he takes any action to free St. Denys, though whether he does or not may prove nothing, since we have no proof he knows anything of St. Denys's plots." Teodoro settled his hand on the hilt of his sword. "Until we know who this mysterious conspirator is and can render him powerless, Cristian will remain under my protection."

Raúl nodded slowly. "We have a name, but nothing else to go on with the lover, and even less with his coconspirator. We will have to remain on our guard." They neared the constable's office. "Do you want me to come in with you or would you rather go alone?"

"Neither Narvaez nor St. Denys know of your involvement," Teodoro said thoughtfully. "I would prefer to keep them ignorant, I think."

Raúl nodded. "I will wait for you at home, then," he said. "Join me there when all is in order." He wanted to ask Teodoro about the night, about Christian and the odd mood his friend seemed to be in, but that could wait until after Teodoro had delivered the letters to the authorities.

Teodoro shifted his shoulder as he neared Raúl's lodgings, the half-healed wound throbbing beneath its bandage. Like him, Raúl did not live in a fashionable quarter of Madrid, and the exterior of his rooms was unremarkable. Unlike Teodoro's rather barren quarters, however, Raúl's chambers were filled with exotic and colorful furnishings. Brightly patterned throws and artfully carved pieces made up the eclectic decor, and a spicy scent of herbs and incense teased the senses. After climbing the steps, Teodoro rapped a pattern of knocks and leaned against the door frame, waiting for Raúl to answer.

When he heard Teodoro knocking, Raúl rose from his chair, set aside his pipe, and opened the door. "Well?" he asked, shutting the door behind them. He resumed his seat, offering the pipe to Teodoro. "Is it done?"

"St. Denys has been taken," Teodoro affirmed, motioning to decline Raúl's offer, "though not without threats to see me in his place."

He tossed his hat onto an intricately detailed chair and straddled another. "Narvaez was quick to seize him as soon as he understood the import of the documents I brought him. I have no doubt his star will rise after making such a notable arrest."

"And these threats?" Raúl asked, more concerned about what evil St. Denys could bring to bear, even from behind bars. "Were they empty posturing, or do we need to be concerned? We know he wants your Cristian. Does he have a long enough arm to reach him even from prison?"

"He may be powerless to act himself, but he is not friendless," Teodoro admitted. "Narvaez allowed him to send a message before delivering him to the castle prison, though he would not tell me to whom he wrote." Teodoro rubbed his shoulder absently. "It could have been his lover, or his partner in the conspiracy—if they are not one and the same. He'll be questioned to see if they can learn anything else from him, though with proof of the plot against the king, he'll be executed within days. But his death won't put Cristian out of danger."

"How is *el vizconde* today?" Raúl asked. He had promised he would not push any more on the subject of the two men's mutual interest, but Teodoro was on edge, more so than he would have expected from dealing with St. Denys, which meant the young *inglés* was the cause.

Despite himself, Teodoro felt his pulse quickening as he recalled the erotic dream from which he had awoken to an impossible reality. Reminding himself that Christian saw him only as a mercenary to be paid for his services, he frowned. "He thought the threat against him would be ended once St. Denys was arrested," he answered. "He is not best pleased that he must remain under my protection until we can uncover the rest of the conspiracy."

Raúl's eyebrows flew up in surprise. "It seems I misjudged him," he said with a frown. "I would not have thought him eager to leave. I am sorry, *amigo mio*. I truly thought he was different, that he saw you as more than just a blade. Have you talked with him about what to do next? I do not imagine you want to keep him around any longer than necessary."

Raúl would be surprised if he knew what he really wanted, Teodoro thought, but knowing those wishes were fruitless, he pushed them from his thoughts. "He has seen the letters, and I have tried to make him understand the threat that still remains while St. Denys's counterpart is free. We need to find out more about the old man's associates. The sooner we identify his partner in the conspiracy, the better. We cannot fight an assailant we cannot see."

Raúl nodded. "We have the name of the lover. At the very least I can see what I can find out about *el conde* de la Rocha. That may give us a place to start, and if it does not, we will have eliminated the lover as a suspect. Did Narvaez show any interest in trying to find the other conspirator?"

"So long as we deliver the partner's head to him on a platter, he will be happy to take the credit," Teodoro growled. "You should know by now the high constable is too lazy to expend any effort of his own if he can rely on someone else to do it for him."

Raúl grimaced. "I will see what I can learn," he repeated. "St. Denys knows you are responsible for his situation. Would it be prudent for you to disappear for a few days? I would hate for this to rebound on you."

"And leave *el vizconde* unprotected? You cannot search for information about St. Denys's partner and guard Cristian at the same time." Raúl was the only man other than himself Teodoro would trust to keep Christian safe, but even so he would not leave Christian's side unless utmost necessity demanded it.

"Take him with you," Raúl replied equably. "I never meant to suggest otherwise. Surely you know some small town where the two of you could stay until such time as I know more."

"Where would you have me take him that would be any safer?" Teodoro protested. "Narvaez may be indolent, but he is marginally honest, and he will listen and respond if I must send for him. In a strange town, where the authorities are unknown to me, and I to them?" He shook his head. "The risk would be greater than if we remain here, where at least the threats are known."

"As you will," Raúl answered. "Will you at least stay close to home where you have friends? I will be able to do my job easier if I do not have to worry about your safety."

"I do not intend to let Cristian out of my chambers until we are certain it is safe," Teodoro replied, though he wondered privately how long they would both endure the close proximity. "So if you do not wish us to kill each other, you will find who St. Denys's partner is quickly."

Raúl chuckled. "I will do my best," he promised, "for I would not enjoy a world without my best friend."

By the time he returned home, Teodoro's entire arm was nearly numb but for the stabs of pain that radiated from his shoulder with every movement. He debated stopping to purchase a bottle of wine in the tavern, knowing it would deaden the pain, but he was unwilling to risk numbing his senses as well. He would just have to endure the discomfort; he would not imperil Christian's safety for his own assuagement. After unlocking the door to his lodging and latching it securely behind him, he hid a grimace as he unbuckled his sword belt and hung it beside the door.

"You are home," Christian exclaimed, flying from his seat to Teodoro's side, searching for new rents in his skin. "Are you well? Did they arrest St. Denys? What did he say? Do you know who his partner is?"

"St. Denys is in jail," Teodoro replied, repeating the tale he had told Raúl but omitting St. Denys's threats. It would do no good to add to Christian's fears. "He said nothing to indicate who he was plotting with. Perhaps the high constable will learn something from him during questioning. Raúl is going to see what he can discover as well, beginning with—" Teodoro paused, hesitant to allude to what had transpired between them that morning by speaking of St. Denys's lover. "Beginning with the one addressed in the letter we burned."

Christian nodded, taking in all the news. He was glad St. Denys was in prison, glad Raúl was acting to find the cur's partner, since he did not want to spend his life with that threat hanging over his head, but his real concern was Teodoro. "I owe you an apology," he said firmly, thinking of the way they had parted that morning. "I did not mean to insult you earlier. We will not speak of money again, for I do not want such a thing to come between us."

Teodoro stooped to pull off his boots, careful of the cracked, worn leather. "A mercenary cannot afford to take insult," he replied shortly. "But I will not take payment from you, when if I had not wounded your—friend, you would still be under his protection."

"Gerrard was my friend, I suppose," Christian agreed, "but I would rather be here with you. And you are so much more than simply a mercenary to me. You do realize that, do you not?" He rested his hand on Teodoro's shoulder, not quite caressing, but letting Teodoro feel his interest.

"Where has Esteban gone off to?" Teodoro moved to the window, away from Christian's too-tempting touch. He drew the curtain aside, checking for anyone watching the residence as much as he was looking for Esteban, but the street below was empty. "I expect he had quite a head when he finally awoke. He is not accustomed to drinking as you are."

"He said today was market day," Christian replied, neglecting to mention that he had provided Esteban with coin for the purchases from his own purse. "And yes, he had a bit of a headache when he awoke. Isabel gave him a cup of something, and he was much more himself after that." He walked to Teodoro's side, returning a hand to his waist. "Do you see anything?"

"Nothing," Teodoro answered. The remaining gold he had received from St. Denys was in the pouch at his belt; if Esteban had gone to the market, it could only be because Christian had given him the money. His pride stung at the knowledge that, even with the old man's tainted fee, what he could provide was inferior to the luxuries to which Christian was accustomed. "Then you will eat better, at least, until we discover St. Denys's partner."

Christian frowned. This was not going the way he had hoped. Deciding an argument would at least clear the air, he stood in Teodoro's face. "Where did you get the idea that I am a helpless babe who must depend on you for everything? I understand that you feel honor bound to protect me because you wounded Gerrard, but who do you think supported whom in Valencia? I do not need or want a nursemaid, Teodoro. That was why, while I considered Gerrard my friend, I never looked to him for more than that. I want someone who will treat me as an equal partner. I know my strength is not swordplay. In that respect I do not pretend to be as worthy of your regard as Raúl or someone like him, but that does not make me a dependent child. Why are you trying to make me one? I am twenty-three years old. If not for the threat posed by St. Denys, I would already have my first diplomatic posting. And before you say anything else, I am not staying with you because of that threat. I am staying with you because I. Want. You." He punctuated each of the last three words with a finger against Teodoro's ribs.

"You think I see you as a child?" Teodoro could not hold back a bark of laughter. "Esteban is a child. You are not. Believe me, I am only too aware of how much of a man you are." He turned to gesture out the window at the shadows waning in the late morning sun. "But you do not know this city, or the plotters and schemers who control who goes free and who lives in fear, the way that I do. Raúl and I are trying to keep you safe, not because we think you are helpless, but because—" He broke off, knowing he spoke for himself alone. "Because I would not see you come to harm. You have your life ahead of you, and I would be sure you are able to return to it."

"And I will follow your advice because I know you are right," Christian said, stroking up and down Teodoro's chest. The admission warmed his heart. "But at least let me help when and as I can. As for my ignorance, I freely admit it, but I want to learn more of this place that is now my home. I have every intention of living out my life to the fullest. I cannot spend it cowering in your apartment out of fear of the unknown."

Christian's hand tracing over Teodoro's chest was spreading a growing heat that radiated down his abdomen, tightening his groin. Catching the wandering fingers, he took a step back from the window, putting some space between them. "I will take such help as you offer," he agreed, "but there are risks I cannot allow you to take."

"Such as?" Christian asked, closing his fingers around the hand holding his. "What risks must I not take?"

"Until we know who St. Denys was plotting with, and find proof to bring to Narvaez, you must not leave these apartments unless Raúl or I are with you," Teodoro insisted. "Not because I think you are helpless or a child to be coddled, but because you needed a bodyguard even before we learned that this plot threatens the king himself. It is not only your safety at risk, but the interests of both our countries at stake." He held Christian's gaze, the intensity deepening as Christian met his stare boldly, his expression offering more than mere acquiescence to Teodoro's fiat. Christian stroked Teodoro's scarred knuckles with his thumb, the gentle caress sending tendrils of heat coursing along his nerves. Pulling his hand free, Teodoro winced when the sudden motion wrenched his shoulder, pulling at the bandage.

"Is your shoulder still bothering you?" Christian asked immediately, reaching for the laces on Teodoro's shirt. "Come into the bedroom and let me take a look at it."

Teodoro wanted to protest, but he knew that as long as his wound was not fully healed, it would be foolish to deny it. He needed assistance changing his bandage if nothing else, and since Raúl was not around, he would have to rely on Christian's help. After shrugging off his jerkin, he reached behind him with his left hand to pull his shirt over his head, baring his chest and the bandage twisted around his shoulder.

"Sit," Christian ordered, his gaze tracing every line of Teodoro's torso. He grabbed the unused bandages and the herbs Raúl had prescribed to help the injury heal. Once he'd dipped the herbs in the ewer to dampen them, he handed them to Teodoro. "Hold this while I remove the old bandage." He slid his hands up Teodoro's back until he found the knots that held the cloth in place. He worked them free, using every opportunity to brush his knuckles over the bare skin.

Taking a seat on the edge of the bed, Teodoro braced himself with his uninjured arm, holding the handful of moist herbs in his right palm, resting on his thigh. He could feel Christian's breath against his back as he worked the knot, the warm exhalation stirring his skin to gooseflesh. A golden curl fell to his shoulder, tickling him, and without thinking he reached up to tuck it behind Christian's ear, the movement causing him to lean back against Christian as his weight shifted on the mattress.

Without thought, Christian shifted to support Teodoro's weight, wrapping his arms around him to remove the bandage. He leaned forward to peer at the wound from over Teodoro's shoulder, his fine goatee brushing the other man's skin as he did. "It looks a little better," he commented, his lips teasing Teodoro's ear as he spoke. "Raúl's herbs must be working."

Raúl would encourage him, Teodoro knew, allowing himself to lean into Christian's arms as he unwrapped the bandage. Knowing this might be his only chance to feel Christian's arms around him, he told himself it would be safe, just this once, to indulge his longing. Even when he heard Christian's voice against his ear, so close he could feel the brush of his lips, he did not pull away.

Surprised at not having been pushed away yet, Christian decided to press his luck. He plucked the herbs out of Teodoro's hand and smoothed them over the healing laceration, tightening his arms around Teodoro's chest as he worked. Then he picked up the bandage and folded the piece of cloth, hands still in front of Teodoro, arms still around him, and used it to cover the cut. After tying it in place, he grabbed another rag and slid it slowly over Teodoro's stomach, wiping away the sweat of the day.

Teodoro let his eyes slide closed, focusing on the other senses assailing him: Christian's scent in his nostrils, mingling soap and sweat and the faint smell of arousal; the soft exhalations of Christian's breath against his ear; the caress of Christian's hands as he bound the pad to his wound and then drifted lower, over the planes of his chest and lower still, stroking, tantalizing. In his imagination he could taste the sweetness of Christian's mouth as he claimed him for a kiss.

The closed eyes and the head resting on his shoulder were an invitation Christian could not refuse. Slowly, giving Teodoro a chance to pull away, he aligned his cheek with Teodoro's until their lips met softly. He could taste the faint trace of spices from whatever Teodoro had eaten to break his fast, but mostly, he just savored the flavor of the man.

The kiss began so softly that at first Teodoro thought it was part of his imagining, the brush of Christian's lips demanding nothing, opening naturally to the pressure of his. Teodoro traced the contours of Christian's mouth with his tongue, committing its dimensions to memory, though he knew he would never forget the velvet texture of Christian's lips or the way their tongues met, gently, hesitantly, circling each other in a wordless dance of advance and retreat.

A soft moan vibrated in Christian's throat as Teodoro kissed him so sweetly, so tenderly. He could almost let himself believe the previous argument had not happened, that Teodoro was finally accepting him as a lover. He tightened his arms slightly, pulling Teodoro against his chest a little more snugly. Before he could make another move, though, the outer door to the apartment slammed open and Esteban called their names. Christian muffled a curse and lifted his head. "This is not finished," he promised before rising from his spot. "In here, Esteban," he called. "I was just tending Teo's shoulder."

Teodoro inhaled sharply, then let out a slow breath, berating himself for the rush of warmth at the simple intimacy of hearing his forename on Christian's lips.

TEN

TEODORO COULD have cursed Esteban's untimely return, but in his heart he knew it was best they had been interrupted before he let things go too far. He pushed to his feet, recovered his shirt, and strode toward the common room, pulling it over his head. Esteban was dropping an armload of provisions on the battered table and chattering about what he had purchased, too caught up in the luxuries they were so rarely able to afford to notice anything amiss between the two older men.

"Look, Teo, they had oranges! I bought six, enough for each of us to have two. And I bought drinking chocolate for you. And lamb! Fresh from the farm it is, the shopkeeper said, and it looks so much more tender than *cabrito*, I though perhaps we could ask Isabel to roast it... and sweetmeat! I couldn't decide between them, so I bought some of each!"

"I see you took advantage of my purse," Christian commented from the doorway, his smile teasing Teodoro gently.

Esteban had been watching Teodoro's face as he pulled out each purchase, and at Christian's words his expression fell. "I hope I did not spend too much?" he said uneasily, his gaze flickering to Christian. "I thought they were things that would make Teo feel better...." He trailed off, his innate honesty forcing him to admit he was looking forward to the treats as well.

"Not at all," Christian replied smoothly, walking to Esteban's side and bending his head close. "But if your father disagrees, we'll just keep his share for ourselves. How does that sound?"

"I agreed to accept such help as you can offer," Teodoro countered, meeting Christian's gaze with a wry smile. "And if you think you can keep my share of that drinking chocolate, I may need to test your prowess with a sword."

"Teo has a sweet tooth," Esteban told Christian with the air of one disclosing a grave secret. "I knew he would like the chocolate best of all."

"Then perhaps I should give him my share as well," Christian suggested to Esteban. "I would rather not have him challenge me to a fight over chocolate."

"One day we will measure our lengths against one another," Teodoro answered, his lips twitching when he saw the flush that rose in Christian's cheeks at the suggestive phrase. He would not normally tease with anyone but Raúl in such a manner, but seeing the happiness Christian's generosity had brought Esteban loosened some of the restraint he kept on his emotions. Would it be so terrible to let Christian see beneath the mask he habitually wore, just this once? Esteban's presence would assure they did not go beyond teasing words. "But not this day—we will share the chocolate evenly, as soon as we get hot milk from Isabel to brew it."

Christian could not stop the flush from staining his cheeks, but a smile followed immediately at being invited to bandy words the way he had seen Teodoro do with Raúl. He moved closer to where Teodoro stood, pitching his voice so only he would hear. "I look forward to it," he replied suggestively. Before the situation could progress beyond words, he turned back to Esteban. "Shall we try one of those oranges?"

"Esteban, take the lamb and sweetmeat to Isabel and ask if she will prepare them, and invite her and your uncle to join us for the meal when it is ready," Teodoro instructed.

The moment the door closed behind Esteban, Christian was at Teodoro's side, pressing his body against Teodoro's, brushing their hips together. "Measure our lengths?" he teased, lifting his mouth for a kiss.

"We did tell Beatriz at the tavern that you were looking for fencing lessons," Teodoro countered, allowing their lips to brush against each other in a gentle, languorous touch until the sound of Esteban's returning footsteps on the stairs forced them apart.

"Tío Inocencio is with an ailing soul," Esteban told them when he came inside, "and Isabel's family is expecting her home for their midday meal."

"We will save them some to enjoy this evening, then," Teodoro declared, in truth not displeased that they would not have to share this time together.

Esteban could not remember ever seeing Teodoro's rare smile as often as he did that afternoon. The lamb was roasted on the kitchen's broad hearth; the sweetmeat was used to fill *empanadillas dulces*; hot milk was procured to brew a pot of dark, sweet chocolate; the oranges were peeled and every fragrant, juicy section devoured amid much teasing and laughter. He could not help but be grateful to Christian for providing the means for such a delicious repast. If Raúl had been present, the day would have been nearly perfect.

Leaning back in his chair as he drained his cup of chocolate, Teodoro watched Christian pop a wedge of orange between his lips. A surge of desire flashed through him as the strong white teeth bit the slice in two, releasing the sweet juices. Christian's tongue flicked out to capture the flavorful droplets, and Teodoro remembered the honeyed taste of that tongue in his mouth when they kissed earlier that morning. He shifted against the hard wooden seat, reaching for an *empanadilla* in place of the treat he would really like to claim.

The shared laughter did much to dispel the unsated desire that tormented Christian, but the sight of various delicacies slipping between Teodoro's lips reminded him all too often of what had been interrupted. He was not about to order Esteban out of his own home so he and Teodoro could pick up where they left off, not least because he knew his lover would never accept such a suggestion, but he could not help but hope that Esteban would have another errand to run or some other reason to leave again. It was only midafternoon. Christian knew he would never make it until nightfall.

Hearing the church bell toll across the square, Teodoro glanced up at Esteban. "You will be late for afternoon prayers, whelp," he observed, grateful that he would not need to make up some reason to get Esteban out of their rooms. The hunger that gnawed at him had not been satisfied by the luxuries they had indulged in. Nothing but another taste of Christian would slake it, and he feared even that would not be enough to satisfy him.

Esteban jumped up from the table, flushing at the thought of being late. He grabbed his hat and rushed out of the room, not wanting to suffer a penance for his tardiness. "Gracias," he called as the door slammed shut behind him.

"'Tis not every day I see a lad so eager for religious services," Christian commented with an arched eyebrow, his mind racing as he wondered how long he and Teodoro would have alone while Esteban was at his prayers.

"Inocencio ensures that Esteban is raised as a good Catholic. He assists his uncle as an altar server once a week, and *el cura* has little patience with tardiness," Teodoro answered, his mind already dismissing Esteban as he wondered how he was going to withstand the temptation to pull Christian back into the bedroom and resume where they had broken off.

"And how long does *el cura* usually keep Esteban?" Christian inquired with deceptive casualness. He did not want to be interrupted as rudely as they had been before.

"Until evening prayers," Teodoro replied with equal composure.

Christian's grin turned rakish. "Then we have several hours alone." He rose from his seat and prowled toward Teodoro. "I believe we have unfinished business." Not giving him a chance to protest or pull away, he closed his lips over Teodoro's, tasting the chocolate and sweetmeat.

Teodoro could think of any number of reasons why they shouldn't continue, but none of them could stand against his need to taste Christian again. He pulled the younger man down to his chair and molded one arm to his back, tangling his other hand in the blond curls to hold his head steady as he plundered deep into Christian's mouth, the sweetness of the oranges and the spicy tang of the sweetmeat flavoring the kiss.

The sensation of Teodoro welcoming him, opening to him, went straight to Christian's head. He parted his lips eagerly to allow his lover entrance, giving Teodoro free access to his mouth. Careful of the wound even in his passion, he encircled Teodoro's shoulders with his arms to offer free access to his body as well.

Christian's encouragement started a coil of heat tightening in Teodoro's gut. Each time he kissed Christian it became harder to resist, harder to remember why he should not simply take what he wanted so desperately—what Christian was offering so freely. He moved both hands to cradle Christian's face, turning it to allow him to delve even deeper into the kiss, stroking the smooth cheeks and tracing the curve of ears beneath the tousle of curls that escaped his queue.

Excited beyond words by Teodoro's positive responses, Christian dropped his hands to his lover's shirt, pulling eagerly at the laces. He had touched Teodoro's strong chest the night before under the pretense of massaging his wounded arm, but that had only whetted his appetite. He wanted more, wanted to see and taste as well as feel. Parting the linen, he let his hands wander freely, hoping Teodoro would take his actions as an invitation to reciprocate.

The touch of Christian's fingers sliding beneath the fabric of his shirt to explore his chest made Teodoro's groin tighten with desire. His conscience began to whisper a warning, but he ignored it, leaning back in the chair without breaking the kiss to allow Christian greater access. Just a little longer, he told himself, his breath catching as the tantalizing fingers splayed across his skin. They were only kisses, only touches—he would stop soon. Soon… just a little longer… another kiss….

Teodoro's new posture was a temptation Christian could not resist, especially not when his roving hands brushed the tip of Teodoro's erect cock. Passion spinning out of control, he lowered himself onto Teodoro's lap, straddling him, rubbing their groins together provocatively. He broke the kiss, trailing his lips across Teodoro's cheek so he could whisper, "I cannot wait to feel you inside me. I have wanted you since I first saw you."

The provocative words and the fierce surge of lust that flared when Christian rubbed against him snapped Teodoro from the sensual haze he had allowed himself to drift in ever since Esteban's departure. Grasping Christian's shoulders, he pushed him backward, the move dragging their cocks against each other as he tried to put some distance between them. "We go too far," he muttered thickly, rubbing his hand across his lips as though he could wipe away the enticement of Christian's kiss.

Christian jerked back, the words stinging him hard. He had hoped, believed, that the kiss in the bedroom earlier and the kiss now were signs that Teodoro had moved beyond his resistance, but it seemed he was wrong. Hurt stiffening his body, he pulled back and turned away, unwilling to let Teodoro see him like this. "I thought you were different from everyone else," he said slowly, trying to keep his voice from trembling as he spoke. "You said you didn't see me as a child, and I believed you. I thought I'd finally found someone who would see me for myself, who would care for me—the real me—instead of the pampered aristocrat everyone thinks I am. I would have done anything for you, you know, would have stayed here without a second thought, if only you had been that man. But you're not." He turned back to face Teodoro accusingly. "You're just like everyone else, determined to push me away for my own protection. Fine. If that's what you want, I'll leave. I'll go back to England and prove you all wrong in the end."

The last thing Teodoro wanted was for Christian to leave, especially with the danger that still threatened, but he knew trying to convince Christian of that would only anger him further. He ran his hand through his hair, trying to find the words to explain why they had to stop, when something Christian had said finally registered. "You would stay?" he asked slowly.

"I would have," Christian agreed, his voice heavy with regret as he thought of all that might have been, all he had hoped would be, "but it doesn't matter now. I should be used to it, you know, being sent away. My father sent me here rather than let me take part in the negotiations. Gerrard sent me away rather than letting me stand by him in a fight. I don't know why I thought this would be any different." He started toward the bedroom, shoulders bent in defeat, to gather his things and leave.

"Cristian," Teodoro rasped, his voice husky with remorse and desire. He rose to his feet, his heart pounding beneath the open lacing of his shirt. As Christian turned, he swallowed and met his eyes, the cerulean depths shimmering behind their long lashes. The thought that he had caused the hurt and doubt that filled that gaze cut him like a sword stroke. "Stay."

"Do you mean that?" Christian asked, incredibly tempted by the outstretched hand and the words he wanted to hear: his name—he would never tire of hearing Teodoro say "Cristian"—but also the invitation. "I don't want to be another responsibility, another ward, albeit older. If I stay, it will be as equals." He paused and took a deep breath, putting his heart on the line. "As lovers. If that's not what you want, tell me now so I can go while I still have some dignity and self-respect left."

Teodoro raised his other arm, holding them open, his dark gaze burning with intensity as he willed Christian to return to him. "Como amantes," he promised, knowing the decision had to be Christian's. "I won't push you away again."

Christian searched Teodoro's face for a moment, then flew into his outstretched arms, tilting his face up to invite the kiss that would seal their promise.

Teodoro closed his arms around Christian, melding their bodies together as he lowered his head to take Christian's lips in a slow, deep claiming. As fiercely as the promise of making Christian his lover aroused him, his lips were tender, his fingers gentle as he pulled the queue loose from Christian's hair and threaded into the silky locks. There would be time for passion, but this kiss was an apology and a pledge. He stroked his tongue against Christian's in an age-old dance, made new by emotions Teodoro was not yet ready to name, even to himself. He broke the kiss softly, his lips quirking into a smile. "You still taste of oranges," he murmured, returning again and again to press short, moist kisses to Christian's sweet lips.

Christian chuckled between kisses, the tenderness in Teodoro's gestures making him feel cherished as nothing else ever had. "And you taste of chocolate," he observed, chasing the flavor into the recesses of Teodoro's mouth. He could feel his passion simmering beneath the surface, but he ignored it for now in favor of the gentle intimacy of the moment. Knowing that it would be sated gave him the patience to wait and anticipate each moment leading up to the culmination. He moved his hands slowly over Teodoro's back, working his way down to the shirttails and beneath, to coast over his lover's hard muscles and soft skin.

As much as he meant to take things slowly, the touch of Christian's hands on his bare skin sent the flame of desire Teodoro had struggled to keep banked flaring to life. He slid a hand down the rich material of Christian's doublet until he cupped the firm curve of his buttocks, drawing him closer to press their groins together as he moved his lips to the soft skin of Christian's neck. "You have on too many clothes," he muttered, trying to work a hand in between them to open buttons without drawing away from their embrace.

Christian's giddy laughter pealed through the room as he kissed Teodoro quickly. "How much shall I remove?" he asked coyly, hoping he knew the answer. He did not wait for a reply before attacking the laces on his doublet and shirt.

The sound of Christian's laughter was a balm to Teodoro's heart. "Remove them all," he answered with a short smile as he shrugged out of his open shirt, letting it fall to the floor. His gaze raked over the smooth pale skin he had the right to look at openly for the first time. The large, pink disks of Christian's nipples tempted him, and he brushed over one with the back of his knuckles, grinning to himself when it tightened into a hard nub. "And then you can remove mine."

Christian did not have to be asked twice. He shed his clothes with alacrity, baring himself to Teodoro's unabashedly appreciative gaze. He took his time with his lover, though, opening the laces of his breeches slowly, caressing each bit of skin as it was revealed, enjoying the moment of anticipation. That he had seen Teodoro naked, or nearly so, when he was feverish, did not enter Christian's mind. That had been a matter of necessity. This… this was a matter of pure pleasure, and he intended to make the most of it. He pushed the breeches and smallclothes down Teodoro's thighs, trailing his fingers over hard, hair-dusted flesh as they went, until he had to kneel to slide them down farther. He helped Teodoro out of them and his thin stockings before turning his gaze upward again, to the swelling cock in front of his face. Feeling daring, he leaned forward and swiped his tongue across the tip.

A hiss of surprised pleasure escaped Teodoro's lips when the rasp of Christian's tongue swept over his cock. He knew Christian was no innocent, but he had not expected him to be so bold. Remembering his demand to be accepted as an equal, Teodoro resisted the urge to pull Christian to his feet and order him into the bedroom. He splayed a hand in Christian's hair and grasped the chair back firmly with the other, giving Christian command of their lovemaking—for the moment.

Christian half expected Teodoro to wrest control away from him immediately. Gratified when that did not happen, he lingered for a moment over the latest and best of the day's treats, licking up and down the hard shaft, learning its contours and its flavor. Teodoro smelled faintly of sweat, but mostly of desire, sparking Christian's already eager arousal. Working his way to the tip, he sucked lightly at the smooth skin before drawing the head into his mouth, tracing the slit and pushing back the foreskin with his tongue, lavishing pleasure on Teodoro.

None of the fantasies Teodoro had conjured during the nights since Christian had entered his life, not even the fevered illusions of his delirium, were as arousing as the reality of the blond beauty kneeling before him, pleasuring him. His fingers tightened in the honeyed curls as he watched the sculpted lips close around the length of his cock, the tantalizing flickers of Christian's tongue sending coils of fire dancing through his veins. Not even the moist suction of his lover's mouth drawing him deeper, deep enough to feel his head nudging the back of Christian's throat, was enough to quench the need to feel himself surrounded by even greater heat, even tighter friction. He felt his release building too quickly, and he was not ready to give in to it yet—he had too much of Christian's delectable body to explore first, too much pleasure he wanted to bestow in return before indulging in his own. With a low growl, he pulled away, urging Christian to lift his head. "Too much," he said softly, drawing Christian to his feet and wrapping him in a hard embrace, savoring his own desire glossing his lover's lips. "I would taste more of you, *corazón*."

"All of me, if you want." Christian pushed himself more tightly against Teodoro. He wanted anything, everything Teodoro would give him, and he wanted it now. He had a feeling, though, that Teodoro would refuse to rush, and that sent anticipation singing down his nerves. "Shall we take this to bed?"

"Do you know how many nights I watched you sleep and longed for the right to lie beside you?" Teodoro asked, nuzzling the silken curve of Christian's throat from below his ear to the arch of his collarbone. "And on those nights I did lie beside you, how I struggled not to take you in my arms, not to touch you and taste you as I am now?" A slight smile crossed his lips as he raised his head, meeting azure eyes that shone with desire as much as he was sure his own burned with it. "*Sí*, let us to bed."

"As many nights as I longed for you to lie beside me, to take me in your arms and touch me, taste me as you are now," Christian replied fervently, his hand never leaving Teodoro's as they moved into the bedroom and onto the bed. Lying back, he stretched his arms out, welcoming Teodoro down onto his eager body. "Give us what we've both desired since we met."

Kneeling on the bed, straddling his lover, Teodoro paused, drinking in the vision of Christian holding his arms out to him, his flawless skin golden against the worn bedclothes, his hair a wild halo against the pillow. Sliding his knees apart, he bent closer, letting his lips trail over the honeyed smoothness. He teased at the pulse that fluttered in the hollow of Christian's throat, tracing up and down the tendons of his neck, then suckling at the knot that bobbed up and down as he swallowed anxiously. He nipped at the bones of his shoulders and down the muscles of his arms, lingering at the bend of each elbow and wrist, pressing moist kisses into each smooth palm and mouthing the fingers as though they were his favorite sweetmeats.

Christian undulated slowly beneath Teodoro's teasing touches, drifting on a swell of passion he had not known existed. He was no innocent, but no lover had ever touched him the way Teodoro did, lingered over him like some special treat, savored him like a delicacy without compare. He wondered vaguely what made the difference, whether it was Teodoro's experience or something else less tangible. Whatever it was, Christian knew one thing for certain: he never wanted to be without Teodoro again.

Watching Christian's face as he nipped his way back up a slender forearm, Teodoro was fascinated by the expression of need on his features and the flutter of dark lashes on his closed eyelids. He rose enough to claim one brief kiss, brushing his stubbled cheek against Christian's neatly trimmed goatee, before returning his attentions to Christian's smooth chest. He let his breath ghost over one of the pink nipples, his lips twitching when it hardened from only that delicate touch. Teasing at it with short, hard kisses, he resisted the temptation to close his lips around the rosy pearl until Christian was moaning beneath him.

"Por favor," Christian begged, burrowing his hands into Teodoro's hair as he urged his lover's mouth against his chest. Teodoro had found his weak spot, the place on his body that reduced him to mindless pleading. The sensation of Teodoro's moustache teasing his skin only added to the already overwhelming sensations. He could feel his cock begin to leak and knew that if Teodoro continued, it would not be long before he came. "Please," he begged again, "oh God, please!"

As much as he wanted to prolong their mutual pleasure, Teodoro was not proof against Christian's pleas. He sucked the tightened nub between his lips, letting his teeth graze it before capturing it with a gentle tug that wrenched a cry from Christian's throat. His strong hands held Christian down against the bed as he licked a trail to the other side of his partner's chest, repeating the rough caress. Every sound of pleasure he coaxed from Christian enflamed his own arousal. His cock was a throbbing weight against his belly, but he ignored its insistent demands in favor of tasting his way down Christian's quavering abdomen, toward the equally hard length that curved from between Christian's spread legs.

Christian's back arched off the bed when Teodoro's lips found his aching shaft. Even his babbling pleas faded into incoherency, words completely beyond him as the wet heat of Teodoro's mouth surrounded him. He wanted to thrust up into the moist depths, but Teodoro restrained him, leaving him to twist and toss helplessly beneath the lash of overpowering sensation. "Teodoro!" he wailed before he brought his hand to his lips to muffle his own shouts as he fought to hold back, to keep from coming down Teodoro's throat. He ached with the need for release, but he struggled to wait, to hold on until Teodoro was with him, inside him, filling and completing him as he knew instinctively Teodoro would do.

Christian tasted exactly as Teodoro had imagined, salty with sweat and musky with desire, and he thought to himself that of all the delicacies he had consumed that day, this was the one he would crave again and again. As much as he wanted to bring Christian to climax and savor the hot tang of his release, the need to bury himself deep inside his body was even stronger. Letting the shaft slide from his lips with a final lap at the milky fluid that seeped from it, he pushed himself up on one elbow, reaching toward the armoire.

Feeling Teodoro's weight leave him, Christian moaned in protest, his hands clenching reflexively at his lover's shoulders. "Don't," he begged, thinking something he had done was causing his partner to pull away again. "Please, *amante*. Don't go."

"Te deseo," Teodoro rasped, the pain in his shoulder where Christian unthinkingly clutched it subsumed by his aching need to claim Christian in the most primal of ways. "But I must get something to ease the way." His fingers closed around a small flask of the oil he used to care for his sword blade. Kneeling back between Christian's legs, he stroked Christian's unblemished thighs with battle-scarred hands, coaxing them to part further before dipping into the flagon of slick fluid. His gaze never left Christian's face as he parted the damp crease of his buttocks, circling the pucker of flesh that quivered beneath his touch.

"Por favor," Christian begged shamelessly, pulling his knees toward his chest, opening himself as completely as he could to Teodoro's hands. "Touch me," he added, so there could be no confusion over what he wanted.

That was a request Teodoro could not deny. Spreading one hand over the planes of Christian's abdomen, Teodoro eased the tip of his finger forward until it penetrated the clenching muscle. The sight of his thick finger disappearing into the pale flesh fired his blood, imagining that heat and pressure squeezing his cock as he claimed Christian completely. Rubbing his thumb over the faint line of hair that arrowed toward Christian's cock, he worked his finger in deeper, stroking the sides of the tight channel, watching Christian's expression lose its initial tension from the intrusion as his body relaxed to accept him.

Christian arched and writhed beneath the confident caresses, losing himself completely in Teodoro's enticing touch, Teodoro's burning gaze. The finger inside him stretched him, but not enough. He wanted, needed more. He needed Teodoro's—

"Teodoro! Get dressed and get out here. Esteban's in danger!"

ELEVEN

MUTTERING A curse, Teodoro rolled to his feet, struggling against the urge to ignore Raúl, ignore everything but the need to claim Christian at last. He ran his hand through his sweaty hair, pushing it back from his face, turning his head for a moment to take in the sight of Christian sprawled in wanton abandon across his bed before turning back toward the door to the common room.

"Wait!" Christian protested, realizing Teodoro intended to walk into the other room naked. "At least put the sheet around yourself."

"It's only Raúl," Teodoro answered dryly. "From the way we left our clothes scattered all over the floor, I'm sure he has no illusions about what we're doing."

"That's not the point," Christian pointed out. "Would you want *me* to walk out there naked?"

Teodoro wasn't sure he understood what Christian was concerned about, but he could tell from the expression on his face that this was important to him. After wrapping the bed linen around his waist, he raised an eyebrow at Christian as if to ask if he were satisfied before stalking through the doorway. "What has happened?" he demanded.

Raúl raised a sardonic eyebrow at Teodoro's unusual attire, but his news was too pressing to take his usual time to tease. "Where is Esteban? I overheard one of *el conde* de la Rocha's men asking about him. It seems *el conde* and St. Denys have a taste for young boys."

His expression hardening, Teodoro began to gather his clothes and Christian's. "And if *el conde* cannot strike at me or Cristian, he will target a defenseless boy? *Bastardo*! Does he know where Esteban is now?"

"Perhaps not at this moment," Raúl replied, his expression matching Teodoro's. "But the *hijo de puta* who answered *el conde*'s man told him you and Esteban reside with *el cura*."

"If any harm comes to him, I will—" Teodoro broke off and glanced back at the bedroom, then met Raúl's eyes with a steely glare. "I must be sure Esteban is safe. Will you remain here and watch over Cristian?"

"Of course," Raúl replied. "It will give me a chance to get to know your young man a little better." He paused and then asked, "Is he your young man now?"

"Had you arrived five minutes later, he would have been," Teodoro answered dryly. "*El conde* de la Rocha will have much to answer for, should we ever meet." With a dour grin, Teodoro turned back to the bedchamber and tossed Christian's clothes onto the bed.

"You would not have wanted me to wait even that long with the news I had," Raúl commented to Teodoro's retreating back.

Inside the room, Christian looked up when Teodoro walked in. "What's wrong with Esteban?" he asked immediately.

"I hope nothing, but I cannot take that chance," he said quietly, pulling on his breeches. "Raúl overheard one of *el conde* de la Rocha's men asking about him. They know we reside with Don Inocencio. I must see that he is safe. Raúl will stay with you until we return." He met Christian's gaze as he fastened his shirt, hoping Christian would not think he was making a choice between them.

"De la Rocha?" Christian asked. "Isn't that the man St. Denys was writing to, the letter we burned?"

"Sí," Teodoro acknowledged as he dressed, "Jimeno Garbajosa y Terrillas, *el conde* de la Rocha. He is a well-known figure at court, though no hint of scandal has attached to his name before this."

Christian's face tightened. "Then perhaps it is time that happens, or we may never be free of their plots," he muttered, lust fading in light of the threat to the boy he had befriended. Getting his breeches fastened, he went to Teodoro's side and kissed him swiftly. "Do what you must. I'll be here waiting for your return."

Though he knew he must hurry, Teodoro could not resist tightening his arm around his lover's shoulders, holding him close for just a moment. They *were* lovers now, regardless of whether they'd completed what they had begun. "Once Esteban is safe, nothing will stop me from loving you," he vowed, softly enough that only Christian could hear.

"Nor I from loving you," Christian swore in return. "Go. Bring him home safely."

After tugging on his boots, Teodoro retrieved his dagger from the armoire and tucked it into his waistband. Returning to the main room, he buckled on his sword and reached for his hat. "When I return, we will decide how to deal with *el conde* de la Rocha," he told Raúl. "I want this threat ended once and for all."

Following Teodoro into the room as he pulled his shirt over his head, Christian nodded in agreement. He had said everything he could to Teodoro in the bedroom, but he didn't want to lose sight of him any sooner than necessary.

"Bring Esteban home safe, and we will make plans then," Raúl agreed, glancing at Christian once before turning his attention back to Teodoro. "I have learned much this afternoon."

"*Bien.* Keep him safe." Teodoro's eyes met Christian's once more, and then he turned out the door and was gone.

"As if he were mine," Raúl said softly, though he knew Teodoro could not hear him. With a grim smile, he set his pistol on the table within easy reach and motioned for Christian to join him.

Christian took the offered seat, his fingers tapping nervously on the rough edge of the table as he tried not to think of the danger Teodoro could well be facing alone, as he tried not to imagine Esteban at the hands of the *conde* and his mercenaries.

"Teodoro is one of the best swordsmen I have ever met," Raúl said, breaking the silence and offering Christian the words of comfort he didn't know he needed. "There is no one I would trust at my back more than him."

"At your back or on your back?" Christian muttered under his breath, jealousy sinking its claws into him hard. The gypsy certainly hadn't seemed upset to have interrupted him and Teodoro earlier, before they could make love.

If Raúl heard the remark, it didn't seem to trouble him. "Are you perhaps wondering if we were lovers?" he asked easily. "We were, of course—between battles, men take such comfort as they can where they can find it, especially in such a hell as the Flemish campaigns. But Teodoro, though he would take another sword in his shoulder rather than admit it, is a romantic at heart—he believes in love, and though we have shared much in the years since I have known him, neither of us has ever imagined we were in love."

"Am I wasting my time with him, then?" Christian asked plaintively, searching Raúl's face for reassurance. He wondered where his jealousy had gone, but it seemed to have been extinguished by Raúl's simple honesty. All that remained was the fear that Teodoro still did not imagine himself in love the way Christian did. "Am I foolish to hope that he loves me?"

"I have seen Teodoro take many lovers," Raúl answered. "Seldom have they lasted more than a few nights, unless it was very clear that neither's heart was involved, and most of those were before Esteban was old enough to question the presence of another person in their rooms." He smiled at Christian, whose openness was such a contrast to Teodoro's reticence to display his emotions. "I have never seen him fight his attraction as he has toward you. If he felt nothing, he would have taken what he wanted from you long before now."

Christian blushed and looked away. "You must think me such a child, demanding reassurances from you this way. It's just...." He paused, trying to decide how much to say. In the end, it seemed nothing but total honesty would do. "It's just that I've never felt for anyone what I feel for Teodoro. It would kill me to find out he did not feel the same way."

The confession having done much to ease Raúl's concerns for Teodoro, he did not hesitate to offer Christian his own reassurance. "He wrapped a sheet around himself earlier because you asked him to, did he not?"

"How do you know that?" Christian demanded defensively, feeling even more insecure now than he had before. Had Teodoro told Raúl? Had they laughed about it together while he paced the room worried about Esteban?

"Because it's the first time he has ever bothered with modesty." Raúl grinned, then sobered as he read the expression in his companion's eyes. "He did it because he cares for your feelings," he continued. "Believe that, for it is more consideration than I have seen him show anyone, even Esteban."

Christian nodded slowly. He wanted to believe that Raúl was right, and certainly from what he had seen, the gypsy knew Teodoro better than anyone else, but a part of him would not believe it completely until he heard the words from Teodoro's mouth.

Sitting back in his chair, Raúl withdrew his pipe from his pouch and began to fill it. He had hoped to gain a sense of Christian's feelings toward Teodoro, but he had learned more from the *inglés*'s questions than from any he might have asked himself. Feeling well satisfied, he turned his mind toward the problem of how to disarm the *conde* de la Rocha, so that Teodoro might enjoy the treasure he had found.

THE COBBLES rang beneath his boot heels as Teodoro strode down the dusty alleyway toward *la iglesia de San Pedro*. Though his eyes darted from side to side when he reached the square, assessing the passersby out of habit, in his mind he saw only Christian as he had looked just before Raúl's arrival, his honeyed skin flushed with heat, his blond hair tangled on the pillow, his face transformed with longing as Teodoro made ready to claim him. Even now the fever still sang in his own veins, urging him to move faster, to be sure Esteban was safe so he could return to his home, his bed—his Christian.

He saw nothing out of the ordinary outside the church, so rather than interrupt afternoon prayer, he leaned against the fence that surrounded the small churchyard, waiting for Esteban to exit. Once more, while he remained alert to everything that went on around him, he could not keep a part of his mind from imagining the pleasure that awaited him when he and Christian were next alone. He would strip Christian from his clothes again, baring each inch of his warm skin to his fingers and lips. Perhaps this time, when he took Christian into his mouth, he would not stop until he had tasted all of him. The corner of Teodoro's lip curled as he imagined Christian's face as he came undone at the touch of his mouth. Then, when he was utterly sated, Teodoro would take him, would slide with aching slowness into his hot, tight channel. His cock swelled as he imagined Christian squeezing around him, imagined the cries he would wring from his lips as he filled him, as Christian's long legs wrapped around his waist and they found the depth, the rhythm that would bring them both to bliss....

Finally free of the *cura*'s demands, Esteban raced out of the church with all his usual boisterous energy, calling his good-byes to the other altar boys as he did. He skidded to a halt when he saw Teodoro waiting there. "Did I...," he began, his mind searching for something he might have done that would explain Teo's presence. "Is something wrong?"

Another quick glance around the church's surroundings showing nothing untoward, Teodoro exhaled sharply and nodded for Esteban to follow him. His sword slapped against his thigh as his long strides ate up the short distance back to the parish residence. Esteban, despite the energy of youth, was hard pressed to keep up with his speed.

As he walked, the rapid pace doing little to cool his ardor, Teodoro considered how to answer Esteban's question. The boy was not wholly innocent, but even so, Teodoro recoiled from exposing him to the *conde* de la Rocha's and St. Denys's intentions. Raúl had not had time to share any details, but Esteban needed to hear enough to understand the danger he faced. Teodoro also had to decide what to tell his son about Christian. He had brought home few lovers since Esteban had grown old enough to be aware of their presence; more, until now they had all been female, and it had been clear none of them were anything more than someone to warm his bed and sate his need. Teodoro suspected Esteban would care less that he had taken a male lover this time, despite the church's strictures, than he would care that Christian was obviously much more to him than just another meaningless fuck. He could hardly explain to Esteban what his future with Christian might be when he did not understand it himself. What would happen to them once the threat of the *conde* and St. Denys was ended? Christian had said he would stay, but for how long? Teodoro knew the two of them needed to talk—later, after they had finished making love.

They had reached the head of the alleyway to the residence's back entrance when Teodoro's keen hearing caught the sound of a number of booted feet approaching. Retreating against the wall of the alleyway they had just crossed, he motioned Esteban behind him, his hand dropping to the hilt of his sword.

Obediently, Esteban moved as Teodoro bid, canny enough to know he did not want to appear in any way to interfere with the city guards or the Inquisition soldiers, squadrons of both roaming the streets at will. He sank back farther into the shadows when the patrol rounded the corner and approached them.

"Teodoro Ciéza de Vivar?" the captain of the guard asked.

Teodoro had been prepared to face a pack of the *conde*'s soldiers, but these guards were clad in the red-and-white livery of the constables of the Holy Office. For just a moment he contemplated drawing his sword in any case, estimating the odds of overpowering them; then his gaze fell on Esteban. Whatever happened to him, he needed to be certain Esteban was safe, and that Christian was warned. Taking a step forward, he inclined his head, waiting to see what would come next.

"You are under arrest by order of the Grand Inquisitor," the captain intoned gravely, gesturing for his soldiers to approach. "Do not make your situation worse by resisting."

Not even as fearless a man as Teodoro Ciéza de Vivar could prevent a shiver from running down his spine at the thought of falling into the clutches of the Inquisition. "Go," he whispered to Esteban, not turning his head to see if he was obeyed. "Tell Raúl." Raising his chin, he stared at the guard from beneath the brim of his broad hat. "What is the charge?" he demanded.

"Sodomy," the captain replied with unholy glee. It had been some weeks since he had gotten to watch the Inquisitors torture a confession from a sodomite. This one looked strong and stubborn. He would enjoy watching them wring the truth from this godless abomination.

TWELVE

THE SILENCE between Christian and Raúl was companionable, each man comfortable enough in his own skin not to need to fill the time with empty conversation. Christian's thoughts drifted, sliding inevitably back to the moments before Raúl had arrived and brought a sudden halt to the interlude between Teodoro and himself. He slipped deeper into the memory of the taste of Teodoro's flesh, the smell of his skin, the feel of his lover's fingers on his body, inside his body. He did not blame Raúl for the interruption, not given the news he had brought, nor did he resent Teodoro's departure. To leave Esteban in such danger would have been unconscionable. He did, however, ache for Teodoro's return, his mind throwing up image after image in which the passion between them finally played out to its inevitable conclusion.

Shifting in his seat, he imagined Teodoro's actions, his lover stripping him where he sat, leaving him sprawled in the wooden chair, legs splayed wide as Teodoro devoured him. He could come from that, letting himself go in Teodoro's mouth. Or he could hold out, fighting back his release until Teodoro took him to bed and ravished him properly, the way he had been about to when Raúl arrived and interrupted them.

Raúl saw the slight flush of color warm his companion's cheeks; he hid a smile but said nothing. He had already interrupted Christian's pleasure once, albeit inadvertently. The least he could do was allow him his memories now. Reaching for his pipe, he rose to light a twist of paper when a hard knock sounded at the door. Christian started, and Raúl waved him back with a silent gesture. Teodoro or Esteban would not knock at their own door, and they weren't expecting anyone else.

Christian tensed, starting to rise to his feet at the knock, only subsiding when Raúl gestured for him to stay seated. His hand reached automatically for the hilt of his sword, only to realize it was not within reach. Cursing silently, he watched Raúl for an indication of what he should do.

Quietly, Raúl paced to the heavy wooden door and pulled it open without warning, surprising the large, dark-haired man who stood in the shadowed corridor.

The door opening caught the big man off guard, but he recovered quickly. He pushed past Raúl, dismissing the slighter man as unimportant, as he drew his sword, searching for his erstwhile adversary. Not seeing the Spaniard he sought, but instead his former charge, he gestured peremptorily for Christian to join him. "Let's go. We can escape before he comes back."

Raúl's dagger was out of his boot and pressed against the swordsman's throat before the big man had finished speaking. Threading his fingers into the crisp dark curls, he pulled the man's head back, smiling calmly as he spoke into his ear. "You turned your back on another man in an unfamiliar situation. You made an assumption, perhaps, that he was harmless? That was foolish, and if I were also given to making hasty assumptions, you would already be dead."

Christian shook his head as he watched the exchange. It highlighted, more than ever, the incredible caliber of man Teodoro was. Gerrard had taken one look at Raúl's unassuming attire and slender build and dismissed him, never seeing the deadly edge beneath the surface. Teodoro would never have made such a mistake. "It's all right, Raúl," he said. "This is Gerrard Hawkins, my former bodyguard. I thought he'd returned to England when he was wounded. Teo took over his role as my protector."

"Protector?" Gerrard spluttered. "He kidnapped you! Whether he wanted you for ransom or for some other nefarious purpose, either way, I couldn't just leave you!"

"I went with Teodoro willingly," Christian countered, "and in the time I have been with him, he has managed to get St. Denys arrested and is trying to end the rest of the threat against me. That is far more than you ever did. Now, apologize to Raúl for misjudging him and then tell me why you've come."

"You make your livelihood hiring your sword?" Raúl marveled as he lowered his dagger, still holding the bigger man's head back with his other hand. Hawkins's dark eyes flared in anger, and Raúl laughed, letting his hand drop. "You must be wiser than you look to have survived this long, but I will not judge you by first appearances." He held out his hand and raised an eyebrow, waiting to see how the other man would respond.

Slowly, not sure what to make of this suddenly changed landscape, of a Christian who had no qualms about ordering him around, Gerrard took the extended hand. "Gerrard Hawkins."

"Raúl," the gypsy answered, settling back comfortably into his chair. "Now that we have finished the pleasantries, you still have not answered *el vizconde*'s question, Señor Hawkins."

"I brought a letter from your father," Gerrard explained, turning his attention back to Christian. "It arrived after you left Valencia, and I've spent days asking for Ciéza de Vivar in Madrid until I found someone who could tell me where he lived." He handed Christian a folded missive. "I hope you have explained the situation to His Grace, because I have no desire to do so."

"You were wounded and I found another protector, exactly according to the terms of your contract," Christian replied simply, opening the letter. He skimmed it quickly, reading the unwelcome news that his father had arrived in Spain for the final stage of the negotiations. He hoped it would mean an end to the interest of the *conde* de la Rocha in their lives, but it could well take away his excuse for staying close until he and Teodoro could resolve things between them.

Before Gerrard could renew his protests, the door banged open again, startling all three men. "Cristian!" Esteban shouted, eyes wild with panic. "Have you seen…. Raúl!" He took a few more steps into the room and collapsed at Raúl's feet. "The Inquisition," he gasped. "Teo!"

Helping the shaking young man to stand, Raúl grasped Esteban's head in both hands and caught his eyes with his steady gaze. "Calm, *mijo*. Breathe." He waited until the boy's heaving gasps eased and then released his head with a ruffle of the shaggy locks. "Now, was he taken?"

Esteban nodded. "There were too many of them," he replied. "He didn't even try to fight. He just told me softly to go and tell you."

Christian flinched as if struck at hearing the news. He had no idea what Raúl could do in such a situation. The Inquisition was incredibly powerful, and only the king and queen were beyond the reach of its authority.

Frowning, Raúl stroked his goatee as he pondered their options. He knew well enough that it would be useless to try to break Teodoro out of the ancient fortress in which the Inquisition held its prisoners, but perhaps there was another way to win his freedom. "I must see what I can learn, though I expect *el conde* has a hand in this," he declared.

Looking pointedly at Christian, he added in a tone that would brook no argument, "You and the boy stay here. Teodoro will have my head if anything happens to you while he is imprisoned."

"Hurry," Esteban pleaded. "The guard said the charge was sodomy. They will not wait long to question him."

"Sodomy!" Christian exclaimed. "They will torture him! Raúl, he cannot stay there. He is only barely recovered from his shoulder injury. We have to do something."

"We will, *amigo mio*, I promise," Raúl vowed. Though he was not at all certain yet what they would be able to do, he would find some way to aid Teodoro, even if the most he could do was smuggle him in some way to end his own suffering. He would not see Teodoro tied to a stake in the public square as far too many of the Inquisition's victims had perished.

He would be damned if he would allow it to come to that!

"I must go," he told Christian, reaching out to lift Esteban's chin and look into the youth's frightened eyes. "Teo is strong and smart. Do not fear for him."

"I can stay with them," Gerrard offered, not completely sure of all the dynamics in the room. One thing, though, he understood perfectly: Christian was once again without a protector.

Looking up into the larger man's eyes, Raúl searched them for a moment, then nodded, satisfied with what he had seen there. "I trust you to keep them safe, my new friend," he said quietly. "Do not prove me wrong." He turned toward the door, tossing over his shoulder as he opened it, "And do not be so quick to discount your opponents in the future."

"I won't," Gerrard replied softly, more than a little embarrassed at having been so lax in his haste to get to Christian. "I'll keep them safe."

When Raúl was gone, Christian slumped back in the chair, letting despair wash over him. It seemed Fate was determined to keep him and Teodoro apart. His frown deepened along with the feelings of helplessness. Raúl, at least, could do something, even if it was only searching for information. Christian was stuck in that little room with a boy and a swordsman who would do as he asked, but who wouldn't have the slightest idea of his own how to help Teodoro.

Somehow, seeing that Christian was as upset by Teodoro's capture as he was himself helped to steady Esteban's own fear. He drew a chair next to Christian's, reaching out to squeeze the nobleman's hand. "Raúl is right. We should trust him and not be frightened. He is almost as clever as Teo himself. Between the two of them, they will find some way to save him. They will—I know they will!"

"How?" Christian asked baldly. "This is not some minor charge in the local court where a few well-placed bribes would see him free. This is the Inquisition!" He did not repeat the charge, not wanting to hear Esteban deny that Teodoro would do such things when he had been about to commit the very act for which he was charged. At least Teodoro could face the Inquisitors and tell them honestly that he had not buggered Christian senseless. Somehow, though, he didn't think that would make much of a difference.

Burying his head in his hands, he let the hopelessness and helplessness wash over him. He could feel tears threatening, but he fought them back. If their situations were reversed, Teodoro wouldn't be sitting there on the verge of crying. He'd be trying to find a solution. Christian might not have Teodoro's prowess with a sword, but he wasn't helpless. Teodoro had shown him that, had believed in him. Pushing aside his doubts, he struggled to find some thread of hope, some way to influence this turn of events. He was an outsider, not bound by the rules of the situation. Barring an accusation of treason, he was outside the jurisdiction of the Inquisition, his father's position giving him diplomatic immunity, as well. He sighed, wondering if he should swallow his pride and ask his father for help. Except that his father would laugh at him for asking that he use his influence for such a personal matter; that is, after he'd called Christian every manner of name for taking a male lover in a country ruled by the Inquisition. His father... St. Denys... the *conde* de la Rocha.... He was so tired of being a pawn of powerful men.

Powerful men....

His head jerked up. Why not? He had the perfect example in his own father. He simply needed to claim some of that power for himself. "Esteban," he said softly, "do you think you could get me some new clothes if I give you the money?"

Esteban stared at the Englishman in disbelief. Could he have been so mistaken about Christian, that when Teo's life was in danger, he could still think of his own appearance? Was he planning to leave after all? "I do not know if the market would have anything fine enough for Your Excellency," he snapped, his disappointment clear in his voice.

"Don't give me that," Christian snapped back. "Did Teo tell you who my father is?"

"What does it matter who your father is?" Esteban said scornfully. "Unless he is King Philip, he won't be able to help us."

"Not quite," Christian replied, "but close. He is the Duke of Ranleigh, England's chief negotiator to the Spanish court. And as his son, as the Viscount Aldwych, I should be able to command the attention of the Inquisition. If I look the part."

A glimmer of hope lit Esteban's eyes; then he ducked his head in embarrassment. "I'm sorry," he muttered, "I should have known you were trying to help Teo. I will buy you the finest clothes I can find, even if I have to threaten every tailor in the city!"

"They don't have to be the very finest," Christian cautioned. "Only fine enough. I want to look like the son of a powerful nobleman, a powerful man in my own right, not like a ridiculous popinjay." He turned to Gerrard. "You should go with Esteban, to keep him safe while he's out."

"I don't need a nurse!" Esteban protested indignantly. "Besides, they have Teo now. Why would they bother with me?"

Christian hesitated, torn between revealing what he knew of the *conde*'s vile predilection and protecting Esteban's innocence just a little longer. In the end, he shrugged. "I just don't want anything to happen to you. Teo would never forgive me if it did."

"Perhaps, perhaps not," Gerrard interjected, "but it's my job to protect *you*. That's what your father hired me to do, and that's what I intend to do."

Christian collapsed back in the chair. So much for his attempt at projecting an aura of command! He couldn't even get a child and a hired sword to do his bidding. Maybe this mad scheme was doomed to failure after all. "Do you still have my purse?" he asked Esteban, not quite willing to give up yet. Teodoro's continued safety might depend upon him.

"Sí," Esteban admitted, ashamed that he had not been above "forgetting" to return Christian's purse when he still thought of him as an adversary rather than an ally, even a friend. "Will it be enough?" he asked, proffering it back to Christian.

"It should be," Christian replied, feeling the weight. "Just remember, fine, but not the finest. And haggle like you always would. I can't do anything tonight no matter how quickly you return, so take your time. We don't want to draw attention to what you're doing."

"Stand up, then, so I can see how your size compares to mine," Esteban countered. "We can't waste time having them made to order, so I will have to find a tailor who has something almost completed that will fit you."

Christian rose and let Esteban take the measurements with his eyes. If the new clothes were slightly large, he could disguise it with a few well-placed stitches, but much more than that would be beyond his skill.

"Good, you are not too much bigger than me. That will make it easier." Esteban reclaimed the coin pouch and turned toward the door. "I will ask Isabel if we can join them for dinner tonight," he added. "Perhaps Tío Inocencio will have some ideas as well." At Christian's accepting nod, he headed down the stairs on his errand.

"So," Gerrard said when they were finally alone, "do you want to explain all of this to me?"

Christian shook his head. "Not really, but I don't suppose you'll take that for an answer."

"What do you expect?" Gerrard asked. "This Ciéza de Vivar kidnaps you after nearly killing me, and suddenly you're acting as if he…." He hesitated, stumbling for words to describe his companion's inexplicable behavior. "The man is a mercenary of the worst kind—if he was helping you, it's obviously only as a way to gain as much from you as he can. You don't owe him anything. You should take this chance to get away. If St. Denys has been arrested, as you say, it should be safe for you to return to England now."

"No," Christian declared firmly. "It's not that simple. St. Denys isn't working alone, and it's his conspirator who got Teodoro arrested, I'm sure of it. As long as the *conde* de la Rocha is on the loose, I'm in as much danger as I was when St. Denys was hunting me. But even more than that, I won't leave Teodoro. Think what you like about him, but he wouldn't take my money when I offered it, wouldn't let me pay him at all. The only thing he's agreed to let me pay for, and then only when I didn't tell him until after the fact, was a few victuals. He fought off another set of St. Denys's hirelings, getting wounded in the process, yet still he worked not just to protect me but to end St. Denys's threat once and for all. For that alone, I owe him a debt of gratitude that I could never repay. But it's not like that between us. It's not a question of debts and balances. I...." He paused, trying to decide how much to say. Gerrard had been his friend, his confidant, even, during the time they had been together in Valencia. He could be honest now. "I love him."

Letting out a low whistle, Gerrard shook his head. "You know in this country that's a death sentence," he protested, lowering his voice even though he and Christian were alone in Ciéza's chambers. "And someone must have discovered it, to have set the Inquisition on him. We're damn fortunate they haven't come for you as well."

"If they were coming for me, they would have been here by now," Christian countered. "It's no secret where Teodoro has his lodgings."

"Who would have known that the two of you are—" Gerrard broke off. "Surely you had sense enough to be discreet?"

Christian flushed. "There is nothing to be discreet about," he admitted softly. "Yes, I love him, but circumstances have conspired to keep us from becoming lovers. As for who might know, Raúl is the only one, and he would never use that knowledge against Teodoro. If anything, he has encouraged us."

"Then who would want the Spaniard out of the way badly enough to have made up such a lie about him?"

"He has foiled St. Denys's plans since he took me under his wing," Christian replied thoughtfully, "and as I said, if Teodoro and Raúl are right, St. Denys wasn't working alone. The *conde* de la Rocha is a very powerful man who would surely have the ear of the Inquisition. Teodoro got St. Denys thrown in prison for plotting against the king. He's since been executed. Then today, Raúl found out that the two of them enjoy young men, probably against their will. I wouldn't put it past the *conde* to accuse Teodoro of his own sin for revenge, and perhaps to take out a barrier between them and me. As fixated as St. Denys was on me, I wouldn't be surprised if the *conde* shared his obsession."

"It seems as if you both have made some powerful enemies," Gerrard asserted. "What do you plan to do to try to rescue your Teodoro?"

"Take a page from my father's book," Christian replied with a hard smile, "and beat them at their own game."

THIRTEEN

AN ESPECIALLY strong jolt over the rough roads awoke Teodoro from his uneasy doze. He had learned early in his stint as a soldier to sleep no matter how dire the circumstances, though he had faced few as dire as this. He had not offered any resistance to his arrest by the agents of the Inquisition, but even so they had not been gentle as they seized him, stripped him of his weapons, and manacled his wrists and feet. As soon as his hands were secured, they had beaten him with the butts of their muskets, forcing him to his knees before dragging him into a waiting carriage, adding a few more blows for good measure as they chained his shackles to a bolt in the floor. There had been too many of them to overcome in any case, and the longer their attention was focused on him, the more chance Esteban had to get away, or at least so Teodoro had thought at the time. Since then he had plenty of opportunity for second thoughts as the carriage jostled over the rutted track, carrying him closer to a confrontation that would strike terror into the heart of any man.

Shifting in a vain attempt to find a less painful position for his aching shoulders, Teodoro considered his options. They were slim. He would watch for a chance to break free when they took him from the carriage, but he knew the odds were against his winning more than a few moments of freedom. These were not ill-trained and half-starved enemy troops he would be facing, but hardened soldiers of the Inquisition. They would be expecting him to try to break free once they arrived in Toledo, before he was buried in the dungeons from which no one had ever been known to escape. Of course, just because the odds were against him did not mean he would not try. Meeting his end in such a manner would likely be preferable to anything he would endure once the Inquisitors got their claws in him.

Teodoro was not a man given to brooding over a future he could do nothing about, but turning his thoughts to what he left behind was little better. This was surely an attempt to remove him as Christian's protector. The Inquisition would have no knowledge and no proof of anything that might have transpired years before. He could not help but recognize the irony of being charged with the one crime he could with all honesty claim he had not committed with Christian. That his innocence was solely due to bad luck and worse timing was no consolation. Of all the regrets of his misspent life, the thought that he might die without ever loving Christian the way he longed to do was the only one he could not dismiss. Still, he would be able to profess his innocence with a clear conscience, and if his denials could keep Christian from harm, it would be worth whatever fate befell him. He only wished he knew with certainty that Esteban had gotten away safely, and that the soldiers had been too intent on guarding against his escape to think to try to seize the boy—or Christian—from their lodgings.

A droplet of sweat trickled down Teodoro's face, stinging his eyes as he tried to blink the moisture away. Christian would not take the news of his capture well, he feared. At least Raúl would know better than to let Christian run headlong into danger. He did not know if there was anything Raúl could do toward freeing him, but as long as Raúl saw that Christian was safe, that would be enough. Teodoro was not an especially pious man either, but he offered a prayer nonetheless for his lover's safety. Shifting again, he closed his eyes and tried once more to sleep, knowing he would need all his strength and all his wits to face what was to come.

"ESTEBAN," ISABEL called through the door, "Don Inocencio is ready for dinner if you and your friends wish to join us."

Esteban led Christian and Gerrard down the interior stairs to the kitchen and from there into the modest sitting room that doubled as a dining room for the priest. Don Inocencio was already seated at the table, the last of the lamb from earlier in the day on a tray along with fresh vegetables and bread. Christian took the offered seat, the reminder of the meal he had shared with such laughter and delight with Teodoro just a few hours ago leaving his stomach roiling. He forced himself to remember his manners and thank Don Inocencio for his hospitality once again, but the lamb he had enjoyed so much earlier would taste like ash in his mouth now.

"You bring an unfamiliar face to my table, *vizconde*," the priest commented once he had said grace.

"Don Guzman, this is Gerrard Hawkins, my former protector who came to Madrid to bring me a message from my father. Gerrard, Don

Inocencio Guzman, *el cura*, our host, and Esteban's uncle," Christian said by way of introduction.

"Welcome to Madrid, Señor Hawkins," Don Inocencio said with a nod of his head. "I hope the news was good?"

"Better than the rest of my news," Christian said with a sigh. "Did Esteban tell you about Teodoro?"

"He did." Don Inocencio's expression grew grave. "I fear the good Lord would not recognize what his church has become."

The comment was the first criticism Christian had heard of the Church and the Inquisition since arriving in Spain. That it came from a priest only made it more shocking. "There is nothing you can do to help him, then?" he asked, afraid he already knew the answer.

"I will offer my testimony to Teo's character and protest his seizure, but I fear my words will carry little weight," Inocencio said softly. "San Pedro is not a wealthy parish, and my role as its pastor carries little influence. And sadly, that means as much or more than innocence to those who wield the power of the Inquisition for purposes it was never intended."

Isabel gasped and crossed herself piously, glancing around as if to make sure the Inquisition did not have spies hidden in the walls and woodwork.

"Then they can be influenced, if the right power is brought to bear?" Christian verified, heart pounding as he considered his ruse.

"It may be so, but I do not know of any with such power who might be persuaded to intercede on Teo's behalf."

"Viscount Aldwych, son of the Duke of Ranleigh, chief legate of His Majesty, King James I of England, at your service," Christian said with a sketchy bow, investing his voice with all the pomposity he'd always hated in his peers.

Don Inocencio's eyes widened, and a glimmer of hope awoke in them. "My prayers will go with you, my son."

The rest of the meal passed in tense silence, everyone at the table picking at their food, with the exception of Gerrard. When a seemly time had passed, Christian excused them, saying he needed to prepare for his appearance tomorrow if he had any hope of convincing the Church authorities to listen to him. Gerrard returned to his post at the entrance of the narrow stairs while Christian and Esteban returned to their rooms.

Christian was trying on the articles of clothing Esteban had obtained for him when Raúl returned, slipping silently into Teodoro's quarters.

"Fine feathers," Raúl observed, watching as Christian tried to judge the fit of the dark blue velvet doublet in Teodoro's small shaving mirror.

"*El vizconde* is going to save Teo," Esteban insisted before Christian could reply to the comment. "You should hear his plan, Raúl. Teo himself couldn't have come up with anything more clever!"

"And what is this clever plan?" Raúl asked as he turned a chair toward Christian and reclined with easy grace. "Were you planning on sharing it with me before you executed it?"

"Of course," Christian replied defensively. "But I needed the clothes for it to work, and you weren't here to ask." He took a deep breath. "Teo told you who my father is. As his son, I should be able to demand a certain amount of attention, should be able to demand Teodoro's release, but I can't do that if I look like another hired sword. If I learned anything from my father, it's that people pay attention to the image you project, especially people in politics. Dressed like this, with Esteban as my page and Gerrard as my bodyguard, I should be able to project a powerful enough image, especially if I mention my father, to get what I want."

"You will certainly look the part," Raúl admitted, rubbing a thumb over his close-trimmed moustache. He knew the chances of Christian's plan working were slim, maybe even none, but he was even more powerless in this situation than the Englishman, his Romani blood a curse rather than a blessing should it come to the attention of the Inquisition. Everything hinged on Christian's ability to play the part convincingly, and Raúl didn't want to say anything that might make the young nobleman doubt himself. "It has a better chance of success than anything I can think to try."

"I will go first thing in the morning, and Teodoro will be safely home with us by nightfall," Christian declared firmly. He refused to consider any other outcome. Failure was simply not an option.

"He is no longer here," Raúl replied quietly. "They have taken him to Toledo, to the dungeons of the Grand Inquisitor himself."

"What?" Christian exclaimed. Immediately, images assailed him of faceless men torturing Teodoro, wielding whips, chains, brands. The rack. Even in England, he had heard tales of the incredible cruelty of the Inquisition. The idea that Teodoro, still wounded, might be subjected to such merciless horrors added to the urgency he had felt since hearing his lover had been taken. "How far is that? We should leave immediately!"

"Over a day's ride each way, though a carriage will take two. We must make haste, since Teo must be out of their grasp before Wednesday or he will be beyond our help...." At Christian's look of dismay, Raúl explained, "The Grand Inquisitor apparently has a special devotion to the Virgin Mary. Each year, before the Feast of the Assumption, he clears the prisons in her honor." He shook his head at the idea that the Holy Mother would look with pleasure at the torment and death of countless innocents. "Any prisoners remaining under accusation will be tried—and sentenced—by this Wednesday, before the feast on Thursday."

Christian digested that information slowly. "What does that mean in terms of my plan?" he asked after a moment, not sure how to go forward now. "Can it still work?"

"Tomorrow is Sunday. I have arranged to hire a carriage in Your Excellency's name. We will leave at first light and arrive by Monday evening. You will have two days to persuade the archbishop in Toledo to release Teo."

"Why do we need a carriage? Wouldn't we arrive more quickly on horseback?"

"Yes, but we will need to bring Teo home, and it is unlikely he will be able to ride," Raúl said. "It is easier to hire a carriage here than to make arrangements to return one if we hire it in Toledo."

Christian flinched at the thought of Teodoro being too injured to ride, but he pushed the image aside. He had to focus on saving him, not on the possibility of losing him.

"I will continue to learn what I can, but I doubt anything I might find could sway the agents of the Holy Office." Raúl held Christian with a steady gaze, knowing the pressure he was placing the younger man under, but judging he had earned the right not to be sheltered from the truth, however harsh. "Your influence may be the only hope we have."

Christian nodded, his resolve hardening. Raúl wasn't pretending this would be easy, wasn't patting him on the head and trying to pacify him. That thought buoyed him. Raúl wasn't treating him like a child, but rather like an equal, one capable of acting to save Teodoro. "Then I will have to be the kind of powerful man who wields that influence." He looked at Raúl, then at Esteban. "I won't let you down."

The evening passed slowly. Christian knew he must be driving Raúl to distraction with his fidgeting, but he could not sit still, not knowing

Teodoro was imprisoned while he sat warm and fed in the relative comfort of their home.

"Come, Cristian," Raúl urged. "Challenge me to a game of chess to pass the time."

"*Gracias*, Raúl," Christian demurred, "but I wouldn't be able to concentrate enough to give you a poor game, much less a good one." Raúl said his name with the same distinctive roll of the tongue that gave Christian such shivers when Teodoro said it, but it had no such effect when it came from Raúl's mouth instead.

"You call yourself Teo's lover and you can't even play a decent game of chess?" Raúl scolded. "I have a book you must borrow—and study—so you can keep him occupied during the long days of his recovery."

"A book?" Christian asked.

"Yes, a book. I do know how to read," Raúl reminded him. "*Repetición de Amores y Arte de Ajedrez*. It will teach you how to play chess. Not simply the moves, but the strategy behind them."

"What does love have to do with chess?" Christian inquired, pondering the title of the book.

Raúl laughed. "Love, like most of life, is one big chess game. Most people are simply too shortsighted to see it."

With a sigh, Christian fetched the chess set from the bedroom, his thoughts fixed on the man who had carved the wooden pieces rather than on the moves they could make or the strategies that would allow him to win a match. He set them up and sat down facing Raúl across the board, quite sure he'd lose the game in no more than a few moves. To his wonder he found himself caught up in the maneuvering of the match, to the point he was surprised when Esteban announced he was tired and going to bed so he would be ready for their trip the next day.

"Thank you for the distraction," he said. "I would not have made it through this evening without your help."

"I will have the carriage here at dawn. Try to get some sleep yourself," Raúl advised. "We have done all we can until we arrive in Toledo, and it will not serve your plan to confront the archbishop if you are exhausted." He clapped Christian on the shoulder and took his leave.

Christian went into the bedroom to pack his traveling bag with his new clothes so he would be ready when Raúl arrived in the morning. He glanced at the armoire that held Teodoro's belongings. On impulse he opened the doors and pulled out Teodoro's spare shirt and breeches. After several days at the mercy of the Inquisition, he would need them. If Christian took comfort from the scent that lingered on the fabric, he counted that an extra blessing.

TEODORO HAD been in jail before, had been held prisoner before, but he had never felt the unnerving, unreasonable dread that tried to take possession of his spirit from the moment he passed under the oppressive stone portal of his destination. He endured being stripped and searched with stoic reserve, given scarce time to pull on his breeches before he was manacled again and led shuffling and clanking into a small, dark chamber, the only contents of which were a plain table, a candle in a wrought iron stand, and a massive, grotesque crucifix mounted on one wall. Two men clad in unrelieved dark robes sat behind the table. One of these was obviously a scribe, prepared to set down every word of the proceedings; the other had the grim expression and hard, gleaming eyes of a true believer—or a fanatic. Teodoro suspected in this case they were one and the same.

The Inquisitor studied the man brought before him. Naked to the waist and barefoot, bound hand and foot in heavy chains, the prisoner nonetheless projected an air of defiance that had him smiling inwardly in anticipation. This one would not break easily, providing him with hours of enjoyment. "State your name for the record," he intoned gravely.

Finding the most comfortable stance he could on the cold stone, Teodoro met his questioner's gaze coolly. "Teodoro Ciéza de Vivar," he answered, certain the cleric knew exactly who he was and judging he would gain nothing by refusing to answer.

"Señor Ciéza, you stand before us accused of sodomy, a crime second only to heresy. What say you to the charges?" He knew the answer, of course. No one ever admitted their crimes immediately. It would take some persuasion to convince the man to admit his guilt.

Teodoro allowed himself to slouch a little more as he answered. "I do not know where Your Excellency obtained this information, but you are misinformed."

"Misinformed?" the cleric repeated incredulously. "I assure you, the accusation comes from a reputable source. Name your partners in this heinous crime, and we shall consider leniency."

"As I am not guilty of the charges, I have no partners, Excellency," Teodoro pointed out reasonably.

"So you do not know one Christian Blackwood?" the Inquisitor challenged.

Teodoro's eyes narrowed, surprised at the Inquisitor's failure to give Christian his proper title. "Señor Blackwood hired my services as his protector," he replied, not volunteering to correct the error.

"A hired sword, are you? And how often have you sheathed your... steel... in him?" the cleric demanded.

Teodoro's eyebrows rose at the crude insinuation. "I can assure Your Excellency that Señor Blackwood and I are not lovers," he averred. Not for lack of intent or desire, it was true, but that was not what the Inquisitor had asked.

"No?" the priest questioned. "Then you will not care if he is brought here to stand trial as well. Perhaps he will see the wisdom of cooperation, though you do not."

For the first time since the questioning began, Teodoro felt a flicker of true fear at the thought of Christian in the clutches of these zealots. Reminding himself that the Inquisitor was only making random threats, hoping to strike a reaction from him, he forced his expression to remain one of bored indifference. "Does Your Excellency not know who Señor Blackwood is?" he asked, feigning surprise. "I would have thought your information more complete than that. He is an Englishman—a noble Englishman—the son of the chief legate to the court of King Philip, in fact. And as such, he of course has diplomatic protection from any accusations that might be raised, however falsely, against him."

The Inquisitor frowned. It was unlike his minions to be less than thorough, and having this fish slip through his fingers was most unpleasant indeed. That did not mean the man before him would fare so well, though. "Then perhaps you sate your unnatural lust with—" He made a show of looking at his notes. "—Esteban Guzman."

Honest incredulity nearly made Teodoro laugh at the Inquisitor's allegation. "Esteban? He is my son, and even if he weren't, he is little more than a child!" In truth Esteban was already older than Teodoro himself when he left his home for the Flemish wars, but again, that was more information than his questioner needed to know.

"Esteban Guzman is the son of Margarita Guzman and Bernardo de Celadilla y Zarzaguda," the cleric pointed out calmly. "Your murder of the boy's father does not change his paternity. Nor does it incline this court to believe your protestations of innocence. You would hardly be the first to despoil a child simply because he was near to hand."

A roil of anger began to burn in Teodoro's gut as he realized his questioner was serious. "Your Excellency is once again misinformed. Don Celadilla y Zarzaguda was killed in a duel—an affair of honor. Perhaps Your Excellency is unfamiliar with the concept. In any event, he is not here to dispute the fact that Esteban is my son."

"I am Eliseo de Celadilla y Zarzaguda, and I am well aware of the facts surrounding the 'affair of honor,'" the Inquisitor spat. "Son or not, the boy would not be safe from your obvious depravity."

Sickened, Teodoro shook his head. No matter how he answered, this perverted excuse for a man of God would find some way to twist his words against him. He recognized the name, if not the man himself— some cousin or such of Margarita's ravisher. He could expect no mercy from one who would clearly not hesitate to use his position for personal revenge. Lowering his gaze to contemplate the cold stone floor beneath his feet, he determined not to respond to any more of his questioner's taunts.

"You have no answer to that?" the cleric challenged. "Perhaps we can loosen your tongue. Guards! Bring the whip!"

Drawing a breath, Teodoro braced himself for what was to come. He had known it would come to this in the end—in truth, he was surprised the Inquisitor had traded words with him as long as he had. He had endured beatings before; he would endure this one. Setting his teeth, he waited for the first blow to fall.

The guards entered, whip in hand, looking to the cleric for direction. "Begin with ten," the Inquisitor instructed. "Then we will see if he can be reasonable. If not, we will try again."

His knees locked, Teodoro forced himself to relax the muscles of his back and chest, knowing tensing them would only allow the whip to cut into his flesh that much sooner. He bit back any sound from escaping his throat, though his hands clenched into fists at his side and his legs were trembling by the time the tenth blow was struck.

The Inquisitor surveyed the damage impassively. Welts had formed immediately, several of them open and bleeding now from the multiple blows. To his surprise, the prisoner had not cried out, but he could see the toll it had taken. "I charge you again to confess to the sin of sodomy, and to name your partners in this heinous deed. And before you refuse to answer, remember that my guards can do this all day."

And probably would, Teodoro recognized grimly, but nothing would force him to answer his tormenter any further. Only by silence could he be sure that he was not giving the Inquisitor any ammunition to use against Christian and Esteban. If that meant letting the guards beat him to death, well, there were worse causes for which to spend one's life.

Surprised but grudgingly impressed at the prisoner's stoic silence, the Inquisitor stepped back, gesturing for the guards to begin again. He specified no number this time. Perhaps when the man had been driven to the floor in pain, he would speak. And if not, they had ways of making him stand for the beatings to begin again.

NEW CLOTHES fitting uncomfortably but allowing him to project the aura of command he had often admired in his father, Christian swept into the palace of Cardinal Juan Carlos Rouco, archbishop of Toledo, demanding an immediate audience as if such were his due and the need to ask beneath him. Gerrard and Esteban, the younger man dressed for the role of page in one of Christian's less elegant garments, walked purposefully behind him, enhancing his air of importance.

Esteban hoped the trepidation he was feeling did not reflect in his expression, which he kept downcast, as a servant should. He had watched the *vizconde* prepare this morning, pacing the tiny room of the inn where they had taken lodging as he went over his plan again with Raúl. Christian had asked Raúl to accompany them, but the gypsy had replied that Christian had enough of an entourage already, and that his time would be better spent finding a market to replenish his supply of herbs. "And I find it safest not to draw the Church's interest," Raúl admitted, grasping Christian's shoulder in reassurance. "You will do well," he added before turning toward the door. "You make quite a convincing nobleman, my friend." Esteban had to admit that Raúl was right, at least when it came to Christian's appearance, but he had privately doubted the *vizconde* would be able to talk his way into an interview with the archbishop. It seemed he was to be proven wrong—from the instant they stepped foot on the cathedral grounds, Christian's entire attitude had changed to one of arrogant self-assurance.

"I am aware that the cardinal is a busy man," Christian replied haughtily when a gray-haired cleric informed him the archbishop was not to be disturbed, "but I am as well, and this is a matter of some importance. I think he would prefer to speak to me rather than having the king hear that he refused to grant me an audience."

The priest frowned. "And who are you to make such demands?" he asked. He hesitated to disturb the archbishop after having been given orders not to, but if this man did indeed have the ear of the king, it might prove dangerous to ignore him.

"Christian Blackwood, Viscount Aldwych, son of the Duke of Ranleigh, England's chief negotiator with the Spanish crown," he replied as if it should have been obvious. "Someone owes me an explanation as to why my most valued attendant was carried off by the Inquisition without so much as a word to me—or to my father—on trumped-up charges with no evidence whatsoever. The cardinal can give it to me, or I can ask the king to look into the matter. I can assure you, neither he nor my father would be pleased with having their negotiations disrupted by this attempt to smear my name and reputation."

Even more convinced that this was not someone it would be safe to ignore, the priest nodded. "Wait here, Excellency," he said. "I will see what can be done for you." Tucking his hands into the sleeves of his robe, he hurried off.

Keeping his arrogant mask in place, Christian glanced back at Esteban and Gerrard behind him. He doubted Gerrard truly cared about the outcome beyond keeping Christian safe, but Esteban had as much, perhaps more, to lose than Christian did. He wanted to whisper an encouragement to Esteban, anything to assure him that, contrary to appearances, this was going exactly as he had expected. He would have been suspicious if the archbishop had immediately agreed to see him. No, this slow bend beneath his influence was much more what he had come to expect as he observed his father move in the rarefied circles of political power.

Before more than a few minutes had passed, the priest returned. "The cardinal's adjutant will see you," he announced, motioning for Christian to accompany him.

Allowing himself to be mollified, Christian gestured for Gerrard and Esteban to wait for him where they were before following the priest deeper into the palace. They walked the ornate halls designed to show the Church's wealth and authority until they reached an office. The priest announced him to the room, then left with a much more respectful bow than he had accorded Christian earlier.

The cleric who greeted Christian was obviously no mere priest. His scarlet robe was trimmed with costly Flemish lace, and an ornate golden cross hung at his chest. A signet ring of the same rich metal adorned one of his long, slim hands. "I am Fray Antonio Maria Gordo, Archbishop Rouco's personal adjutant. What business do you have with the cardinal, *vizconde* Aldwych?"

"Business of a personal nature," Christian replied, determined not to let this man see him as anything less than an equal. "I assume you will transmit everything to him faithfully so I will not have to repeat myself when he and I finally meet."

"Perhaps you will tell me what your business is, so I can better judge whether we can assist you," the adjutant answered.

"My attendant, Teodoro Ciéza de Vivar, was taken in Madrid on Saturday by the Inquisition," Christian stated baldly, "depriving me of much-needed protection given the delicate state of the negotiations between our respective countries. I want an explanation, and then I want him released."

"The name is unfamiliar to me," Fray Gordo mused. "But if your attendant has committed heresy, there is nothing to be done for him."

"The charge was not heresy," Christian averred immediately, "and while his name is perhaps unknown, there is another I think you might recognize. Does the name St. Denys mean anything to you?"

"The Englishman who was executed for conspiring against the king? If your servant was part of that plot, there is even less I can do for him."

"On the contrary," Christian replied coolly. "St. Denys was caught and executed thanks to my attendant. He brought the documents incriminating St. Denys to the attention of the authorities, and this is how Spain expresses its gratitude? Accusing him unjustly of sodomy, handing him over to be tortured until he admits to crimes he did not commit? And I am supposed to stand by and let it happen? I think not, and unless the cardinal wishes me to express my displeasure to the king, he will see that Señor Ciéza de Vivar is returned to me immediately."

"The Inquisition does not answer to the cardinal, or even to the king in matters of faith," Fray Gordo answered. "If this Ciéza de Vivar is truly innocent as you say, he has nothing to fear."

Christian snorted. "Come, Fray Gordo, we are men of the world, you and I, despite the robes you wear, and we both know that the Inquisition does not release its prisoners because they are innocent. Instead they torture them until they confess to end the pain or until they die from it, neither of which is an acceptable option. We also know that everyone, even the Inquisition, answers to someone. So either you and the good cardinal can provide me what I need, or I can interrupt my father and the king, which will, if you are fortunate, merely slow the negotiations between our countries. If you are not so fortunate, it will disrupt them entirely. Do you really want to be the one responsible for that?" Not giving the adjutant a chance to reply to the rhetorical question, he added, "St. Denys had an accomplice in his plot, though we could not find his name. You realize this accusation is not about sodomy at all, but about revenge for St. Denys's execution. Señor Ciéza de Vivar is also the king's best hope for finding the second conspirator and ending this threat to the Spanish throne once and for all."

The cleric stroked his goatee as he considered the Englishman's words. "I will take your concerns to the archbishop," he agreed at last. "Come back tomorrow. I should have a response for you by then."

"A 'response' is not good enough," Christian declared. "I know how the Inquisition works. Tomorrow they will execute any prisoners they still have in their custody before the feast on Thursday. I will come back tomorrow morning, but I expect an order for my attendant's release. I will *not* allow the Inquisition to execute Señor Ciéza de Vivar."

FOURTEEN

CHRISTIAN MANAGED to keep his façade in place and his feet beneath him until the door to their rented rooms shut behind Esteban, Gerrard having stayed below to arrange for a midday meal. As soon as he heard the latch click, his knees folded, collapsing beneath him as the magnitude of what he had attempted, the depth of what he'd implied, washed over him. All the emotions he had not let himself feel, all the fear he'd pushed aside to project his mask of arrogance, came rushing back at him all at once, leaving him trembling on the floor.

Esteban knelt beside him, reaching out a hesitant hand to Christian's ruched sleeve. "What is wrong, Cristian?" he asked, afraid the reaction meant he had failed. "Did they not listen to you? Is Teo still in danger?"

Christian tried to control his breathing, tried to slow the gasps to normal speed, but he couldn't seem to get enough oxygen into his lungs. "They… listened," he managed to say. "Tomorrow…. We go… back… tomorrow." He wanted to say more, to reassure Esteban in some way, but he had no more words, no more bravado. It would still be so easy to fail. His father knew Christian had hired Teodoro as his protector, but nothing more. If the adjutant or the cardinal did more than verify his identity—or his father's—if they sent someone to ask for confirmation of all he had said, his carefully constructed house of cards would come tumbling down around him, Teodoro would be executed, and his father would probably disown him for daring to invoke his name for something so personal.

He couldn't do this. He couldn't be strong anymore. Reaching blindly for the back of a chair, he struggled to his feet, then stumbled toward the bed and all he had of Teodoro right now. His lover wasn't there to hold him, but maybe he could draw on Teodoro's strength anyway. He reached for his knapsack and the one connection to Teo he had carried with him.

Esteban followed, certain now that Christian cared for Teodoro as much as Esteban did himself. "Surely you convinced them," he said, reassuring himself as much as Christian. "You look more noble than any of the *hidalgos* attending the king at the bullfights. They would not dare to deny you."

"I pray you are right," Christian replied, curling up on the bed, his face buried in Teo's spare shirt, letting its scent surround and soothe him. Reminding himself that Esteban didn't know what lay between them, he lifted his head a little. "Would you mind going down to the tavern and asking Gerrard to bring a bottle of wine with supper?"

"Of course, Cristian," Esteban agreed, turning toward the door. He looked back at the *vizconde*, not so many years older than he, wondering if his own nerves would have let him carry out such a risky bluff. "Teo will be proud when he learns what you did," he added before heading downstairs.

Esteban's words tore a sob from Christian's throat, his fear finally getting the better of him. "Be alive," he begged the empty room. "Don't let them steal your will to live." He couldn't begin to imagine the pain and terror Teodoro had to be going through at that very moment. Tears wet his lashes as all the horror stories he had ever heard about the Inquisition and its tortures came back to him: spikes in the flesh, bones crushed, skin flayed from muscle or else burned to a crisp…. "Whatever they do to you, I'll still want you, still love you. Just hold on until tomorrow. Hold on until I can tell you I love you."

"Teodoro is strong." Raúl spoke from the doorway, though Christian hadn't heard him enter. "He has his responsibility to Esteban to hold him to life, and now he has you. He will hold on, for both of you."

Christian wiped his eyes surreptitiously, not wanting Raúl to see him as weak. "Do you truly believe that?" he asked softly.

"I do not have to believe." Raúl smiled. "I know."

TEODORO FOUGHT against the blackness that threatened to consume him as yet another blow tore into the bloody skin of his back. He had long since lost count of how many stripes the guards had laid across him; when his legs would no longer hold him and he had fallen to his knees, they had strung a rope through the manacles on his wrist and tossed it over a rafter, hoisting him upright until only by stretching his legs to their limits could he keep his toes touching the floor. The next set of blows had robbed him of even that. He had tried to grip the *strappado* to keep the strain from tearing his arms from their sockets, but the rope had grown slippery with blood, and he no longer had the strength to hold himself up. Each stroke of the whip, delivered with enough force to set him swinging, sent red-hot fire burning along his nerves. He had bitten his lip until the blood ran down his chin, unable to hold back the hoarse grunts of pain at each crack of the whip. Closing his eyes, he tried to conjure an image of Christian lying in his bed, smiling at him, his arms opening in welcome. "For you," Teodoro vowed, his lips moving silently as another vicious blow curled around his ribs, stealing his breath.

"Enough," the Inquisitor said in disgust. "Beating him is gaining us nothing. Take him back to his cell for the night, but be warned, Señor Ciéza, if you have not changed your attitude come morning, we will see if you like the rack any better."

He tried to respond, but a backhand from one of the guards filled his mouth with blood. Spitting it onto the reddened stone before the Inquisitor's bench, he collapsed as soon as the rope was released. The guards' harsh grip on his tortured shoulders was yet another agony as they dragged him back to his cell.

Long after the iron portal had closed behind him, he lay on the cold stone floor, his chest heaving as he struggled to find the strength to push up onto his hands and knees. Eventually he was able to move enough to pull his legs beneath him and wrap an arm around his shins to sit upright. He was trembling from the cold, but there was no way he could bear even the weight of his shirt on his flayed back.

Teodoro wasn't sure how long it took for him to realize the moans he heard were not all coming from his own throat. Lifting his head, he could make out another shape in the near-dark of the cell, huddled against the opposite wall. Slowly he crawled across the filthy floor, thinking at least the two of them could rest against each other and share their bodies' warmth. No doubt the Inquisitor would take such an act as further proof of his alleged sin, were they observed, but at the moment his need to alleviate the cell's bone-chilling dankness outweighed the risk.

"St-stay away from me," the other man stuttered, backing even farther into the corner.

"Believe me, I don't have strength enough to harm you, even were that my intent," Teodoro rasped unevenly. "I only thought the two of us could share our warmth against the cold."

"You have not been here long if you have that much kindness left in you still," the man commented. "Come closer, but carefully. We can sit together, but my arms are useless to me now."

"I doubt mine are much better," Teodoro observed grimly, grunting with the effort to raise himself to the rough wooden seat the other man rested on. His elbow folded beneath him, and he fell against his companion with a muffled curse.

A high-pitched scream escaped the other prisoner's lips as Teodoro's weight crashed into his damaged shoulder.

"Maldita sea!" Teodoro muttered. "Forgive me, my friend." He pushed away carefully, returning a gentle hand once he was sure he could hold himself upright. "Your shoulder is disjointed," he told the other man as his fingers lightly probed the distorted socket. "I can put it back for you—there will be a moment of sharp pain but you will be able to move it again when I am done."

The injured man considered his options for a moment. He had no illusions that he would escape more torture and eventually death, but the idea of a night with less pain was tempting. "What do I need to do?"

"Lie on your stomach," Teodoro instructed. "Let your arm relax as much as you can." Letting himself slide back to his knees on the uneven floor, he grasped his unfortunate companion's forearm with one hand, the other resting on the shoulder joint. "I'm going to pull, slowly, until I can push the ball back into the socket."

The prisoner did as Teodoro directed, trusting in the air of confidence he projected. It would hurt, but it could hardly compare with the unrelenting pull of the rack. "I'm ready."

Leaning back on his heels, Teodoro did his best to apply a slow, steady pressure to stretch the damaged arm downward, biting back another curse at the strain on his own overtaxed sinews. At length he felt the rounded end of the bone begin to move, guiding it with his other hand until with an audible click it popped into its cradle. Teodoro let his own arms drop as he struggled to catch his breath, too weary to even try to move back onto the bench.

The sharp pain materialized, just as his comrade had said it would, but then it was gone, leaving a different kind of ache in the injured man's shoulder, one he could live with. Moving his arm tentatively, he smiled. "It worked." Seeing that his companion did not move, he slid carefully off the bench to sit next to the other man. "Javier Montega," he said by way of introduction, moving close enough to share what little heat they each had in their bodies.

"Teodoro Ciéza de Vivar," he returned, letting himself relax against his cellmate's uninjured shoulder. Less injured, he corrected himself; he doubted either of them had an uninjured limb between them. "The *strappado*?" he asked, though he suspected he knew the answer.

"No," Javier replied, "the rack. They want me to admit I have Jewish blood in my ancestry. I am a good Catholic along with all my family, but they do not believe me. They will make me confess soon, I know. I am not strong enough to take much more. What of you?"

"I am not so good a Catholic, perhaps," Teodoro answered wryly. "In any case, they do not approve of my choice of companions." That was true enough, and vague enough that it could be understood in several ways. He was not ashamed of what he felt for Christian, but he was wary of revealing anything that might place his lover in any more danger than he already faced.

Javier nodded. "Do not tell me more than that. The Inquisitors sometimes ask about other prisoners as well when they interrogate me, and I would not wish to repay your kindness by letting slip something you would rather they not know."

"You are wise, my friend," Teodoro agreed. Closing his eyes, he let his head drop toward his chest and tried not to think about the questioning that was sure to resume with the daylight, tried not to imagine the injuries his new companion had suffered wrought upon his own body. Once again he turned his thoughts toward Christian, the memory of lying in his lover's arms his refuge from the hell in which he was trapped.

CHRISTIAN TOOK a deep breath and pulled his mask into place before entering the archbishop's palace. Gerrard and Esteban walked a respectful distance behind him, as they had before, but Christian still felt the lack of the most comforting presence in his life at the moment. He had pleaded with Raúl to accompany him, but the gypsy had declined, repeating his desire not to bring his existence to the attention of authorities who might be less than pleased with his "heathen" ways. The comment had shocked Christian, who had long since stopped thinking of the other man in those terms, but he understood Raúl's wisdom. "I will come with you when he is released, for though they have had only two days to question him,

I fear he will need what assistance I can provide," Raúl had said. That thought left Christian unsettled, but he could not let it show now. He had to be strong... for Teo's sake.

"I have an appointment with Archbishop Rouco," Christian haughtily informed the priest who challenged his presence. "You may announce me."

The foreigner's peremptory command sent the cleric scurrying out of the ornate drawing room, to return a few moments later. "Fray Gordo is expecting you," he announced in a slightly breathless voice. "This way, please, Excellency."

Christian followed the man into the same study where he had talked with the cardinal's adjutant before. "Fray Gordo," he acknowledged, "not that I expected you to be absent from this meeting, but I did expect to have a more... august interlocutor as well. The archbishop *will* be joining us, will he not?"

"His Eminence has too much to do in preparation for tomorrow's holy celebration to meet with visitors," the adjutant replied, "particularly when they are not even members of the true faith." His gaze spoke eloquently that had it not been for Christian's family connections and his father's position, he might well have been facing his own questions from the most Holy Office, rather than here importuning the archbishop with his demands. "You are fortunate he agreed to consider your petition at all."

"And did he do more than simply consider it?" Christian demanded, heart pounding now that the moment of truth was at hand. "Or do I need to speak to the king?"

Fray Gordo glanced through the sheaf of papers on his desk, selected one, and read it over. "This order will permit you to claim your servant's freedom," he conceded. He signed the parchment and then dropped a dollop of candle wax beside the endorsement before pressing his ornate signet ring into the cooling sealant. "The accused will be taken to the public square for judgment this afternoon. You may meet the carriages at the Plaza de Zocodover."

Christian took the order and scanned it quickly. Deciding everything was in order, he pocketed the precious document and bowed politely to the adjutant. "I will not forget your assistance, or the archbishop's, when next I speak to my father," he offered in way of thanks and parting.

"I would suggest you ensure that your attendant does not have cause to be accused again," Fray Gordo answered. "I doubt His Eminence the cardinal could be persuaded to assist you a second time."

Christian nodded his understanding and took his leave. Gerrard and Esteban fell in step behind him without any prompting, playing the roles of good servants. Christian could see the question in Esteban's eyes, but he said nothing until they were safely in the carriage. He didn't want anyone in the palace wondering about his relationship with his "servant."

When the carriage rolled out, he dropped the façade of the arrogant nobleman. "He signed the release order," he told the Esteban, relief leaving him trembling slightly. They still had much to do and so many ways things could go wrong, but they had a chance now.

"You did it!" Esteban cried, crushing Christian in an embrace as relief overwhelmed him. "I knew you would convince them!" Feeling the English bodyguard's gaze turn to them from where he sat on the box of the carriage, he drew back awkwardly, hoping he had not angered Christian with his reaction.

"I'm glad one of us had faith in me," Christian muttered, returning the embrace. "A few more hours and he will be back with us where he belongs. We must collect Raúl and go immediately to the Plaza de Zocodover. I don't know what time the executions will begin, but we must free Teodoro before they do."

"Raúl will know," Esteban assured Christian. "He knows everything."

Two weeks ago Christian would have questioned that assertion, but no more. He had seen enough since meeting Raúl to know that there were more things in heaven and earth than he could have dreamed existed.

THEY ARRIVED at the Plaza de Zocodover long before the executions were expected to begin, but Christian couldn't stay cooped up in their rented rooms. "What now?" he asked Raúl.

"We wait," Raúl replied, though in truth his own patience was beginning to be stretched thin.

The morning hours dragged slowly as the crowd in the plaza grew in anticipation of the auto-de-fé. Christian shuddered to think of people choosing to watch the executions, but he had more important things to focus on.

Christian had noticed how carefully Raúl packed his pockets and satchel with herbs and bandages and strapped a small canteen of water about his waist. His heart pounded as he wondered what state Teodoro would be in when they finally saw him. He said a final prayer that the damage, whatever it was, would not be permanent.

A little past noon, the rumble of wagons drew their attention. Christian stepped forward to hail the lead vehicle. "We have orders for you," he told the guards atop the first wagon when they questioned him.

"What orders?" the largest guard growled. "These are prisoners of the Inquisition, to be sentenced at the auto-de-fé."

"Not all of them," Christian insisted, showing the order to the guard. "Not anymore."

Eying the official-looking document with the seal of the archbishop at the bottom, ordering the release of Teodoro Ciéza de Vivar, attendant to *vizconde* Aldwych, the guard shrugged. "You can look in the wagons," he conceded. "If he's still alive, he'll be in one of them."

That thought was simply too cruel to contemplate. After all they had done, Teodoro had to be alive. Christian approached the lead wagon, gagging at the stench of blood, unwashed bodies, and rotting flesh that wafted over him. For the first time in his life, he was glad of the pomander his father always insisted he carry. He held it to his nose, aware that it added to his image of a pampered, pompous noble, while at the same time warding off the overwhelming odors. Under the circumstances, he didn't care what anyone else thought. "Teo?" he called softly, examining the wretched, pain-racked faces in case Teodoro was there but could not reply.

Seeing no familiar shaggy head, no thick moustache, he moved down the line to the next wagon, bracing himself for another spectacle like the one he had found in the first. His stomach wrenched painfully as he searched among the abused bodies for that of his lover, but Teodoro was not in the second wagon either. Forcing himself to walk to the next, Christian could not stop the stumble that tangled his feet on the cobblestones as despair ate at him. Even if Teodoro was there, would they be able to keep him alive? He did not see how anyone could recover from the horrors inflicted upon the poor souls in the first two wagons.

Raúl's hand shot out to catch Christian's arm, steadying him. "Be calm. He is here."

"Yes, but in what state?" Christian whispered back. "Did you see…?" He could not finish the sentence, could not put words to the pierced bodies and shattered bones. Reminding himself of his vow to love Teodoro no matter what had been done to him, he approached the third wagon.

Vaguely Teodoro had registered that the wagon had stopped moving, but the constant jolting over the rutted road had left every muscle in his body screaming in pain. The small part of his brain that still held out any hope told him this was his last chance for escape, but he was too weak to do more than lift his head. The sun's rays surrounded the face that filled his vision, burnished curls framing beloved features in a halo of light. Not sure he wasn't hallucinating, Teodoro tried to stretch out his hand to touch the wavering illusion. "Cristian," he rasped, little more than a whisper escaping his raw throat.

Heart swelling with relief and love at hearing his name again in Teodoro's voice despite the weakness that left it raspy, Christian shouted, "Here! Come release him!" His gaze, though, never left Teodoro.

"My friend," Teodoro whispered, gesturing to Javier, who lay unconscious beside him. He did not know how Christian had managed to arrange for his release, but he could not leave the other man to his death if there was any way to secure Javier's freedom along with his own.

"His name," Raúl murmured, appearing at Christian's side, mind racing as he worked out how to do as Teodoro asked. "Tell me his name."

"Javier," Teodoro answered, knowing Raúl would find a way to manage the situation. "Javier Montega."

"Tell the guards to release both of them," Raúl murmured. "I have an idea."

Bemused, Christian nodded. "Here they are," he said, all sign of doubt gone from his face and voice as he turned to face the same guard who had challenged him before. He knew Raúl would never do anything to endanger Teodoro, so if he said it could be done to save both men, Christian would just have to trust him and play along as best he could. "Teodoro Ciéza de Vivar and Javier Montega." He indicated the two men with a sweep of his hand.

The guard frowned. "What game are you playing? The order is for one man—Teodoro Ciéza de Vivar."

Christian froze, not sure what to say. Before the guard could notice, though, Raúl had taken the order from his hand, waving it vaguely under the man's nose. "Look again," he insisted, catching and holding the guard's gaze, putting every ounce of his persuasive power into the words. His voice lowered just a little, slowing to a hypnotizing lull. "I think you'll find that it says Teodoro Ciéza de Vivar and the attendant to *el vizconde* Aldwych. Javier Montega is his attendant."

Catching on to the game Raúl was playing, Christian drew his noble arrogance around him like a shield. "Those orders came from Cardinal Juan Carlos Rouco himself. Perhaps you would like to explain to His Eminence why you refuse to carry them out as written?"

Hesitating, the guard's gaze flickered from the order, to the huddle of broken bodies in the wagon, to the two men standing expectantly before him. What did it matter, after all, if he let the poor bastards go? They were going to die anyway, as badly as they had been tortured, and the Inquisition would never miss one more of them. "Take them," he muttered, waving his hand toward the stink that rose from the wagon. "Take them so I can get rid of the rest."

Reaching into the wagon, Christian grabbed Teodoro's hand to help him out. Behind him he could hear Raúl shouting for Gerrard, but Christian had eyes only for his lover. Teodoro was covered in blood, moving feebly, but he was moving, a fact that kept Christian from giving up hope. He raked the strong body with his gaze, looking for the kinds of wounds he had seen on other prisoners, but Teodoro's limbs all appeared intact. Helping Teodoro to stand, he stayed close while Raúl and Gerrard lifted Javier's unconscious body from the wagon, checking softly with Teodoro to make sure they had the right man.

Christian's grasp tore at his pain-racked arm, but nothing short of death itself could have made Teodoro release his lover's clasp. Struggling to stay on his feet, Teodoro nodded as the periphery of his attention noted Javier being lifted from the wagon, his gaze never leaving Christian's face, half-afraid that if he looked away, the vision would transform back into nightmare.

Esteban had been given strict instructions from both Christian and Raúl to wait for them to return to the carriage, but when he saw Teodoro pulled free, he could not stop himself from running to his side. "You are safe," he whispered, breathing a prayer of thanksgiving as he moved to help support Teo, lifting a bloodied arm to encircle his shoulder as the other still embraced Christian.

Christian hushed Esteban sharply as he dismissed the guards with a haughty wave.

"In the carriage, quickly," Raúl murmured at his elbow. "Before they change their minds."

Christian nodded and started toward the waiting coach, bearing as much of Teodoro's weight as he could. Ahead of him, Gerrard had simply scooped the unconscious Javier into his arms and was now depositing him on one of the seats. "On the box with me, lad," he told Esteban. "There's not room inside for all of you."

"I want to stay with Teo," Esteban protested.

"The sooner you get on that box, the sooner we can get Teo back to the inn where you can fuss all you like," Raúl scolded. "Use your head, Esteban, as well as your heart. Cristian is our lord. He cannot very well ride outside, and both the others need care only I can give them."

Abashed at having to be corrected, Esteban nodded glumly and climbed to the top of the carriage with the big Englishman, who flicked the reins and started the coach moving away from the gate as soon as the door was closed.

Inside the carriage, Raúl began pulling out herbs from various pockets and pouches about his person. "What did they do to you?" he asked Teodoro, though he was not entirely sure his friend would be able to tear his thoughts away from Christian long enough to reply. He still asked, though, because whatever Teodoro could tell him would make it that much easier to treat.

"Beatings," Teodoro muttered, lifting a shaky hand to Christian's face, his fingers leaving a ruddy stain as he trailed them down Christian's soft cheek. "Rack." He brushed away the tears that escaped from beneath feathered lashes with ragged fingertips.

Raúl frowned, though he doubted either of the other men saw it. "Help me get his shirt off," he told Christian. "I'll deal with that first. If his shoulder's separated, that's best tended to at the inn."

Christian nodded, reaching blindly for the laces on Teodoro's shirt, tilting his head into the caress of his hand, his eyes never leaving the dark gaze that held his like a lifeline. "It's over," he murmured. "You're safe now. I won't let anything happen to you."

"Mi amor," Teodoro whispered, leaning into Christian's touch. "You kept me alive, only you...."

Tears welled in Christian's eyes at the whispered words. Teodoro was such a strong man, so fiercely independent. To have him admit, willingly, to such emotion redoubled the tears that leaked from the corners of Christian's eyes. He wanted to return the sentiment, to whisper words of love and devotion to the man who had become his entire life, but Raúl's presence held him back. Raúl wouldn't care—that wasn't Christian's concern—but he didn't want an audience the first time he told Teodoro that he loved him. Instead he leaned forward and touched his lips lightly to the cracked bow of his lover's mouth, ignoring the swelling, the dried blood, the lingering stench of the Inquisition dungeon. His hands stilled in their task, his attention focused entirely on the tender contact he had feared lost.

Teodoro's lips moved against Christian's sweetness, drinking in his breath, everything else fading at the impossible beauty of this moment he had nearly given up hope of ever experiencing again. He groped for Christian's shoulder, pulling himself closer, deepening the kiss.

Despite the relative urgency of seeing to Teodoro's injuries, Raúl looked away, giving the two men what privacy he could in the cramped quarters of the carriage. He had never seen Teodoro this needy, but he thought perhaps a brush with death might do that to a man. If it meant that his old friend finally stopped fighting what was in his heart and embraced the love he and the young *inglés* shared, perhaps the pain was worth it after all. When they showed no signs of separating, he sighed. "Teodoro," he prodded, "let me tend to your wounds. You can ravish His Excellency when you get back to our quarters and I'm done with you."

Raúl's words coaxed a bark of laughter from Teodoro when he finally brought himself to release Christian's lips. "You think to ravage me first?" he grated, his words trailing into a spate of broken coughing.

"No," Raúl retorted, "I think to heal you enough that you can finish what I interrupted before I sent you on the fool's errand that landed you in this mess in the first place. Now take off your shirt and let me see what I can do for your back."

Releasing Christian's shoulder with reluctance, Teodoro tried to shrug out of his shirt, but the linen clung to his bloodied back. Despising the weakness that prevented him from the simplest of actions, he wordlessly implored Christian's help.

The frustration and helplessness on Teodoro's face tore at Christian's heart. Gently he helped Teodoro free his arms from the shirt before trying to loosen it from his back without tearing the scabs that had formed. Every wince, every groan pierced his soul, but he knew it had to be done. "Lean against me," he said finally. "Raúl will have to pull it off you. I'm sorry."

Needing no encouragement to rest against Christian, Teodoro eased forward. "A little more pain is nothing," he murmured, drawing strength from Christian's heartbeat beneath his cheek.

"That may be true," Raúl interrupted, "but you don't need to bleed any more than you already have. I'm trying to make you stronger, not weaker. Stay where you are and let me see what I can do."

"As if I would let him move," Christian retorted, tightening his arms around Teodoro.

No longer able to keep Christian's gaze, Teodoro let his eyelids fall shut. The sounds of the coach, the sure and gentle touch of Raúl at his back faded, only his arms around Christian and the tenderness of his lover's fingers stroking through his hair holding him to consciousness.

Watching Teodoro relax in Christian's arms, Raúl smiled softly, taking the canteen from his belt to dampen the cloth covering his friend's back. Carefully he worked the fabric loose, the water softening the scabs enough that most of them stayed in place even when the garment was removed. He hoped Christian was not looking, though he had no doubt the younger man would see the mess that was Teodoro's back eventually. Not an inch of flesh was unmarked. Stifling a curse so he wouldn't draw Christian's attention, he drew out the herbs he had brought, applied them to Teodoro's back, and covered the shredded flesh with soft, clean bandages, sliding his hands between the two men to secure them in place. After glancing up to make sure the lovers were lost in each other rather than paying attention to him, he closed his own eyes and murmured softly in the secret language of his ancestors.

Slowly the constant agony that accompanied Teodoro's every breath began to lessen, not gone, but becoming remote somehow, as if the herbs and Raúl's gentle touch and most of all Christian's presence were suffusing him, shielding him, healing him. He tried to force his eyes to open, not willing to lose a moment of being held in Christian's embrace, but the wave of lethargy was too much for him to battle, and he slumped forward into unconsciousness.

"Raúl!" Christian hissed when he felt Teodoro collapse against him.

From his seat on the opposite bench, Raúl opened his eyes and shook his head. "He's sleeping," he told Christian wearily. "He needs it to heal. Hold him until we get to the inn. Then we'll rouse him so he can go inside. I've done what I can. Now rest and your arms around him will have to serve him."

In truth, he might have given Teodoro a little more of his strength, but there was another injured man to consider. He had dealt with the worst of his friend's injuries. Time would heal the remainder. He turned his attention to assessing Javier's condition.

"Would it not be better to leave for Madrid now?" Christian asked. "We did take more of their prisoners than they intended. Putting as much distance between us and the Inquisition as possible seems wise."

"Spending two days in a carriage over rough roads may be more than either of them is ready to endure. Give them a night to rest peacefully and regain some strength. We can leave for Madrid in the morning."

Christian reminded himself to trust Raúl, and the feeling of Teodoro's labored breaths snuffling against his neck provided the rest of the reassurance he needed. He could not pretend Teodoro wasn't in danger still, from infection and loss of blood, but he clung to the solid reality of the body against his, promising himself it would only be a matter of time before Teodoro returned to full strength. Then they would lie like this again, bodies aligned from chest to knee, to far more pleasurable ends. Letting the tension of the past week seep away, Christian pressed a kiss to Teodoro's grimy temple and shut his eyes as well, storing up his energy for the battles still to come.

FIFTEEN

THE CARRIAGE slowed as it neared its destination, the change in movement rousing two of its occupants. Christian looked across the dim space to where Raúl sat, still and silent. "Should I try to wake him now?"

Raúl nodded. "We're almost there, and it will be easier if he can help us move him."

Christian moved his fingers with more deliberation now through Teodoro's hair, stroking him gently awake, not wanting to startle him into any sudden movements that might cause more pain. Christian had not seen the injuries inflicted on Teodoro, but the simple extent of the bandages covering his back spoke volumes of how badly he was hurt. "Teodoro, *querido*, can you wake up for me?"

Half fearing to wake from another dream to the dank cell in the Inquisition dungeon, Teodoro opened his eyes slowly. To his relief he was still in the carriage, still pillowed in Christian's arms, the ceaseless agony that had racked his body for the past two days muted to a dull ache. "Cristian," he husked, even his voice sounding stronger in his ears.

"We are almost to the inn," Christian murmured when he saw Teodoro's eyes open. He would never tire of hearing his name spoken in Teodoro's delightful accent. "We need to move you inside."

When the carriage arrived at the inn, Christian eased Teodoro from the carriage with Raúl's help. Teodoro swayed despite Christian's arm around his waist but managed to stay on his feet. Gerrard climbed down from the box, eyeing Teodoro doubtfully.

"Can you walk well enough to make it up the stairs?" Christian asked Teodoro. "Or do you need Gerrard's help as well?"

Teodoro supposed he should be grateful that the English bodyguard had somehow returned to serve as Christian's protector in his absence, but by hell, he would not let the big man lay a hand on him. "I can walk," he growled, taking an unsteady step to prove his point.

"Esteban, help your father," Raúl instructed. "Gerrard will take Javier to my room for the night." Gerrard scooped the still unconscious

Javier into his arms and started toward the inn. "Teo, let them help you," Raúl added before following the Gerrard inside.

"We have a room where you can rest, Teo," Esteban said quickly. "You'll feel better once you can lie down for a bit."

Teodoro's head swam, the words buzzing in his ears, but he understood enough to know he needed to move. Grasping the hand Christian had wrapped around his waist, he planted one foot in front of the other, sheer determination driving him until they halted in front of a door. Esteban opened it and Christian led him to a bed, where he dropped in exhaustion.

"Teo!" Christian cried as Teodoro collapsed on the bed, but his words met no response, not even a fluttering of eyelashes. He frantically checked Teodoro's breathing, relieved to feel it huffing against his palm. He needed something to do, some way to help.

"Is there water in the ewer?" he asked Esteban.

"A bit," Esteban responded, bringing the pitcher and bowl to him. "I can fetch more if you need it."

"We can't do much for him, but we can clean his hands and face," Christian said. "He will rest more easily if we do."

"I'll go right now," Esteban said and suited actions to words. Christian waited only for the door to close before falling to his knees next to the bed. He clung to Teodoro's unresponsive hand and sobbed out the tension that had kept him moving since Teodoro was taken. He only had a few moments before Esteban's return, when he would have to be strong again to keep Esteban from worrying, but he took the chance this solitude gave him to press another tender kiss to Teodoro's chapped and bloodied lips.

When he heard footsteps in the hall outside, he rose and searched for some scraps of cloth to use as washrags.

"Here's the fresh water," Esteban said. "The cook warmed it up for me a little."

"Thank you," Christian said. "Do you want to wash his hands and feet? I'll take care of his face. Get them as clean as you can, but don't disturb any cuts or bandages."

The warm cloth moving over his skin drew Teodoro from his torpor. He forced his eyes to open and saw Christian hovering over him, wiping his brow. "I didn't dream this," he managed to murmur and tried to raise a hand to stroke Christian's hair, but even that movement was beyond him.

"It's no dream," Christian promised. "You are safe. Rest now. You need to regain your strength, for tomorrow we must return to Madrid." Seeing how weak Teodoro was, he hated the idea of subjecting him to two days in the carriage, but he would not feel truly safe until they were once again ensconced in Teodoro's apartments.

THE TWO days of travel were excruciating for them all. Javier moaned at every bump in the road, despite not regaining consciousness for more than brief moments. Teodoro bore the journey in stoic silence, but Christian could see the toll it was taking in the deepening lines around his mouth and eyes. He seemed to regain some energy each time Raúl changed his bandages, but the rags still came away bloodied, and the journey could not end soon enough for Christian. The sun was setting as the carriage rolled back into Madrid on Friday night.

"We are almost home," Christian murmured when he saw Teodoro's eyes open and heard his name on his lover's lips. "Can you tell us about your friend? Does he have some place to go?"

"I cannot say," Teodoro answered slowly. "He told me he had been falsely accused of having Jewish blood. I do not know if any of his family escaped being taken as well." He looked to Christian, hoping he would understand. "He helped me, offered me warmth and comfort. I could not let him be killed if we could help him in turn."

"Of course you couldn't," Christian soothed, not even caring why Teodoro had acted as he had. Teodoro had asked for his help, and he had given it. He trusted that the reasons were sound. "We'll just have to find something to do with him until he can tell us his story. Your apartments are already crowded as it is."

"I have space in my rooms," Raúl offered, "though it may be disconcerting for him to wake there with no familiar faces. But he can stay with me until he's well enough to be on his own again."

"I suspect Javier hoped not to wake at all," Teodoro admitted. "I am sure he will cope with strange surroundings when he learns he is free of the Inquisition's sentence." His gaze moved to Raúl's face. "*Gracias*, my friend," he murmured, knowing Raúl would understand he meant more than just offering to take Javier in.

Raúl shrugged. "As I said, you have no space in your rooms for another stray, and I have plenty of space in mine. As for the rest, you would do the same for me, but most of the thanks go to your young man. Without him, I would have been trying to smuggle you a knife so you could end your torment before they carried you to the stake." As the carriage rolled to a halt, he glanced up toward where Esteban was perched next to the other bodyguard. "I'll take Esteban with me," he said. "He can help me with the herbs while I care for your friend, and then bring fresh ones back to your rooms later. I imagine you can do without his hovering for a few hours."

"If you can convince him to go," Teodoro agreed, grateful to Raúl for recognizing his need to be alone with Christian. "Is it safe?" he added for Raúl's ears only. "I am a poor guard at the moment."

Raúl nodded subtly. "Take him upstairs and make him rest, Don Cristian," he said aloud, teasing the *inglés* gently. "Our Teo has seen better days. And take Hawkins with you to stand guard. I will deal with Esteban."

Christian jumped down from the carriage and turned back to offer his hand to Teodoro. He could ignore Raúl's teasing the same way he ignored the way he said his name. Esteban appeared at his elbow instantly, wanting to help as well.

"Esteban," Raúl called from inside the carriage before either of them could speak, "come in here with me. I'll need your help with Teo's friend. He is still unconscious, and I cannot handle him alone."

Esteban's worried gaze darted back to Teodoro, who nodded his agreement. "Go, Esteban, help Raúl with Javier. I promise I will survive until you return."

The young man's eyes met Christian's, seeking assurance that Teodoro would receive all the care Esteban would offer himself.

"You know I'm hardly likely to let anything happen to him now that we have him back," Christian assured him, ruffling Esteban's hair lightly. Leaning down, he added softly, "Javier helped Teo in prison. The least we can do is take good care of him now. Since Teo cannot, it falls to you, his son, to show our gratitude in his place."

"*Sí*, I will help Raúl with your friend, Teo," Esteban agreed. "I will bring you back news of him once he is better."

Esteban taken care of, Christian turned his attention to his former protector. "Guard the stairs," he directed Gerrard. "I don't think the Inquisition will send anyone after us, but that doesn't mean our other adversary will be so generous. I doubt he'll hear the news tonight, but we can't afford to take chances."

Gerrard nodded and took up his place at the base of the stairs leading to Ciéza's rooms. He'd had his doubts when he first arrived in Madrid, but the transformation in his erstwhile charge had convinced him that the Spaniard was good for the viscount. He would do all he could to protect them a little longer.

"Let's get you upstairs," Christian murmured to Teodoro. "You'll feel better once you've had a chance to rest."

"I already feel better," Teodoro asserted, though he still found he needed to lean on Christian to manage the narrow stairway to his rooms. A light sweat coated his skin by the time the heavy door finally closed behind them. "Lock it," he instructed, leaning against the frame to catch his breath.

Christian threw the heavy bolt, then turned to wrap his arms around Teodoro's neck. "Come lie down," he urged, kissing Teodoro tenderly, twining his fingers in the sweat-tangled hair. Neither the inn in Toledo nor the one on the road home had offered enough privacy for Christian to sleep in Teodoro's arms as he longed to do. Instead he had spent the nights dozing in a chair, waking every few minutes to make sure Teodoro still breathed and did not need anything. He had nodded off in the carriage at times during the day, but he was ready for a night of uninterrupted rest in Teodoro's arms.

Reaching up to Christian's face, Teodoro's attention was drawn to the traces of blood on his fingers. Disgust at the foulness that clung to his body filled him. "I must bathe first," he insisted. "I reek of the dungeons. I would not have that filth anywhere near you."

"They cannot touch us," Christian assured him, "but I understand why you would want to be clean again. Come into the bedroom, and we'll see what we can do. You cannot sit in the bath with your back the way it is, but we can surely wash away some of the grime."

Letting Christian lead him, Teodoro began to lower himself onto the bed, pausing when he glanced down at the blood and dirt staining his breeches. He had refused the clean clothes Christian had brought to Toledo, not wanting to soil them with the filth that still begrimed him. "Help get these off me," he asked, working at the fastenings with awkward fingers.

Despite the seriousness of Teodoro's injuries, despite his weakness, Christian could not help the grin that split his face at the thought. Kneeling at Teodoro's feet, he unfastened the breeches and slid them down, leaving Teodoro in his smallclothes. "The rest of it as well?" he asked huskily, unable to stop his reaction to the thought of Teodoro naked regardless of the situation.

"All of it," Teodoro answered, anxious to be rid of anything with the taint of the Inquisition prison clinging to it. "Esteban will need to boil them before I can wear them again."

Esteban would buy him new ones, Christian decided instantly, though it was a discussion he would have with Teodoro later. For the moment it was enough to pull the soiled cloth from Teodoro's body and leave him bare but for the bandages. "These should stay until I have more of Raúl's herbs to put on them, if you can stand to have me wash around them."

"Just bring me some water and a cloth. I will manage." Teodoro would prefer not to face an irate Raúl by disarranging his bandages.

"You will sit there and do nothing but try to relax," Christian insisted, beginning to remove his own garments. "You wouldn't deprive me of the opportunity to touch you, would you?"

"You look so fine in those clothes, it seems a shame to soil them," Teodoro replied, easing himself carefully onto the mattress.

Christian turned back to Teodoro as he set aside his doublet and reached for the tie on his breeches. "I won't be soiling them." He let the breeches fall and pulled the linen shirt over his head, leaving him dressed only in his smallclothes. "Now, can I please take care of you?"

"I thought you hired me to take care of you," Teodoro answered, trying not to stare at the enticing figure of his nearly unclothed lover. Despite his weariness, his body was trying to react; he shifted uneasily, willing away the inappropriate response, certain Christian could only be sickened by his damaged state.

Christian frowned. "*I* thought we were lovers, equal partners who took care of each other as the situation warranted." He stroked Teodoro's face to soften his next words. He feared if he let any distance grow between them, he would have to start over again. "Or did the Inquisition change your mind?"

"I would not have you see me like this," Teodoro replied truthfully, though he could not help but lean into the soothing touch.

"Like what?" Christian asked, knowing the answer but wanting to reassure Teodoro. "Naked beneath my hands? Moving into my touch? Why wouldn't I want to see you that way? Why wouldn't I *want* you that way?"

"Injured," Teodoro countered, though he could not prevent the desire that shivered through him at Christian's words. "Helpless. Useless to you."

Christian kissed Teodoro again gently. "I know you're hurt. I know they did unspeakable things to you, but I don't care. I don't need you to be 'helpful.' I don't need you to be 'useful.' I love you. All I need is you here with me. Let me show you?"

All his arguments melting away at Christian's words of love, Teodoro nodded, opening his arms and his heart to his lover. "Querido," he murmured, tangling one hand into the blond curls as he leaned into the offered embrace. "Te amo, solamente a ti."

"And I only you," Christian vowed, gazing deep into Teodoro's eyes. He was tempted to forget about Teodoro's bath in favor of even more intimate activities, but Teodoro had been very specific about why he wanted to bathe, and Christian could understand his reasoning. Not looking away, even for a moment, he felt blindly for the pitcher of water and rag that he knew were on the nearby sideboard. Besides, he doubted Teodoro was truly well enough for anything more strenuous than a bath and sleeping in Christian's arms.

Having given in to his body's demand to hold Christian, Teodoro begrudged even the momentary loss of his embrace. "What is wrong?"

"Not a thing," Christian replied, picking up the supplies he needed. "But I believe you wanted a bath." He set the pitcher on the floor by the bed and dipped the rag inside. "Your servant, señor," he teased gently, wiping the cloth across Teodoro's face. It came away red with blood and black with grime, but he ignored the twinge in his heart at the thought of what his lover had suffered. Teodoro did not want his pity, and Christian would not demean him by giving it. Instead he would use this time to show Teodoro how much he admired his courage and fortitude in surviving his terrible ordeal.

The rough nap of the rag was harsh against Teodoro's bruised and broken flesh, but it was Christian's hand holding the cloth, Christian's voice whispering to him as he gently wiped the gore and sweat from his skin, the pain outweighed by the simple effect of Christian's hands on his body. There was nothing intentionally erotic about the touch, yet Teodoro found his arousal growing with each swipe of the cool cloth.

"Am I hurting you?" Christian asked, concern heavy in his voice when he felt Teodoro shift beneath his hand. "I know you wished to be clean, but I would not cause you pain. The bath can wait until you are better."

"Don't stop," Teodoro insisted. "I would be clean when I hold you against me." No pain would prevent him from feeling Christian curled against him as they slept.

"I want nothing more than to be in your arms again," Christian averred, rubbing the cloth down Teodoro's arms, carefully avoiding the bandages over his shoulders. He could see the swelling around Teodoro's joints and knew that had to come from the time he had spent on the rack. He pushed down the rage that surged within him, knowing he could do nothing to change the horrors of the Inquisition. He would have to be satisfied with having thwarted it this time.

"I dreamed of that—of returning to you here, in my arms, in my bed," Teodoro admitted. "Though I thought it no more than a dream—I held little hope you would succeed in freeing me."

"I slept in your spare shirt," Christian admitted in return. "It smelled of you, and I needed that comfort to settle enough to doze. I know Esteban thought me mad, but otherwise, fear of not being able to help you kept me from resting." He turned his attention to the furred chest, wiping all the skin not covered by the tied ends of the bandages. He would have to repeat the process when Raúl came to change the dressings, for there was much he could not reach, but he would do what he could.

"But you did help me." The cloth brushing over his chest, scratching his nipples, which pebbled as it swiped over them, started a warmth growing lower in Teodoro's body, spreading through his limbs as Christian moved the rag down his ribs. To distract himself, he continued, "How were you able to gain an order for my release?"

Turning his attention to Teodoro's legs, Christian picked up one foot, beginning to wash it as he replied, "I pretended I was a man like my father, a man like you—a powerful man with enough influence to demand the release of my attendant." He realized what he had said and glanced up frantically, meeting Teodoro's gaze. "I don't think of you as my servant, but if I'd told them you were my lover, I'd never have been able to help you."

"It was no more than the truth," Teodoro reassured him, his breath catching as Christian began running the rag up his calf. "And you do not have to pretend to be a powerful man. You were obviously convincing enough to win my freedom."

Christian shrugged diffidently. "They feared the possibility of my father's displeasure far more than they cared about your fate. And while it was no more than the truth, it was also far less than the whole truth." Returning to the task at hand, his gaze fell to the juncture of Teodoro's thighs and the swelling there. A smile growing on his face, he brushed the cloth across Teodoro's cock. "I thought you'd be in too much pain."

This time Teodoro made no attempt to hide his gasp as Christian caressed him. "I would have to be dead not to respond when you touch me like that."

Christian's heart leaped at the flattering words. Encouraging Teodoro to spread his legs, he knelt between his knees, washing him thoroughly before dropping the rag to the floor. "Shall I touch you some more?" he asked teasingly, his lips close enough that his breath wafted across the burgeoning shaft.

"Do not play with me, Cristian," Teodoro rasped, holding himself back from the desire to push Christian's head down onto his cock. "Touch me, *querido*."

Christian complied immediately, closing his lips around the leaking tip as he slid his hands up Teodoro's thighs to cradle his heavy sac. His own body quickened as he lavished pleasure on Teodoro in all the ways he'd dreamed of doing while they were separated. The salty flavor assaulted his senses as he took the thick shaft deeper into his mouth, imagining what it would feel like to have it inside him, though he didn't dare hope that would happen tonight. The last thing he wanted to do was overtax Teodoro's strength. He could wait a little longer for that pleasure, knowing it was only a matter of time and allowing Teodoro to heal.

Teodoro groaned deeply as Christian took him in his mouth, teasing his tongue over his most sensitive flesh, cradling his sac in soft hands, making his balls tighten in anticipation. It would be so easy to find his release this way, but Teodoro had imagined their first night of lovemaking far differently. Cursing his body, which was so quick to rouse and yet, he feared, too weak to give his lover the same pleasure, he stroked a hand through Christian's silken curls, not to pull him closer but to ease him away from the all-too-enticing sensations.

Christian looked up. "What is it?" he asked. "Do you want me to stop?" He didn't want to, not with Teodoro's taste on his lips and scent in his nose, but he would. Teodoro's well-being came before any lust on his own part.

"I want to kiss you." Teodoro coaxed Christian to return where he could reach him. "I want to hold you in my arms, to share the pleasure you are giving me." He drew them both down onto the mattress, careful to lean his weight on his side, which had sustained the least damage from the whip and the rack.

Christian offered his mouth willingly, twining his arms around Teodoro's neck again, hoping that there, at least, they would cause no more pain. "You give me pleasure simply by being here," he insisted. "Everything else is extra."

Teodoro feasted at the banquet of Christian's lips, the taste of his own saltiness a reminder of the intimacy he longed to share with him. He tangled his legs with Christian's, drawing them closer, aligning their bodies as he relearned the smooth planes of Christian's back with his hands.

Christian rubbed himself eagerly against Teodoro's hip, the brush of linen against his cock a sudden reminder that he had not finished undressing. He pulled away only long enough to strip off his smallclothes before returning quickly to Teodoro's arms. The sensation of their swollen shafts bumping together nearly undid him. "I want you inside me," he told Teodoro bluntly. "Can we manage?"

"I don't know," Teodoro said. He frowned, tightening his arms when Christian misread his expression for pain and tried to pull away. "This is not how I wanted the first time I made love to you to be," he confessed, "but I cannot wait another night. We've already waited too long."

"We have," Christian agreed. "It doesn't matter how we position our bodies tonight or any other night. Making love comes from the heart, and mine is entirely in your care. However we lie, however we touch each other, it will be making love." He pulled away enough to roll to his other side, rubbing his bottom provocatively against Teodoro's groin. "Make love to me."

The friction of Christian's buttocks against him made Teodoro's cock surge with blood, but he ignored its demands for the moment.

Burying his head in the nape of Christian's neck, he inhaled the sweet, clean scent, the curls tickling his face as he pressed small, soft kisses over the fragrant flesh. "You smell much better than my last bed," he murmured, muffling a hiss of pain as he raised up a bit on one elbow to circle Christian's chest with the other arm, searching for the sensitive nipples with his fingers.

"I'd be worried if I didn't," Christian murmured in reply, his hiss of pleasure echoing the one from Teodoro's lips. He angled his shoulders to give Teodoro better access to his chest. "Lie back down," he urged, hearing the hint of pain Teodoro tried to suppress. "Lie still and move me to get what you want. That way I won't be distracted by worrying that I'm making your pain worse."

"*Mi amor*, there is pain if you do nothing at all," Teodoro answered, rolling a tightened nub between his thumb and forefinger. "Pleasuring you at least gives some purpose to it."

A low moan escaped Christian's lips. "You do give me pleasure," he assured him as he turned to his back, slipping his fingers beneath the ties of the bandages to reciprocate the caress. "Just by being here and alive, you give me pleasure."

There was no mistaking Teodoro's sigh for anything but contentment at Christian's gentle touch. Fanning his fingers to find and tease the other pebble of flesh, Teodoro kissed his way across Christian's shoulder, the sweet taste more refreshing than cool water, more intoxicating than wine.

Christian skimmed his hand lower, feeling the bandages come to an end at Teodoro's hipbones. Scooting closer, he stroked the bare skin of Teodoro's hip and upper thigh before reaching around to cup the firm muscle of his buttocks. He wanted to touch, to taste everywhere, but he accepted that wouldn't be possible tonight. This, at least, he could do, bringing Teodoro's cock back into contact with his own hip. He kneaded gently, watching for signs of pain. He couldn't feel any open wounds, but that didn't guarantee anything.

Grunting softly as he shifted to press into Christian's caress, Teodoro bent forward, the bristles of his moustache brushing over a rosy disk before he flicked at it with his tongue. With his free hand, he gave a final tweak to the pearl he had been playing with before trailing lower, following the faint trail of hair that bisected Christian's abdomen, winding in and out of the wispy curls and tracing the perimeter of the thicker patch to which it led.

Christian groaned when Teodoro's lips and moustache brushed his nipple. When the agile fingers started teasing around his cock, he arched his hips eagerly. "Touch me," he pleaded, his grip on the firm flesh beneath his palm tightening. "Now."

"I am touching you." Teodoro smiled, groaning when the attempt to stretch farther to lave Christian's other nipple strained the wounds across his back. "Roll closer."

He moved with Christian until he could close his teeth around the delectable nugget. All the while he continued his desultory exploration of Christian's groin, winding the wiry curls around his fingertips, combing through the tangle to outline the base of the rigid shaft, drifting lower to the delicate skin that enclosed the hardening sac.

Christian might have caviled had Teodoro not moved his hands as he did. As it was, he canted his hips, crooking one knee to leave his most intimate regions open to Teodoro's sure, lingering touch. Slipping his hand between them, he found Teodoro's cock, and his fingers danced along its length, hoping to convince Teodoro to hurry. The fear and tension of the past few days had taken their toll on Christian's patience, and he needed their impending joining to chase away the last of the nightmares that haunted him.

Teodoro had thought to draw out their lovemaking, the warmth of Christian's flesh beneath his fingers and the soft sounds of enjoyment he was coaxing from Christian's lips grounding him, proof that they had cheated the fate that threatened them; but his lover was too enticing, and he feared he would not have the strength to continue much longer. He ached to straddle Christian's lean hips, to plunge into the roseate opening that even now clenched beneath his seeking fingers, but his arm was already trembling with the strain of holding himself upright. Circling the hot, tight portal, he once again cursed his weakness as he sagged back onto his side, lifting his hand to Christian's face.

"If we are to do this, you will need to find something I can use to make you ready for me," he murmured. "Taking you with nothing but spit would hurt both of us."

Christian glanced around the room, mentally ransacking his valise for something they could use, and his gaze landed on the flagon of oil on the sideboard. "You didn't get much of a chance to use this before," he commented slyly, grabbing it and then bringing it back to bed with him. "Let's hope we aren't interrupted this time." His heart raced as he remembered what it had felt like to have Teodoro's finger inside him. His entire body thrilled with the prospect of being filled by something even more satisfactory.

"I think Raúl has seen to it that we will not be," Teodoro answered, watching Christian remove the stopper from the glass vial. "Unless your other protector feels the need to check upon you?"

"I only have one protector," Christian averred, "and he is right here with me, about to make love to me. Gerrard is not a fool. He'll stay downstairs and leave us in peace." After setting the stopper aside, he offered the oil to Teodoro. "Forget about him and come ravish me properly."

As he dipped his fingers into the viscous fluid, Teodoro paused a moment in appreciation of the embodiment of every dream that had kept him alive during his days in the Inquisition's dungeons—Christian, lying in a pose of wanton invitation on his bed, reaching for him, his eyes kindled not only with desire but with love. Ignoring the pain that accompanied his every movement, Teodoro bent to kiss the hollow of Christian's abdomen as he worked his fingers into the crease between Christian's widespread legs, circling the puckered entrance, coating it with the slickness that clung to his fingers. Not until Christian was twisting and pleading beneath him did he breach the opening with the tip of one thick digit, the tightness a tiny foretaste of the bliss to come.

Christian sobbed his readiness, his desire, his need, writhing desperately beneath the long-desired touch. "Teo," he entreated, digging his fingers into Teodoro's hip as he tried to draw him closer. He reached blindly for the cock that nudged his hip, hoping to urge Teodoro to pick up the pace.

Biting back a groan at the stab of pain in his swollen joints, Teodoro raised his head to nuzzle at the slender shaft lying in a pool of clear fluid, the salty taste on his tongue and the curl of Christian's fingers around his own cock encouraging him to work a second finger into his lover's tight passage. He would have reached for more oil, but he needed his other hand to hold himself upright, so he settled for twisting and stretching the clinging walls as best he could, willing his strength to hold out long enough to let him love Christian the way they both hungered to be joined.

"Enough," Christian gasped. "I want you inside me when I come, not just your fingers." As much as he wanted to be able to watch Teodoro's face as their bodies came together for the first time, he knew it would be easiest on Teodoro if he turned onto his side. Giving him one more, lingering kiss, he rolled away and pressed his back to Teodoro's chest. "Please."

Vowing that as soon as he was stronger he would make love to Christian the way he deserved, Teodoro pressed a kiss to his lover's shoulder and settled back onto his side. "Hand me the oil, *querido*," he requested, withdrawing his fingers to dip them again in the proffered flagon and anoint his already leaking shaft. He moved his lips to Christian's ear as he positioned himself to slip inside, his breath ghosting over the whorled shell as he pressed slowly, easing the tender flesh open with exquisite gentleness. "Let me inside you," he murmured. "Let me love you, *mi amor*."

Christian repressed a sob at the tender epithet, consciously relaxing his body as much as he could. He leaned back against the hard flesh spearing him, taking it deeper into himself, letting it fill him, complete him, join them together in the most elemental of ways. "Te amo," he gasped as he fought not to climax the first time the tip of Teodoro's cock brushed the sensitive spot inside him.

The words of love, even more than the tight heat welcoming him, set a match to the conflagration burning in Teodoro's belly. Clenching his teeth even as his lips still moved over Christian's neck, he spread his legs to align their bodies even closer, stirring his hips gently, each motion rocking him minutely inside the tight channel. He circled Christian's shaft with his hand, stroking it firmly, whispering endearments against the glistening skin as he drove them both toward their fulfillment.

Christian rocked eagerly back against Teodoro, spurred on by the hand on his cock, the breath in his ear. His heart swelled with love as his proud lover bared his soul in this intimate moment. He didn't care if he ever heard the words again. To have Teodoro say them now, to know that this moment meant as much to Teodoro as it did to him, left Christian overcome with emotion, his own words of devotion pouring from his lips in a babbling litany.

The flames were licking at Teodoro's nerves, pain and pleasure melding together, consuming him, stealing his breath, overwhelming his control. He fought to mold himself to Christian, tightening his fist around Christian's cock, stroking it as his hips thrust to the rhythm of their pounding heartbeats. "Mi corazón," he gasped, fighting the instinct that sought to overpower him.

Christian gave in to the needs riding him, Teodoro's hand and cock driving him toward the moment of release, the precipice beyond which there would be only bliss and completion. A part of him wanted to prolong the moment, to hang on to the novelty of their union, but his body had reached its limits, his control stretched thin by the week of tension and fear, and now by joy. Letting go of his hold on his passions, he arched against Teodoro, his climax rolling through him in long, lingering waves.

As soon as the first hot splash of Christian's release slickened his fingers, Teodoro gave in, crushing Christian to him as he convulsed around him. Heedless of pain, his emotions soared, his senses lost to anything but the flare of ecstasy that blazed within him, coursing along his nerves, leaving him shuddering with each aftershock that racked them both. With a final heaving breath, he slumped against Christian's back, his strength exhausted.

Pushing back the lethargy brought on by his own release, Christian turned over immediately to check on his lover. Teodoro's face was wan, but a smile bowed his lips, reassuring Christian as nothing else could. "Sleep," he urged softly, pillowing Teodoro's head on his shoulder. "Everything else can wait until morning." He kissed the broad forehead. "Te amo."

Teodoro tried to reply, but exertion and exhaustion had taken their toll and he lapsed into blackness, safe in the haven of Christian's arms.

Sixteen

A PLEASANT satiation filled Christian as he stirred from sleep, his lover—finally and truly his lover—still curled against him. His body ached in the most pleasurable of ways, reminding him of how well and thoroughly Teodoro had loved him last night, despite the constraints of his injuries. That thought made Christian frown. He hated knowing that Teodoro was wounded, that he had suffered because of him. Shifting slightly, he stroked Teodoro's hair gently, afraid to touch anywhere else for fear of hurting him worse. His eyelids started to drift shut again when a flash of red caught his attention. Easing Teodoro's head to the pillow, he sat up, reaching out to touch the sticky stain.

The loss of the warm skin and reassuring heartbeat beneath his cheek pulled Teodoro from the restful lassitude he had been drifting in. "Come back to bed," he murmured drowsily, admiring Christian's sleep-rumpled beauty from beneath hooded lids. "'S too early to be up."

"You're bleeding," Christian protested. "We shouldn't have—"

"A cut or two pulled open," Teodoro interrupted, dismissing the concern before Christian could continue. Despite the pain he still felt, he could not regret a moment of the previous night's activity. "It signifies nothing. Raúl will draw more than that when he changes the bandages." He pushed onto one elbow and reached to draw Christian back down to the bedding, his blood heating as his body began to stir.

"But I hurt you," Christian whispered, still stricken at the sight of blood on the sheets, though he did not fight his return to Teodoro's arms. He dared not, for fear of causing even more pain.

"You drove the pain away," Teodoro countered, tipping Christian's head upward to meet his hungry gaze. "When I was inside you, I felt nothing but joy, *mi amor*," he murmured, stilling any further protest by the simple expedient of covering Christian's mouth with his.

Christian had no hope of resisting the kiss, reacting to Teodoro's touch like tinder to a brand, heat engulfing him instantly, overruling all his hesitations. He arched against Teodoro wantonly, feeling the morning erection nudging his thigh. He parted his legs eagerly, inviting

Teodoro to renew the intimate caresses that had brought them such bliss the night before.

The unrestrained eagerness of Christian's response strengthened Teodoro's spirit as much as the night's rest had begun to restore his body. Rolling over, he let his weight settle on Christian's pliant form, deepening the kiss, his hips shifting to increase the friction as they pressed against each other's growing arousal. He had just palmed a handful of delectable backside when the outer door to the apartment slammed, sending Teodoro pushing to his feet. "Stay here," he hissed to Christian as he moved toward the main room, all too aware that his sword and dagger were still in the hands of the Inquisition.

"Don't be stupid," Christian retorted, launching himself out of bed after Teodoro. "Gerrard would have shouted a warning at least if there were danger. It's Raúl and Esteban, I'm sure. I'm impressed Raúl kept him away this long." He caught himself before he slid beneath Teodoro's arm, wanting to urge his lover to lean on him but afraid to reawaken his prickly pride. He would just watch and be ready to help if Teodoro truly needed him. "Put some clothes on and go reassure your son."

With his free hand, Christian reached for Teodoro's spare pair of breeches from his bag and offered them to him. Moving slowly but without assistance, Teodoro pulled them on stiffly before entering the common room. "Once again, your timing is less than ideal," he groused to Raúl as Esteban ran to his side, anxious for proof that he had not worsened while they were apart.

"Short of tying him to a chair, there was no way I could keep him away any longer," Raúl replied, running his own assessing gaze over Teodoro. However his friend had passed the night, it did not seem to have done him any lasting harm.

"He has every right to be worried," Christian agreed, coming into the room, breeches in place but bare from the waist up. "Sit down, Teodoro, and let the lad see you. And while he's doing that, Raúl can check your back. It still worries me that you bled through the bandages during the night."

"Some bleeding is to be expected. It will wash out any poisons," Raúl said calmly, "but I will see when I change the dressing." He knelt in front of Teodoro, untying the knots that held the linen strips in place.

Immediately Christian and Esteban moved to help, Christian sliding his hands over Teodoro's chest with easy familiarity and a sureness of his welcome that left Esteban standing uncomfortably to one side, unsure of his place in this suddenly shifting reality. Last night Teo had sent him away in favor of the *vizconde*, and now Teo turned to the Englishman instead of to him for something that would surely have been his task a few weeks ago. He frowned uneasily, wondering how he had been supplanted.

"We should finish your bath while the bandages are off," Christian told Teodoro. "I did the best I could last night, but you'll feel better if you're completely clean. Esteban, can you get the pitcher and a rag from the bedroom?"

Eager to help, Esteban hurried into the bedroom to retrieve the requested items, only to draw up short at the sight of the rumpled bed, sheets in complete disarray. He looked around the rest of the room, taking in the clothes scattered haphazardly on the floor. Not sure how to interpret what he was seeing—not wanting to interpret it the way he would have if a woman like Aldonza were the one in the other room—he grabbed the pitcher and a clean rag.

The last knots worked free, Raúl eased the bloodied bandages from Teodoro's back, careful to dislodge as little of the clotted skin as possible. "Let us see how much damage you managed to inflict on yourself overnight."

"I was not the one on my back," Teodoro murmured, his eyes meeting Christian's with a glint of warmth Raúl had never before seen in his friend's expression.

"I wasn't either," Christian retorted immediately, turning bright red as he realized what he had said and who had heard him. Despite his budding friendship with Raúl, he was not completely comfortable with the idea of the gypsy knowing about the full extent of their relationship. All thoughts of being embarrassed disappeared as he turned to look at Teodoro's back. A stifled sob escaped his lips as he stared at the torn flesh, finally seeing the damage wrought by the Inquisition. "The bastards!" he cursed, reaching out as if to touch, held back only by the realization that anywhere he touched would only cause Teodoro more pain.

"It is over," Teodoro insisted. He caught Christian's hand between both of his and was raising it toward his lips when a cry from behind him made him turn toward his horrified ward.

Esteban stood in the doorway between the rooms, pitcher and rag in hand, staring at the scene in front of him. He couldn't decide which was worse—Teo's back or the fact that Teo was holding Christian's hand so tenderly. Setting the items he'd been sent to fetch on the table with trembling hands, he dipped the rag in the pitcher, intending to wash Teo's back, to tend to him as he had always done when Teodoro was injured. He reached Teo's side only to have the rag taken from his hands. He watched for a moment as the *vizconde* ran the cloth tenderly over Teodoro's face before sliding it lower to wipe at the bloodstained skin of his chest. The gesture, combined with everything else he had seen that morning, snapped something inside him, and he bolted for the door. His world was crumbling around him, and he could not stay to watch.

"Esteban!" Teodoro commanded, his voice forceful enough to make the youth stop in his tracks. His expression softening, he beckoned Esteban closer. "Beatings always look worse than they feel," he told the boy, hoping he would never have cause to learn differently. When Esteban's worried look did not ease, Teodoro reached for him, pulling him into a rough hug. "I'll live," he assured him, holding his gaze until he saw the concern begin to lessen. "Perhaps you could ask Isabel for breakfast for us—enough for the other Englishman too," he asked, knowing Esteban would fret less if he was kept busy.

Esteban nodded slowly, the security of being held by his adored guardian easing some of his fears. He clung a few moments more before rising to his feet and leaving the room at a pace resembling normal.

"Your back is not all that worries him," Raúl observed, removing a handful of herbs from his pouch as Christian carefully cleaned Teodoro's torn skin.

Teodoro grimaced as he rested his hands on his knees, baring more of his back to Christian's ablutions. "I will speak with him," he said, though he was not entirely sure what he could tell Esteban. It was not as if he and Christian had made any promises to each other. While Teodoro believed their lovemaking had meant as much to Christian as it did to him, he could not see any way they could remain together once the threat to Christian's life was ended.

"Would it be better if I made myself scarce while you talked?" Christian asked, finishing his task and then stepping aside so Raúl could check on Teodoro. "I can keep Gerrard company for a while if you'd like."

"It would be easier," Teodoro admitted, though having reminded himself that their time together was limited, he begrudged even those moments they would spend apart—especially when Christian would be spending them in the company of the big Englishman.

"I cannot see any sign of infection," Raúl said with relief after examining Teodoro's back. He applied fresh herbs over the worst of the torn skin, holding them in place with clean bandages. "Try not to engage in anything too acrobatic for a few days, so you can begin to heal."

"If he does, I'll just tie him to the bed," Christian replied with a wink for Teodoro as he imagined everything he would do while he had him in such a position.

Raúl shook his head, pulled a heavy tome from his satchel, and handed it to Christian. "Challenge him to play chess instead."

Christian looked down at the embossed cover, seeing the title Raúl had mentioned the night before they left to rescue Teodoro. "I think the other would be more fun," he muttered, setting the book on the sideboard for safekeeping.

Before Teodoro could reply, the door from the hallway opened and Esteban came back in, arms laden with a heavy tray full of pastries for breakfast. Christian moved to help him, offering the youth a tentative smile. "Shall I take some down to Gerrard?" He picked up one of the tarts and bit into it with relish before wrapping a few more into a napkin. Their nocturnal activities had left him with an appetite now that he knew Teodoro would be all right, given time to heal.

Raúl packed up his bandages and rose also, lifting a pastry from the tray as he accompanied Christian to the door. "I must check on your friend Javier, and then I have a few more avenues to explore regarding *el conde* de la Rocha," he added. "I will return to change your bandages this evening and let you know what I have learned."

"Bring me an *ensaimada*?" Teodoro asked as the door closed behind the two men, leaving him and Esteban alone.

Esteban was quick to put several of the light pastries on a plate and set them before Teodoro. "Here you are, Teo," he said softly. "You should eat so you can get better quickly."

"Gracias," Teodoro said, realizing how truly hungry he was after he took a bite of one of the pastries. The food—if the few crusts of moldy bread could be called that—provided while he was imprisoned had been barely edible, though he had forced himself to eat since his rescue to regain his strength. After pushing the rest of the flaky tart into his mouth, he smiled at Esteban. "What would I do without you?"

"You seemed to do fine last night and this morning," Esteban muttered, telling himself the resentment he felt was unworthy of the efforts the *vizconde* had gone to on Teo's behalf and yet still feeling betrayed by Teo's obvious preference for Christian's company.

"Come here, Esteban." Teodoro gestured for the young man to sit beside him. His moustache twitched as he frowned, searching for a way to reassure his son. He was a man of action, not of words, but he knew he owed Esteban an explanation of Christian's place in his life. If only he understood it himself. Drawing a breath, he held Esteban's gaze and motioned toward his back.

"Until this heals, I must rely on you, and Raúl, and *vizconde* Aldwych for help," he began. "*El vizconde*—Cristian—he is…." He shook his head, his eyes softening as he realized there was no way he could explain what was in his heart to Esteban. "He is very special to me," he continued, lifting a hand as Esteban started to speak. "He is very special, but once the danger facing him is gone, there will be no reason for him to stay in Spain."

Esteban snorted in disbelief, his hand flying to his face to hide the disrespectful sound. "You did not see him this past week," he countered, remembering Christian's determination to help Teodoro, and his fear that it hadn't worked. The image of Christian falling to his knees after they first returned from the archbishop's palace haunted his thoughts. "I think…." He flushed a little as he considered all the implications of what he had seen and heard in the past few days. "I think you are very special to him too. If it weren't for me, you could go with him even if he does return to England."

Teodoro might hope that Esteban was correct, but even if it were true, it changed nothing. "What place would I have in England?" Teodoro shook his head. "My life is here, in Madrid, with you. *Vizconde* Aldwych cannot change that."

"I'm sorry," Esteban said softly, able to see the pain Teo felt now that his own fears had been allayed. "You're so much happier since he's been with us. Maybe… maybe he'd stay? If you asked?"

And offer him what? A life of poverty, of taking whatever job would pay enough reales to keep clothes on our backs and a meal on the table? Teodoro knew he couldn't answer Esteban that way, so he merely shrugged. "That must be *el vizconde*'s decision," he said, tousling Esteban's hair. "Now, perhaps you could take my clothes to Isabel to be washed?"

Esteban nodded, eager to help. He hurried into the other room and returned with the bundle of soiled cloth. "She'll have to mend them too," he observed, seeing the rents in the seams and smelling the foul moldiness of the dungeons. "I still have *el vizconde*'s pouch, from when I bought him clothes so he could convince the archbishop to let you go. I'm sure he wouldn't mind if you got something new to replace these."

"See what Isabel can do with them first," Teodoro directed, the innocent comment another reminder of how wide the gulf was between Christian and himself. He rose stiffly, cursing the weakness that made his head reel for a moment until he grasped the chair back to steady himself. Waiting had never been one of his strengths; waiting helplessly for his body to heal was going to drive him mad.

Esteban nodded again and carried the clothes downstairs, calling out a greeting to Christian and the other Englishman as he passed.

Seeing the bundle Esteban carried, Christian beckoned to him. "Are you taking those to be burned?"

"No," Esteban replied, "Teo wants Isabel to wash them."

Christian shook his head. "Burn them and buy something new for him. You still have money from earlier in the week, don't you?"

"*Sí*, but Teo said—"

"Teo is too proud for his own good," Christian replied before turning to Gerrard. "He'll need a new sword too, and a long dagger. Do you think you can find a good set for him?"

"I could," Gerrard said, "but if I go to look for them, I'll be leaving you unprotected."

"I'll lock the door," Christian promised. "We'll be fine for a few hours. He'll feel much better knowing he has weapons at hand again, even if he's really not strong enough to use them."

"I can take you," Esteban suggested shyly. "I know where Teo bought his last sword. Surely we would find something there that he would approve of. And if not, I know another shop that sells good swords too."

"Very well, lad," Gerrard agreed, clapping Esteban on the shoulder. "Lead on." He paused to glance back at his erstwhile employer over his shoulder. "Be sure you lock the door, and don't go out alone for any reason."

"I learned your lessons well," Christian joked as he started back up the stairs. "Don't worry about us. We'll be fine." He couldn't stop the smile as he climbed, knowing they would be gone for a couple of hours at least and Raúl was not expected back until evening. A couple of hours alone with Teodoro… what a tempting prospect!

Once Christian reached the apartment, he walked inside, locked the door behind him, and crossed the room to Teodoro's side. He was relieved to see the tray almost empty, a sure sign Teodoro had eaten something. "How are you feeling?" he purred, hoping to convince Teodoro to return to bed with him. "Did you manage to reassure Esteban?"

Reflecting that he had not so much reassured Esteban as he had discomposed himself, Teodoro shrugged. "He needs to feel useful," he said, pushing his doubts to the back of his mind. He would not allow them to affect the time he had with Christian, however long that might be.

"Then I did the right thing by sending him to the market," Christian replied with a relieved sigh. He did not want to cause tension between Teodoro and his son, not when he could see how important they were to each other, not when Esteban had rapidly become so important to him as well. "Gerrard went with him, to help him find you a new sword and dagger."

Teodoro's head snapped up at Christian's words. "To do *what*?" The knowledge that Gerrard's departure left Christian unguarded was less disturbing than the idea of being dependent on Christian to replace his weapons. He knew he would need to acquire a new sword and dagger soon, for Christian's protection as well as his own livelihood, but he had hoped to make some arrangement with Raúl. That Christian had stepped in before he could do so in no way filled him with gratitude. "There is no need. I prefer to acquire my own weapons."

"They've already left," Christian replied with a shrug, sliding his hand down Teodoro's arm to take his hand. "If you don't like what Gerrard brings back, that's fine. We'll look for something else, but Esteban said he knew where you'd gotten your last sword. Surely they'll have something that meets your exacting standards."

"And how is Esteban to pay for this sword?" Teodoro asked shortly, knowing to a *reale* how much money he had to his name—not enough to cover the cost of a decent *daga izquierda*, let alone a length of good Toledo steel.

"He still has my purse from Saturday, when I sent him to buy me new clothes so I could bluff the archbishop. There's enough in there for a sword for you," Christian said, tugging gently on Teodoro's hand. "You don't need to worry about Esteban. Come back to bed."

"I am not an invalid to lie in bed all day." Teodoro refused to concede to the pain in his joints and back.

"I think you proved that quite well last night," Christian retorted. "I was rather hoping you'd be interested in proving it again."

Despite his irritation, Christian's suggestive comment, and the seductive tone in which he delivered it, sent a wave of heat through Teodoro. How could he wish to ravish his lover and to throttle him at the same time? But however strong the desire that tempted him to take Christian to bed and forget everything but the pleasure they could bring one another, his pride would not allow him to let the matter go.

"Before we attempt to demonstrate my recovery, there is something you must understand." Teodoro pushed to his feet, his brown eyes smoldering as they met Christian's. "I earn my living by my sword. I am not always proud of the things I have taken pay to do, but I had not only myself to provide for, but Esteban as well, and so I have done what I must."

"Of course you have." Christian wondered why Teodoro felt the need to point out to him something he had known from the first days of their acquaintance. "I have always known that, but don't you see? Those days are over now. You don't have to worry about money anymore."

"No!" Teodoro insisted, his eyes flashing in anger. "You cannot simply toss your purse at me and expect me to thank you for it!"

Christian stared at Teodoro, flabbergasted. They had had this conversation once before, and he had thought the issue resolved. Apparently he had been wrong. "Is that what you think I'm doing?" His own anger began to flare. "I can't change the way we met, nor would I if I could. I can't change our pasts or even our relative fortunes, and I won't pretend to be something I'm not. You told me you would take such help as I could offer, told me you would let me be a partner to you, not another charge, yet the first time I do just that, you slap me down as if I've done something wrong. Make up your mind."

"Partners?" Teodoro growled. "I do not recall you asking whether I wished you to provide me with a sword. You simply informed me and expect me to be grateful for your munificence."

Christian's temper flared again. "And if I had come up and discussed it with you, would you have accepted? Or would we still be arguing over money and wasting time that Gerrard is now using to find you a sword?" He ran his hands through his hair and sighed when Teodoro did not answer him right away. He had the sinking feeling his dreams were slipping through his fingers like so much sand through an hourglass. His pride, his anger didn't matter when compared with what he hoped to gain. Letting them go, he looked up and met Teodoro's eyes.

"I know you're a proud man," he added more softly, "and it's one of the many things I love about you, but if we're to have any hope of building a life together, we have to resolve this. Tell me what would make it better. Would it truly help if I gave up my fortune?"

"I would not have you give up anything." Teodoro's own anger faded at the sorrowful note in Christian's voice. The words of love, of building a life together, bolstered his spirit, though this argument only emphasized the gulf between their worlds. "Your generosity is but proof of your kindness of heart. But you have never known what it is not to have whatever you desire immediately at hand, so perhaps you cannot understand how difficult it is for one who has labored for everything he owns to accept that generosity without feeling lessened." He frowned, covering Christian's hand with his as he struggled to make him understand. "What do I bring to this partnership you seek, when I cannot even serve as your protector? What can I offer you in return?"

Christian stared at Teodoro in silence for a moment. Did he not know, not realize...? "You really don't see what you give me, do you?" he whispered in amazement. "Teodoro, you give me so much more than mere coin could buy, even all the gold in the king's treasury. You believe in me. Every time you touch me, every time you look at me, I feel like I can do anything, be anything. I told you how my father views me, how Gerrard saw me. You're the only one who has ever believed in me, and that gave me the strength to challenge the Inquisition for you rather than cower helplessly, to face down the guards to save your friend rather than let him go to certain death. Don't you see what that means to me? With you at my side, I might actually *be* a powerful man. Without you, I'm exactly what my father fears I'll amount to: nothing. My money is nothing compared to what you give me, because what you give me, no amount of money could ever buy. It comes from you and you alone: your faith in me."

Stunned by Christian's words, Teodoro lifted a hand to his lover's cheek, tracing the smooth jawline and trimmed goatee with his abraded knuckles. "How can you doubt your strength?" he asked, his pride forgotten in the need to make Christian see himself for the man he was, not the man his father and his life until now had taught him to believe he was. "It is as obvious as your beauty and of far greater worth than all your gold."

"You are the only one who has ever looked beyond my beauty to see it," Christian reminded him, leaning into the gentle caress. "Your belief in me brings it out because I want to be the man you see when you look at me, a man who might be worthy of your time, your regard, your love."

"Tienes mi amor." Teodoro closed the space between them to claim Christian's lips, the kiss as much a promise as his words. "It is I who fear I am not worthy of you."

Christian leaned into the kiss, relieved the argument seemed to be over. "Perhaps that is a debate we could save for another time?" he teased gently. "I can think of a far better way to spend our morning alone."

"As can I." Teodoro followed the curve of Christian's neck to his bare chest with his hand. He was sure there were still issues of importance they needed to discuss, but he was finding them harder to remember as he felt Christian quiver beneath his touch, as he watched his ruddy nipples tighten at the mere approach of his hand.

"Come to bed, *mi amor*," Christian urged, leaning into the questing fingers. "We will both be more comfortable there." He mimicked Teodoro's gesture, easing beneath the ends of the bandages to slide through the curls on Teodoro's chest, seeking taut flesh. Smiling seductively, he took a step back toward the bedroom, then another, waiting to see if Teodoro would follow.

Pausing only to confirm that the door was bolted, Teodoro turned to the bedroom, his eyes holding Christian's as he enticed him, the sultry azure gaze promising much more than mere comfort. As he reached Teodoro's bed, Christian was already working the fastenings of his breeches, leaving him bare for Teodoro's hungry stare. His gaze swept from the still sleep-tousled golden hair crowning Christian's face, down his graceful neck, strong torso, slender flanks, and long legs and up again, pausing at the unmistakable evidence of Christian's desire. "Hermoso," he murmured, stalking forward with a predatory stride.

Smile still in place, Christian lay back across the bed. "What are you waiting for?" he teased huskily when Teodoro did not immediately undress. "An invitation? Or were you hoping I'd do it for you?" He stroked across his abdomen, brushing under the tip of his swelling cock, lifting it slightly, issuing the invitation in case Teodoro needed more incentive.

Teodoro kicked off his breeches, hissing slightly at the reminder of stiff muscles. Moving more carefully, he knelt on the bed, cradling Christian's hips in his hands as he bent forward to lick the head of the slender shaft, unable to resist what was so clearly being offered. Savoring the salty tang, he moved upward, his lips following the trail of hair that arrowed up Christian's abdomen.

"Don't tease," Christian pleaded, quivering under Teodoro's amorous assault, the rasp of his moustache only heightening the sensation. He tangled his fingers in Teodoro's shaggy hair, needing the connection amidst the waves of sensation rocking him.

Dipping his tongue into the sweet declivity of Christian's navel, Teodoro shook his head, scraping his stubble over the smooth flesh. "I dreamed of this all the time we were apart," he rejoined, circling the tiny pucker, sliding his hands below Christian's buttocks to lift him into the kiss. The weight was too much for his weakened arms to support for long, and with a muttered curse, he lowered Christian back to the mattress, mouthing a moist path up the planes of his chest. When he reached a ripe nipple, he let his breath caress it, coasting his palms up Christian's torso until he could tease the pebbled nubs with his thumbs.

Christian gasped at the tickling sensation of Teodoro's moustache against his chest, lifting into the kiss. When he felt Teodoro's muscles give out, an idea struck him even as he arched into the callused fingers. Scooting over to make room for Teodoro on the bed beside him, Christian patted the mattress. "Lie down," he suggested, wanting to be able to reach more than just Teodoro's head and battered shoulders.

Though he could not admit it, Teodoro was grateful to ease onto his side, taking the weight off his swollen joints. As soon as he had settled, he reached for Christian, frowning as Christian pulled out of his reach. "Come back here," he growled impatiently. "I'm not done with you yet."

"I'm not going anywhere," Christian soothed, shifting so his feet brushed the headboard. "I simply want to be able to touch you as well." He lowered his head and brushed his lips across Teodoro's belly. "You wouldn't deny me that, would you?"

Teodoro gasped, his cock leaping when Christian's mouth opened against his stomach. "I can deny you nothing," he asserted, drawing Christian's hips closer to nuzzle the tawny curls surrounding the base of his shaft, now easily within reach of his hands and his mouth. Taking his time, he explored the gracefully curved length with his lips and tongue, bathing every inch in moisture, capturing the pearls of fluid that seeped from the smooth tip.

Christian cocked his knee, opening himself to Teodoro's hands and lips, wanting to give him complete access. He consciously refrained from rocking his hips into Teodoro's mouth, not wishing to choke him. He couldn't, however, stop the hiss of delight that escaped his lips at finally feeling the brush of Teodoro's silky moustache against his most sensitive skin. "Teo," he moaned in encouragement.

Spurred on by Christian's sounds of enjoyment, Teodoro parted his lips, letting the head of the shaft slide into his mouth, teasing back the foreskin with his tongue, tracing the slit to coax out more of the milky fluid. With each breath he slid lower, taking in more of the length, cupping the pendant sac in a large palm. As Christian's moans deepened, he drew his teeth gently over the taut skin, easing back and then down again, and again, until Christian was writhing against him.

Determined to give as much pleasure as he was receiving, Christian dipped his head as well, mimicking the gestures Teodoro bestowed on him, licking and sucking, working his tongue along the sensitive vein on the underside of Teodoro's cock. He reached around Teodoro's hips, closing over the firm flesh of his buttocks, kneading provocatively as he urged him to thrust deeper into his mouth.

Rocking into Christian's caress, Teodoro couldn't hold back a deep groan as he pushed into the warm friction of his mouth. Letting all his concerns about their future together dissipate, he gave in to the emotions driving him and the desire he had held in check for so long. Taking Christian's cock in hand, he moved his lips lower, first laving and then sucking the loose skin of his sac, taking each globe into his mouth in turn, relishing the musky taste. Letting the taut flesh slide from his lips, he tongued the sensitive skin behind it, stroking Christian as he parted his lover's cheeks with his other hand, his moustache brushing either side as he licked down the crease.

Christian quivered with delight as he realized Teodoro's intention. He tightened his grip on Teodoro's hips, working his mouth with even greater enthusiasm along the length of his cock. He dared not reciprocate this particular caress, not sure Teodoro would accept it, but that did not stop him from tracing his fingers along the divide between the muscular cheeks as he swallowed the length of Teodoro's erection.

His pride swelling at Christian's responsiveness, Teodoro found the target he sought at the same moment Christian slid his fingers between his buttocks. Wetting the small portal well, Teodoro sucked it lightly before breaching it with his tongue, stroking inside with the same sure rhythm of his hand over Christian's shaft. His own fever rising as Christian's mouth enveloped him, he pressed deeper, needing to assure his lover's pleasure before capitulating to his own.

Christian moaned around the thick shaft in his mouth at the feeling of Teodoro's agile tongue working its way inside him. His body ached for release, and he knew it wouldn't take much more. Not quite ready to succumb, though, he concentrated on increasing Teodoro's pleasure, bobbing his head slightly to keep a constant pressure on the tip of Teodoro's cock. Emboldened by his passion, he dipped his fingers a little deeper into the sweaty crease, barely brushing the tight entrance. He made no move to penetrate the tiny ingress, nor would he without discussing it with Teodoro first, but he knew how pleasurable attention to even the outer ring could be.

Even the lightest touch of Christian's fingers was enough to nearly snap Teodoro's tenuous control. Responding in kind, he traced a fingertip around Christian's rippled entrance, his lips twitching in a slight smile as it clenched around his probing tongue. Gently, he worked the callused digit inside the damp passage, careful not to cause Christian pain. The long finger could reach where his tongue could not, and he rubbed the small nub of nerves at the same time he caressed the head of Christian's cock with his thumb, willing him to come.

The friction against his sweet spot destroyed what little remained of Christian's control. With a muffled shout around Teodoro's cock, he came hard, the creamy fluid splattering over his hand and chest, staining the ends of the bandages. He swallowed hard, hoping it would be enough to trigger Teodoro's climax in return.

Christian's release was the catalyst Teodoro had waited for, the convulsive tightening of his lover's mouth around his cock setting off his own explosive orgasm. Arching deep into the moist heat as he came, the involuntary thrust of his hips allowed the tip of Christian's finger to penetrate him, prolonging the waves of ecstasy that washed through him.

Teodoro's release hit Christian's tongue in wave after hot wave, filling his mouth as he tried to swallow it all. The movement of Teodoro's hips caught him off guard, his finger slipping inside past the clenching muscle, the tight heat spawning images of replacing his digit with another, more sensitive appendage. He groaned at the thought, his cock twitching dryly as he imagined what it would feel like. Reminding himself not to ask for more than Teodoro would be willing to give, he turned his attention to cleaning his lover's shaft.

Sated and drained, Teodoro sank back to the mattress, lifting his hand to his lips to savor the taste of Christian's release. Seeing Christian watching him, he beckoned him to return to his embrace. "Come here," he murmured. "Let me hold you until the others return."

Swiftly Christian shifted so he could settle Teodoro against his chest, nuzzling his neck tenderly. "Te amo," he whispered as he draped his arms around Teodoro, trying to position them so they would not cause any additional pain.

"Siempre." Teodoro's eyelids drifted closed as he fell into peaceful sleep.

SEVENTEEN

EAGER TO show Teo the new garments he had purchased and to tell him about the sword he and Señor Hawkins had selected for him, Esteban pushed open the door to his guardian's bedroom, his arms full of clothing. The sight that met his eyes made him stop in the doorway, his words of greeting dying on his lips. Teodoro lay on his side, Christian drawn against him, their arms and legs intertwined with each other and the rumpled bedsheets in an unmistakably intimate embrace. Esteban stared for a moment, stunned by the steady rise and fall of the two men's breathing; then he realized what he was seeing and backed away silently, dropping the garments on the table in the common room and moving uncertainly to the apartment's small window.

There had been rare occasions when Teo had brought home women. Esteban knew too, though Teo thought he did not, of the arrangement Teo had with Aldonza de la Cerda to provide protection at the brothel when funds were low. He was not child enough to still be ignorant of a man's needs. His heart told him that what he had just seen was different. He had felt it, the emotion growing between Teodoro and Christian, without needing the confirmation he had just seen to understand the threat. Gazing out the window at the dusty street below, he wondered how he would support himself when Teo left or asked him to go.

The sound of a door closing roused Christian from his slumber. Taking care not to disturb Teodoro, who definitely needed the rest, he slid from the bed and into breeches and a loose shirt. Walking into the other room, he found Esteban standing by the window. "Did you get what we needed?" he asked softly, keeping his voice down so he wouldn't wake Teodoro.

"Sí," Esteban answered without turning, nodding toward the garments on the table. "A sword and dagger too—we have to go back to get them once they are sharpened."

"Good," Christian declared. "We'll give them to Teo when he wakes up." He examined the clothes on the table, approving the quality and workmanship. They were good clothes, but not so fine that Teodoro would feel uncomfortable wearing them. "You know him well," he observed. "He'll like these, I think."

"Sí," Esteban repeated dully, thinking back on his life with Teo. He had never doubted that once he was old enough, he would join Teo in his adventures, fighting at his side—now he felt lost, unsure what the future would hold for him. He could not return to the sleepy rural village where he was born; nor could he imagine remaining with his *tío* Inocencio without Teo. Swallowing down the fear that threatened to choke him—after all, hadn't Teo been just a little older than Esteban was now when he first joined *la compañia del Castillo*?—he cast his mind for some means to make his way on his own.

Christian frowned at the curt answer. Usually Esteban was much more talkative. "Did something happen in the market?" he asked, wondering what was bothering the youth.

"No, nothing," Esteban replied, knowing he was being rude but unable to summon the energy to care. Suddenly he couldn't stand to remain with Christian while his guardian—his *former* guardian—slept. "I think I will go see if any of my friends are about," he muttered, turning from the window toward the door to the stairs.

"Esteban, wait, please," Christian asked, cursing his sleep-fuddled brain for not letting him figure out the puzzle in front of him. "Something is bothering you, and it wasn't when you left to go shopping. Teodoro said he talked to you and that everything was all right, but it's not. Tell me what's wrong, please. Maybe I can help."

"Nothing is wrong," Esteban insisted. "I am glad Teo found someone to make him happy."

"I'd like to think I make him happy," Christian admitted softly. "He certainly makes me that way, but he wouldn't be happy if he thought you'd run out of here upset without talking to one of us about it." He paused and considered the situation for a moment, trying to see it from Esteban's perspective. "Is that the problem? Are you afraid that now that he's found me, he won't want you anymore?"

"Neither of you will want me around, will you?" Esteban asked, fighting not to lose control of his emotions in front of Christian. "I'm not a child. You don't have to pretend in front of me. I know I will have to leave."

Christian frowned. "What gave you that idea? Did Teodoro say something to you to make you think he felt that way? I'll admit we haven't talked much about the future, but I can't see him abandoning you like that. I know I won't. You mean too much to me, to both of us. I don't know what I would have done without you this week, Esteban, and that's not going to change just because Teo is out of prison." He shrugged a little. "Spain may not be the safest place for any of us given how often we've thwarted *el conde* over the past few weeks, but whatever we decide to do, we will decide it together, all three of us, as a family. Unless you don't want to be around us now that you know?"

"No!" Esteban protested quickly. "I mean—you—he—I did not think you would want me around." He did not think Teo would send him away on his own, but he had been sure Christian would not want him to stay; far less had he expected to be offered any say in their decisions. Embarrassed at having misjudged the *vizconde* so badly, he dropped his eyes to his feet in awkward silence.

"I'm sorry if I made you feel that way," Christian replied. "I certainly never meant to. You were my rock this week, and I'd like to think we've become friends since I got here." He held out his hand, palm up, an invitation and a gesture of peace. "Amigos?"

"Amigos," Esteban agreed shyly, taking Christian's outstretched hand. He had expected a soft, pampered grip, but Christian clasped his hand strongly and reached for his shoulder with the other, the sincerity of his words made manifest in his embrace.

The absence of Christian's warmth and the muted sound of voices awoke Teodoro. After pulling on his breeches, he stopped in the entry to the common room, a small smile playing over his face as he watched his son and his lover assert their friendship. "I suppose I must now guard against the two of you conspiring together," he observed, leaning against the door frame.

"Only if you try to separate us." Christian's gaze raked over Teodoro's form, observing the lessened swelling in his shoulders. "Are you sure you should be up?" He didn't want to coddle Teodoro unnecessarily, but he also knew he would need to be in better shape than this if they had to deal with any new threat from the *conde*.

"The bed is empty without you," Teodoro murmured, moving forward until he could place an arm around both Christian and Esteban. While he would not embarrass Christian in front of Esteban, neither would he hide what he felt for the one who had captured his heart. They would still need to face some hard decisions, but hearing Christian declare he would not leave either of them had done much to ease the doubts that still assailed him.

Still feeling a little shy in the face of all the revelations of the past few hours, Esteban peeked up at Teodoro nonetheless, seeing the emotion in his eyes. "You can kiss him if you want," he murmured, his gaze dropping as a flush spread over his cheeks. "I don't mind, and I won't tell anybody. I promise."

Squeezing Esteban's shoulder, Teodoro ruffled his hair before turning to Christian and taking his lips in a kiss of tenderness and promise. "Te adoro," he murmured, softly enough for only Christian to hear.

Christian returned the embrace in the spirit it was offered, leaning into Teodoro with all the love in his heart. He was careful, though, not to release Esteban's hand, not wanting the boy to feel dismissed. The whispered words of love elated him, making him wish they were alone so he could show Teodoro how he felt, but there would be time for that later, when doing so would not risk alienating the youngest member of their family. Pulling back before he lost all control, Christian smiled at Esteban, grateful not to have to hide his feelings any longer. "Do you want to show Teo what you bought him?" he suggested to Esteban, knowing that if he didn't put some space between himself and Teodoro, he couldn't be responsible for his actions.

Mindful of their earlier conversation, Teodoro bit back his uneasiness at being dependent on Christian's largesse and complimented Esteban on the shirt, breeches, jerkin, and boots he had selected.

"We purchased a sword and dagger too. The merchant remembered you and promised to have them sharpened and ready before dinnertime," Esteban added. "Señor Hawkins said he had never seen so many fine swords before. I am sure you will be pleased with the one we picked for you."

"I am certain you chose well," Teodoro agreed, his words underscored by a loud rumble from his stomach. "It seems I still have several missed meals to make up for," he added with a twist of his lips. "Perhaps you could add to your usefulness by fetching us some luncheon?"

RAÚL KNOCKED as he waited at the head of the stairs, alerting the inhabitants of the apartments to his presence. He looked at the man leaning against the wall, his chest heaving with the effort it had taken to get there. "A few moments more," he assured Javier, "and you can rest again."

"I must rebuild my strength," Javier insisted, though his voice shook slightly as he fought to catch his breath. "You have been more than kind to take a stranger under your care. I cannot continue to impose on you."

"You helped Teodoro in prison," Raúl replied simply. "That makes you far more than a stranger and deserving of any help I can give you." The door opened before he could say more, Esteban appearing in the doorway. "Ah, *mijo*, you remember Javier. I think he'd like to see your father, if you can help him inside."

Esteban smiled and stepped into the hallway, offering his arm to the older man. "Señor Montega," he said with a slight bow, "won't you come in?"

"Gracias." He gave a small, stiff bow in return before taking Esteban's arm. "Are you Teodoro's son?"

"Sí," Esteban replied. Javier might have aided Teo, but no one other than *tío* Inocencio, Raúl, and now Christian knew that was not the full truth. "I helped Raúl take care of you last night, but I don't think you were awake enough to remember. Thank you for taking care of Teo in prison." Esteban could tell by Javier's raised eyebrows that he wondered at what he no doubt considered a lack of filial respect. "Teo made me promise to call him by name when I was old enough to understand. He said being called *padre* made him feel too old."

"He saved my life. I won't return the favor by criticizing how he raised his son. And he tended to me first, teaching me the way of it on my own shoulder," Javier admitted, suspecting his new friend would not have boasted of his own acts of compassion. "Helping him in return was the least I could do to repay him."

Esteban shrugged. It didn't matter whose kindness had come first. Teo considered the señor a friend, and that was all that mattered to Esteban. "Come and sit down," he insisted, walking slowly so as not to strain Javier's strength. He had spent enough time watching Christian help Teo that he thought he knew what to do now. As soon as he had Señor Montega settled at the table, he looked at Raúl, sprawled comfortably on a nearby chair. "Teo is resting," he said as evenly as he could, "and Cristian is... with him. Shall I go get them?" He could not stop the blush that stained his cheeks as he remembered the sight that had met his eyes the last time he had opened the bedroom door.

"I'll wake them," Raúl replied, rising from his seat and starting toward the door.

"No," Esteban pleaded, but he subsided when Raúl's gaze met his.

"It's all right, *mijo*. Teo and I have no secrets from one another," Raúl assured him, pleased to see that Esteban's protective attitude extended now to Christian as well.

Javier saw Esteban glance at him uneasily and smiled in reassurance. "Your father saved my life," he said softly. "He did not ask for proof of my innocence before helping me. I will not condemn him for his choice of companions—he could be guilty of a hundred worse acts, and I would still owe him my loyalty and respect."

Raúl's smile widened as he stepped into the bedroom. It seemed Teodoro's knack for winning the hearts of those around him had not failed him. His gaze softened as it landed on the sight before him, the two men wrapped tightly around each other, the sheet kicked down to their feet. Their shirts lay on the floor, but their breeches remained in place. Chuckling slightly, he rested a hand on Teodoro's foot. "Is *el inglés* teaching you modesty?" he teased when Teodoro's eyes opened immediately.

"I'm still too damned weak to do more than sleep," Teodoro grumbled. "This time," he added, a warm smile playing at the corners of his lips as he watched Christian's eyelashes flutter against his cheek, their voices beginning to waken him.

Reluctant to wake, Christian buried his face in the crook of Teodoro's neck, not wanting to slip out of the dream he'd been having, the dream of Teodoro hale again, making love to him without limits. "Don' go," he mumbled sleepily, feeling Teodoro shift as if to move away.

"Raúl is here," Teodoro murmured, pressing a kiss to Christian's burnished curls before tilting his head up to brush his lips. "I must speak with him." His lips against Christian's ear, he whispered a salacious promise for later in the evening before forcing himself to pull from the tempting embrace.

Christian groaned at Teodoro's words, his cock thickening eagerly. He tried to settle back into the pillows, but it was pointless, he decided quickly. He wouldn't be able to rest again so soon without Teodoro's arms around him. Grousing under his breath, he sat up and pulled a shirt over his head. "So what have you learned?" he asked Raúl.

"Why don't we go back in the other room?" Raúl suggested rather than answering right away. "I think Javier would feel much more comfortable once he's seen for himself that his friend is also on the mend."

Shrugging the new shirt Esteban had brought over his bandaged shoulders, Teodoro walked into the common room to greet his companion. "I am glad to see you are doing better, my friend," he said, clasping Javier's hand. "We did not know if you had family in the city to inform of your freedom."

"Those who resided in Madrid have already fled or been taken," Javier replied grimly. "I would not know how to reach any of them, if they still live."

"Are there others?" Raúl suggested. "Perhaps out of town, where you would be safe?"

"Perhaps," Javier said hesitantly, "though I do not know if any place can be called 'safe' any longer when one can be denounced without proof or even knowing who one's accuser is. And *el conde* de la Rocha is not known to be tolerant of suspected heretics living on his estates."

Around the table, the other men's faces grew grim. "So you too have had dealings with *el conde*," Raúl observed, glancing at Teodoro to see if he considered it safe to talk in front of Montega.

"I think Javier has proven that he cannot be forced to speak against his will," Teodoro replied dryly. "But perhaps you are not so eager to risk your life again by becoming entangled in our concerns. I will not fault you for telling me a second time that you do wish not to hear any more."

"I have never heard anything good of *el conde* de la Rocha," Javier admitted. "Certainly he never treated my relations who farmed his lands with anything but contempt. I owe you my life—if there is anything I can do to repay that debt, you have my word I will assist you."

"How well do you know de la Rocha's estate?" Raúl asked, thinking of the tidbit of information he had gleaned that afternoon. "*El conde* has extended an invitation to the king for the treaty negotiations to be concluded there."

Teodoro's dark eyes met Raúl's lighter ones in understanding. "Thus bringing both sets of negotiators within his purview," he murmured. "There can be little doubt left that de la Rocha is St. Denys's partner in conspiracy."

Raúl nodded. "The negotiators won't be leaving the city immediately. I don't know if I can learn anything useful by visiting *el conde*'s estate before they arrive, but it seems worth a try."

"I grew up on my grandparents' farm before my parents moved to Madrid," Javier replied. "My grandmother used to bring vegetables to the cook at *el conde*'s estate, and I would drive the cart for her when I was old enough. I have even been inside the *pazo* itself—once, when *el conde* was at court, I snuck inside while my grandmother was visiting with her friend."

Raúl's gaze sharpened, and he began to ask questions about the land surrounding the estate, the outbuildings, the entrances, drawing out every detail Javier could remember and storing it all away to use in his own attempt to get inside the house. When he was convinced he knew everything Javier did, he leaned back in the chair. "I'll tend your back before I leave," he told Teodoro, "but you'll have to make do with Cristian's tender care for the next several days."

"That is no hardship, but I do not like the idea of you going there alone," Teodoro protested. "If anything goes wrong, we would have no way of knowing, and you would have no one to assist you. Perhaps it would be wise to wait a few days."

"A few days will not make that much difference in your condition," Raúl pointed out reasonably, "and in that time, *el conde* could well have returned to his estate. This will only work if he is not in residence when I arrive."

"You could take Gerrard with you," Christian suggested. "At least that way you wouldn't be going alone and unprotected."

Raúl rolled his eyes. "What is it with you *payos*? You think that because you can't go with me, I will have to go alone. I'm not stupid, as you well know, Teodoro. I won't take unnecessary risks, and I won't leave myself open to de la Rocha's treachery. I am hardly the only Rom in Madrid, after all."

He rose, effectively ending the conversation, and moved to stand behind Teodoro. "Take your shirt off," he directed. "I want to check your back one more time before I leave."

Recognizing a battle it would be impossible to win, Teodoro shrugged off his shirt, baring his torso. The twinges of pain as Raúl eased the bandages off reminded Teodoro that he was not the only one recovering from the Inquisition's depredations. "If Raúl leaves, are you recovered enough to manage alone?" he asked Javier.

"I will be fine," Javier insisted, determined not to add to his new friends' burdens.

"I could come and help you," Esteban offered softly, even though a part of him did not want to interfere in the adults' conversation. This was something he could do, though, to help against the *conde* and to give Teodoro some privacy over the next few days. "I'm not Raúl, but I can at least change your bandages and keep an eye out for infection. I've learned a few things about treating wounds from him and Teo." He kept his gaze firmly fixed on the newest arrival, not daring to meet Teodoro's eyes as he spoke.

"Esteban," Teodoro protested, "it is not safe for you to be alone." He knew Esteban was offering them privacy, and as much as he longed to take advantage of the gift his son was proffering, he could not risk exposing the boy to de la Rocha's perfidy.

"We've been careful," Raúl reminded Teodoro, spreading a fresh poultice across the stripes on his back. "My name hasn't been connected at all with your investigations. He is probably safer with Javier in my rooms than he is here with you, especially right now." He leaned closer so that only Teodoro heard his next words. "Accept his generosity. It is a huge step for him to offer it."

Teodoro acknowledged that, though it went against his every instinct to leave Esteban unprotected. "You must not leave Raúl's rooms unless it is an emergency, and then only to come here to us," he ordered as Raúl tied clean bandaging around his chest.

"Teo," Christian scolded gently, though he understood his qualms, "Esteban is hardly a child who needs to be reminded of every little precaution. You can trust him not to do anything reckless like exposing himself to danger unnecessarily. You've raised him well, you know."

Meeting Esteban's eyes with a rueful smile, Teodoro nodded. "It is hard to accept you are nearly a man," he admitted, the pride he felt clear in his voice, "when it points out how many years I carry myself."

After tying off the last of the bandages, Raúl patted Teodoro's shoulder reassuringly. "You forget what babes we were when we left for Flanders—or when we came home. Now, since all is settled here, I suggest you gather what you'll need, Esteban, and we can be off. I've done half of Cristian's work for him, but I rather imagine he'd prefer to be alone to finish it."

"Gracias." Javier extended his hand to Teodoro, recognizing the trust his new friend was placing in him. "I swear I will die before I let any harm come to the boy."

Teodoro clasped Javier's hand in return. "Regain your strength, my friend—we may yet have need of it."

Esteban stood quickly and gathered his spare clothes into a bundle. "I'm ready," he announced, moving to the door. Raúl's comment had reminded him again of his unstated reason for leaving the apartment for the next few days. As happy as he truly was for Teodoro and Christian, he was not quite ready to sleep in the room next to them, knowing what would surely transpire during the night.

Javier and Raúl both stood as well, then joined Esteban by the door. As they made their way out, Raúl turned back to Teodoro with a wink. "Don't overdo it while I'm gone. I will need you recovered soon, and you'll be no good to us if you've let your *inglés* tire you out." He shut the door behind him before Teodoro could reply.

Christian turned to Teodoro, a blush staining his cheeks again. "Have I tired you out, *querido?*" he asked, mostly teasing, though with an undercurrent of seriousness. "I wouldn't want to be responsible for making Raúl angry when he returns."

"Of course we must not make Raúl angry," Teodoro agreed, his voice lowering as his arm circled Christian's waist, drawing their bodies into alignment. "Perhaps we should return to bed, *mi amor.*"

Christian's smile lit up his face. "What a wonderful idea!" he purred, rubbing against Teodoro encouragingly.

TEODORO PACED from one side of the common room to the other, feeling the confines of the small space as he never had before. Pausing before the window, his gaze raked the street outside the parish residence once again, seeking in vain for a sign of Raúl's return. "He should be back by now," he muttered to himself, resuming his pacing.

Christian stood in the doorway with the tray of food Gerrard had fetched from the tavern for their dinner. Ever since Raúl had left for the country, Teodoro had been like this: restless, leery, edgy. Except when Christian distracted him. He'd found only two things that kept Teo's mind off Raúl's absence: trouncing Christian at chess in an attempt to teach him more than the basic movements of the pieces, and making Christian scream in ecstasy as he used his hands, lips, and moustache to drive him past the point of no return. Deciding dinner could wait, Christian put the tray on the table and set about distracting his lover. He crossed the room and wrapped his arms around Teodoro from behind, pleased when the contact between his chest and Teo's back did not elicit a flinch. He moved his hands slowly over Teodoro's abdomen, stroking invitingly. "Come to bed."

Leaning back willingly in Christian's embrace, Teodoro groaned softly at the slow, teasing touch. "We have scarcely left the bed for five days," he murmured, a hint of laughter in his voice as he shifted his stance to encourage the caress, rubbing against the growing arousal that prodded his backside. "I thought you wished me to eat to keep up my strength."

"You are much stronger than you were five days ago," Christian pointed out, as if resting was how they had spent their days. In truth, he had never been loved as Teodoro had loved him, and he looked forward to a lifetime of such care. "And we will eat. Later." He drew Teodoro toward the bedroom, already planning how to return some of the attention Teodoro had lavished on him despite his infirmities.

"I would eat now," Teodoro insisted, settling his mouth on the honeyed skin of Christian's neck as he let him lead them back to their bed. He moved his lips up the graceful throat, nipping between words as he spoke. "I find myself... very... hungry."

Christian tipped his head back, offering himself to Teodoro. "I shall have to see what I can do to... satisfy you," he teased, divesting Teodoro of his clothes easily, eagerly. After pushing gently until Teodoro sat on the bed, Christian straddled his hips and leaned forward. "What would you feast on this evening?"

Once he removed the obstruction of Christian's shirt, Teodoro tasted the bounty spread before him. "You never... fail to... satisfy me, *querido*," he asserted, closing his lips around a peaked nipple, savoring it as though it were the sweetest chocolate. Supporting Christian's back, he arched the willowy body, shifting it at his pleasure until he had sampled every bit of Christian's smooth chest.

Christian let Teodoro move him as he pleased, since Teo's pleasure always assured his own as well. Eventually, though, he found himself wanting more. Pulling back for a moment, he worked off his breeches, leaving him as naked as his lover. He moved to straddle Teodoro again, rubbing their groins together provocatively as he slid his hands over Teodoro's taut abdomen, enjoying the sensation of skin against skin.

Leaning back on his elbows to grant even more access to his body, Teodoro rocked his hips slowly, each motion brushing them together, soft hair against silky flesh. "Take what you wish," he murmured as Christian's hands slid lower, the boldness inciting his own heated response.

"What I wish?" Christian mused aloud, wondering if he dared ask for what he truly wanted. *Not tonight*, he decided. Tonight was about distracting Teodoro, not adding to his edginess. "What I wish is to feel you beneath me as I ride you, to feel your eyes on me as I take you inside me, as you stretch me and fill me like no one else has ever done." He leaned forward to grab the bottle of oil from the table near the bed. "Watch while I make us ready."

Teodoro captured Christian's mouth as it came within reach, moving his lips hungrily over the softness, dipping his tongue inside to tease at its counterpart before letting his head fall back. Watching from beneath hooded lids, Teodoro's gaze never left Christian as he poured the oil over his fingers, then reached behind himself, gliding his other hand over his abdomen as he breached himself with one slender digit.

Thrilled at Teodoro's acquiescence and emboldened by the desire on his face, Christian took his time, shunting his finger in and out of his passage slowly, seductively, while languidly stroking his cock. Eventually he added a second finger, stretching the entrance for Teodoro's girth. They had made love often enough in Raúl's absence that his muscles relaxed quickly. After withdrawing his fingers, he slicked Teodoro's erection and positioned it at his entrance. "Do you want me, *mi amor*?"

"Foolish question," Teodoro groaned as Christian's body opened for him and he sank down by agonizingly slow degrees, squeezing his cock in wet satin until he had taken him in completely. Bracing his hands on Christian's slender hipbones, he canted his pelvis slightly, watching his lover's mouth form an *O* of rapture as he shifted in the tight embrace. "I awake wanting you. I pass the day wanting you. I sleep and want you in my dreams." Each sentence was punctuated by a subtle movement and another blissful exhalation. "The only time I do not want you... is when... I am having you."

Christian shifted slightly in Teodoro's grip, angling his hips so his cock hit his bundle of nerves with each tiny thrust. "You don't want me now?" he teased, reveling in the thick length piercing him so lovingly. "Your body tells a different story." He leaned forward and licked Teodoro's taut nipples. "Your body says it wants me now most of all."

"Perhaps my body should speak for me, then," Teodoro rasped, unable to deny Christian's assertion. Pretty speeches were not his strength in any case—he much preferred action to words, but he had told Christian to take what he wished, and he would not retract that acquiescence. The kittenish laps at his nipples whetted his hunger to taste Christian in the same way, tempting him to flip them over so he could sate himself, but the vision of wantonness straddling him, hair tossing as Christian gasped at a particularly strong flex of Teodoro's hips, was a sight he wished to burn forever in his memory. Letting his head fall back, he watched Christian ride him from beneath lowered lids, allowing him to set the pace, using his thumbs to caress the muscles that bunched and jumped beneath his grip.

Christian undulated provocatively above Teodoro, intent on driving every thought out of their minds but this moment. A part of him never wanted it to end, wanted to stay as they were in that instant, bodies joined in the sultry summer evening, love and lust simmering in their eyes as they strove together to find the perfection of release, but the physical demands of the flesh were stronger than his will, pushing him closer and closer to the inevitable point of no return. He fought it with everything he had, with every ounce of experience, slowing his movements when he felt himself skating too close to the edge, focusing his attention outward, on Teodoro's needs, Teodoro's pleasure.

Teodoro fought to prevent himself from seizing control each time Christian eased his movements. He was no more eager than Christian for this moment of complete communion to end, but his body had other ideas, the heat in his blood growing more intense with each delay, until he felt as if he were again in the grip of a fever—one only the beautiful young man in his arms could meliorate. "Tesoro," he husked, biting his lip as the urge to thrust became almost unendurable. "Mi vida…."

Christian cried out at the tender words, his ability to hold back melting like butter in the heat of their combined passion. He closed one hand around his cock as he began to rock in earnest, driving them hard toward their release.

Letting go of a slender hip, Teodoro tugged Christian's hand away from his shaft, closing his own around it instead. His head dropping forward, he covered Christian's lips with his own, plunging his tongue deep into the beloved cavern, stroking in time with the urgent rhythm of their bodies as they strove at last for completion.

Christian might have had some hope of resisting his own caress, but the moment Teodoro's hand replaced his, control was a thing of the past. Combined with the potent aphrodisiac of Teodoro's lips, he lost the battle with his passions, his release spraying forth to cover Teodoro's hand and abdomen, his passage clenching tightly, rhythmically around the shaft that continued to plow deeply into him.

Teodoro gentled his hand but didn't still, letting the creamy fluid ease his strokes as the shuddering contractions around his cock brought him closer and closer to his own fulfillment. Breaking away from the kiss to draw a heaving breath, he leaned forward to guide Christian's head to his chest, the change in angle driving him just a fraction deeper, Christian's teeth closing around his nipple the last stimulus he needed to trigger his own shattering orgasm. Waves of sensation pounded through him as he emptied himself in what felt like an endless climax, until he had poured his very soul into his lover's keeping.

EIGHTEEN

ADJUSTING HER bodice so that it showed far more of her cleavage than she would ever leave visible outside her establishment, Aldonza de la Cerda climbed the stairs to see her favorite employee, even if he insisted he no longer needed the job. She knew Ciéza had been injured recently, but she hoped he would soon be well enough—and insolvent enough—to return to her bed. She missed his strength, his virility. None of her other occasional lovers satisfied her nearly as well. Rapping lightly on the door, she called softly for him. "Teodoro!"

Teodoro looked up from tending the new blade Esteban and the big Englishman, Hawkins, had obtained for him. Raúl was overdue to return from his scouting of the *conde* de la Rocha's country estate, but the gypsy had his own unique knock, and Teodoro was expecting no one else. Hawkins was supposed to be standing guard, but despite Christian's assertions, the bodyguard had yet to win Teodoro's full trust. He set the rag he'd been using to oil the blade on the table, rose, and crossed to the door, sword in hand. Surprised to hear Aldonza's voice, he set the blade against the wall and opened the door to the brothel keeper.

Stepping inside when the door opened, Aldonza glanced around, looking for Teodoro's son, not wanting the youth to interfere with her plans. Finding the room empty, she smiled, moving closer to Teodoro. "You have not come to see me again since your return to Madrid," she purred, running her hand up his arm from wrist to shoulder. "If I didn't know better, I might think you had grown tired of me. You haven't taken a new commission since then. Surely you could use the coin a night or two would earn you."

Before meeting Christian, Teodoro would not have hesitated to return the procuress's bold overture. While no longer the beauty she had been in her prime as one of the most sought-after courtesans in Madrid, Aldonza de la Cerda was still a desirable woman, and Teodoro had found it no hardship to share her bed. Now everything was different, but he could not afford to raise suspicions by spurning his former lover—nor did Aldonza deserve such treatment. She had always been more than generous to him, whether with employment or with her body, and he would not rebuff her harshly now that he no longer needed her for either.

"The last few weeks have been… difficult," he replied, removing her hand from his shoulder and bringing it to his lips with courtly charm.

Aldonza turned her hand in his, sliding it over his slightly stubbled cheek. "All the more reason for you to avail yourself of the ease I can offer," she scolded gently, draping her arms over his shoulders as she moved closer still, brushing provocatively against him. "Surely I could have relieved some of your tension."

Christian's eyes narrowed as he heard the harlot's words and watched the familiar way she touched his lover. He wanted to cross the room and tear her from Teodoro's arms, but he remembered his lectures on discretion and knew they applied to the woman as well as to anyone else other than Raúl and Esteban. He settled for clearing his throat loudly and striding into the room as if he had every right to be there. "Excuse me for interrupting," he said, an edge of sarcasm hardening his voice. A part of him wanted to put her in her place for daring to touch what was his, but he could hardly blame her for an attraction he felt as well. Then again, if her behavior and her attire were any indication, she was the type who didn't need attraction to bed a man. He wondered how she'd gotten upstairs when Gerrard was supposed to be guarding the stairs, but while his former bodyguard was proof against bribery, he had a terrible soft spot for women. "Perhaps I should go downstairs and give you some privacy."

His lips twitching beneath their heavy moustache, Teodoro tempered his response as he took a step back from the clinging brothel mistress. "That will not be necessary, Excellency," he countered, his hooded gaze sweeping over Christian's bare chest before returning his attention to Aldonza. "The English gentleman has run afoul of his companions and engaged my protection," he explained in a lowered voice, as if not wishing Christian to overhear. "We thought it best for him to disappear from their notice for the moment."

"I'm not sure you've been protecting him very well," Aldonza said coolly. Her eyes raked over the admittedly attractive form, settling shrewdly on a bruise on the noble's collarbone. She looked up at Teodoro sharply, experienced enough to recognize a bite mark when she saw one, but his face was its usual composed mask, revealing nothing. She was no ignorant miss, but Teodoro had been far too enthusiastic in her bed for him to be one of *those* men. The bruise surely had another origin, an injury of some sort. "How long will he be here? I've had problems for several nights without anyone to run off boisterous customers. I need your sword back at work."

"It will be some time before *I* have finished with Señor Ciéza de Vivar's sword," Christian interrupted haughtily. "And I'm quite sure you can't match my price, señora." He slurred the last word, turning the honorific into an insult.

Teodoro met Aldonza's gaze with a roll of his eye for the airs of nobility. "He's laid claim to my bedchamber," he murmured confidentially, in case she wondered at his charge's half-dressed state. "But the pay is sufficient to bear with his peccadillos."

"I know of more than one bed where you would be most welcome," Aldonza purred, pressing her breasts against his chest in silent invitation. "And I won't even charge you for it if you find a few hours to monitor my girls."

"*El inglés* demands my full attention, *preciosa*," Teodoro demurred with every evidence of regret. "Though I would be most… grateful… should his presence here remain unremarked until his departure."

"Grateful enough to return to work once he's gone?" Aldonza bargained. "Perhaps even to leave him in the care of the big man downstairs for an evening?"

All too aware he still had no assurance of what kind of life he and Christian could share, Teodoro refused to look beyond ending the *conde*'s threat. "Who knows what tomorrow will bring?" he answered with a shrug that implied much and promised nothing.

"I suppose I shall have to be satisfied with that," Aldonza complained, leaning up to kiss Teodoro before she left. If she could not talk him into her bed, she could perhaps seduce him there. He turned his head, though, so her lips only brushed his cheek.

"Gracias, preciosa," Teodoro said with a smile as he graciously ushered the proprietress out the door and into the hallway. Barring the door behind her, he turned to raise an eyebrow at his obviously jealous lover.

"Preciosa?" Christian hissed when the door shut behind the woman, stalking toward Teodoro. "Strumpet is more like it, draping herself all over you like you belonged to her." He backed Teodoro against the door. "She can't have you. You're mine." He brought their mouths together in a bruising kiss, his jealousy pushing him to stake his claim as he had never dared do before, invading Teodoro's mouth with his tongue, ravishing it forcefully as his emotions slipped his control and ran rampant through him. "Mine," he ground out again before renewing the embrace.

Deciding it would not be wise to acknowledge to Christian that both his statements concerning Aldonza had at one time been true, Teodoro remained silent and gave himself willingly to Christian's assault, the demanding kisses firing his blood in return. Tongues and teeth met and clashed in a near-brutal conflict that Teodoro answered with equal ferocity, pulling Christian against him to drag their erections together, proving his own hunger. "Sí, yours," Teodoro rasped when they broke apart finally to draw breath into heaving chests. "Tuyo nada más." Hopeful that Christian had burned off enough of his jealousy to hear his words, he pressed his bruised lips gently over the livid bite on Christian's shoulder. "Only you share my bed any longer. Only you bear my mark, which you flaunt so boldly without regard for the risk to which you expose us both." Judging from Christian's sudden gasp that he had not realized the danger of his action, he gentled his voice. "Only you are the one I love."

Teodoro's words acted like a splash of cold water on Christian's passions. The reassurances that he wanted—needed—to hear paled in comparison to the danger he had not even considered when he had stepped out of the bedroom, so caught in his jealousy that he had forgotten the mark Teodoro had left on him the night before. "I'm sorry." He caught Teodoro's face with his hands and met his eyes. "I didn't think…. All I could think about was her trying to entice you, and you not pulling away. I'll be more careful. I promise."

Shifting his legs to nestle Christian even closer between them, Teodoro combed a hand through his lover's tousled hair. "Aldonza has been very good to me," he admitted. "I owe her my gratitude and my respect." He traced the trimmed line of Christian's goatee, lingering to hover just below his lips. "And while I do not believe she would consciously betray us, she is not above gossip. A careless word to the wrong ears could imperil us both."

"I know," Christian replied, crestfallen. "I know better than to act without thinking, always, but especially here and in this situation. My father pounded that into my head from the time I was old enough to think. I guess it's a lesson I still need to learn. Maybe he's right about me after all."

Teodoro tightened his hand around Christian's chin, forcing it up to meet his implacable gaze. "He is *not* right about you, *querido*. That I am here to love you is proof of that." He lowered his head to Christian's lips, the kiss less fierce but no less impassioned, pouring all the love he could never find the words to express into his actions. "Come to bed, *mi corazón*."

It was a request Christian would never deny. How could he when he so desperately needed the reassurance implicit in Teodoro's words? If Teodoro still wanted him, he could not be as worthless as he sometimes felt. Nodding his agreement, he let Teodoro walk him into the bedroom, never releasing him from the tight embrace. Feeling his legs bump against the bed, he paused, wondering if he should reach for his breeches, or Teodoro's, or just wait for Teodoro to act.

It did not matter that Christian had shared Teodoro's bed every night—and most of the days—since he had been saved from the Inquisition. Teodoro would always marvel that such an image of perfection—young, noble, flawlessly handsome—should choose to offer himself to a grizzled mercenary such as he, but he had stopped protesting against his fortune. He would treasure it for as long as it was his to hold. After stripping the breeches from Christian's body, he eased him back onto the rumpled bedding, etching the vision of long, honeyed limbs and tumbled golden curls into his memory as he quickly dispensed with his own garments. Kneeling on the bed, he ran a worshipful hand down the lithe curves of Christian's chest. "Te amo," he murmured, bending to follow the same path with his lips.

Christian stared up at Teodoro's strong, handsome features, committing to memory every crease on the striking face, every line of the powerful body that moved over his. His breath caught in his throat as he imagined what the next minutes would bring. He and Teodoro had made love frequently since Teodoro's return from Toledo, but until now, Teodoro had been too weakened by the torture he had endured to support himself above Christian as they made love. That weakness seemed a thing of the past as Teodoro crouched above him, cherishing him with hands and lips. Christian's breath rushed out in a low moan as he imagined finally feeling Teodoro's frame bearing down on him, pressing him into the mattress, surrounding and protecting him. Then Teodoro's hips settled against his, and he groaned, reality even better than his fevered imaginings. "I love you too," he gasped, all other thought, all other words stripped from him by the inconceivable pleasure of Teodoro's weight atop him.

Days of learning his lover's body had taught Teodoro where Christian was most vulnerable to his touch, and he exploited that knowledge with callused hands and moist kisses, with the rough scrape of his tongue, the soft brush of his hair, the gentle nip of his teeth, every caress an avowal of desire and adoration. Days of loving eased his acceptance into Christian's body, the slow glide into welcoming flesh as much a spiritual union as a physical one. Teodoro gradually let his full weight settle onto Christian, let Christian's smooth skin cradle him, let Christian's strength support him. He moved in long, slow strokes, letting the passion build and spiral between them, never wanting this moment of communion to end.

The sensation of having Teodoro above him, in him, both surrounding and filling him, soothed the jagged edges of Christian's self-doubt. Surely such an amazing man would not love him unless he was worthy of it. He arched into the caresses, the kisses, the tickle of Teodoro's moustache, the hints of teeth, each an additional balm to his heart. As Teodoro slid inside him again, Christian let himself believe his words, his jealousy fading to nothing in the face of such trenchant desire. No one could love this way and still harbor thoughts of another. Meeting the leisurely, maddening strokes, he tightened his internal muscles, wanting to add to Teodoro's pleasure. He knew it would speed their climax, yet he could not hold back, desperate now for release, for that timeless moment when nothing existed but Teodoro and himself. Body tightening, rapture overtook him, and he cried Teo's name.

No sound was sweeter to Teodoro's ears than his name called out in Christian's impassioned voice, no victory more rewarding than seeing Christian's face transformed in bliss, feeling his body tighten and convulse around him. Stilling his motions as if he could stop time, he let Christian's ecstasy wash over him, through him, until his own enflamed senses could withstand no more. Still trembling with the intensity of his climax, he rolled to his side, keeping Christian wrapped in his embrace. "Never doubt yourself, *mi corazón*," he murmured hoarsely. "Never doubt my love for you."

Christian immediately regretted the loss of Teodoro's weight above him, but the loving embrace continued, and he moved with Teodoro, staying as close as they could possibly be. Looking up, he met Teodoro's dark eyes. "Keep reminding me," he said softly.

"Always," Teodoro promised, beginning to believe it might be possible, that somehow they would find a way to remain together even after the threat of the *conde* de la Rocha's machinations was ended. That thought reminded him they had still not seen or heard from Raúl, and that in turn drew him to sit up and reach for his breeches.

Seeing Teodoro rising from the bed, Christian sighed and sat up as well, deciding he should speak to Gerrard and see why he thought it acceptable to let Señora de la Cerda come upstairs. Once he'd pulled on his own breeches and shirt, he kissed Teodoro one more time because he simply couldn't resist and went to the door. "Gerrard!" he shouted down the steps. "Get up here!"

"Is something wrong?" Gerrard asked, hand on the hilt of his sword as he entered the room.

"I don't know," Christian said. "You tell me. A short time ago, we had a visitor, a somewhat importuning one at that, and I have to admit to some curiosity as to why you simply let her come upstairs without even accompanying her to make sure her presence was welcome."

"I—" A flush reddened Gerrard's cheeks. "She was—that is—she said Ciéza de Vivar worked for her. I didn't think she could do any harm."

"Fortunately, she didn't," Christian said, "but that doesn't mean she won't. She knows I'm here now, a fact that was mostly secret. If she chooses to bruit it about or even if she simply slips and mentions it in the wrong ear, we could well be the center of some unwelcome attention again."

"I'm sure she wouldn't—perhaps I should go speak to her," Gerrard offered.

"Take your purse," Teodoro advised wryly.

"My purse?" Gerrard asked, brow wrinkling in confusion.

"The señora runs a brothel," Christian said bluntly. "She'll give you as much of her attention as you can afford to pay for. Go if you want. Lock the outer door behind you if you do."

"Of course I'm not going to leave!" Gerrard protested. His hand moved from his sword to slide inside his doublet. "I nearly forgot," he added with another flush that left little doubt as to the cause of his forgetfulness. "The priest gave me this for you—it was delivered this morning." He handed a folded letter to Christian with an apologetic nod before returning to his post below stairs.

"I wonder why Don Inocencio didn't bring it up himself," Christian wondered aloud as he opened the letter. "We've been here the whole time."

Teodoro shrugged. "Perhaps it is just as well he did not," he murmured. "He might have heard something he would be best not suspecting."

Christian blushed as he remembered the passionate lovemaking they'd engaged in that morning. "It's your fault, you know," he teased. "You touch me and I forget everything else, including caution and decorum."

"It is acceptable to forget decorum but not caution," Teodoro warned. "Not until we have pulled *el conde*'s claws, in any case." He gestured to the missive still in Christian's hands. "Are you not going to read your letter?"

"As if I want to hear anything my father has to say," Christian muttered, having recognized the duke's bold scrawl. He scanned the text automatically, expecting it to be the same empty platitudes and admonishments that such epistles usually contained. The letter started the same as always, urging Christian to be careful, to stay out of sight and in the presence of someone who could protect him, but the second paragraph caught his eye.

"Look at this," he murmured softly. "Raúl had better hurry. According to my father, they're moving the negotiations to *el conde* de la Rocha's estate this weekend, and the king will be there to sign the treaty." He finished reading over the letter, crumpling it in his hand when his father ended by telling Christian that shortly he would no longer have any value as a bargaining tool and so could come out of hiding at last.

The reminder that Christian would soon have no further need of a protector no longer disturbed Teodoro as it would have once—the past days of recovery and lovemaking had done much to strengthen the belief that somehow he would retain a place in Christian's life. Of more concern was the intimation that events were quickly drawing to a confrontation. "It is no chance that the king will be there. De la Rocha must be planning to strike." He pulled Christian back against his chest, stroking his long hair. "We cannot wait for Raúl to return. I will have to find a way into *el conde*'s town house myself and hope to find some proof of his treachery."

Christian smoothed the parchment back out and read the pertinent words again. "The king won't arrive until this weekend according to my father," he observed. "It's only Wednesday. That gives us a couple of days before we have to act. You're much stronger than you were, but we can afford to give Raúl another day to return before going after *el conde.* I don't want anything to happen to you."

"We still do not know exactly what de la Rocha has planned," Teodoro protested. "We must hope to find something in his rooms to betray him—but even if we do not, to have any chance to forestall his plot, we must ride for his estate by Friday."

"Which means we could still search tomorrow night," Christian pointed out as reasonably as he could, fear for Teodoro's safety making him feel anything but rational. "We don't even know if *el conde* has left for his estate yet. If you try to search his town house tonight, you could well find him still resident and yourself back in prison. I got you out once, but it won't work a second time." He turned in Teodoro's embrace, tightening his arms around his torso. "I can't lose you."

Tilting Christian's face upward to brush his lips, Teodoro shook his head. "De la Rocha would surely want to see to arrangements for a royal visit personally," he countered. Seeing the stubbornness on Christian's face, he smiled wryly. "If it will ease your mind, perhaps your other watchdog can call upon *el conde*'s residence to confirm if he has left Madrid." His own expression resolved, Teodoro added, "But if he has gone, I will search his rooms tonight. We must have time to make plans if I find nothing."

Christian nodded slowly, appreciating the fact that Teodoro would discuss the issue with him rather than simply overruling him. "I'll go talk to Gerrard in a few minutes, then. And Raúl could still well return before nightfall." He did not mention that one way or another, he intended to accompany Teodoro on his search. There would be time for that argument later. "But if de la Rocha is still in town, promise me you'll wait until he leaves."

"I am not so rash as to press a frontal assault against one with *el conde*'s influence. Not until we have no other choice."

"Or incontrovertible proof," Christian added. "And then my father will have to accept that I'm more than just a helpless child to be protected."

It was more important for Christian to accept that himself, Teodoro mused, than anything his father believed. "No helpless child could have rescued two convicted men from the Inquisition," he observed, pushing up from the bed. "Let us send Hawkins off to *el conde*'s apartments so we can make our plans." He only hoped Raúl would return before they needed to leave Madrid.

THE SUN had just started its descent toward the horizon when a familiar knock sounded at the door. Christian jumped to his feet and rushed to the door, unlocking it and then swinging it wide. "You're back!" he exclaimed, seeing Raúl standing on the threshold, looking as unflappable as ever. "We were getting worried."

Raúl's smile was rakish as he stepped into the room and shut the door behind him. His gaze raked over Teodoro, searching for signs of renewed health. To his delight, everything he saw proclaimed his friend well on the road to recovery. "I am sorry," he replied with a bow of his head. "I was delayed."

"What did you learn?" Teodoro asked, no less relieved than Christian, if less demonstrative at his old friend's safe return.

"*El conde* arrived at his estate last night," Raúl informed them. "With the recommendations and introductions that Javier provided, I was able to leave several of my friends in de la Rocha's employ. Now all we have to do is find enough proof to hang the man."

"Then his town house should be empty but for servants," Teodoro said approvingly, confirming what Hawkins's visit had indicated. "A search may turn up something we can use against him."

"We will go as soon as it's dark," Raúl agreed.

"I'm going with you this time," Christian interrupted, marshalling his arguments for the inevitable discussion that would follow, but he refused to be left behind this time.

"Of course you are," Teodoro and Raúl both said at the same time. His moustache twitching with suppressed laughter at Christian's startled expression, Teodoro took his hand. "Raúl and I will both be able to search if you are standing guard for us," he explained.

Christian's gaze darted back and forth between the two men's faces, searching for any sign of doubt or condescension in their expressions, but he found only confidence and determination. "You'd trust me that much?" he asked in disbelief.

"Why wouldn't we?" Raúl asked simply. "You've more than proven yourself this past week. And the more quickly we can search, the more quickly we can return here to safety."

"Join us for dinner," Teodoro suggested. "We can get a meal at the tavern—it will be good to get out of these apartments and see what news we can gather." His eyes met Christian's as he spoke, trusting he would not hear his comment as a complaint of how they had spent their time while confined to his rooms.

"And then when we're done we should go by my rooms as well to check on Javier and Esteban. If I know your son, he'll be almost as worried as you were."

Christian followed the two men down the stairs, letting the banter between them wash over him as he invited Gerrard to join them for dinner. His mind spun with amazement as he considered their words to him in the past few minutes. He had been prepared to argue his case, to convince them—Teodoro, especially—that it would be far safer for him to accompany them than to stay at his lodging, but Teodoro had not even questioned his presence on their search. The reasons they gave, no matter how logical, were unimportant. All that mattered to him was their unquestioning acceptance of him at their side. No one had ever treated him that way before, as an equal rather than as a burden. Teodoro knew of his insecurities, but he had not spoken of them to Raúl, so the gypsy was certainly not humoring him by letting him come along. He didn't think Teodoro was either, honestly. His lover had proven far too protective of him in the past to have suddenly decided to indulge Christian. His acceptance had to be genuine. And that brought a smile to his lips.

Entering the common room of *la taberna Castellán*, Teodoro looked around for Beatriz as they took their seats at a back table that gave a clear view of the rest of the room. He lifted an eyebrow as he spotted Aldonza de la Cerda at another table, beckoning with a smile to the big bodyguard, Hawkins. He supposed he should not have been surprised— the *burdel* proprietress had always had an eye for attractive men. That it drew her attention from trying to entice Teodoro back into her bed was good; that Hawkins gave every appearance of returning her interest was even better, easing the pang of jealousy Teodoro felt when he considered that Hawkins, or anyone else, might once have been Christian's lover.

Raúl met Teodoro's gaze with a twinkle in his eye before turning to Christian. "Now I understand why Teodoro was able to spirit you away so easily," he teased the young *inglés* softly. "If your former protector wasn't any more diligent in Valencia, then bringing you here must have been child's play."

"I think he understands that I have a far better protector now than he could ever have been," Christian replied with complete seriousness, fighting the temptation to reach for Teodoro's hand beneath the table, "and so he lets himself relax in a way he would not if he didn't know Teodoro was here." He took in the scene with an indulgent smile, relieved to see that the procuress had apparently given up on pursuing the man at his side, at least for the moment. "She will entertain him far better than I could, that is certain," he added, hoping Teodoro would understand that while he and Gerrard had become good friends, they had never been anything more.

"Well, he will need to delay his entertainment a little longer, if he wishes to be fed this evening," Teodoro answered with a twitch of his lip, rising to capture the innkeeper's attention long enough to request their meal. He judged that Hawkins's purse would indeed be lighter before the night was over.

THE SOUND of a key turning in the lock thrilled Esteban. He had worried and fretted for days over Raúl's extended absence, with no one to share those concerns with. Javier did not know the gypsy, couldn't share his fears or his faith that somehow Raúl would still return. And with the wounded man in his care, Esteban could not seek out Teodoro for reassurance either. He therefore jumped to his feet in his excitement at seeing not only Raúl but Teo and Christian as well. "You're back!" he exclaimed, hugging Raúl impulsively before taking a step toward Teo. He hesitated for a moment, suddenly unsure of taking the same liberties he had as a child.

Teodoro stepped forward, clasping Esteban's shoulder in the same soldier's embrace he would offer Raúl. As hard as it was for him to believe, his son was no longer a child, but well on the way to becoming a man himself. *God help me, I've done my best by him, Margarita*, he thought, though he was sure the boy's mother would find as much to be proud of in her son as Teodoro did. Stepping back, he offered his hand to Javier, waving him back when the older man tried to rise from his seat at Raúl's curiously inlaid table. "You look better than the last time I saw you, my friend."

"Your son has insisted I do nothing but eat and sleep," Javier avowed with a smile for Esteban. "With such care as that, I could do nothing but get better."

"I tried to care for him as Raúl showed me," Esteban said, both honored and humbled that Teo had greeted him as a man—as an equal—and vowing to never do anything to forfeit that respect. "You look much better as well, Teo," he added with a smile, though his voice remained steady as he glanced over Teodoro's shoulder to meet Christian's amused gaze.

"You weren't the only one with specific orders from Raúl on how to care for a patient." Christian didn't add that his orders had been a little different than the ones Raúl gave Esteban. He didn't need to. He was quite sure no one in that room had any illusions about what his and Teodoro's relationship involved. And if that had Teodoro looking and feeling better, he saw no reason, here among friends, to be ashamed of it.

"Time is short if we are to pay a visit to *el conde* de la Rocha's residence tonight," Teodoro counseled, uncomfortable with the intimate tone of the conversation. Esteban knew how matters stood with Christian now, and he had no secrets from Raúl, but though he trusted Javier completely, he did not care to speak so openly before him. In any case, it was not safe for them to fall into the habit of showing their emotions for each other freely, even among friends. "Tell us what you learned at *el conde*'s country estate," he told Raúl as he pulled a chair from the table and straddled it.

Raúl flashed Teodoro a raffish grin that hinted at news of some import. With an inclusive wave of his hand, he gathered the others to the table, waiting for them to take their seats before he began. "*El conde* has a weakness, it seems."

NINETEEN

"WHAT IS it?" Christian asked, voicing the question on the minds of everyone in the room.

Raúl's grin broadened. "His vanity," he replied. "With his desire to impress the king, he has hired a number of new servants temporarily. Thanks to Javier's introductions, most of those men are my people. When the time comes to confront *el conde*, we will not face him alone."

Javier flushed with pride at Raúl's acknowledgment. "I am glad I could be of some help," he said softly. "I fear my fighting days are behind me, but I would do what I can to repay my debt to you all."

"There is no debt between friends," Teodoro insisted, clapping Javier gently on the shoulder. "And do not count the worth of your aid so cheaply. It will take more than just blades to put an end to *el conde* de la Rocha's treachery."

"Indeed," Raúl agreed. "We would be in much worse straits without your aid. None of our plans will do us any good, however, if we cannot find some proof of *el conde*'s treachery, and while we know he was St. Denys's lover, we have no proof even of that, much less of what we believe to be true. And de la Rocha is too well connected for the king to listen to us, even to Cristian, without something to back up our claims."

"We can't just let him succeed," Christian protested. "If he does, none of us will be safe, but Teodoro especially."

"Then we need to find some proof we can bring to the king," Teodoro agreed, leaning forward to rest his elbows on the table. "Hawkins scouted de la Rocha's town house for us earlier," he admitted, still uneasy at relying on the big Englishman for something he would normally have done himself. "*El conde* took most of his servants with him to his estate. There is only one left here, from what he could determine. It should be easy enough to get past him so we can search."

"What do you hope to find?" Javier asked, a little in awe of what his compatriots intended.

"Proof that he is the coconspirator in a plot against the king," Raúl replied honestly. "The other one is dead already, thanks to proof Teodoro provided, but while we know there is a plot and suspect *el conde* de la Rocha of being involved, we can't yet prove it. Hopefully he will be as careless as his lover and will have left something around for us to find. If not, we will have to hope we can prevent whatever he has planned and unmask him that way."

Honored by the trust shown to him, Javier nodded. "I wish I could be of more help to you," he said sadly. "My family is gone, my possessions seized by the Inquisition. All I have left is my knowledge and my memories, but I will share them with you gladly."

"We will call on them both again before we leave for *el conde*'s meeting," Teodoro answered. "For now, we need to decide how best to gain access to his residence here in Madrid." He glanced at Raúl, his gaze thoughtful. "Perhaps the direct approach is best. It would be easy enough to overpower a single servant."

"Is the servant male or female?" Raúl countered. "We could overpower one servant easily enough, but that tips our hand if the servant has any loyalty to *el conde*. It's only Wednesday, which leaves two days for word to get to him of our presence."

Teodoro looked to Christian, who had spoken with Hawkins when the bodyguard returned, with a raised eyebrow. "Given *el conde*'s proclivities, I assumed male."

"No," Christian replied with a shake of his head, "Gerrard said it was a girl. He was surprised enough by that to remark it in particular. De la Rocha must have taken all the male servants with him."

Raúl smiled. "Are you up for a walk this evening, Esteban?" he asked. "I always prefer distraction to force when possible."

"Me?" Esteban stammered in disbelief. It had always been his greatest wish to join Teo on his adventures—he could scarcely believe Raúl was actually offering him this chance. He looked to Teo for confirmation. "You want me to help you?" Teo inclined his head in agreement, transforming Esteban's nervous hesitation into a fierce determination to prove himself worthy of their trust.

"Better you than Cristian," Teodoro countered, the thought of watching his lover flirt with another, for any reason, sparking a flare of possessive jealousy. Teodoro smiled at Esteban reassuringly. "You have only to draw her away for a time, long enough to allow us to search."

"I will not fail you," Esteban assented proudly.

"You haven't seen her yet," Raúl teased gently. "She could be old enough to be your grandmother and look like the witch from your childhood fairy tales."

"It doesn't matter what she looks like," Esteban vowed, though he couldn't repress a shudder at the thought.

Christian took pity on Esteban. "I haven't seen her either, but Gerrard said she looked young—younger than he is, anyway. I'm sure she'll fall for your charm immediately."

"And when she does, Raúl and I will see what *el conde* may have left for us to find," Teodoro added, hoping that de la Rocha would prove as indiscreet as St. Denys.

TEODORO WAITED in the gathering darkness until Esteban and the *conde*'s maidservant had disappeared around the corner of the quiet street. Were the circumstances not so serious, he might have smiled at the ease with which Esteban had captured the serving girl's interest after knocking on the door with the pretext of having a message to deliver to the *conde*. He would need to have a talk with his son about the ways of a man with a maid soon, it seemed. Nodding to his companions, he stepped from the shadows toward the opulent apartments de la Rocha kept as his residence when in attendance at court. Christian couldn't swallow his smile at the sight of Esteban and the girl. "She's pretty enough for even the most discerning young man," he commented softly as he followed Teodoro and Raúl across the street and took up his post just inside the portico to the *conde*'s residence.

Pausing to allow Raúl to precede him, Teodoro's body blocked the view from the street, allowing him to risk running a long finger down Christian's cheek. "Whistle if there is any danger," he murmured, holding Christian's gaze and rubbing the fingertip over his moist bottom lip before stepping away and following Raúl inside. He reminded himself that Christian had proven well able to care for himself, but that did not make leaving him unprotected any easier, even for the few minutes it would take to search the *conde*'s rooms.

Christian shivered at the touch, wishing he could lean in and kiss Teodoro, but even the protection of his broad shoulders was not enough to hide that gesture. Instead he nodded, hoping Teodoro could read his emotions—and his desire—in his eyes.

Raúl couldn't stop a smile at the show of affection between the two men. He had known the *inglés* would be good for his friend. He just hadn't realized how good. When Teodoro joined him at the top of the stairs, Raúl grinned. "In his eyes, you are a knight as noble as Amadís de Gaula."

Teodoro muffled a snort at the fanciful allusion. "Let us hope our quest does not prove as foolish as those of Cervantes's knight instead."

"We are both of us too sane, not to say too fond of our skins, to tilt at windmills," Raúl countered. "Nor is our target so unassailable. Shall we see if *el conde*'s arrogance extends to leaving papers lying around?"

At Teodoro's nod, Raúl tried the door, finding it locked. "The boy still has some things to learn if he can't distract a girl enough that she forgets to lock the door behind her," he commented teasingly, bending to pick the lock. In a matter of moments, it opened to his skilled hands.

"Let us hope he has many years ahead in which to learn," Teodoro responded dryly, the idea making him feel his years.

"We'll make sure of it," Raúl promised. Teodoro had been the one to offer his name to Margarita, but Raúl had helped her give birth to Esteban and felt the same responsibility for his well-being, having been unable to stop his mother's death. "Let's get this done. It's been far too easy, and that makes me nervous."

"I have no desire to impose on the hospitality of the Inquisition, or even the high constable, again," Teodoro agreed. His keen eyes scanned the room, seeking the most likely places to begin their search. "See if you can find *el conde*'s personal chambers," he suggested. "I will begin here." He crossed the entrance hall to a formal sitting room and began pulling out drawers to examine their contents.

Raúl shook his head at Teodoro's sardonic humor and disappeared down the hall, opening doors as he went until he found an opulent bedchamber that was surely the *conde*'s domain. Shaking his head again at the squandered fortune that could have been much better used improving conditions for the tenants on de la Rocha's estates, Raúl began a methodical search of the room, pulling out drawers, riffling through linens, ransacking every possible hiding place. The *conde* had more than one secret, he quickly discovered, but none of them would serve as evidence of his plot against the king. When he found a riding crop in among the cuffs and toys, his face tightened. He sincerely hoped Teodoro was having better luck, but one way or another, he was determined to see *el conde* de la Rocha brought down. Finding nothing else in the bedroom, he headed back toward the entrance hall, crop in hand.

Teodoro raised a brow at the ornate gilt and silver chess set on the sideboard of the drawing room. It seemed they had indeed found St. Denys's gaming partner; he hoped the rest of their search would be equally fruitful. The first drawer Teodoro opened contained nothing but invitations to various balls and dinners. The second was filled with an assortment of writing paper and quills. In the third drawer, however, he found a cache of letters. Sitting back in one of the luxuriously padded chairs, he scanned them rapidly, his gaze narrowing as he took in the purport of the missive in his hand. "Raúl!" he called softly, anger tightening his voice at the nobleman's arrogance in not only putting his filth into writing, but leaving it where the simplest search could find it. "*El conde* has been most reckless—he has given us just what we hoped to find."

"And more," Raúl replied with a moue of disgust, holding out the crop for Teodoro to see. "What does he have to fear? He thinks you're dead, he doesn't know about me, and I'm quite sure he didn't expect Cristian to come into his own the way he has this past week."

"De la Rocha keeps only carriage horses in town," Teodoro retorted with a scowl that said he knew very well that the uses the *conde* had for a whip did not involve riding. "His letters make quite clear what use he thought to put Cristian to." Teodoro rose, stuffing the sheaf of letters angrily into the breast of his jerkin, more determined than ever to bring the *conde* to justice for his sins. "Let's get out of here. The very air stinks of his taint."

"We have what we need, don't we?" Raúl asked, face hardening at the thought of the young man he had come to know and respect at the hands of such a monster. Teodoro nodded. "Then there's no reason to linger."

Despite Raúl's words, Teodoro paused long enough to cross the room to the chessboard, once again putting the darker king in check. The move had proved a good omen in their dealings with St. Denys; perhaps it would be equally prophetic for de la Rocha.

Teodoro's taut nerves eased a bit when they exited the *conde*'s rooms to rejoin Christian, still watching the street from the shelter of the shadowed portico. Unbidden, the sight of his lover was for a moment replaced with the vile images from de la Rocha's letter, filling his throat with bile.

"Any luck?" Christian asked, not sure how to read the tight expressions on their faces.

"Sí," Teodoro assented, his visage grim. "*El conde* was as careless as we hoped. He left a stack of correspondence to be found." He would not share details in the street, but his grimace made his opinion of the content clear. "I need a drink—that tavern off the plaza has a courtyard. We can watch for Esteban to return from there." He strode away angrily, his cloak snapping behind him.

Raúl let him go, shaking his head when Christian would have gone after him immediately. "Give him a moment to calm down," Raúl advised. "He doesn't take any threat to you lightly, but *el conde* is worse than most."

Christian's eyes followed his retreating lover. He understood Teodoro's reaction—he had felt the same way when he'd heard about Teodoro's arrest. He simply nodded at Raúl, not wanting to discuss such things in public. He let Raúl set the pace as they walked down the street to the tavern.

As it was, they had barely ordered a bottle of wine from a serving girl quite pleased to serve three such handsome *caballeros* when Teodoro spotted Esteban, heading back toward the *conde*'s dwelling with the young housemaid on his arm.

Seeing Esteban at the same time, Raúl waited until they were well within view and then let out a loud, appreciative whistle. That he generally preferred male company to female was irrelevant at the moment, and the girl really was quite lovely. She would be flustered but would otherwise think nothing of his expression of appreciation.

Esteban looked about, indignant at the insult to the young woman he was escorting. Constanza was very friendly, and Esteban was already thinking of visiting her again once matters with the *conde* were settled. He scanned the patio of the tavern across the street, recognizing Teo, Raúl, and Christian at one of the tables. He held Teo's gaze for a moment and then bent to murmur a reassurance to Constanza, assuring her of his protection against such crude advances.

Holding his ward's eye and nodding in Raúl's direction, Teodoro picked up the bottle to take with them, tossing a few coins on the tabletop. "Esteban will know to meet us in your rooms. We can examine the letters more closely there."

They made their way quickly back to Raúl's lodgings, the swords at their waists and their confident strides ensuring no one bothered them, even in the more dangerous section of the city that lay between the *conde*'s apartments and their goal. When the door to Raúl's rooms had shut behind them, Christian turned to Teodoro. "What was in those letters?"

"Let us see," Teodoro answered, tossing the packet onto the inlaid table. "We did no more than scan them at *el conde*'s lodgings, though that was enough to see they could be the proof we need." As he pulled around a chair and reached for one of the letters, Teodoro reminded himself how damning St. Denys's correspondence's had proven to be. He had already read enough to know the *conde* felt even less need for discretion than his deceased lover.

"This is from St. Denys," Teodoro said as he worked through the Englishman's scrawl. "It says—" He paused for a moment, his jaw tightening. "—he has found a hireling to bring *el vizconde* Aldwych back to Madrid." At Javier's puzzled expression, Teodoro explained, "That is how this began—St. Denys paid me to find Cristian, claiming he had run away from his family." He did not add that St. Denys had intimated that Christian had run off with his lover—or that he himself had not been too scrupulous to take the money in any case. "He is sure that once they have the chief negotiator's son in their hands, he will be more amenable to listening to reason."

Seeing Teodoro's expression, Christian gave in to the temptation to squeeze his hand soothingly. "And you helped me avoid their trap. Is there anything else in that one? Knowledge of one Englishman conspiring against another will not be enough to condemn *el conde*, even if it proves he helped."

Judging that St. Denys's salacious comments about the charms of the chief negotiator's son would do nothing but fan the flames of his own anger, Teodoro shook his head and reached for another letter. "This is from St. Denys as well—the *bastardo* he hired will not give the boy up." The corner of his heavy moustache twitched in a wry smile. "He has hired two more *bravos* to take him from me." The smile twisted as he remembered the outcome of that confrontation—one man dead, another wounded, and a sword through his own shoulder to keep Christian safe.

"This one is far more damning," Raúl interrupted. "It seems to be from de la Rocha and it's unfinished, but he writes that if they cannot get the boy, they will just have to influence the negotiations another way." He read a little more, then let out a low whistle. "He means to blame the negotiators for his crime."

Christian's face grew grim. The threat to the Spanish king bothered him only in the power it would give to de la Rocha—and what that represented for Teodoro's future. The threat to his father, however difficult their relationship, was something entirely different. "Is it enough to denounce him? Does he specify what he intends to do?"

Raúl shook his head. "St. Denys knew their plans. There would have been no reason to lay them out again, but the collection of letters might be enough. After all, St. Denys was convicted of plotting against the crown, and these place de la Rocha in definite contact with the late, unlamented *cabrón*." Reading the final paragraph, Raúl frowned before passing the letter to Teodoro. "It was no accident you were taken by the Inquisition."

"What?" Christian exclaimed, rising from his seat to peer over Teodoro's shoulder at the cramped writing.

"I did not imagine it was," Teodoro answered, skimming over the more ornate script. "Someone with *el conde*'s standing would find it easy to drop a word in the Grand Inquisitor's ear. Though he has *cojones*, I give him that, to accuse me of what he is guilty of himself—" His voice bit off suddenly at an extremely explicit description of the ways de la Rocha and St. Denys might amuse themselves with the chief negotiator's son until matters were settled in their favor. No wonder the *conde* had not denounced Christian to the Inquisition as well! He handed the missive back to Raúl. "There is enough here to convict him of sodomy, if not of treason," he growled, vowing that whether the *conde* ultimately answered to the king or to the Holy Office, he would answer to Teodoro Ciéza de Vivar first.

Christian had protested denouncing St. Denys for sodomy, but now, seeing the perversions the two men had planned for him and knowing that the *conde* was not above using any lie to achieve his ends, he set his scruples aside. In this case, the ends most certainly justified the means. Before he could voice that opinion, though, a knock sounded at the door.

"Hide the letters," Raúl ordered as he rose from his seat, tucking the paper in his hand into his jerkin.

Esteban swept into the room, his high spirits at winning his first kiss from a lovely young woman fading at the grim expressions of the men gathered around the table. "What did I miss?" he asked.

THEY FILLED Esteban in, leaving out the details he didn't need to hear, then took their leave of Raúl and Javier. Christian had seen Esteban's hesitation, but with Raúl returned, the youth had no reason to stay with Javier any longer. Hoping to ease the tension, he had twitted the lad gently about the time it had taken him to return to Raúl's rooms. In his haste to defend himself, Esteban had followed them without thinking. Now back at their lodgings, Christian felt the awkwardness return as he and Teodoro left Esteban to sleep on his cot while they retired to the bedroom. Their time of total privacy had come to an end. "It's not quite the same with Esteban in the next room, is it?"

After tossing his garments in the armoire, Teodoro shrugged and stretched out on the bed, waiting for Christian to undress and join him. "He is not so much of an innocent as you think." Though it gave him no pleasure to admit it, Esteban surely knew Teodoro was no monk. He had always done his best to behave discreetly before the boy, but there had been nights when he had not slept alone in his bed. "So long as we are quiet, we will not disturb him."

Christian finished undressing and slid into bed next to Teodoro, stretching along his side, enjoying every point of contact. He chose not to reflect on those who had been there before him. He had no claim on Teodoro's past, regardless of his plans for his lover's future. Those former lovers were gone. He was the one in Teodoro's bed now. "That is easier said than done," he joked. "You make me forget everything but your hands on me. You'll just have to find a way to keep me quiet."

"I suppose I could gag you," Teodoro mused, hiding a grin at the flare of shock in Christian's azure eyes. "But that would prevent me from doing this." He rolled them over, ignoring the twinges of pain from barely healed muscles, settling between Christian's legs and pinning their joined hands on either side of the head of golden curls while muffling Christian's mouth with his own. He swept his tongue possessively through the moist cavern, coaxing Christian to answer in kind, feeding the hunger that had built throughout the day despite the urgency of the tasks they faced.

Christian arched into the kiss, his surprise at Teodoro's comment fading quickly beneath the passionate onslaught. All thought of Esteban in the next room, indeed of anything outside their bed, disappeared as he gave himself over wholly to Teodoro's care. They could do nothing else about the *conde* tonight anyway, but even if they could have, he needed this interlude, this reaffirmation of their unspoken promises, too much to let anything intrude. He broke the kiss long enough to whisper, "Make me yours."

As much as I am yours, Teodoro would have answered, but his lips were already molded to Christian's again, his body rocking in an unconscious rhythm that brushed their cocks together, silken skin sliding over steely hardness. Releasing Christian's hands, he mapped the muscles of forearm and bicep with his palm, measuring strong shoulders before coasting down the smooth chest, finding hardened nipples through touch alone. He rubbed and tugged until Christian writhed beneath him, swallowing the moans that shook from Christian's chest with each tweak of the sensitized flesh.

Christian tried to stifle his moans, but that was an exercise in futility with Teodoro driving him wild. He squirmed beneath Teodoro, wanting his hands lower but not willing to break the kiss to issue the request. Instead, he slid his own hands lower, clenching them tightly on the firm globes of Teodoro's buttocks, using that pressure to urge him on.

Humming his approval of Christian's hands clasping him closer, Teodoro's movements intensified, each thrust of his hips dragging their leaking erections against each other and against the slickening skin of their bellies. He was tempted to slide downward to taste that harsh creaminess, to sample it directly from its source, but that would mean giving up Christian's mouth, and that was something he could not bring himself to do. Instead he freed a hand and dragged it through the dampness between them, gliding over their cocks for a moment before the sensation became too much for him to bear without losing control. Raising his hand back to his mouth, he lapped at it without releasing Christian's lips, his tongue gathering the pearlescent fluid to share with his lover, the sharp taste mixing with the sweetness of Christian's mouth, intoxicating him with the mingled flavors.

Christian gasped as he tasted himself on Teodoro's hand and tongue. He thrust up harder against his weight, wrapping his legs around Teodoro's hips and grinding them together. He needed Teodoro inside him, driving strong and hard into his depths. Blindly he reached for the oil on the bedside table and pressed it into Teodoro's hand. He hoped Teodoro would take the hint, would take him, and soon.

His need spiraling with each nudge of Christian's legs against his backside, Teodoro fumbled to open the oil without lifting his head, spilling some on the bedsheets in his haste to coat his fingers. He slid a slick digit into the channel between Christian's legs, too ardent for subtlety as he worked to stretch the opening to receive him, his tongue mimicking the strokes and swirls of his fingers in the tight passage. Sooner than he knew he should, he pushed to his knees, spreading Christian's legs apart and positioning himself to press inside. "Mi tesoro," he whispered against his lover's lips, a single firm thrust surrounding him in Christian's embrace, a shudder of pure bliss racking his frame at the perfection of their bodies' joining.

Christian shouted his pleasure into Teodoro's mouth as he felt himself claimed again. His grip tightened as he flexed his inner muscles. He broke their kiss long enough to whisper "Harder!" before attacking Teodoro's mouth in the hopes of inspiring the pounding he desired. He braced his feet on the mattress to get the leverage he needed to participate fully in his own reaming.

The excitement of the day's events, and the very real possibility that, if things went ill, this could be the last time Teodoro made love to Christian, lent an urgency to their coupling that Christian's wanton movements only intensified. The whispered plea snapped any pretense of control, and Teodoro cupped his hands beneath Christian's buttocks and slammed their bodies together, rocking with a primal fever to bury himself, brand himself on Christian's skin, fill him so completely that Christian would never be free of him, no matter what transpired tomorrow.

Christian's grunts sounded in time with Teodoro's thrusts as he met each ingress with his hips, their bodies slapping together in a rhythm as old as time. Christian had no idea what the next few days would bring, but whatever happened, he intended to have these memories to hold onto. He dug his fingers into the muscles of Teodoro's back, heedless of the still-healing stripes. He clung to Teodoro's strong frame like a lifeline, needing that connection, every possible connection, against the storm of uncertainty that faced them.

All too quickly Teodoro felt his climax welling in his groin, threatening to overpower him. Pinning Christian to the mattress with the force of his thrusts, he worked a hand between them to grasp his lover's shaft, cradling the back of Christian's skull with his other hand as he ravaged his mouth and his cock, intent on bringing him to the same fierce peak of ecstasy. The long, slow groan as he orgasmed swallowed in their kiss, he clutched Christian to him, tremors shaking through them both for long moments after.

The rush of heat as Teodoro's release filled him made Christian moan with the sense of communion at this intense sharing of body and soul. He hadn't known what it was to make love with someone until he met Teodoro. He collapsed beneath his weight, too sated to care if he could breathe or not. He cared only about extending the moment as long as possible. "I love you," he murmured against Teodoro's lips.

"Te adoro," Teodoro answered in a voice heavy with satiation. Claiming a final, slow kiss, he rolled to one side, carrying Christian with him in a tangle of limbs. He still ached from the depredations of the Inquisition, but every torment he had suffered was worth this moment of repletion. Resting his chin in a bed of blond curls, he exhaled deeply, the peace of the moment seeping into his bones and strengthening him for the demands of the days ahead.

TWENTY

CHRISTIAN STIRRED slowly. He couldn't have said what awakened him, but he knew what was keeping him awake. He burrowed closer against Teodoro, the warmth of his body lulling him into a drowsy half sleep where his arousal was a low hum in the background, enough that he was aware of it but not so strongly that he felt the necessity of acting on it. Not yet, anyway. It wouldn't take much, but for the moment, he was content to drift in and out of consciousness at Teodoro's side.

Although he normally awoke with the dawn, Teodoro found himself reluctant to open his eyes and disturb the rare calm of this moment. Though he would never admit it to Christian, he was still weakened from the Inquisition's tortures, and the previous day's exertions had wearied him. It felt good to lie abed, not sleeping but not yet wholly awake—his body relaxed, the constant ache of his abused muscles had faded, soothed by the warmth of Christian's frame nestled against him, lulled by the soft susurration of his breathing. Though he knew he should rise and prepare for their departure later that morning, for the moment he allowed himself to linger, his thoughts drifting free of the usual check he held on them, memories of the past weeks with Christian mingling with images of the future, of a time when they would be free of the dangers that beset them.

The pressures of the day finally interfering with his dozing, Christian opened his eyes fully and stared down at Teodoro's relaxed face. Someday, they wouldn't have to worry about what that day would bring. Someday, they would have the luxury of lolling abed until noon if it suited them. "Someday," he whispered, not wanting to awaken Teodoro, "we'll be able to enjoy a morning like this without hurrying."

The quiet words were so expressive of his musings that Teodoro thought at first he had dreamt them. When a warm breath stirred the air near his cheek, he opened his eyes to the sight of Christian's face, his eyes soft and yearning, his hair a tousled halo around his head. Still not sure he wasn't dreaming, Teodoro parted his lips and raised a hand to brush a lightly stubbled cheek, the touch enough to coax Christian to lower his head and let their lips meet in a slow, gentle kiss.

Telling himself Teodoro simply hadn't heard him and so hadn't agreed for that reason rather than some more sinister one, Christian sank into the soft kiss. Teodoro loved him. That had to count for something. Slowly he mapped Teodoro's mouth with his own, storing up memories against an uncertain future. He didn't know what tomorrow would bring, but he knew he would do everything in his power to ensure them a life together, and he invested their kiss with that faith, that determination. It had carried him through the hellish days of Teodoro's imprisonment. It would carry him through whatever they faced at *el conde* de la Rocha's estate and beyond.

The reality of Christian's mouth moving against his stirred him more than any dream, making Teodoro believe as nothing else could that perhaps the future he imagined was possible. "Someday," he averred softly, meeting the blue eyes that regarded him so lovingly with a gaze free of the cynicism in which he usually guarded himself. "God willing, it may be so."

"Amen," Christian replied, echoing the simple prayer. Today was not that day, though, and so after another soft kiss to Teodoro's lips, he rose from the bed and started to dress, feeling the leftover twinges from their energetic lovemaking the night before. He was tempted to slip back into bed and encourage Teodoro to ravish him again, but they had to ride today, and he would be sore enough as it was.

Teodoro allowed himself one more moment to observe Christian's graceful frame disappear beneath his garments, then stretched to loosen his joints, hiding a grimace at the twinges of pain this entailed. He rolled his neck as he reached for his breeches and stepped into them. "We should stop at the tavern for a large breakfast before we meet Raúl," he suggested, pulling on his shirt. "I do not know what chance we may have to eat once we depart for de la Rocha's estate."

Christian chuckled. "I wonder if we will find Gerrard already there, since he did not return here last night," he mused as he finished dressing. He didn't say anything aloud for he knew well his lover's prickly pride, but he would keep an eye on Teodoro and make sure the ride was not too tiring for him. Teodoro would surely resent the coddling, but it was self-preservation on Christian's part. He knew his own weakness with a sword. He wanted Teodoro at his best should it come to a fight.

"If he is not, we may have to retrieve him from Aldonza's," Teodoro answered, confident enough to tease a little now that Christian knew matters between him and the brothel's mistress were ended. He turned to open the bedroom door, adding over his shoulder, "The problem may be prying Hawkins from her bed so that we may depart."

"And is that likely to be a problem? I wouldn't know," Christian replied tartly, giving no thought to Esteban in the other room, "never having been in either of their beds."

About to reply in kind, Teodoro caught the interested expression on Esteban's face as they entered the common room and bit back his response, raising a quelling eyebrow at his son. Esteban quickly affected an innocent demeanor, glancing toward Christian and asking solicitously whether he had slept well.

"Teo made sure I was quite comfortable," Christian replied without thinking, a blush staining his cheeks as soon as the words escaped. Esteban couldn't hide a knowing smirk at Christian's discomfiture, knowing full well—courtesy of the sounds he had overheard despite their best attempts to muffle them—exactly how Teo had seen to his comfort.

"Impudent cub," Teodoro growled, cuffing the back of Esteban's head, though his eyes glowed with humor. "Get dressed—we will be leaving soon."

Before Esteban, rubbing the back of his skull, could act on Teo's request, a heavy knock sounded at the door. Motioning for Christian and Esteban to stand back, Teodoro picked up the new dagger from the sideboard, holding it at the ready while throwing back the bolt to crack open the portal. Though he hadn't honestly expected a threat to announce itself by knocking, he was relieved to see only the other Englishman, Hawkins, standing in the narrow passageway. Lowering the blade, Teodoro stepped aside to let the bodyguard enter.

"Where did you disappear to last night after dinner?" Gerrard began. He looked around the room at the three occupants, trying to make out the dynamics between them. He knew how Christian felt about Ciéza, but the rest remained unclear to him.

Teodoro glanced at Christian, uneasy admitting too much to the big stranger. After all, Hawkins had scouted de la Rocha's rooms for them— he ought to have been able to figure it out for himself. "Back to search *el conde*'s rooms," he said shortly, slipping the dagger into his belt.

Frustrated, Gerrard ran a hand through his thick, dark hair. "I could help, you know," he declared, turning to Christian. "If you'd trust me enough to tell me what's going on, I would gladly help. You used to confide in me. You used to let me protect you."

"He no longer needs your protection." Teodoro glowered, his voice no less dangerous for being quiet.

"Perhaps not," Gerrard conceded, "but that's no reason to refuse my friendship. Or was I wrong when I believed we were friends?"

"He is my friend," Christian told Teodoro, leaving the final decision up to his lover. While he hoped Teodoro could accept that and Gerrard's offer, he knew the outcome of any choice to be made between them. His love for Teodoro would win over his friendship with Gerrard, no matter what. "We could use another sword."

"You would gamble your life for a cause you know nothing about?" Teodoro asked. While Hawkins's sword would undeniably be useful, he could not risk their future, or Christian's safety, unless he was sure he could trust him completely. "For... friendship?" Teodoro had come to believe Christian's repeated insistence that he had never shared Hawkins's bed, but he could not forget that Hawkins had been hired as a mercenary, just as Teodoro himself had been—before falling in love.

"If Christian believes it a worthy cause, then I know it is worth taking a risk," Gerrard pointed out, guessing where Ciéza's hesitations sprang from. "He would never endanger *you* if it weren't."

"There is danger to both our countries, but most of all, danger to Cristian," Teodoro admitted reluctantly. "If you accompany us, it will be to ensure his safety, above all else."

Gerrard nodded his agreement. "That has always been my first concern. So will you explain what's going on now?"

Taking Teodoro's words as acceptance, Christian pushed down his reaction to Teodoro's voice—he doubted he would ever get used to it—and joined the conversation again, explaining de la Rocha's plot against the Spanish king and his intention to cast the blame on the English delegation. "None of us will be safe here if he succeeds," he finished. "We ride for *el conde*'s estate as soon as we break our fast, in the hopes of thwarting him before he has a chance to act."

Teodoro buckled on his sword, settling it against his hip with the ease of long practice. "*El conde* thought to use Cristian as a pawn to sway his father's negotiations," he added. "He had... other intentions for Cristian himself." His expression hardened as he remembered the vile perversions de la Rocha had described in his letter to St. Denys. Had the *conde* succeeded in his plans, he would be retrieving his intestines from the point of Teodoro's sword.

Gerrard frowned. "We suspected the former," he observed. "St. Denys tried several times to kidnap Christian. That's why his father hired me in the first place. So when do we leave?" He didn't comment on the latter, seeing no reason to prod Ciéza's temper.

"We'll meet Raúl after we've eaten," Teodoro replied. "He is arranging horses for us—we will hope the stables can find another mount for you."

"Can I come with you too, Teo?" Esteban broke in. He had never dared ask to accompany Teodoro before, but he hoped that after being allowed to help them last night, he had proven he was ready to take part in their adventure.

"Not this time, *mijo*," Teodoro said, shaking his head at Esteban's impatience, though he well remembered his own desire to prove himself at that age. "You will stay with Javier until we return. I do not expect any trouble to come to him, but if it should, he will need someone to defend him." Pleased that Esteban did not continue to argue, he squeezed his shoulder. "Sometimes the hardest duty is to remain behind."

"I will keep him safe until you return," Esteban pledged. In the week since Teo's and Javier's rescue from the Inquisition, he had grown to respect Javier, who never treated him like a child. "Though I would rather be fighting with you."

It wouldn't be long, Christian knew, before Teodoro would stop saying no to Esteban. He watched their interaction with a pang, thinking of the differences between their relationship and the one Christian had with his father. Esteban had no idea how fortunate he was to have Teodoro taking care of him. Teodoro would never make Esteban question his worth the way Christian's father had done. Turning away to hide the rush of emotion that he didn't care to share, he applied himself diligently to his final preparations, the sooner to end the conversation and speed their departure. Maybe this time he would finally win his father's unconditional approval.

"I HOPE you can abide my company for a few more days, Señor Montega," Esteban said, trying not to let his disappointment sound in his voice after Teodoro had explained their plans. "We are being left behind while the others have all the adventures."

"I will be glad of the company," Javier answered with a warm smile. "Esteban has taken such good care of me, I almost feel as if he is one of my own grandchildren." As it had been with his own boys, he knew it would be his job while Ciéza and the others were gone to keep Esteban from falling into trouble out of boredom. "Do not worry for us. We shall watch out for each other."

"Where are your grandchildren?" Christian asked, hoping they could see Javier reunited with his family. It seemed a small enough thing to do after his aid to Teodoro in prison and to all of them against de la Rocha.

The smile withered from Javier's face. "Taken, or scattered and hiding," he said, his voice heavy with sadness. "Our family's lands were seized by the Inquisition. I would not know where to begin to search for them, yet I cannot remain in the city or I risk being taken again myself." He shook his head slowly; Ciéza and his comrades had saved his life, but he had no life to return to. "I do not know what I shall do once I am well enough to leave here."

"Taken?" Christian repeated, aghast. "But they were only children! What crime could they have committed?"

"The Inquisition is not concerned with guilt or innocence," Raúl reminded Christian gently, "only with its own power. You know that guilt by association is one of their favorite conclusions. It's one of the reasons I make sure not to come to their notice. They would not take kindly to my... differences. As for the future, you will certainly have some decisions to make, Señor Montega, but they can wait a few more days, at least until our return. It's part of my calling to tend to the injured. You're welcome here as long as you need my hospitality."

"I shall wait anxiously for your return, and for the success of your quest," Javier said. "I will pray for right to prevail."

"Yet even right must rely upon might," Teodoro said dryly. "We will need another horse, Raúl. Señor Hawkins is accompanying us."

"One day, Teodoro, you will ask something of me that I cannot simply conjure from thin air. Señor Hawkins's horse is waiting with the others, though I had some trouble finding one strong enough to bear him," Raúl replied archly, casting an appreciative eye over the big Englishman.

"How did you know?" Gerrard asked in surprise. "We didn't decide until just before we came here this morning."

"Raúl always knows," Esteban said with a grin at Hawkins's bafflement. "It does no good to ask how—he will never tell his secrets."

"Another sword will be useful. I knew Teo would see that sooner or later," Raúl demurred, not ready to open himself up to more speculation than necessary. "It was a logical conclusion, nothing more."

"And if you had not come, he would never have mentioned arranging for another horse," Teodoro offered with a raise of his eyebrow that was the closest he would come to a smile until he was more confident of Hawkins's nature. "Now, we should put as many miles as we can toward *el conde*'s estates while it is light. I would prefer time to scout the grounds before the king's arrival."

THE HORSES Raúl had arranged for them were hardy but unremarkable animals, their saddles well-worn and serviceable, but as an hour turned into two and two turned into three, Christian began to see their value. The leather conformed to his seat, allowing him a degree of comfort he rarely found in borrowed gear. The horse's gait was steady, rocking him rather than jarring him, a relief given the pounding he had taken so willingly the night before. The long strides ate up the road effortlessly without overtaxing horse or rider. Still, Christian kept watch over Teodoro out of the corner of his eye, intimate knowledge of every cut and bruise on his lover's magnificent body making him poignantly aware of how far Teodoro still had to go before he recovered completely from the Inquisition's mercies.

For his part, Teodoro kept an equally cautious eye on Christian. While his years in the king's service were mainly as a foot soldier, he had spent his share of time in the saddle; it was soon apparent to him that Christian was a more accomplished rider, moving with his hired mount as effortlessly as if they were old acquaintances. Watching Christian's slender body rise and fall with the horse's steady gallop, he could not help but remember the ride from Valencia to Madrid, with Christian's reluctant body stiff against his on their single mount. He would be stiff for a different reason if they shared a horse now, Teodoro thought with a self-satisfied smile. Christian had proven himself a skilled rider in the bedchamber as well.

The ride stretched on, league upon league. Christian's watch never wavered, but Teodoro didn't falter, increasing Christian's respect for his stamina. He doubted he would fare so well were he riding with such injuries. Christian knew what Teodoro would say to that—it had to be done so he did it—but it didn't change Christian's reaction. If anything, it strengthened it. As his concern eased, though never faded completely, other emotions assailed him with memories of sharing a horse with Teodoro, of being pressed against that hard body for hours on end. What he would give to be pressed there now! He knew their need for haste precluded such pastimes—the double weight would seriously slow their mount—but he yearned nonetheless. Shifting uncomfortably in the saddle, he wondered how much longer until they could reasonably stop for lunch and to rest their horses. When they did, he would find a way to be alone with Teodoro even if it meant following him into the privy.

Raúl glanced back from where his horse led the way, gauging the state of his companions, and called over his shoulder, "There is an inn just ahead where we can stop for a meal and to rest the horses before we ride on."

Christian swore to himself he wouldn't blush, but he could feel the heat staining his cheeks. He only hoped the distance would keep Raúl from divining his thoughts. The smirk that played around Raúl's lips told him he hadn't been successful.

Though he would not admit it aloud, Teodoro was glad of the opportunity for a rest. Not wanting to draw attention to themselves, they had kept to a steady pace that, allowing for an overnight stop, would bring them to the *conde*'s estates the morning before the king was to arrive. Though the ride had not been particularly demanding, his battered body ached from the constant motion, something he suspected had not escaped Raúl's attention. "A jug of Valdeiglesias to wet our throats would be not be amiss," he said, arching his back to stretch the tightly drawn muscles.

Christian's gaze sharpened as he watched Teodoro move gingerly. His determination to spend some time resting grew. They all needed to be at their best when they arrived at de la Rocha's estates, and Teodoro was starting at a disadvantage. "That sounds wonderful," he agreed, the dust of the road gritty in his throat and on his skin. He didn't imagine he'd get a bath, even when they stopped that night, however much he wanted one, but at least the wine would ease his throat.

A meal of hot soup and *empanadillas*, accompanied by a mug of rich red wine, did much to reconcile Teodoro to the prospect of several more hours of riding. The inn they would stop at for the night was an even more attractive prospect, and he felt himself stirring at the thought of holding Christian in his arms again, even if they did nothing more than rest. His moustache twitched as he remembered their earliest nights together, when he had to fight against the first stirrings of desire for the stranger he was returning to Madrid against his will. How little he had suspected what a passionate and responsive lover that stranger would prove to be! As little as he had expected to lose his heart to that same alluring Englishman. Before his body's reaction to the direction of his thoughts became unmanageable, he rose and cracked his knuckles. "I'm going to wash the dust from my face," he announced, hoping some cool water would cool his mistimed arousal as well.

"That sounds like a wonderful idea," Christian declared, following Teodoro out the door quickly, his desire heightening in a rush at the unexpected possibility of getting his lover alone for even a few minutes.

Reasoning that most inns had a source of water near their kitchens, Teodoro skirted the building, finding a pump as he expected midway between the kitchen and the stables. A few strokes of the handle yielded him a stream of clear water, and he had just filled his cupped palms when a pair of arms encircled him from behind, the touch unmistakably Christian's. Letting the water spill from his hands, he wrapped them around the slender wrists, holding them motionless. "You need to work on tracking your quarry silently—I heard you coming as soon as you rose from the table."

"It might have looked a bit odd if I slunk out of the inn after you," Christian pointed out, nuzzling the sweat-stained collar of Teodoro's shirt and jerkin. "Better to simply walk out as if it were nothing worth noticing, don't you think?"

The arousal that had begun to subside as a result of the cool water rekindled instantly at the gentle caress. As much as he wished he could simply turn and pull Christian into his arms, they were still too exposed for Teodoro's comfort. "Were one of the scullery maids to walk out of the kitchen now, she might notice something," he said dryly, releasing Christian's wrists. "We cannot forget discretion simply because we are no longer in Madrid. The Holy Office has eyes and ears everywhere."

"Then let us find somewhere they will not see us," Christian proposed, stepping away, but not before brushing against Teodoro's hip, letting him feel his arousal. "You wouldn't make me ride like this, would you?"

Glancing about to the seemingly deserted stables, Teodoro pulled Christian along to an empty stall at the rear of the shadowed structure. After kicking the wooden door closed behind them, he pulled Christian into his arms, capturing his lips with all the hunger of hours spent watching and wanting. He burrowed one hand into the bright curls that had escaped from their queue and delved the other beneath the hem of Christian's doublet to cup his buttocks, pulling his body close so that their erections met in frustrated tension.

Christian moaned into Teodoro's mouth, hungry for his taste beneath the flavor of the wine they had drunk with lunch. Their tongues met and danced, twining around each other as their bodies did the same. Soon, though, it wasn't enough for Christian, the craving for a different taste growing swiftly. He tore his mouth away, reaching between their straining bodies to open the placket of Teodoro's breeches. He closed his hand around the leaking shaft as he dropped to his knees, inhaling the musky fragrance. He licked his lips in anticipation.

"*Sangre de Dios*, you would tempt a saint," Teodoro murmured, knowing this was madness but unable to resist the wanton provocation. He threaded his hands back into Christian's windblown hair, adding to its disarray as his fingers clenched at the first touch of Christian's mouth to his straining cock.

Inside the inn, Gerrard pushed back from the table they had shared for their meal. "I think I'll wash up as well," he decided.

"You don't want to do that right now," Raúl informed him. "They wouldn't appreciate you disturbing them at the moment."

It took a moment for comprehension to dawn on Gerrard's face. He dropped back from his half-risen stance, a flush staining his cheeks. "Maybe later would be better," he stammered uncomfortably.

"Very wise," Raúl agreed affably.

Teodoro's husky words, the fingers tightening in his hair, and the hitch in Teodoro's breathing all combined to stoke the fire in Christian's loins. He wanted to linger over his treat the way one lingered over fine wine, but he knew their time was limited. As he released his own aching shaft, he worked his lips down the upstanding rod, taking Teodoro as deep as he could, his eyes closing in bliss as he pushed them both closer to the peak of passion.

His dark head thrown back against the rough stable wall, Teodoro gasped for breath as Christian's lips and tongue played over him, the heat in his loins spreading through his veins until his entire being was aflame with need. It had never felt like this before. Teodoro had known the sudden lust of stress-driven coupling before battle, the need to prove one's self alive after a day of savage fighting, but he had never felt a hunger that consumed him to his very core like this, until body and soul ached to unite with Christian. Biting his lip to keep from howling as his release erupted, he shuddered against the constant suction of Christian's mouth, emptying himself in a pulsing wave that left him shaking. Grasping Christian's shoulders, he pulled him up into his embrace, crushing his mouth, still bitter with the taste of his own seed. He wrapped a callused hand around Christian's cock, needing only a few sharp tugs to bring him to completion, hot fluid coating his fist.

Christian's climax shuddered through him, the scent and flavor of Teodoro's essence merging with the heat of his hand to set Christian's nerves to riot. Only Teodoro's strong arms around him kept him upright in the trembling aftermath. He leaned his head heavily against the leather-clad shoulder, drinking in Teodoro's closeness, needing the solace of this moment against whatever was to come in the next few days.

After one more deep breath, Teodoro nudged his shoulder until Christian looked up, and he dropped a swift kiss on his reddened lips. "They will miss us if we don't return soon," he said quietly, reminding himself that they would be sharing a bed again at the end of the day's ride. Straightening his garments, he opened the door to the stall, gesturing Christian to precede him. "And this time we will really need to wash up," he added with a glint in his eyes.

"It's not my fault my lover is too desirable to resist," Christian retorted softly as they left the haven of the empty stall. He didn't protest, though, because he knew Teodoro was right.

Quirking his lips at Christian's jest—surely he knew he was the irresistible one—Teodoro worked the pump handle while Christian washed his hands and face, then quickly rinsed himself clean, the cool water restoring enough of his control to allow him to face the others again. He suspected Raúl would know what they had been doing, but he found the thought didn't bother him. Safety demanded they act with discretion, but he could not hide what he had come to feel for Christian from his closest friend.

Christian did his best to school his expression as they walked back into the inn, though he suspected anyone who knew him would read his satisfaction beneath the affable smile he wore. They found Gerrard and Raúl exactly where they'd left them.

"Ready to ride?" Raúl asked, his smile innocent, though the gleam in his eyes was anything but.

"I am much refreshed," Teodoro answered with equal coolness. "Perhaps you would care to avail yourself before we depart?"

"The wine was enough to refresh me," Raúl teased. "The other amenities are less... suited to me, I think, though they obviously met with your approval."

"If there's time, I wouldn't mind refreshing myself," Gerrard interrupted. "I have yet to grow used to this miserable heat." He rose before any of the others could comment and left the inn. Christian tried to hold back the burst of laughter that bubbled up within him, but meeting the other two men's gazes, he gave that up as hopeless, his laughter welling free, releasing a little more of the tension that had gripped him all morning.

Meeting first Raúl's eyes and then Christian's, Teodoro shook with silent humor. "A pity he must find his refreshment alone," he murmured solicitously.

Their laughter had barely subsided when Gerrard came back inside. "That didn't take long," Christian commented, trying to keep a straight face. That lasted until Raúl started coughing next to him as he struggled to contain his own mirth, setting off another bout of laughter on Christian's part.

"What's so funny?" Gerrard asked curiously.

As this served only to set Christian to a fresh round of laughter, Teodoro shook his head reprovingly and motioned toward the door. "Vamos," he said shortly. "We still have many miles to travel before nightfall. And," he added softly as the others filed out the door, "I shall be looking forward to a bed at the end of our ride."

"Getting old, *amigo*?" Raúl asked with a wink. "I remember when you looked forward to other things than your bed at the end of a day's ride."

"You assume that will be the end of the ride," Teodoro retorted, softly enough for only Raúl to hear.

"All the more reason to hurry," Raúl agreed equally quietly as they stepped out of the inn and into the stable yard. They had just finished reclaiming their horses when the loud clatter of galloping hooves on the cobblestones drew their attention. Looking up, they saw a man not much older than Christian, but with the typical swarthy skin of a gypsy.

"Raúl," he cried, out of breath, "*gracias a Dios que te encuentro*! The king arrived this morning!"

"No!" Christian shouted, swinging onto his mount's back and then reining him toward the road, images of his father hanging for treason flashing through his mind. "Teo, we have to ride!"

"Maldita sea!" Teodoro mounted with a curse, spurring his horse after Christian at a gallop. There would be no inn and no bed that night.

TWENTY-ONE

THEY HAD ridden at great speed through the night, the horse's steady rhythm lulling Teodoro into a half-torpid state, his eyelids heavy despite his efforts to remain watchful. He needed to move, to act—the long, tense wait before a battle was always harder on him than the fighting itself. Forcing back a yawn, he noticed the first light of dawn brightening the horizon. They had to be nearing the *conde*'s estates, surely? He looked to Raúl, riding on his left, but the gypsy shook his head, interpreting Teodoro's glance without words. Nodding in acceptance, Teodoro turned his head toward his right, where Christian clung to his horse's reins with weary determination. It had better not be much farther to de la Rocha's *pazo*, he thought grimly, or they would be too exhausted to confront him.

Christian prayed hard as they rode, the energy that had come from hearing the news that the king had arrived early having long since worn off. He only hoped it would return when they reached the estates, for he was in no shape for a swordfight now, his skills only passable at the best of times. He kept his gaze focused on the road ahead, the slowly brightening light allowing them to pick up their speed even more. Beneath him, his horse puffed hard but kept the pace. When this was over, if he survived, he would owe the animal a great favor.

Raúl could see Teodoro and Christian both tiring, but there was nothing to be done for it. They had to ride on and confront de la Rocha as quickly as they could or else they could be too late. Glancing back, he sought the other *inglés* with his eyes to see if he fared any better than the other two.

Gerrard's horse was slower than the others, trying to drop back to an easier pace whenever his attention wandered. Seeing the gypsy looking back at him, he waved them on, digging his spurs into his reluctant mount's side. After all but demanding to join their undertaking, he would not be the one to hold them back. He thought he glimpsed a flicker of approbation as the exotic eyes held his for an instant before returning to the road ahead of them.

As they scrambled around a curve in the road without breaking stride, Teodoro's mount's sides heaved, its muscles trembling beneath his thighs. "How much farther?" he called softly to Raúl. "The horses will not last much longer."

"Another hour, perhaps," Raúl replied. "If we are lucky, we will catch *el conde* and his guests at breakfast still, before they lock themselves in some hall for their negotiations."

"The horses will last that much longer," Christian assured the others, "though probably not much more."

Teodoro grinned, teeth flashing beneath his heavy moustache. Christian was the surest horseman of them all—if he felt their mounts could endure, they should take advantage of it. "Then let us ride hard, and save our breath to convince the king of de la Rocha's treachery," he called, urging his tired steed to push on just a little faster.

The last hour was the hardest, nerves stretched taut against any danger, senses on full alert, hoping they would be in time. When they reached the boundaries of the *conde*'s estate, Raúl slowed his horse. "Quietly, now," he warned the others. "We will do ourselves no good if we alert de la Rocha to our arrival too soon."

The others reined their horses in, following Raúl's lead as they wound their way through the forest that bordered the property. Before long, the manor house came into view. Christian whistled softly under his breath. "De la Rocha doesn't believe in modesty, does he?" he muttered as he perused the immense structure. "We'll never find the king in there without *el conde* finding us first."

"This is where our friend Javier's knowledge will prove of use," Teodoro countered. "There is an entrance near the kitchens that is used only by servants. One of Raúl's men should be able to get us inside."

"And tell us where the king is," Raúl added. He pulled the horse to a stop and dismounted agilely. Checking that his sword hung loosely in its sheath, he turned to the others. "Shall we beard the lion in his den?"

Adjusting his sword belt so the hilt was in easy reach, Teodoro pulled the *daga izquierda* from his saddle bag and tucked it into the back of his waistband before twitching his brown leather jerkin into place. His breeches were powdered with dust from the road, his tall boots splattered with mud, the bandanna that covered his windblown hair stained with sweat. A glance confirmed his companions looked little better; even Christian's more fashionable attire was creased and travel-stained. He twisted the end of his moustache with a bark of laughter. "'Sblood, we are a fine set of courtiers to seek audience with the king!"

"We shall hope he can see beyond our clothes to the import of the message we bring," Christian replied, brushing ineffectually at his travel-marred clothes. He wished in vain for the outfit Esteban had purchased for him to wear as he faced down the cardinal in Madrid, but the trek would have ruined that as well. Clothes did not make the man, he reminded himself, glancing at Raúl and Teodoro as proof of his silent assertion, for if they did, those two would be dressed in the finest garb in the land.

An almost imperceptible crackle of dry leaves caused both Teodoro's and Raúl's heads to snap up, hands falling to their weapons as a slender man dressed in the livery of a groom stepped from the trees beside them. Raúl raised a hand to wave the others back and clasped the younger man's shoulder with a smile. "What news, Fonsi?" he asked softly.

"Joachim arrived several hours ago to warn us you were coming," Fonsi answered. "I'll take your horses to the stables. There is quite a gathering here already. No one will question a few more nags. Emilio is watching for you from the kitchen. He'll see you safely inside."

"Treat the horses well," Christian requested. "We have used them roughly."

"And keep them ready, in case we need to make a speedy escape," Gerrard suggested.

Raúl didn't say—he doubted he needed to—that escape was probably not in their future. They would either confront *el conde* de la Rocha and put their proof before the king or they would die trying. He saw no other options before them. "Let's not keep Emilio waiting," he said to the others, continuing on toward the side door Javier had told them would provide unannounced entrance into the house.

Another of Raúl's confederates met them at the door and guided them through a kitchen bustling with activity. "*El conde* has ordered a special breakfast to celebrate His Majesty's presence," Emilio told them, leading them down a wide, empty hallway. Teodoro frowned at the echo of their boot heels on the polished marble flooring. "All the guests are seated in the grand dining room." Their escort pointed to the ornately carved double doors at the end of the corridor. "Several of our men are inside, serving as footmen," he added to Raúl before turning back toward the kitchens.

Teodoro's gaze locked with Raúl's for a moment; then he gave a small nod. Between them, no words needed to be said. He spared an appraising glance for the big Englishman standing quietly behind Raúl, recognizing that despite his doubts, Hawkins had kept up with their punishing pace without complaint. The larger man met his stare unflinchingly, and Teodoro nodded again, satisfied he had made the right decision allowing Hawkins to join them. Finally, his gaze slid to Christian. His lover's slender frame was all but vibrating with suppressed tension. He brushed a smudge of dust from one cheek, his touch lingering. "You will convince him," he said softly. "The king will listen to you."

As always, Teodoro's faith in him settled Christian's nerves. "I can only pray you're right," he replied with equal softness, tilting his head into the gentle caress. He wished he dared kiss Teodoro one last time. If they failed, it wouldn't matter—they would be dead men. If they succeeded, though, they could not afford anything that would later endanger them. "If not, I fear it will cost us all dearly."

Despite the danger, Teodoro could not let Christian take the final step that might lead to their deaths without tasting his lips one more time. Wedging his boot against the doors to prevent them from opening, he lowered his head for a swift, sweet kiss. "This is worth the cost," he insisted. "If we were to fail, it would all be worth it, only to have known this." He gripped Christian's shoulder in a soldier's embrace. "But we shall not fail."

Christian drew strength from the sudden kiss and the confidence in Teodoro's eyes. Taking a deep breath and drawing himself to his full height, he pushed open the doors to the dining room and strode inside. "Your Majesty!" His voice echoed through the ornately decorated space, breaking through the hum of desultory morning conversation. Every eye in the room turned his way, but he refused to let the startled gazes deter him. "A moment of your time, if you will!"

The king's guards stepped forward as if to stop him, only to find their way blocked by footmen of various descriptions. "I wish only to speak with you, Your Majesty," Christian continued, advancing into the room with his hands far from his sword, trusting Teodoro, Raúl, and Gerrard to keep him safe. He had one priority only: convincing the king to hear him out. Even his father's voice, demanding to know what he was doing there, had no power to distract him now.

His Most Catholic Majesty Philip IV clearly had not expected to face any danger at a private breakfast in the home of one of his most powerful noblemen. His ceremonial guards might perhaps have been forgiven for being taken by surprise by the sudden interruption, an advantage Raúl's gypsies were quick to exploit, disarming the three men before more than one of them could even pull his sword from its scabbard. A babble of voices erupted from the shocked guests around the table, increasing in volume as Christian stopped near the head of the table, his three companions aligning themselves protectively around him.

"Who do you think you are, daring to disturb my household and guests this way?" a man Christian presumed to be *el conde* de la Rocha demanded, rising from his seat and then stepping out from behind the table. His clothing alone proclaimed him a member of the high nobility—only the king's pourpoint was more luxurious—but his bearing was even more unmistakable. The patrician cut of his features under heavy, graying brows and the confident, even arrogant, expression on his face declared him an aristocrat of the first water. He might have been considered handsome—he was certainly stately—but Christian was too aware of the evil that lurked beneath the surface to be swayed by his appearance.

"You mean you don't recognize me, *conde*?" Christian rebutted. "And you've tried so hard to make my acquaintance. Christian Blackwood, Viscount Aldwych at Your Majesty's service," he finished with a low bow to the king.

Philip raised an eyebrow, glancing down the table at the chief English negotiator. "A relation of yours, Ranleigh?" he asked, his attention piqued by the young man's persistence.

"His son," Christian replied, not giving his father a chance to intervene. "I'm sure Your Majesty has heard of the plot to assassinate you. We've brought proof of the other conspirator's identity."

"Another conspirator?" the king questioned, looking toward de la Rocha. "Did we not deal with the Englishman involved?"

"He had a partner among your courtiers," Christian explained. "We found letters in the man's own hand. Ciéza?" He gestured for Teodoro to present their evidence to the king.

Stepping forward toward the king with a deep bow, Teodoro slipped a hand beneath his jerkin to retrieve the letters. He had, of course, seen the monarch from a distance many times but had never approached this close to the royal personage before, and he found he was not particularly impressed. Philip's heavily pomaded hair waved back from a high, pale forehead, his narrow features aloof and indolent, as if even the continued threat against his life was not of enough import to disturb his dignity. Teodoro could not help but contrast this waxwork of a man with Christian's passionate energy. What might his lover accomplish if gifted with Philip's power and authority?

At that instant *el conde* de la Rocha lunged forward, his sword hissing from its scabbard, the blade arcing in a deadly path toward Christian's chest. Teodoro whirled, clutching for his sword hilt, knowing even as he did that neither he nor Raúl would be able to reach the *conde* in time to block his attack. Nor did Christian or Hawkins have the skill and lightning reactions needed to counter such an unexpected strike. He shouted Christian's name in warning, cursing himself for not anticipating that de la Rocha might panic, even though the *conde* had surely damned himself by his desperate action. Teodoro's heart clenched in horror at the inevitable outcome, when suddenly Hawkins launched himself, not at the *conde*, but at Christian, knocking him from his feet.

Hawkins's weight bore them both to the ground, leaving the *conde*'s blade slicing through empty air in a slash that a fraction of a second earlier would have pierced Christian's heart. The tip, however, caught Hawkins's shoulder, a bright splash of red appearing on his sleeve as he fell. Before de la Rocha could recover, Teodoro's sword met his with a dissonant clang, parrying the blade upward in an attempt to wrest it from the older man's hand.

Christian grunted as Gerrard's weight crushed him into the floor. Then it was gone when Gerrard rolled them under the table, taking refuge there as the clang of swords echoed above them. His heart was pounding wildly in his chest, the nerves that arose from facing the king replaced first by fear for his own life and then fear for Teodoro's. He had seen Teodoro fight, knew that he could hold his own in a fair engagement, but the odds were stacked against them now. They weren't on neutral territory where the spectators would observe but not participate. He fully expected to hear the sound of booted feet at any second, the *conde*'s guards coming to his aid. Then too, Teodoro was still at less than full strength, and the wild ride to get here had surely not helped. Pushing Gerrard off him, Christian moved to the edge of the table so he could watch. He noticed immediately that Raúl and the other gypsies had formed a protective circle around the combatants, wisely not drawing their own swords, for to do so in the king's presence bore the penalty of death. Christian could only hope that if Teodoro survived the fight with de la Rocha, the king would view Teodoro's actions through the lens of the *conde*'s treachery.

The door opened and the sounds of shouts reached his ears as soldiers, the king's or the *conde*'s, he couldn't tell, came running. Either way, Christian clambered to his feet, ready to defend Teodoro as his lover had defended him. At his side Gerrard rose as well, hand on the hilt of his sword.

"Hold!" Philip commanded the guards and gypsies, though neither swordsman so much as paused. The *conde*'s actions had done much to condemn him already, and the king did not want to see his defender slain by any outsider. "Do not interfere if you value your lives."

Christian breathed a sigh of relief. That assuaged one of his fears. Now it remained only for Teodoro's strength to hold out.

Teodoro circled de la Rocha warily, letting the *conde* bring the attack to him. It was always wise to assess one's opponent's skills, and he knew he would need to conserve his strength. The *conde* might be at least a dozen years older than Teodoro, but he was lean and agile and had obviously been well tutored in swordplay. Teodoro would not be surprised if the older man still sparred regularly—the speed and power of his assault argued frequent practice.

The *conde* feinted right, engaging the foible of Teodoro's steel; then, with a sudden flick of his wrist, the blade skipped free and de la Rocha lunged, aiming for the heart. Teodoro twisted aside, parrying the thrust as he did so, the tip of his sword catching the sleeve of the *conde*'s doublet and slicing a rent in the rich velvet brocade. He took a step back as the nobleman's face contorted in anger, scanning the room around them for further threats. The king's command at least held the others back—he would not have to face multiple opponents or worry for his friends' safety as he dealt with de la Rocha.

Raúl couldn't decide whether to sigh in relief or curse in frustration when the king ordered all others to stay out of the fight. He didn't relish pitting his men against the *conde*'s guards—for, however good they were, he would surely lose some in such a fight—but neither could he now go to Teodoro's assistance if he needed it. He watched de la Rocha critically. The man had skill, obviously, but no imagination, it seemed, all his feints and parries were straight from the fencing master. That heartened Raúl considerably. Teodoro had never felt so constrained.

"Uncouth buffoon!" de la Rocha hissed over the clatter of their blades. "I thought I had rid myself of your interference. How did you escape the Inquisition?"

"Your prey was not so powerless as you thought him," Teodoro answered, nodding toward Christian while deflecting yet another lunge, his pulse already pounding from the brief skirmish.

"St. Denys was a fool to hire you," the *conde* panted, pressing Teodoro back with a flurry of quick cuts. "But then his greed always outweighed his sense. He should have known you'd be tempted to keep the boy for yourself. You have barely enough taste to appreciate him."

"Pederast," Teodoro spat, his lip curling in disgust. "Had you laid a hand on him, I would have cut off your *cojones* and fed them to your own pigs." Catching the *conde*'s blade on the quillons of his sword, he shoved back forcefully, setting de la Rocha staggering. Teodoro drew a deep breath and tucked the hank of hair that fell over his forehead, threatening to blind him, beneath his bandanna, but before he could press his advantage, the *conde* had recovered his footing and resumed the attack.

Christian's breath caught in his throat as Teodoro fell back, only escaping again when his lover pushed the *conde* away. He couldn't tell what words passed between them, but they seemed to incense Teodoro. Christian could see the sweat beading on his protector's brow, dripping from his hair. He was tempted to draw his sword and join Teodoro despite the king's command, but he feared he would be more hindrance than help. He must have made a move in that direction, though, because Gerrard suddenly put a hand on his arm, restraining him.

The sound of steel on steel grated through the room as the two men vied for supremacy. Neither had any illusions as to the mercy of the other. Everyone in the room understood this duel could end only one way: with the death of one of the contenders. Christian could tell Teodoro was tiring, though his face still bore the signs of grim determination. Fortunately, though, it seemed de la Rocha's age was taking its toll as well, for his parries were slowing too.

Teodoro's arm muscles ached near to trembling, his breath rasping from his throat as the pattern of advance and retreat, parry and riposte wore on. He could tell that the *conde* was wearying too, but he dared not gamble on which of them could endure longer. His barely healed shoulder wound from the duel with St. Denys's men, the Inquisition's torture, and their desperate ride to reach the king in time had all eroded his strength to a point he knew was near to exhaustion. He needed to find a way to end this, soon.

Christian couldn't stifle a cry when de la Rocha bent suddenly and drew a wicked-looking knife from his boot, stabbing at Teodoro's side while he had Teodoro's sword locked with his. Teodoro sidestepped quickly, barely avoiding the tip of the blade, and reached behind him, drawing the *daga izquierda* from his belt. Whether the *conde* underestimated the length of the knife or whether he simply wasn't fast enough, Christian couldn't say, but seconds later the *conde* bent double, his hands clutching his belly as he fell to his knees, blood pouring from his abdomen onto the floor.

His chest heaving, Teodoro let his hands drop to his sides, the tip of his blade touching the carpet, the dagger dripping with de la Rocha's blood. The *conde* glared at him with pure, if powerless, hatred. Teodoro's cut had slit him from groin to gullet—a soldier's attack, not a move de la Rocha would have learned from his cultured fencing master, but seeing Christian safe had become Teodoro's own personal war, and he would accept any consequences, knowing his lover was finally free of the *conde*'s threat. "Check and mate," Teodoro murmured softly.

The entire room seemed frozen in shock, a tableau captured by one of Philip's court painters, and then the *conde* crumpled to one side, catching his fall with one shaking arm. Spitting out a curse to rival any Teodoro had heard on the battlefields, de la Rocha curled his lip into a sneer of disdain. "I hope you enjoyed him," the dying man gasped. "You will never keep him now you have served his purpose." Blood-fletched spittle accented a final curse as the *conde* slumped lifeless to the floor.

Christian forced himself to remember where they were and why they were there, despite the nearly overwhelming urge to fly to Teodoro's side and make sure he was unhurt. He wanted to deny de la Rocha's dying claim, but that would condemn them both before the king himself, and no amount of trickery would save them then. Instead he turned to the king. "*El conde*'s actions accuse him as completely as any word in his own hand, but we will lay the proof of it before Your Majesty if you would see it."

As Christian spoke again on their behalf, Raúl broke the protective circle and put a hand on Teodoro's arm to draw him away from the *conde*'s body. Under cover of that innocent gesture, he imbued his touch with as much healing energy as he could without drawing attention to his actions. It wasn't much, but hopefully it would offset the exhaustion he could read on Teodoro's face long enough for them to finish with the king and withdraw. They needed Christian focused on their diplomatic efforts, not worried about Teodoro.

"His actions have condemned him already, else he would never have attacked to prevent you from showing the letters," Philip replied simply. "You have the gratitude of the throne for bringing it to our attention and preventing his crime, but we see you have not arrived alone. Present your companions to us."

Christian inclined his head in acceptance of the thanks the king had offered and gestured for Teodoro, Raúl, and Gerrard to join him. "Teodoro Ciéza de Vivar, formerly a soldier for Your Majesty, Gerrard Hawkins, who came with me from England to protect me from *el conde*'s threats, and Raúl…." He trailed off, not knowing how to describe the enigmatic gypsy.

"Also one of Your Majesty's former soldiers and loyal subjects," Raúl inserted smoothly.

"Our gratitude to you all," Philip declared. "Señor Hawkins, you saved your master's life this morning, taking a blow intended for him." He slipped a simple garnet ring from his finger and held it out. "Such dedication deserves a reward."

"It's only a scratch," Gerrard demurred as he bowed low before the king and accepted the offered token.

"I'll be the judge of that later," Raúl murmured when Gerrard returned to his side. The *inglés* shot him a surprised look, but Raúl ignored it.

"Señor Raúl," the king continued, drawing their attention again.

"If Your Majesty would thank me for my service, then stop the Inquisition from persecuting the gypsies simply because they are Rom," Raúl interrupted. "My people have served Your Majesty loyally these past days while I returned to Madrid to seek the proof we brought you. Grant them your protection."

"Done," Philip declared, taking the time to look more carefully at the servants whose demeanor was suddenly less than subservient. "As for you, Señor Ciéza de Vivar, we should be put out with you for daring to draw your sword in our presence."

Christian tensed, ready to defend Teodoro's actions, but the king went on before he could speak. "By your quick reactions, though, you saved our lives. You shall have a captaincy in the Royal Guard, where hopefully those quick reactions will continue to serve the crown well."

Teodoro inclined his head, fully aware of the distinction the king was offering. Once he would not have hesitated an instant before accepting such an elevated position, but while he had served his king faithfully for many years, he owed his loyalty and his allegiance to another now.

"I am most honored by Your Majesty's consideration, but I must respectfully decline," Teodoro replied, conscious that the king's offer was not truly a request. He and Christian had still not spoken at length about their future, but despite de la Rocha's dying words, Teodoro finally believed they would share one together. "I fear I would fit poorly into your royal household."

Philip frowned, unused to being refused. "It is not wise to reject the patronage of your king," he pointed out, his voice hardening slightly.

Taking a step back, Teodoro stood at Christian's side, resisting the temptation to meet his lover's eyes, sure if he did so his expression would reveal more than the king and his court had any right to know. "I am honored," Teodoro repeated, "but I have already the patronage of a powerful man. My sword is pledged to him, for as long as he has need of my service."

TWENTY-TWO

"IT REALLY isn't anything serious," Gerrard repeated for at least the fifth time as the gypsy followed him doggedly toward the quarters the king had offered them for the duration of their stay at *el conde* de la Rocha's estates. Gerrard didn't think they would stay long, but Ciéza de Vivar needed some rest before they could ride back to Madrid, even at a leisurely pace. He didn't know how the Spaniard was still standing.

"Unless your skills in healing surpass your skills in swordplay, I suggest you allow me to confirm that," Raúl countered, admiring the graceful manner in which his companion moved despite his size. He smiled disarmingly as Hawkins whipped his head around to stare at him, making it clear he was only teasing.

"Be glad Christian likes you," Gerrard growled defensively despite the smile Raúl wore, "or we would test my skills in swordplay." He shrugged out of his doublet and shirt. "Do your worst, gypsy."

"Some would say that is when I am at my best," Raúl riposted, examining the wound. He found Hawkins's judgment was correct; the cut was not serious, beginning as a mere scratch on the upper bicep that deepened as it traced upward to a shallow score across the meat of the *inglés*'s shoulder. The sides of the cut were clean, to be expected from steel as sharp as the *conde*'s, and the wound itself did not appear inflamed. Raúl trailed his fingers gently over the score, feeling no unusual heat. "This should heal well," he said softly as the muscle flexed beneath his fingertips. Powerful men had ever been his weakness.

"I told you it wasn't serious," Gerrard declared, even as the touch of Raúl's hand sent an unexpected shiver down his spine. He looked up sharply, wondering what magic the gypsy had in his fingers to garner such a reaction, but Raúl's face bore no sign of any guile, leaving Gerrard mentally floundering. If it had been Aldonza tending his wound, he would have thought nothing of his reaction, but Raúl was no woman. Of that he was certain.

The shock in Hawkins's gaze confirmed what Raúl had until now only suspected. Smothering a sigh, he reached instead for his herbs and bandages. After pouring some water from the ewer on the sideboard into a basin, he crumbled a mix of healing herbs into the water and dampened a cloth to bathe the wound before binding it.

Gerrard's muscles twitched as Raúl cleaned the wound, though he would have been hard-pressed to say whether it was from the sting of the herbs on the cut or from fighting the urge to lean back into the gypsy's touch. Then the damp cloth was gone and Raúl's fingers were back, spreading a thick, cool paste over the injury. "What's that?" he asked, confusion making his voice sharp.

"Merely a poultice made with comfrey to speed healing," Raúl answered. "Are you always so—agitated—over a cut that isn't serious?"

"I don't like being fussed over," Gerrard retorted, refusing to consider the true source of his unease. "And don't tell me I'm the first person to chafe at your medicines. I don't see Ciéza de Vivar submitting easily to your attentions."

"Teodoro never submits easily to anything," Raúl agreed, unrolling the bandage around Gerrard's broad chest with careful fingers. "Witness how long he fought against his feelings for Cristian."

Gerrard fought the images that assailed him at Raúl's words. He didn't want to imagine Christian in the arms of his lover, regardless of who submitted to whom. The thought was simply too disturbing. Even more disturbing, though, was the idea that Raúl might once have shared similar embraces with Ciéza—and the fact that such a thought bothered him at all. "Did he fight his feelings for you as hard?"

Raúl arched an eyebrow at Gerrard's reaction—it almost sounded as if the *inglés* was feeling the pinch of jealousy. "Friendship is the one thing Teodoro has never fought," he replied, leaning closer to tie off the bandage.

Gerrard couldn't suppress the thrill of satisfaction at knowing Ciéza had no claim beyond friendship. "What magic is this?" he muttered, pulling away and turning to face Raúl, arms crossed protectively across his chest. "What have you done to me that I react to you like a jealous lover? I've never sought the company of men the way Christian has!"

"I have never needed a spell to attract a lover," Raúl answered with an amused smile. "Are you surprised that strength is drawn to strength?" Gerrard's bewildered expression tempted him to step into those strong arms and show the other man what he had been missing, but the first move had to be Gerrard's.

"But why now?" Gerrard demanded even as his body thrilled at the thought that Raúl might return this crazy attraction.

"That is a question even the wisest man cannot answer," Raúl responded, feeling the tremor of muscle where his hand still rested on Gerrard's chest. He took a step closer, ready to back away if he felt Gerrard withdraw, but the *inglés* stood his ground. "Does it matter?"

"I don't know," Gerrard replied honestly, closing his hand over the one against his skin. "I've never felt this way before. I only know I don't want it to stop."

"Only if you ask to stop," Raúl agreed, lifting his other hand to the broad chest and raising his head to brush his lips softly against Gerrard's.

Gerrard's breath caught in his throat, his entire being focused on the sudden connection between them. Slowly, as if he had to convince himself this was really happening, he lifted his hands to Raúl's shoulders and then into his thick black hair, tilting his head to better mate their mouths one to another.

"A POWERFUL man?"

Teodoro muffled a grunt of pain as Christian maneuvered the sweat-dampened shirt over his head. "After today, how can you still doubt yourself?" he asked, leaning back against the headboard of the luxurious bed in Christian's quarters. "Even the king himself recognized it."

Christian shrugged, uncomfortable with the king's gratitude, though it had only extended as far as praising his courage and agreeing to leave Teodoro in his employ, as he pushed at Teodoro's shoulder so he could examine his back. Between the wild ride and the fight with de la Rocha, Christian was sure Teodoro had to be bleeding. No red rivulets stained his skin, though. "Good," he said with a sigh of relief. "You haven't torn open any of the wounds. I would have had to call Raúl, and I really want to be alone with you right now."

That was a desire Teodoro definitely shared. "No doubt Raúl has other things to command his attention at the moment." He captured Christian's hand and drew it to his chest. "As do we, no?"

Christian spared a thought for the wound on Gerrard's shoulder and decided it wasn't serious, or if it was, Raúl would send for them if he needed their assistance. Raúl had already seen to all their privacy by stationing his men to guard the wing they had been assigned to rest.

They would bar anyone short of the king himself from disturbing them. Then he turned his full attention to the man in his bed. "We do indeed," he agreed, tilting his head to kiss Teodoro firmly, eagerly. He didn't think he'd ever get enough of Teodoro's taste, but thanks to their exploits today, it looked like he would have a lifetime to try. "Te amo," he murmured between nipping bites of Teodoro's lips.

"Para toda la vida," Teodoro asserted, threading a hand into Christian's curls to hold his head still and deepen the kiss. As weary as the duel had left him, the blood still surged in his veins, driving the desire that was never absent in Christian's presence. With his free hand, he worked at the fastenings of Christian's doublet, seeking the warm skin beneath.

Christian broke their kiss long enough to tear his garments over his head, leaving himself bare to the waist. He had no patience with slow seduction now. He—they—had faced down death today, and he needed the connection between them to prove to himself that they had succeeded, that they had survived. After pushing his breeches off as well, he returned to the bed, kneeling over Teodoro as he pressed him into the mattress, urgency investing every line of his body.

Teodoro skimmed his hands over Christian's honeyed skin, urging him closer with every touch. His need was too strong to worship Christian in the manner he deserved, but there would be time for that slow lovemaking later. Right now his body demanded he possess Christian in the most basic of ways, to restake his claim and reinforce the primacy of their union. Lifting his hips from the mattress, he thrust down his breeches far enough to free his straining erection, and pulled Christian to rut against him urgently. "Mi alma," he rasped, desire stealing his breath, "need you now."

Yesterday Christian would not have dared. A week ago he wouldn't have dreamt of it. But today, flushed with success, high on the reality of breaking free of the shadow that had hung over his life for months, Christian dared, reaching for the flagon of oil, not to give to Teodoro, but to slick his own fingers as they dropped between his lover's legs. "Let me," he said, sliding his fingers over the tight pucker of muscle.

His body flexing instinctively at the intimate caress, Teodoro shifted his legs to open himself to Christian without hesitance. Normally a dominant lover, everything in his being longed to feel Christian filling him, claiming him as the equal partners they were, in loving as in life. "Sí," he assented, taking Christian's lips in a hungry kiss. "Soy tuyo."

Relief flooded Christian along with the desire that already swamped his senses. He had not known how Teodoro would react to his request, but now, permission granted, he hastened to take the liberties he'd hesitated to take before. He swiped his fingers back and forth across the clenching flesh, teasing, tantalizing, waiting for Teodoro to relax enough to let him in. He had no idea how long it had been since Teodoro last welcomed someone this way—he didn't want to think about anyone else touching *his* Teodoro. Regardless, he needed to take his time, to treat Teodoro with as much care as his lover had always showed him. Feeling the muscle finally give a little, he slid one finger inside, gasping as the tight heat scalded him. "You feel so good," he murmured, breaking their kiss to study Teodoro's face as he prepared him. He wanted to see every emotion cross the strong features.

Willing his body to relax, Teodoro hitched his hips to take the probing digit deeper. "More," he demanded, gliding his hand down Christian's flank, encircling the shaft he would soon feel inside him. The initial burn of penetration fading, a single finger was not nearly enough to satisfy him. Only Christian filling him could slake that hunger. "Want you—all of you."

"Soon," Christian promised, adding a second finger. "Just let me make you ready."

"I will always be ready for you, *mi amor*." Teodoro reached for the oil and slickened Christian's cock. The quick intake of breath at his touch convinced him Christian's need was as urgent as his own. "Now," he insisted, guiding the silken head to where the twisting fingers breached him. He invaded Christian's mouth in demonstration of how he would have Christian claim his willing body.

Christian fought the urge to simply plunge into Teodoro's welcoming heat. Impaling Teodoro slowly, he reveled in the sensation of being joined to his lover again. When he was fully seated, he paused, reining in his rampant passions, giving Teodoro a chance to adjust. The powerful body trembled beneath him, but as Christian pulled back to study Teodoro's face again, there was no mistaking his expression for anything but pleasure. Teodoro's eyes were closed, features set in a rictus of ecstasy, lips parted on a gasp beneath his heavy moustache. Lowering himself so their chests brushed, Christian eased out slowly, only to thrust deeply once more.

It was a different sensation to feel Christian moving inside him, but to Teodoro the sense of communion was even stronger. Giving himself to Christian in an intimacy he had seldom allowed any lover before, and never with this depth of emotion, every touch of their bodies strengthened the connection uniting them. Teodoro felt invincible—joined like this, there was nothing that could threaten them, no power on earth that could separate them. Christian pushed deeper, brushing against the spot that made Teodoro hiss with pleasure. "There," he urged hoarsely. "Harder."

Christian complied eagerly, rocking his hips so that his cock rubbed back and forth over Teodoro's susceptible spot. That moment of consummation convinced Christian finally of the truth of Teodoro's assertion before the king in a way his success against the Inquisition, discrediting de la Rocha, or even the king's approbation, had been unable to do. In that moment he finally felt like a powerful man. He slid his hand between their bodies to encircle the hard flesh that usually pleasured him so well. His control was growing thin, but he was determined to bring Teodoro joy first.

The clasp of Christian's palm around his cock, coupled with the exquisite friction of his lover stretching him, proved Teodoro's undoing. With a wild cry, he spilled himself between them, his body convulsing around Christian's with the power of his orgasm. Even after he had emptied himself, his hips continued to move, drawing out the blissful tremors as he sought to bring Christian the same fierce rapture.

Christian groaned as Teodoro's muscles milked his hard cock, pulling his climax from him in long, wrenching waves. His rhythm broke, his hips thrusting erratically as he filled Teodoro with his seed. His arms giving out, he collapsed at Teodoro's side, not wanting to exacerbate his healing wounds. He pulled Teodoro with him so they remained locked in an embrace, bodies as close as two separate beings could be.

As much as Teodoro longed to sustain this moment of perfect closeness, his reserves of strength were exhausted and his body demanded rest. Spooning Christian in his arms, his chin nestled in a cloud of golden curls and his hand resting over his lover's heart, Teodoro slept.

"WELL?" ESTEBAN demanded as soon as the door to Raúl's apartments shut behind the four men. "What happened?"

"De la Rocha is dead. The king is safe," Teodoro answered as he pulled out a chair and seated himself gingerly at the table.

Taking pity on Esteban's curiosity, Raúl shared the tale with him and Javier in greater detail, ending with the king's expressions of gratitude to the four rescuers. What happened after that did not need to be shared beyond those involved.

"What happens now?" Esteban asked, still marveling that Teodoro had refused an offer from the king himself to join the Royal Guard.

"My father has asked me to relay a message to the English king on his behalf," Christian replied, unable yet to hide his amazement at the change in his father's attitude in his regard. He had slipped from the bed he shared with Teodoro to heed his sire's summons, determined to stand up for himself for the first time. Full of righteous indignation, he had entered the sitting room where the Duke of Ranleigh waited, ready to insist the older man give him the respect he had surely earned. Before he could even speak, his father had handed him the unsealed missive to their king, which contained not only a more detailed accounting of the day's events than the one he had sent by courier immediately, but also privileged information about the status of the negotiations with Spain and a recommendation that Christian be given a diplomatic posting. "We will need to leave as soon as we can put things in order here. If all goes as planned, we will not be returning to Madrid anytime soon."

Javier reached out his hands to clasp Teodoro's and Christian's. "Then I must thank you, once again, for all your kindness to me."

"What will you do now?" Teodoro asked.

"I am not sure," Javier answered slowly. "I fear I am still in danger from the Inquisition if I remain in Madrid, and I no longer have any family to return to on *el conde*'s estates."

"You could come to England with us," Christian suggested. "My family's estates are large enough to support another person, though we must leave with some haste. Perhaps Gerrard would wait and travel with you when you are well."

"Who said I was returning to England?" Gerrard asked archly, resisting the urge to reach for Raúl as he spoke. He almost laughed as surprise replaced confusion on Christian's face. Ciéza, he noticed, didn't seem surprised at all.

"The king offered the gypsies his protection in gratitude for our assistance," Raúl added. "You would be welcome to stay with my people as well."

"I thank you for the offer, but there is nothing left for me here," Javier answered. "I would be honored to serve you, *vizconde*, in any way I can. I can read and write—though not English," he added sadly.

"You can learn English along with Esteban." Teodoro ignored the startled protest from his son. "A nobleman's page would do well to speak several languages, especially if he expects to travel on his master's diplomatic missions."

His eyes as big as saucers, Esteban glanced from Teo to Christian, who nodded his encouragement. Esteban grinned, even the prospect of more studies unable to quell his excitement at the thought of the new experiences that awaited him. "Yes, come to England with us, Señor Montega," he urged. "It will be much better for both of us to learn together."

"We will see whether Javier is well enough to travel when it is time for us to depart," Teodoro said. "In the meantime, we have much to do in preparation."

Christian rose at Teodoro's words and started for the door. When only Teodoro and Esteban followed him, he looked back at Gerrard in confusion. "Aren't you coming with us?"

"You obviously don't need me anymore," Gerrard pointed out, though his words bore no heat. "We'll all be much happier if I stay here."

A KNOCK on the door startled all three inhabitants of the tiny apartment as they were cleaning up from dinner. Christian tensed in automatic reaction before reminding himself that the *conde* was dead, the threat to him lifted for good. "Do you want me to get the door?" he asked Teo.

Teodoro was already on his feet, habit setting his hand reaching for his dagger. He wondered whether he would feel any less protective once they arrived in England. Deciding it would not be amiss to suggest providing fencing lessons to Christian in earnest, he opened the door to Don Inocencio standing on the other side.

"Do you mind if I come in?" the *cura* asked. "I need to speak with you, and I'd rather do it here than have you come downstairs."

"Certainly," Teodoro agreed, senses alert at the unusual formality of Inocencio's manner. "We were just supping. Have you eaten?"

"Isabel insisted I have something earlier," Don Inocencio replied, nodding to Esteban and Christian. "Esteban, perhaps you would go sit with Isabel while I talk with your father and his guest."

Three sets of eyes meeting, Teodoro lifted a hand before Esteban could protest. "Anything you have to say may be spoken before my son, Inocencio." Glancing again at Christian, he added, "We have some news to share with you as well."

"I have always admired you," Inocencio began, not quite comfortable, "and I have many reasons to be grateful as well, not the least because my nephew does not bear the stain of illegitimacy. But I must ask you and your guest to find other lodgings. I will not condemn you for your choices—I owe you too much to even consider doing that— but as soon as you are well enough, you must find somewhere else to live. Esteban is welcome to stay, either here or downstairs with me, for as long as he likes."

Esteban regarded his uncle seriously. "My place now is where it has always been," he said with great dignity. "Where my father makes his home is where I too will reside."

Teodoro smiled at his son, struck again by how much Esteban had matured over the past weeks. Christian's arrival had changed more than his own life. "I understand your reasons, my old friend, and would not wish to place you in a situation you cannot condone. But the news I referred to is that *el vizconde* Aldwych is returning to England, and Esteban and I are to accompany him."

Don Inocencio's eyes widened in surprise. "To England? But why?" Realizing how his words must sound, he turned to Christian. "Please do not think I am ungrateful for your assistance. I know Teo would be dead now but for your intervention, and that would have left Esteban an orphan, but the Holy Office—"

"I have heard enough about the Holy Office to last a lifetime," Christian interrupted, putting his arm over Esteban's shoulders in silent inclusion. "I prefer to take my family somewhere safer, where my good name and my influence will help protect us all. You may trust I'll take good care of them."

If Don Inocencio found it odd to hear Christian speak of protecting Teodoro, he did not remark on it. "I understand your wish to remove from its reach," he said softly, lifting his hand in benediction. "May the good Lord's blessings be with you always."

"*Gracias*, Don Inocencio," Christian said with an inclination of his head. "I should begin to pack. I'll leave you to say good-bye, for you will almost certainly be at *matins* when we leave in the morning."

Having made their farewells, with Esteban promising to write to his uncle as soon as they arrived in England, the priest returned downstairs and Teodoro joined Christian in their bedchamber, closing the door behind him. "So I am to rely on your good name to protect me now?" he asked, the corners of his lips twitching beneath his moustache.

Christian shrugged. "In diplomatic circles, none will question a consul keeping a bodyguard nearby. My position will allow us to be together in a way we could never do here in Spain. Is that going to be a problem between us, Teo? That the rest of the world will see and probably point out regularly the differences in our stations?"

"I have made my peace with your station," Teodoro answered, "so long as it does not prevent us from sharing a bed."

"Never." Christian sealed his promise with an ardent kiss. "Nothing will keep me from your bed." He drew Teodoro in that direction, intending to prove the truth of his words.

"Except perhaps all the clothes presently occupying it," Teodoro commented wryly.

Christian was tempted to simply shove them aside in favor of ravishing his lover, but he'd argued enough over the number of shirts and breeches Teodoro owned. He didn't want to start another discussion now. He returned to his task of folding and packing their belongings. "Will you regret leaving your home, your country? Everything happened so quickly that we really didn't have time to talk about it, much less about how Esteban might feel at being suddenly uprooted."

Tossing his garments into the armoire as soon as the bed was cleared, Teodoro sank onto the mattress with a sigh of relief, his muscles still protesting the activities of the past few days. "Esteban sees it all as a grand adventure. As for me, there is nothing and no one I care about leaving behind, save Raúl, and I suspect circumstances will bring us together again," he answered, stretching out and drawing Christian into his embrace. He wondered now how he had ever slept without Christian's warmth beside him. "Everything else I need will be accompanying me. What then should I regret?"

Christian stripped off the last of his clothes and turned into Teodoro's welcoming arms, nuzzling his jaw before nibbling his way toward his lips, joining their mouths as they would join their lives. "Nothing, it would seem, but I had to make sure. We are partners in this as in all things, and I didn't want you to feel slighted."

"I am most pleased to see your true worth recognized at last," Teodoro assured him. Especially by Christian himself, though he did not add that aloud. "I find seeing you exercise your power most… arousing." He ground against Christian, offering empirical proof of his arousal.

Christian bit back a moan at the erotic friction. "Esteban is still awake," he gasped, not wanting to create a situation that would embarrass all three of them come morning.

"Esteban will need to get used to this," Teodoro retorted, resenting anything that prevented him from hearing Christian's sounds of passion. He sought out the vulnerable tendons of Christian's neck while he spanned the wings of his hips with his hands, increasing the sensual friction. "Since I do not plan to cease loving you anytime soon."

"No," Christian agreed, "don't stop." The brush of Teodoro's moustache over his skin sent shivers of desire through him, wiping away all thoughts of Esteban, of the future, indeed of anything except what his lover was doing to him. He tipped his head back, offering his neck to Teodoro, needing more contact, more caresses, simply more.

"Never." Teodoro nipped down the graceful throat, pausing to suck at the pulse beating in the hollow between Christian's collarbones before dipping lower, seeking the flat, sensitive nipples he loved to worship. "Let me hear you," he urged, the proof of his effect on Christian feeding his own desire.

Between the husky rasp of Teodoro's voice and his own emotions, Christian had no hope of resisting that request. A heartfelt groan slipped from his lips as Teodoro's teeth and tongue toyed with his peaked flesh. He arched his back, wordlessly urging Teodoro to continue.

After eliciting another deep moan from his attentions, Teodoro slid lower, teasing his moustache over the quivering skin of Christian's abdomen. The heady scent of arousal drew him like a magnet to a lodestone, until he could lap at the source of the enticing muskiness. The wail that sounded as he carefully drew his teeth over the silky head of Christian's cock made him swell with his own hunger, but he repressed his need, gorging himself on the taste.

In the main room of the apartment, Esteban rolled over on his narrow cot, trying his best to ignore the sounds coming from the other room. Only Teo's anger if he found that Esteban had left their lodgings at such a late hour kept him from slipping out to give the two some privacy. As it was, he pulled the pillow over his head and resolved to find quarters far, far away from theirs once they began their travels. He didn't need the sound of his new master's begging or his guardian's muffled laughter in reply in his head.

"Please, Teo," Christian whimpered, his hips held in place by Teodoro's large hands. He needed to move, to thrust into the moist heat surrounding his cock, but Teodoro wouldn't let him, set on torturing him all night long, it seemed.

Twisting his head so that the tips of his moustache brushed over Christian's sac, Teodoro worked his tongue up and down the twitching shaft that filled his mouth so deliciously. He'd need to give in to Christian's pleas for relief soon, his own body's demands becoming too insistent to ignore, but he wanted to indulge himself in coaxing out a few more sultry moans first. Stretching out an arm, he found the flagon of oil he'd left uncapped on the sideboard, then dipped his fingers inside to coat them well. Hollowing his cheeks to increase the pressure, he trailed the oiled fingertips up the damp crease below his chin, tickling at the roseate opening.

Christian fought hard against his imminent release, not wanting their lovemaking to end this way. Teodoro's fingers playing over his entrance made him long to be filled with something thicker and harder. The brush of the heavy moustache combined with the suction of Teodoro's sinful mouth, though, made it difficult to concentrate. "Close," he gasped, tugging on Teodoro's shaggy hair, trying to pull him up for a kiss and to give himself a much-needed reprieve. Teodoro, however, refused to cooperate.

Christian's admission was what Teodoro wanted to hear, and he redoubled his efforts, sinking his fingers deeper and flexing when he found the bump of soft tissue that made Christian cry out sharply. He dragged his teeth up the steely flesh until he could circle the ridge below the head with his lips, sucking hard and then taking the entire cock as deep as he could, relaxing his throat until it nudged the back of his gullet. The salty taste teased at him, and he swallowed around the head, growling deep in his throat in anticipation.

Christian tried to resist. Truly, he did, but he had no defense against such overwhelming sensations. His body bowing off the bed, he wailed his pleasure as his engorged cock released its pent-up fluid. Panting hard, he collapsed back onto the sheets, tremors still shaking him as Teodoro continued to probe and stimulate his sensitive passage. He wanted to offer to return the favor, but he couldn't catch his breath enough to form the words. Instead he stroked his fingers through Teodoro's hair and hoped he would read his willingness in his eyes.

Nothing compared to the flavor of Christian filling his mouth, though Christian's cries as he emptied himself gave Teodoro almost as much joy. Swallowing the last pulses of tangy fluid, he moved his fingers gently, prolonging Christian's pleasure as he ensured his lover was well-prepared to receive him. The gasp as his rough fingertips rubbed the spongy mound made him consider bringing Christian to a second release, but his own cock was throbbing too urgently to dally any longer. Letting the softened shaft slide from his lips with a final kiss, he pushed upward to kneel over the delectable body lying indolently below him.

Without hesitation Christian spread his legs wide, offering himself to Teodoro. Languidly he lifted his hand to encircle the rigid cock he hoped would soon be splitting him wide. "Soy tuyo," he murmured, feeling his own erection begin to swell again in response to the continued stimulation.

"Y yo tuyo." Teodoro settled his palms on Christian's sleek hips, holding him down as he knelt between the long legs that welcomed him home. He let Christian guide him in place and then lifted his lover's hand to his lips, laving the hint of his own cream from the palm as he slid inside in one long, slow stroke.

Christian gasped again as he was filled, the moment of communion as strong this time as it had been the first time, as it was every time. He slid his hands down Teodoro's back to clasp his buttocks, keeping him close, completing the circle that held them. He rocked in time to Teodoro's thrusts, meeting every ingress with a push of his own, until the force of their movements set the headboard thumping against the wall.

The clasp of Christian's hot, moist flesh around him stealing his breath, Teodoro bit his lip as he plunged deeper with each stroke, Christian's moans encouraging him to move harder, faster. He threw back his head, his chest heaving for cooler air as he fought to hold back his climax until he could bring Christian to the peak again, this time with him. Only when the shortened cries issuing from Christian's throat changed in pitch, to a tone Teodoro had learned meant he was close to release, did he let his head drop forward, finding Christian's lips roughly, taking his cry into his mouth as they soared together off the highest pinnacle of ecstasy.

His second climax shaking him like a dog with a bone, Christian slumped onto the bed, every muscle limp as Teodoro thrust hard one more time before spilling inside him. He nuzzled blindly at Teodoro's cheek, feeling the rasp of stubble against his lips. He floated on the edge of consciousness, wrapped in contentment and satiation, knowing from Teodoro's even breathing that he felt the same. He wanted to speak, but no words seemed powerful enough to encompass the depth and breadth of his emotions. He would just have to spend his lifetime showing Teodoro how he felt instead.

"Wherever you go," Teodoro rasped when he could speak again. He rolled them over, bodies still joined, easing his weight from his sated lover and wrapping him in a possessive embrace. "Wherever it leads, we will be together."

EPILOGUE

Five years later

THE COURT of Louis XIII, king of France, glittered like few others, and the courtiers had put on their finest feathers, the better to impress the new English ambassador with their wealth and prestige. Christian understood this well, for he too had dressed to impress, but that knowledge did not lessen the impact as he strode confidently down the long hall of the Louvre to make his bow to the king and queen. When he reached the foot of the dais, he bowed low before presenting his letter of introduction to the French monarch.

"Ah, *vicomte* Aldwych," Louis intoned, glancing over the letter before setting it aside, "we have been expecting you. Our royal brother in Spain speaks highly of you."

"Your Majesty is too kind," Christian demurred. "I merely delivered the message."

"You have our gratitude nonetheless," Anne d'Autriche, Philip's sister, insisted. "Be welcome here for as long as you choose to stay."

"Madame." Christian's bow was deep, not merely an ambassador greeting a king, but a man before a queen. He had no interest in women personally, but his father had drilled a deep respect for them into his son. "I serve at the will of my liege and yours."

Louis watched the exchange between his wife and the Englishman carefully. He knew all too well the attraction she held for the men of the court. He chose to believe she was faithful to him, but that did not mean men did not try to dissuade her from that course. This one, however, showed none of the usual signs, making the king wonder where his interest lay. Looking beyond the new ambassador, his gaze raked the man's entourage. A secretary, a page, a bodyguard... all necessary, but nothing near the number of hangers-on he often saw behind other countries' representatives to his court. He wondered what that meant as well, even as his gaze lingered on the bodyguard. Ciéza de Vivar, Philip had named the man when writing to his sister. An able swordsman and independent man. So what had led this independent man to his current position? Louis's gaze returned to the ambassador, still exchanging courtesies with the queen. Could that be the attraction? Certainly it might have been for Louis if his and Ciéza de Vivar's roles were reversed. Aldwych was a fine figure of a man, young still, but not so much as to be mistaken for a boy. He stood with the grace of his upbringing and the confidence of one who knew his own worth, something Louis wished most of his courtiers would learn. Whether they thought too much or too little of themselves made no difference to him. This one, though, was neither fawning nor arrogant, and Louis found that terribly attractive. Now if the Englishman would but return his regard....

Running his fingers beneath the collar of his elegant doublet, Teodoro fought back the surge of jealousy that gnawed him at Louis's admiring gaze. He would be the first to admit that Christian was a fine figure of a man, the deep russet of his doublet favoring the golden cast of his skin, the breeches flattering his long legs, the same legs that had wrapped around Teodoro so strongly in their bed last night. Only that memory allowed him to hold back the insistent urge to wrench Christian away from the monarch's lascivious stare. He trusted his lover completely, but Teodoro did not take well to anyone eying his partner in that way, be he king of all France or a lowly stable hand.

At his elbow, a musketeer jostled him slightly, drawing his gaze. "Clear the scowl from your face," Aristide murmured. "His Majesty considers himself a lover of some skill and so prides himself on seducing rather than ordering his lovers to his bed. He may admire your ambassador, but he will not force him."

"King or no, he would need to kill me first to do so," Teodoro answered just as softly. His introduction to the more exalted ranks of society had taught him that men were no different for having riches and titles—if anything, they were more open about their appetites. Something about the looks of the reddish-blond man in the black tabard of the Royal Musketeers told him it was safe to speak freely, though, even if it was an oblique threat to the monarch this man served. Still, he tried to clear his expression, transferring his gaze from the king to Christian, a sight that never failed to calm his heart even as it warmed his loins.

Aristide inclined his head with a small smile. Strength recognized strength. "Then it is fortunate it will not come to that. While my friends and I would gladly spar with you, we would rather not have to challenge you in earnest. It would not be good for diplomatic relations."

Respecting the easy confidence of a fighter who had no need to boast, Teodoro nodded. "I would be pleased to try my sword against yours, or any of your companions," he replied with an answering smile. "I find diplomatic relations provide little chance for me to keep my arm keen."

"This evening, perhaps?" Aristide suggested. "At the palais of M. de Tréville?"

"I serve at the will of my ambassador," Teodoro answered, sure that Christian's plans for the evening matched his own—and that the sparring they intended would not require their swords. "I do not believe I will be free this evening, but perhaps another day?"

"I look forward to it."

"As do I."

Christian stifled a sigh as he felt the king's gaze undressing him. He supposed he should be used to it by now. In every court they had served in, someone, often more than one man, had followed him with his eyes. So far none had been brazen enough to approach him. He only hoped the king would be equally tactful. Rebuffing him would not be politic, but his heart and his body belonged to one man alone, and that was not the king of France. He tried to resist glancing back to assure himself that Teodoro was at his back, as always. There would be time for them later. It would be hours still before they could slip away, but Christian couldn't stop himself from glancing at Teodoro, eyes dark with promise.

Teodoro bit back a groan at the heated look Christian shot him, hoping no one else had recognized its intent. Seeing Christian assume the trappings of power his position demanded always left Teodoro aching to feel his lover prove some of that power in their bed as well. Widening his stance, he grasped the ornately woven hilt of his sword and hoped the political maneuvering would not go on much longer.

Standing beside Javier, Esteban caught the look passing between Christian and Teo and tried not to roll his eyes. He leaned toward Javier instead, whose face bore an indulgent smile that told Esteban the meaning of that look was not lost on him either. "It's a good thing our quarters are far from the ambassador's," he said under his breath. "It's going to be one of those nights."

Exclusive excerpt

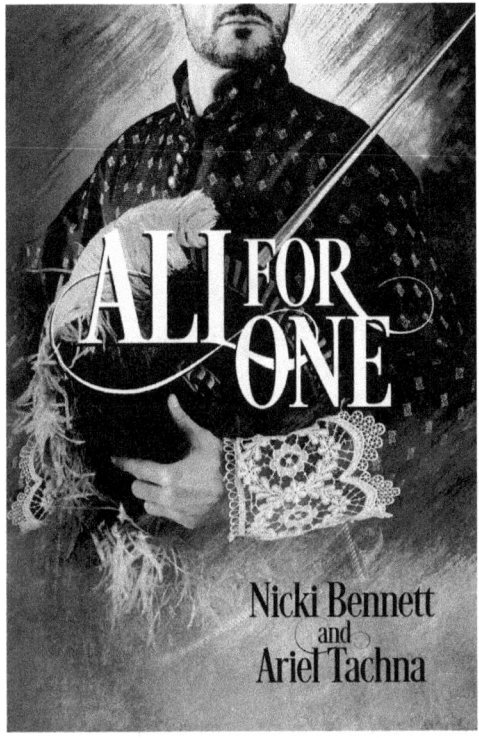

All for Love: Book Two

Aristide, Léandre, and Perrin pledge only three loyalties in life: their king, their captain, and their passion for each other. So when the musketeers discover a plan to accuse M. de Tréville of treason, the initial impulse to kill the messenger, Benoît, is tempered by their need to unmask the plotter. But their first two suspects, the English ambassador and Cardinal Richelieu, prove to be innocent, forcing the musketeers to delve deeper into the inner machinations of the French court.

Meanwhile, Aristide finds himself falling in love with the ill-fated messenger, a blacksmith without a home who rouses all of his protective, possessive instincts. Benoît, however, has no interest in any man. Torn between desire and duty, Aristide must find a way to protect the king and clear his captain's name—all while heeding the demands of his heart.

Coming Soon to
www.dreamspinnerpress.com

ONE

Paris, 1629

"WHEN DID Aristide say he got off duty?" Perrin asked languidly, running his hand down Léandre's naked back. "It's been too long since we last fucked him."

"Sundown, I think," Léandre answered, shifting slightly where he lay between his bedmate's legs. He cupped the dark-haired man's buttocks, tweaking a muscular cheek as he pulled him closer. "Getting ambitious, aren't you? What makes you think Aristide's suddenly going to change his tastes? You should know him by now, Perrin—he'll suck you anytime you like, but he'll not give his ass to anyone."

"Fine," Perrin huffed, thrusting up against the blond. "I'll just have to settle for your ass while he fucks mine."

"Lucky for you, I'm much more flexible than he is," Léandre agreed, wrapping a long leg around Perrin's hips. Reaching down, he took the heavy shaft in hand, stroking it just the way he knew Perrin liked best. "Though I ought to make you take care of yourself for implying that fucking me is 'settling' for anything. This is the finest piece of ass you'll ever sink your cock into, boy, and don't ever forget it."

Perrin smacked Léandre's buttocks lightly, barely enough to sting. "Only because I can't have Aristide's," he retorted, nuzzling Léandre's neck gently to dispel any heat in his words, and then rolled them both until Léandre was beneath him. "And you won't make me take care of myself because then you'd have to take care of yourself, and you hate to do that."

"Damn right. It's the only reason I put up with you. Now shut up and fuck me," Léandre growled, stopping any further conversation by dragging Perrin's mouth to his and kissing him ruthlessly.

Not being one to argue with the voice of authority when he heard it, Perrin slid a hand between them to make sure Léandre was well enough stretched and lubricated for the reaming he wanted. Deciding all was in order, he lined up his cock and pushed in all the way with one solid thrust, enjoying the deep groan that escaped through the torrid kiss.

Léandre could never decide which he preferred more—sinking into Perrin's tight ass or being split wide by the younger man's long, thick cock. Aristide might be a more experienced lover, but Perrin more than made up for his lack of finesse with sheer exuberance. Grabbing on with both hands, Léandre hitched Perrin a little higher, so that each stroke rubbed firmly over his sweet spot. Once he had Perrin exactly where he wanted him, Léandre let his fingers wander the valley between his cheeks, teasing at the puckered entrance.

Perrin reared back when he felt Léandre's fingers on him. As much as he loved fucking, he also loved someone playing with his hole, a fact Léandre knew well. His pace increased as Léandre probed more firmly, driving him wild with lust.

Earning a moan when he withdrew, Léandre spat on his fingers and rubbed them together before pushing back inside with two digits, stretching and searching at the same time. When Perrin's entire body— and a magnificent body it was, all hard, toned muscle—seized with pleasure, he pulled Perrin's dark head down to his and bit at his lips. Clenching his internal muscles around the invasive rod, he arched his hips upward to meet Perrin's thrust, using every trick at his command to prove the truth of his boast.

"Fuck, Léandre," Perrin groaned as Léandre teased him without mercy, leaving him gasping and aching for release. He thrust his tongue hard and deep into Léandre's mouth, ravishing it as he ravished the man beneath him. "So tight." And Léandre was. No matter how often they did this, Léandre was as tight as the first time, and it drove Perrin crazy.

Rocking in counterpoint as Perrin did his best to fuck him through the mattress, Léandre fought the impulse to reach for himself—not that there was a *pouce* of space between their bodies anyway. Instead he worked a third finger into Perrin's ass, stretching him nearly as wide as Perrin was stretching him. His fingers might be a poor substitute for Aristide filling Perrin from behind, but Léandre was determined to bring him to nearly as hard a climax before he came himself. He still had hopes of burying himself in that firm—and now well prepared—arse when he did so. "*Allez*, Perrin," he rasped, tearing his lips away to suck air into his heaving lungs. "Give it up. You know you can't outlast me."

With a frustrated roar, Perrin climaxed. One day he'd manage to stay in control long enough to fuck Léandre to orgasm, but until then, he'd satisfy him some other way. Pulling back as soon as the tremors racking his muscles eased enough for him to move, he rocked onto his knees, intending to take Léandre in his mouth and ease the heavy erection.

Not that Perrin didn't have a supremely talented mouth, but Léandre had another target in mind for his cock. Taking advantage of the Perrin's still-relaxed state, Léandre lunged forward, driving him onto his back. Locking his arms under Perrin's knees, he pulled his legs up and back to open him completely. With a deep, satisfied groan, he drove into Perrin's well-stretched hole, hissing when the walls closed around him in a hot, velvety sheath.

Perrin howled his pleasure as he felt Léandre's cock pierce him, his hips rocking into the thrust mindlessly. "Feel like a real man now?" he taunted, knowing he'd get a more enthusiastic ride if he pricked Léandre's temper. And since he liked it the harder the better, pricking Léandre's temper was essential.

"If Aristide was here... he could stuff something... in your mouth... to shut you up," Léandre panted, hitching Perrin's hips higher and pounding into him with all his considerable strength. His pulse roared in his ears, and though he vaguely heard a bang he assumed was Perrin's skull hitting the headboard, he was too consumed by his impending climax to care. Throwing back his head, he shouted in triumph as his release surged through him, sparking every nerve in his body with pleasure.

Hearing his name, the third member of the trio paused in the doorway, taking in the sight of golden buttocks driving between widespread thighs dusted with darker hair. Léandre fucking Perrin, then. He'd made a mental wager with himself which man would be topping the other when he returned from patrol to the small town house the three of them shared near the musketeer headquarters in Paris. Grinning as his assumption proved correct, he kicked the door closed and leaned against the frame, pulling off his gloves. "Starting without me again?" he drawled.

"He was too impatient to wait," Perrin gasped, back arching as Léandre's hips stuttered against his in release. He turned to look at the tall figure in the door, imposing in his black uniform, and he was aroused all over again. "He's got me all worked up. Come finish me off."

"Just… taking the edge off," Léandre managed to rasp, rolling to his side and patting the mattress between them in invitation. "I'll last longer with you this way," he added, green eyes gleaming lasciviously.

"I was on duty all day, not lounging in bed," Aristide observed wryly, working his tabard over his head and hanging it up carefully before bending to pull off his boots. "I don't have the energy to deal with both of you at once."

"Then let us deal with you," Perrin proposed, sitting up and reaching for Aristide. "Lie back and let us do all the work." Aristide never agreed to that proposition, but Perrin never stopped hoping. He figured if he didn't ask, the answer would always be no.

"I've got Perrin's ass all stretched and slick for you." Léandre smirked, stroking a hand over the come still coating his cock. He might have just climaxed, but watching Aristide slowly reveal his magnificent body as he removed his uniform was a sight that never failed to rouse him, however tired or sated he might be. "Or we can let him suck you for a bit, and then you can fuck a real man."

"Oh, have you got one hidden somewhere?" Aristide taunted, smiling as he tossed the last of his clothing over a chair and stretched mightily. "*Putain*, I'm looking forward to some time off," he groaned, sliding into the wide bed between his fellow swordsmen. "This latest batch of recruits is trying even my patience."

"Salaud," Perrin retorted in response to the insult even as he slid a roving hand up Aristide's thigh. "All the more reason to let us help you relieve some stress." He bent his head and nipped sharply at one pink nipple, hidden in its mat of hair. "We have two weeks to do whatever we want. And tonight, I want to do you."

Aristide and Léandre snorted together as Léandre lowered his head to mouth at the other rosy nub. "Told him to keep dreaming," he muttered around a hardening mouthful.

Aristide groaned and arched to encourage more of the dual attentions. "I think I'm too tired to fuck either of you," he complained. "In fact, you can just keep doing that until I fall asleep."

"And waste this?" Perrin protested, cupping the shaft that was rapidly swelling to hardness despite Aristide's claims of fatigue. He reared back onto his knees and straddled the older man's hips. "Just lie back and relax. I'll do all the work." He reached behind him to stroke Aristide's cock a few times before lifting it upright so he could slide down its length. "Léandre loosened me just enough for you." He smirked at Léandre. "Of course, if he weren't so puny, this wouldn't feel nearly as good."

"If I were any bigger, you wouldn't be able to ride tomorrow," Léandre retorted, easing the sting of his retort by wrapping a palm around Perrin's cock where it bobbed in front of his nose as he kissed his way down Aristide's muscled abdomen. "The only reason you can take Aristide or me is that you're such a cock whore—though you're wasting your time looking for anyone else with our natural gifts."

Perrin snorted, breaking his rhythm on Aristide's cock. "You'd be wasting your time trying to find anyone else willing to 'waste their time' with your 'gifts,'" he snapped back instantly, stroking Léandre's hair to soften the insult.

"Children," Aristide chided with the hint of a chuckle in his voice, "if you can't play nicely with your toys, they'll be taken away." He raised a hand to stroke Perrin's stubbled cheek, then ran his fingers over the full lips. "Surely you can find better use for your tongues than bickering."

Perrin opened his mouth at once to suck the digits inside, making sure to wet them well since he hoped he knew where they would be going next. Léandre, in the meantime, had worked his way down Aristide's stomach to nuzzle the bronzed hair surrounding his cock. Edging closer and leaning with a forearm on either side of Perrin's shins, he licked around the base of the thick shaft where it breached Perrin.

The wet drag of Léandre's tongue drew low moans of approval from both Aristide and Perrin. Aristide pulled his fingers from Perrin's mouth and wrapped his arms around Léandre's hips, using one hand to spread his cheeks while he trailed the dampened fingers down his crease. He could feel the slickness seeping from the eager portal—so Perrin had fucked Léandre first; he'd have won his bet either way—and didn't hesitate to thrust two fingers inside, unerringly finding the spot that would make Léandre howl.

Perrin posted frantically on Aristide's hard cock, the tickle of Léandre's tongue only adding to his arousal. Despite his earlier climax, he was achingly hard again, a tribute to the unquenchable lust his two lovers aroused in him. It only took a touch, a look, and he was ready for them, either to give or take or both at once. He was often the filling in a very delectable *chausson aux pommes*, much to their mutual delight. For now, though, he needed to come again, and he intended to take Aristide with him. Feeling daring, he reached behind him and traced his fingers down the crack of Aristide's ass, dancing across the tight hole.

Clenching instinctively at the touch of Perrin's fingers, Aristide's hips jutted upward, his cock pushing deeper into the clinging embrace of Perrin's passage. When he drew back, Léandre's tongue traced around the base of his shaft, following up its length to dance around the place where he and Perrin joined, trying to wedge its way inside with him. Unable to hold out any longer against the combined attentions of both his lovers, Aristide growled deep in his chest and shook with the strength of his release, his seed filling Perrin's channel and leaking down to be lapped up by Léandre's agile tongue.

Aristide's fingers faltered as his climax shuddered through him, and Léandre tightened around them, dancing close to the edge of his own release. He licked avidly around the softening shaft, rimming Perrin's stretched opening and gleaning as much of Aristide's taste as he could, before pushing up to lap at the leaking head of Perrin's erection.

Any one of the provocations currently pushing him toward release would have been enough for Perrin. The combination of Aristide's hot seed flooding him and Léandre's facile tongue licking it from his ass before moving to the tip of his erection was more than he needed. With barely a shout of warning, Perrin sprayed all over Léandre's face.

Léandre's subsequent yelp, nearly as loud as Perrin's had been, roused Aristide from his lassitude. Pressing a third finger alongside those still stretching Léandre open, he wrapped his free hand around Léandre's cock, the fluid dripping from it letting his fist glide smoothly. A few twisting strokes were all it took to wring another climax from Léandre, who collapsed into the pool of creamy seed on Aristide's belly, his forehead pillowed against Perrin's broad chest. "Good thing you handle a sword better than you do your cock, Perrin," Léandre grumbled, rubbing the come from his face into Perrin's skin.

"It did exactly what it was supposed to," Perrin retorted, stroking Léandre's blond hair lightly. "And exactly *where* it was supposed to." He yawned broadly and shifted around on the bed so they were all lying with their heads on the pillows. "You've worn me out."

"I hope you've saved enough energy to get an early start tomorrow," Aristide countered, using a corner of the sheet to clean himself before settling between his two lovers. "I want to get on the road before M. de Tréville thinks of a reason to keep us here."

"After all the extra training time we've spent with the new recruits, we deserve a fortnight's rest," Léandre protested. "And I can't think of a better way to spend them than tasting the newest vintage at Chablis."

"He's granted us leave," Perrin reminded them. "He won't recall it unless he has no other choice. He knows how hard we've worked, and that we'll work as hard or harder when we get back because we've had a break. Now stop jabbering and let me get some sleep, or I won't be responsible for my actions in the morning."

"You wake up the same way every morning, Perrin—hard," Aristide observed, stifling a yawn. He shifted until he was comfortably spooned between his two partners' warm bodies, his eyelids drifting shut. "Now, both of you, sleep—we ride at dawn."

THE SUN was barely above the horizon, a scant six hours after it had set, when the three musketeers strode into the stable at *l'hôtel particulier de M. de Tréville*. Aristide went immediately to the box where Orphée, his stallion, whickered impatiently. Behind him he could hear Léandre and Perrin arguing over which horses they would ride today. He just shook his head and began saddling his impatient brute. "I'm sorry I haven't been around much," he told the steed as he brushed him. "We'll go for a long run today and show those pretenders what a real horse can do."

"Riding that old nag again?" Perrin asked, coming to stand at the stall door and admire the big bay animal—and its owner.

"I don't ever have to worry about having a mount," Aristide pointed out laconically. Keeping his own steed, rather than having to make do with whatever horse was available in their company's common stables, was the one luxury he retained from his privileged life before joining the musketeers.

"Where's your sense of adventure?" Léandre added, joining the other two men. "I'd get bored with only one ride."

Perrin snorted. "That's why we can't find him some nights. He's gone in search of a new mount."

Aristide just shook his head at the younger men's antics. "Variety is no replacement for quality," he informed them. "No amount of adventure can make up for knowing I can always rely on this 'old nag,' as you call him."

Léandre and Perrin looked at each other and laughed. "Boring," they teased, going to finish preparing the horses they'd selected for the upcoming adventure.

"Horses are like lovers," Aristide mused to Orphée as he saddled the animal. "When you find the perfect match, you hold on to it. There isn't a horse in this stable that's your equal, old boy, so as long as you're game, we'll keep on together. What do you say?"

The horse butted its owner's chest affectionately, eliciting a lighthearted laugh. "Let's go show those two children what real men can do."

Aristide led the bay out into the courtyard and swung onto its back. "Perrin, Léandre!" he shouted. "We're wasting daylight. The vineyards await!"

Perrin and Léandre clattered out of the stable atop two of the company's horses. Aristide shook his head again at their foolery and led the way toward the Porte d'Italie and south toward Chablis. They thundered through the countryside, enjoying the cool morning air on their faces as they rode. Perrin was sure it would be a hot day by the time the sun reached its zenith, but this early the dew still moistened the air and settled the dust, leaving them to ride unhampered toward their destination. They passed through Viry-Châtillon at lunchtime and arrived in Savigny-le-Temple as the sun was setting. The innkeeper was happy to provide a room, food, and drinks for three of the king's musketeers and equally happy to see his boisterous guests on their way the next morning.

It had rained lightly during the night, leaving the air crisp and fresh. Despite the run the day before, the horses were frisky, so the three men gave them their heads and let them gallop on southward toward Fontainebleau, where they intended to stop for lunch.

The sun was almost overhead and breakfast but a distant memory when they pulled abruptly to a halt, dismounting swiftly to come to the aid of an injured man lying on the side of the road.

"Was he thrown from his horse?" Perrin asked as Aristide knelt at the man's side.

"Possibly," Aristide allowed, glancing up from the pool of red spreading over the dampened ground. "Too much blood for that alone, though," he observed, gently rolling the body from where it lay crumpled, facedown. His breath caught as he saw the source of the blood. A dark hole marred the tunic and shoulder of the man in the dirt. "He's been shot."

Léandre and Perrin exchanged somber glances, hands going to the pistols they carried in their belts. "He's still wearing his satchel," Léandre observed. "There may be something in there."

"Check and see," Aristide nodded, tearing a strip of linen from the hem of the man's shirt to staunch the bleeding. "Perrin, see if you can find his horse."

Perrin nodded and searched for any hoofprints not left by their own mounts. Finding a print too deep for their animals, he swung back onto his horse and started off in the direction of the tracks.

Léandre, meanwhile, had dumped the contents of the knapsack onto the road. For the most part, it contained the usual accoutrements of a traveler, but a letter drew his attention. Picking it up, he saw that the seal was broken and the parchment torn. He'd started to put it back down when M. de Tréville's name caught his eye. Wondering what business the stranger could have with the leader of the musketeers, he opened the missive and read its contents. "I'm not sure you should work so hard to save him, Aristide," he said gravely, his expression hardening. "This letter accuses M. de Tréville of treason."

The story continues in

All for Love: Book Three

"Are you surprised that strength is drawn to strength?"

For the last six years, the gypsy healer Raúl has lived a life he never dreamed possible. Gerrard Hawkins has stood at his side, his love a source of silent strength like nothing Raúl has ever known.

When a letter from Gerrard's estranged father forces them in separate directions—Gerrard back to England to make peace with his family and Raúl to Saintes-Maries-de-la-Mer for his annual pilgrimage—Raúl expects to suffer for their parting, but he holds on to their plans to meet again in France when Gerrard has satisfied his father's demands.

When Gerrard left England, he never expected to return, especially after he pledged his life and love to Raúl. Yet he cannot dismiss his father's offer of peace without some acknowledgment. When he arrives in England to find tragedy, his sense of duty toward his family's tenants wars with his promises to Raúl.

As tensions mount and illness spreads in France, Raúl stands as a bastion of hope, but his strength is not limitless. Gerrard is the rock he leans on, and without that strength, Gerrard's arrival in France may come too late.

Coming Soon to www.dreamspinnerpress.com

A Hot Cargo story

Captured and accused of piracy, privateer Blaise Risner, captain of the Golden Stallion, finds himself in a clinch - literally - with Confederation Admiral Peter Keller, who promises to see justice done by way of hard labor. But when the chemistry between them rivals the heat of the twin Talixin suns, the dominant admiral decides he wants to handle the rehabilitation of the provocative pirate himself. After their first close encounter, Blaise figures that serving Keller in such a personal capacity won't be such a terrible sentence.

Keller dispenses his own forms of painful justice and sensual discipline, which usually involve a not-so-resistant Blaise on his knees bound and determined to give as good as he gets. The privateer can't deny that suffering the handsome admiral's punishments makes him burn like the fires of the Horsehead Nebula. Serving in the roles of prisoner and captor defines their 'relationship', but no power can stop a shooting star ... the star of startling passion that flares every time they touch.

Just when Blaise thinks he can navigate the treacherous asteroid field of emotion to find common ground with Keller, an interstellar war tears them apart. Through it all, Blaise's desire for his captor stands as tall and strong as the monoliths of Maraven, and he'll go to the very edge of the galaxy and back if that's what it takes to crack the ice around the admiral's heart.

www.dreamspinnerpress.com

SOMETHING
ABOUT
HARRY

NICKI BENNETT
ARIEL TACHNA

A Hot Cargo Story

Desperate for an edge in the war against the Gavenelians that will keep the Confederation from losing as many ships to the sadistic aliens as they destroy, Sasha Dmitrov contacts the space pirate he knows only as Harry, hoping the mysterious engineer will be able to pull off one more miracle. Having been warned of Harry's disdain for the Confederation, Sasha is prepared for Harry to tell him to jump out an airlock without a space suit. The last thing he expects is an invitation to Nicodemus Vector, Harry's shielded planetoid. What Sasha discovers is an Andromedite empath who sees far too deeply into his soul.

As they race against time for a breakthrough that will tip the scales in their favor, Sasha finds himself more and more attracted to the reclusive mercenary. But duty calls, and Sasha has a war to win before he can even think about returning to Harry's side—assuming that either of them will risk opening himself to the other's empathic touch.

www.dreamspinnerpress.com

UNDER
THE
SKIN

NICKI BENNETT
AND ARIEL TACHNA

Police detective Patrick Flaherty has no illusions about Russian mobster Alexei Boczar, but that doesn't stop his fascination with the bodyguard to one of the most ruthless families in Chicago's growing Eastern European crime community. From the moment Patrick meets Alexei's eyes over the body of another Russian mobster, Alexei is a thorn in Patrick's side, refusing to cooperate with the police and turning all of Patrick's questions back on him. Alexei's hard-as-nails persona whets Patrick's professional determination to get the information he's sure the gangster is hiding, while personally Patrick just wants to get his hands on Alexei's hard body.

The tattoos marking Alexei's skin tell the story of his criminal past, but the more Patrick learns about Alexei, the more he wants to know, until he finds himself over his head in a relationship that might cost him his job and could well cost Alexei his life. Alexei is equally fascinated by Patrick's willingness to overlook his past and even his present associations, but he has secrets of his own that could drive a wedge between them forever.

www.dreamspinnerpress.com

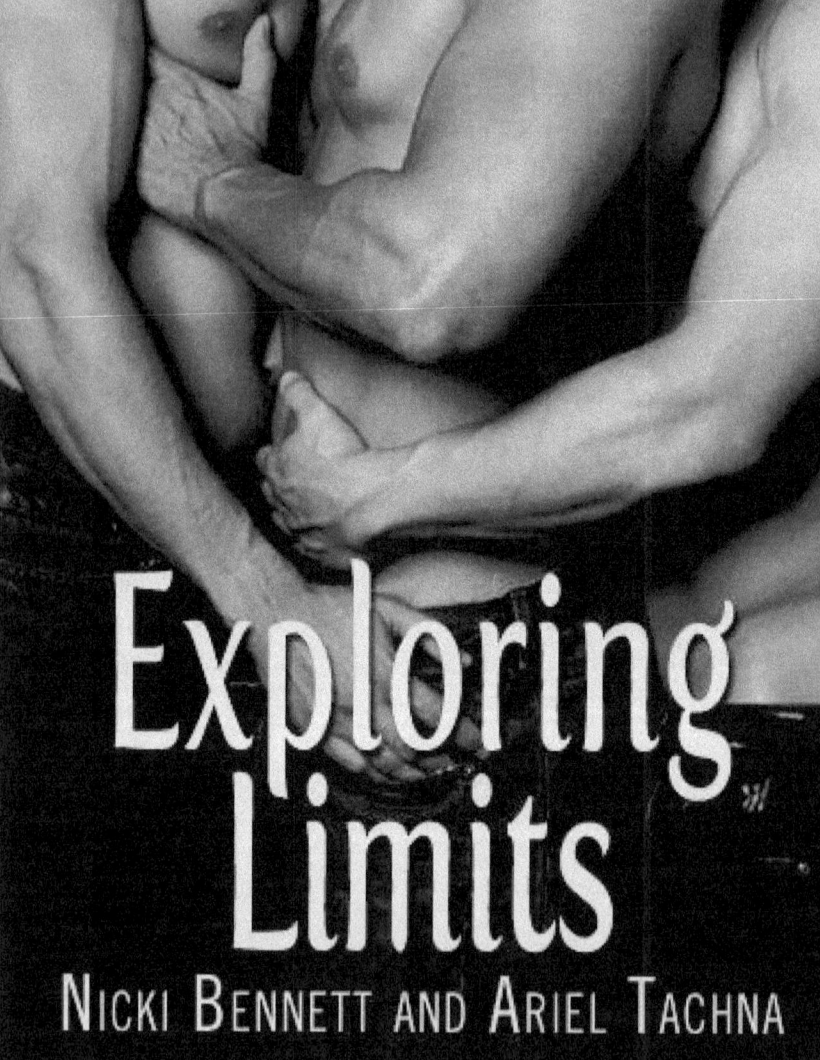

Exploring Limits

Limits

NICKI BENNETT AND ARIEL TACHNA

Exploring Limits: Book 1

Jonathan Braedon's successful acting career and consideration for his young son have always kept him from acting on his attraction to men. Newly cast as King Arthur in a BBC miniseries, he manages to conceal his interest in co-stars Devon Aldridge and Kit Webster—but Kit and Devon are just as interested in him. Rather than fighting over Jonathan, the two decide to seduce him together. Jonathan might have been able to hide his attraction to Devon and Kit individually... but together, they're too much to resist.

The three find themselves deciding what they want out of their lovemaking and their relationship, exploring options they'd never before considered or thought they'd left behind. Add a touch of kink to the mix, and Jonathan, Devon, and Kit discover that the perceived limits of the past are really just the beginning.

www.dreamspinnerpress.com

Growing up in Chicago, Nicki Bennett spent every Saturday at the central library, losing herself in the world of books. A voracious reader, she eventually found it difficult to find enough of the kind of stories she liked to read and decided to start writing them herself.

When ARIEL TACHNA was twelve years old, she discovered two things: the French language and romance novels. Those two loves have defined her ever since. By the time she finished high school, she'd written four novels, none of which anyone would want to read now, featuring a young woman who was—you guessed it—bilingual. That girl was everything Ariel wanted to be at age twelve and wasn't.

She now lives on the outskirts of Houston with her husband (who also speaks French), her kids (who understand French even when they're too lazy to speak it back), and their two dogs (who steadfastly refuse to answer any French commands).

Visit Ariel:
Website: www.arieltachna.com
Facebook: www.facebook.com/ArielTachna
E-mail: arieltachna@gmail.com